DEALGA

LORNA MACDONALD-BRADLEY

THE DEALGA TRILOGY PART I

APS Books
Yorkshire

APS Books,
The Stables Field Lane,
Aberford,
West Yorkshire,
LS25 3AE

APS Books is a subsidiary of the APS Publications imprint

www.andrewsparke.com

3022: 500 Years A.D.F.

CHAPTER ONE

Since the Earth Drought and Earth Famine it was the medication that kept them alive. Without it, slowly and painfully, the plastics would eventually poison them.

Callie threw off her blanket in disgust and swung off the edge of her bunk. Bare feet on the cool floor, she sighed and took a few precious seconds to stretch awake. Her eyes adjusted to the growing dawn light, and she was aware of the dormitory coming to life. Bodies were beginning to stir around her, screwed up faces rubbed awake. At the side of her bunk sat the small, white pill. She swallowed.

One tiny, precious capsule every morning. For everyone. Forever. Now the human population survived thanks to the scientists who had finally discovered a way to combat the effects of the toxins. This time, they were working long term with no apparent side effects.

Twenty minutes freedom till the day began. After shrugging into her uniform and running her fingers quickly through her wayward dark hair, Callie tied it carelessly with a band. She walked along the cool, faded green tiled floor to the end of the dorm. She splashed some cleansing liquid in her face from the rectangular pumps and sink at the end. There was no need to make an effort when all that was ahead was a day at work in the fields. And no need to waste any time when a meal was available. Rather than wince and shiver at the coolness under her toes, Callie enjoyed it, not only because it helped wake her but because it was the only coolness she would find during the long hours ahead.

A few others were already jostling to collect their rations and find a seat at the benches outside. The mornings were comfortable enough to sit out so early and enjoy the coolness in the air. Callie joined the queue, nodding with a tight smile at the girl in front. Reaching the trays, she collected her daily allowance – thin oatmeal and water. Polys of course, as it all was now. To some degree.

Callie spooned the thin porridge into her mouth and felt a few lukewarm, nourishing lumps slide down her throat. She washed the horrid taste away quickly and winced. Water, she thought back to her dream. As if she would ever see, or even hear, waves on a beach. Most of them were gone forever, either destroyed in the drought or resourced until there was none left.

Callie had never seen an ocean for real. She had never swum in a loch or taken her socks and shoes off and paddled in a stream, feeling the liquid trickle over her toes. They rarely had rain here on Earth now. When they did, the pollutants captured it as it landed. What drinking water became available was harvested almost immediately and shipped as rations for EarthMoon. In rare, exceptional circumstances some might be sent to Salthea, the capital city, to help sustain the government. Like the others living and working here, she knew of water from books and videos taught in school about the old times. Before. Now natural, uncontaminated water was too precious for most of those left on Earth. It was only available to the treasured and lucky on EarthMoon.

Callie looked up from her bowl at the farm in front of her. Thorrach. Dry, scorched land, rocky and orange coloured as far as she could see. The mountains in the distance looked the same: dusty and barren. Particles moved restlessly on the haze from the sunrise. It was impossible to tell whether they were dust or artificial pollinators. Patches of rough, dense bushes and shrubs, squat and tough were dotted here and there – leaves and branches dried with the heat and dust. Everything else had been scraped and cleared and flattened in the past, in failed attempts to strip back the land and remove the pollutants. The only other plants growing here were in the fields and fields of corn harvested at Thorrach. Modified corn, natural corn would never exist here now. But the scientists had developed seeds which could grow in these conditions. And Callie was one of the harvesters. Gruelling work – but she preferred it to the labs or greenhouses. The food there was much closer to being fully natural and pure, but Callie always felt being trapped there would be oppressive and smothered. At least here in the outdoors there was the illusion of being free.

Another klaxon went off. Callie returned her empty tray before taking up position in the transportation to the edges of the field. The truck was quiet, most people still waking up or saving energy for the long day ahead. Here and there heads lolled, rocking from side to side as the truck bumped, trying to catch a few more precious moments of sleep. It was starting to get hot already. Dry, relentless heat that constantly irritated the back of your throat, and Callie knew by early afternoon the heat would be stifling. She fiddled with a blue thread coming away from her dungarees, rolling it into a ball between her fingers, letting it go and then rolling it again under her calloused hands. Her palms were dry and at the bottom of her fingers were rough, raised lumps, some cracked and red.

Arriving with a jolt the team unloaded from the van and collected their tools. The quota they were expected to harvest in a day wasn't unreasonable, but it wasn't easy either. Especially with Blight threatening at any time. So far, this farm had been lucky, but it was only a matter of time.

All around her the rows swayed as other harvesters, hidden in the high plants, twisted and tore ears of corn from their stalks. One after another after another. Without question. Not that you were allowed to question – not openly anyway, but Callie sometimes wondered if anyone did. Did they dream of the Old Earth like she did? Did they long to see EarthMoon up close? Or were they simply content with this life? Robots on autopilot, resigned to their situation and position.

It wasn't that she didn't appreciate what the scientists were doing or appreciate that she had a job and shelter – things could be so much worse if she were left to the Caves. Unthinkable. But she had so many questions about life, Earth, EarthMoon and desire to understand what had happened before. This was what had got her in trouble in school and assigned to farming in the first place. Questioning teachers – asking them things they couldn't tell her the answers to. She had been told she was cheeky, unruly, disruptive. When actually she just wanted to learn.

'You ok?' a voice asked, nudging Callie gently in the side. 'You're gazing again.'

Callie turned to see a girl from her dorm, working behind her on the other side of their row.

'Yeah. Hi Bree,' she said, 'Just thinking.'

Bree grinned, wide lipped, 'Don't forget, we get paid to pick, not think!'

Callie nodded, 'Don't I know it.'

Bree was probably the closest thing she had to a friend – if anyone really had friends anymore. It was usually safer not to get too close to another person. There could be a new Reordering, and the Founding didn't particularly encourage friendships, especially groups of them. The old Chancellor and Founding had spent years violently quelling discontent and disorder. Earth no longer had the resources, stomach or bravery to question or rebel. At school children were encouraged to maintain a distance from each other and learn independence. Callie had heard whispers this was precisely because friendships could encourage collusion and resistance against power.

Still, she couldn't help feeling some warmth and affection towards Bree. She was only a few years older than Callie and had been inanely positive since arriving on the farm a few months ago. It was almost impossible for some of that positivity to rub off when they worked together. Strong shouldered despite her slim waist, Bree had the strength and stamina of a small pack horse, even in the mid-afternoon heat, and had often supported other harvesters when they were falling behind. Even at the end of a shift she was able to throw crates onto the back of the truck and stack them with ease, or at the very least, with far fewer groans and grumbles than the majority. She followed the rules without question and didn't seem to dream for anything more or anywhere else. Callie often wondered if she would be better off being more like Bree.

'What was it today?' Bree asked, twisting at a stubborn ear of corn before it gave and fell in her crate. 'Let me guess, snow topped mountains in moonlight?'

'Not today. The beach. Blue sea, smooth pebbles. Don't you ever dream Bree?'

'I don't need to waste the energy, Callie. I can just listen to yours,' Bree said. 'Anyways, if I was going to dream, I think it would be of extra rations, or rainfall,' her voice became a whisper, she flicked her thick, red plaits over her shoulder and leaned closer, 'or the transport driver!'

'Bree!' Callie smiled. 'Really? Yuck! Is she not a bit old for you?'

'Maybe,' Bree grinned, 'but let's face it the gene pool isn't exactly bursting at the seams, is it? Anyway, what about you? Anyone you like? I've seen Thatch checking you out you know.'

'Thatch! Ewww, no thanks! All muscle no brains,' said Callie.

'And what's wrong with that? Nice to look at and you don't have to worry about him being swept off to the labs or EarthMoon.'

'Would that be so bad?'

'What? The labs? I thought you liked working outside.'

'EarthMoon,' said Callie. 'Don't you ever wonder what it's like?'

'I know what it's like,' answered Bree. 'Didn't you listen in school? Cold, craggy, tough, precarious.'

'Unusual, wild, undiscovered, evolving.'

'Don't talk like that, Callie. You know it's forbidden.'

'But haven't you ever wished you could see it, just for a minute?' asked Callie. 'To find out what we are working for?'

'No,' said Bree, sounding slightly uncomfortable, her voice changed now and tinged with seriousness. 'I haven't. We know. We've known all our lives. We are here to support, to supply and to sustain the now and the future. Our work, effort and sacrifice mean the survival of the human race. Will lead to the Unification again one day. If we weren't harvesting rations, then…'

'I know it by heart Bree, but…'

'No, Callie,' she pressed on, 'That is it. We support EarthMoon, they provide for us here. We should be grateful for the resources and care. For the discoveries they make. We could have been just as easily left behind. Forgotten and abandoned.'

'Maybe we were,' whispered Callie to herself. Then smiling and shaking herself off, 'Sorry Bree, you're right. Just ignore me, daydreaming again. There's no harm in that, right?'

'No harm in daydreaming,' said Bree, glancing at Callie perhaps a second too long. 'You sure you're ok?' Callie nodded and Bree's smile returned, 'Great! Let's just get these done before weight check at lunch.'

The girls returned to twisting the ears of corn, hearing the slight crack just as the ears came loose in their hands and filling their crates. It looked like this was going to be an easy, large harvest again, three years in a row.

Soon enough the crates were full, and the harvesters lugged them back to the transport for shipment, piling them high before returning to their rows to reach the daily quota.

Finally, as the sun began to dip lower in the sky and the rays began to glow reds and auburns across the land, the transport returned to the camp. Muscles aching, hands cramped and dirty, the group splashed their faces with cleansing liquid- trying to remove the dust, grime and sweat from the day. Callie could taste the earth in her mouth and each time she blinked she could see rows of waving corn behind her eyes.

Collecting her tray again, she sat with evening rations. Bread and some kind of tepid stew. She had no idea what kind of meat it contained. It was nondescript and tasted as bland as every meal. Padded out with carrots and green beans, judging by shapes and colours. The mush, Callie assumed, was mashed potato. Everything was perfectly safe to eat, thanks to the tablets. But it would never be perfect. Sometimes it was the shape or colour: never as bright or fresh or vibrant. Sometimes it was a texture: too soft, too smooth, too lumpy. There was little variety of taste on Earth now – taste was a luxury kept for EarthMoon and the lucky. Bio science it seems, had not yet found a way to create strong flavours and differentiate between tastes. Food was not enjoyable; it was fuel to stay alive and as healthy as possible. It was also banal and nondescript.

Callie had never eaten natural food, never touched, tasted or smelled it. She could only imagine what it would be like to feel tangy, soured juice squirt from an orange and smell the fruity, citrus. Replica oranges were rare enough, but Callie had tried a segment or two. The colour was wrong, not as vibrant, slightly sickly and the flesh was dry and stringy. But the nutritional value was needed, so they all ate.

What percentage was additives, favouring, vitamins, she wondered, what percentage was bioplastic? There was no natural food available to the survivors on Earth now. Everything for the last three hundred years was at least 90% plastic enhanced, if not more. Bioplastics were the only way humanity could survive – the only way to deal with the shortages after the catastrophes of the past. Like the water, any near-natural food was grown for experimentation for successful farming on EarthMoon or to sustain the population there. For the scientists to try to reduce the pollutants and restore truly natural food. Or the animals took it.

After Earth Drought and Earth Famine the majority of everything was wiped out. 80% of people, of animals, of plants gone. Thick, ample forests and trees grew only in the far reaches of the Wilds, no-one dared enter there. Any animals that survived had adapted and evolved much better than mankind. They did not fear the weakened humans now. For the animals, the planet had taken over again, and it was the people that now struggled to survive.

And the Wilds were where the unspoken of went. They commanded the Wilds now, whatever, whoever 'they' were.

Fresh water too was a thing of near myth or legend, wide areas of the world from before was uninhabitable. The poles melted and slowly evaporated, but not before swathes of land were drowned. Those on Earth deemed themselves lucky the medicine had finally been found to combat the effects of manufactured foods and water. Unlike animals, they had not been so quick to evolve over the centuries.

Callie often worried if it was a twisted karma against humanity. She knew she had been one of the lucky ones; her parents had afforded the cure for her and Tax. They had sacrificed themselves and their future for their children. But she and her brother at least were alive. Although where Tax was, she had no idea. They had been separated two Reorders ago. Another farm she guessed.

She was certain he was still alive. Certain she would feel it if, well, she would not allow her thoughts to take her there and dreamed they would find each other again one day. Until then she had to hope and believe he was safe somewhere, building a life.

CHAPTER TWO

Callie woke with a jolt – confused and agitated: panicking she had somehow slept through the klaxon and would be reprimanded. But it was still night – the sounds that had disturbed her awake came from murmured voices outside the dormitory building. They were hushed but determined and clearly worried.

'Five already in the North East field,' she thought she heard. 'Found yesterday.'

Then another voice, 'Is it certain?'

'Samples have been sent to the labs in Salthea…the colour…the fact there was more than one found…that they were all together in the same stretch of corn…seems definitive,' she could just make out as the voices moved away. The last thing she made out was, 'contamination team.'

Callie was now fully awake and alert. Contamination team, what did it mean? Could they really have found Blight here? What would happen to them and to the farm? The disease was lethal among crops but also highly toxic to anyone who came into close contact with it. Severe blisters and respiratory problems were highly common. And extremely contagious. Should she keep it to herself or speak? A thousand thoughts fired through Callie's brain as she lay, tossing and turning till morning.

She watched through the morning for signs from the staff that anything was wrong and looked to the horizon for any signs of dust indicating vehicles moving. Callie obviously knew all about the dangers and severe problems there could be if Blight attacked, but she couldn't help secretly hoping deep within herself for some excitement.

But there was nothing. No hint of something going on or worry from the staff. The harvesters travelled in sleepy half silence as usual, there was no different in the transport or among the transporters. Callie wouldn't admit it to anyone but herself, but she did feel disappointed.

'You're quiet,' commented Bree as they met together again in the rows. 'You ok?'

'Fine, I'm fine. Just thinking.'

'Let me guess – storming Salthea and demanding better rations?'

'Actually I was thinking of here.'

'What, the farm?' said Bree sounding doubtful.

'Yep. Have you always worked in this section?'

'Why wouldn't I?'

'No reason,' said Callie carefully. 'I was just thinking how huge Thorrach is and if you'd ever been allocated to a different section.'

Bree shrugged,

'Look around, Cal. Corn's corn.'

'I guess so,' Callie agreed. 'I was just wondering. I mean if this is it. I'd still like to see a bit more.'

'You're still lucky, Cal. At least you get to study one day a week. You can bury your head and thoughts in the books you like. I'm stuck here all day, six days a week – seven if I'm really unlucky and the quotas aren't met.'

Callie was sixteen now, seventeen before the next harvest was over. This meant just one day a week spent in school these days. School was now about survival and human advancement. How to best support EarthMoon and the government. How to work the land. How to hunt. Of course, even hunting was rare now. Vast lands belonged to the animals, as it had been millennia ago. They were not scared of humans anymore. They were not farmed or domesticated. Humans and creatures had to co-exist. Animals were respected. And feared. Since the catastrophe mankind had had to learn nature was stronger and human survival was fragile.

Students learned the ways of fishing, trapping and archery. Of tracking. Although now these skills were used for security – against rogue creatures and any civil unrest.

Farming. Hunting. Science. Everything to progress the future. Science of bioplastics. Of Earth and EarthMoon. Human biology and anatomy. Ecosystems and the natural world. Anyone seen to have genius-like knowledge or skills was put under close surveillance. The prodigies left to continue education on EarthMoon; those who excelled finished school and took places in labs in Salthea.

Callie had to admit most of science made her head spin. She wanted the answers but not the processes. She saw it as a class of opportunity and of vision and ideas. Callie loved knowledge – but she wanted to know it all now. Books could only tell her and teach her so much. Callie also got the impression this was perhaps what those in command thought they should know, what was safe to teach people. Often, she was far too restless for indoors – her questions irritated the staff. She wanted knowledge beyond what they knew. Or beyond what they were willing to share. She got into trouble – too quick to question, too sharp too soon. Outside things were easier, less frustrating, freer and left her more clear headed. Callie could challenge herself then; set her own goals and targets. She wasn't always the top student by any means, at least indoors, but what she did have was tenacity and a stubborn determination.

She knew she would hate to work the labs. Cooped up indoors all day. Artificial light; no daylight; restricted in protective suits; painstakingly slow tasks; failed results. Drawing boards. Waiting months, even years, for proof, calculations and solutions. It just wasn't for her. She wasn't sure it was even for Earth.

But the greenhouses. She hoped she might just see them one day. See, touch, smell the more real, organic foods that grew there. Varieties from before. From the greenhouses to EarthMoon.

The hope, the safety, the future lied on EarthMoon. That was where the Chancellor and the government sat; where the strongest, cleverest, fittest and most talented existed. Everyone knew only the chosen, the elite were on EarthMoon. There to re-establish the best of humanity. Stronger. Better.

Those on EarthMoon were resolute and dedicated to finding a way to rebuild and return to Earth. They tirelessly researched ways to counteract the effects of carbon dioxide without medicine; to develop improved bioplastics with the eternal hope of eradicating it completely and return truly natural produce to Earth. To find out how to start over with truly natural plants and food in abundance, ending rations for good. To regenerate the ecosystems, the animals, the birds. To discover how to successfully advance into the future.

They said.

Callie couldn't help wondering how fast they worked, how committed they were. She kept her thoughts deep down and secret. EarthMoon was populated with the smartest, fittest, most skilled and gifted people from Earth. Safe as far as she knew, with everyone down here working to do their bidding. She did sometimes wonder why they would want to come back.

Still, she could never say this to anyone, never trust anyone enough to share her negativity. Callie had heard the whispered myths since she was a young child. How people disappeared in the night. Never found. How people got sick. Fled or were exiled to the caves. Preferring to take their chances in the Wild.

The Wilds were everywhere beyond cities and outside the farms and greenhouses, the places it was forbidden or unsafe to go. Left to rot and struggle and die. Hiding in the caves in uncivilised, rule-less groups. No-one Callie knew had ever seen or heard someone come back from the Wilds, only heard the rumours and stories. Been taught the warnings in school. Of groups returning to pillage harvests and labs and steal with brutality and derangement.

Children were brought up to dread the Wild, to fear it almost above everything else. Unknown, secret and threatening, no-one had reason to travel there except madness, reckless thoughts of rebellion or expulsion. It was said that those who did never returned. Or at least never returned the same. There were whispers of insanity, individuals returning unrecognisable and soon disappearing again. There were stories of groups there, once human but now changed into something primitive and violent, raiding the cities from time to time to loot for medicines and weapons. Altered and transformed by exposure to the plastics and the perilous environment. Legends grew through the decades and evolved through the centuries, holding fast until no-one really knew where the stories ended, and reality started. All that was true was the Wilds were deadly and they were outlawed.

But there could be beauty here again. Callie hoped they did remember this. The lush, abundant forests she had seen in school; countless varieties of creatures, not all of them deadly. Vast seas and oceans. Mountains green in the summer and white capped in the winter. And space. Space to be free. To discover and renew afresh. To develop and care for. So many opportunities. That was what gave Callie the most hope. That one day she would see and experience so much more.

Outside. That was where her talents lay, if you could call them that. Callie certainly didn't, she wasn't vain enough. She needed to feel the outdoors, the freedom, the questions. She loved to track. To solve the problem of hunting down a classmate, looking for tiny clues, her mind racing to piece a puzzle together and complete her challenge and beat another time limit. She wasn't the most agile, strongest or most athletic, although she had the determination and pig-headedness to always try to hold her own, but she was yet to be beaten in tracking.

When the transport was filled for the last journey at the end of the day it was clear the supervisors were not happy. They barked orders, hurrying people up and forcibly pushing stragglers along or onto the back of the transport carriers. As the harvesters returned, dusting down their uniforms and picking callouses on their hands murmurs passed up and down that the quotas had not been met.

Arriving back at the camp once again the stress permeated the air. Callie saw one woman, obviously not quick enough to unload a basket, have it grabbed off her and be pushed to the ground with a grunt 'Out of the way.' A fellow harvester went and helped her to her feet as she wiped her eyes in obvious shock. It reminded Callie how fragile their positions were.

'Stop staring,' a voice beside her said. Turning to the voice, Callie found herself face to face with a harvester she didn't recognise. 'They're really not in the mood,' he continued, nodding gently towards the supervisors. 'I've already been threatened with half rations tonight.'

'What did you do?' asked Callie, moving her attention away from the irritated supervisors. She couldn't help but notice his tanned skin from the hours working outside, brown hair speckled here and there with red highlights from the sun and his athletic frame clearly suited this type of work. She was slightly frustrated with herself for the flutter in her stomach.

'Nothing,' he said. 'Talking and laughing too loud at lunch. Apparently, I needed to wipe the look off my face and get back to work. If I had that much energy, I should be doubling my efforts. I'm Ben by the way, Ben Rhea.'

He put out his hand and she took it in hers. It was ingrained with hard work: scars and stubborn dirt in the knuckles that dinner would no doubt be clearly too important to worry about scrubbing away right now. But it was warm and encased Callie's firmly but softly – she had to admit she was curious about the sensation.

'Callie Rassay,' she replied.

'Rassay?'

'Yes, so?'

'Oh, nothing, sorry. It's just an unusual name. Nice though. Don't think I've ever heard it before.'

'Thanks, I suppose.' Callie answered. 'So why do you think they're so mad?'

'Something over in our section apparently.' Ben said, taking care to lower his voice.

Callie tried not to react or look too interested. Was he serious or just trying to impress her?

'And which section is that?' she asked, beginning to churn with interest inside.

'The North East Quadrant,' said Ben. 'Why, what did you hear?'

Callie's stomach lurched and she could feel the heat rise up her neck towards her cheek. She realised she was holding her breath.

'Oh, nothing really. Just rumours and grumbling on the journey back. Something about quotas, then something else about a blown tyre, then something about a shipment delay. I was too tired to pay any attention,' she lied.

Ben shrugged his shoulders. 'Who knows? All I know is my stomach is rumbling! Nice meeting you Cassie.'

'Callie, it's Callie' she said as Ben disappeared into the dorm, no doubt washing up before rations.

Collecting her meal and looking for a seat, Callie found one beside Bree. She was looking for a different type of news.

'So, who was the boy?'

'What boy?'

Bree teased, 'You know what boy. The one you were talking to when we got back. That looked very cosy.'

'Hardly, Bree. I just met him. He just asked if I knew why the staff were so grumpy. That was it.'

'Well, there were plenty other people he could have asked,' Bree pressed. 'Are you sure that was all he wanted. What was his name?'

'I dunno. Ben, Ben something.' Callie was rescued by the klaxon. This was unusual, it never went off at unmarked times.

Slowly cutlery and food went down on the benches as Superintendent Knox came into the canteen. Tall and wide with a rugged, unimpressed face and critical eyes he was not someone used to being interrupted or within the living quarters of the harvesters. Callie looked on with eager interest as he moved to the front of the room and addressed the group, imposing muscles pressing against the sleeves of his shirt as he crossed his arms across his chest.

Silence hung in the air, the gravitas clipping whispers in its grasp.

'It appears not everyone has achieved their quotas,' he announced. 'This is, unfortunate.' He managed to make the word sound both tragic and dangerous at the same time. 'Quotas, as we all know, must be met. This is vital to our purpose and commitment. Therefore, I will require volunteers. These volunteers will support those who have been unable to harvest to the standards set and ensure the equilibrium between the quadrants is returned. I of course assume there will be a range of willing volunteers. If not, your supervisors will allocate workers to the tasks. I would like to remind you all of our pledge. I do not need to reinforce the problems that could arise should our harvests not be met.' Knox paused to let this shielded threat hang in the air for a few seconds.

'Anyone prepared to support your fellow harvesters in the North East could be looked on favourably in the future.'

As the words 'North East' rang in her ears, she could feel herself rise swiftly from the table and raise her hand, arm trembling.

'Callie Rassay and Bree Crossan,' Callie exclaimed in a sort of yelp-shout before thumping back down hard in her chair and exhaling loudly.

CHAPTER THREE

Leaving the benches and heading back to the dorms, Callie felt her arm grabbed as she was spun around. Bree was glaring at her, eyes wide and furious.

'And what in hell was that?'

Callie sighed. 'What? I thought you'd want to help. No big deal, look he even said there might be rewards for volunteers.'

'Volunteers, Callie. The clue is in the word. When exactly did I volunteer?'

'Sorry,' mumbled Callie. 'I didn't think it would matter so much. Come on Bree, it's a change of scene. A chance to see a new part of the farm. Meet some new harvesters. Explore a little. Where's your sense of adventure. I didn't think you'd mind'.

Bree crossed her arms and shook her head.

'What big adventure, Callie? We are on a farm. Corn is corn is corn. Am I supposed to be happy? I'm sorry, whoopee! Tomorrow, I get to travel to another god-forsaken area. To get splinters in my fingers from different plants. To try and find shade from a different angle. And for what? So you can eye-up a boy.'

It was Callie's turn to look confused and disgusted.

'Boy, what boy?'

'You know exactly what boy, Callie. Ben.'

'Ben,' Callie scoffed in disgust, 'what about him? Do you really think I would drag us across the farm for a boy? Come on, Bree.'

'Well, I'm not happy Callie. Listening to your daydreams is one thing, going on some weird goose-chase for a hot harvester you just met...'

'I just told you; this has nothing to do with him!' Callie cut her off.

'Right. You didn't notice his shoulders, the tanned skin, those eyes looking right into you?'

Callie shrugged.

'Fine, but you not telling me your actual reason is really great Callie, thanks. Thanks for the trust and thanks for roping me into whatever the hell this is. Goodnight.' Bree marched off to the dorms, ignoring Callie's appeal to come back. Turning around she realised she was alone in the canteen room now and the air had turned chilly. Pulling her cardigan around her shoulder Callie headed back on her own.

The atmosphere in there appeared much less frosty. Cautious but free speculation flew around the various groups and through the card games. Those who were trying to read quietly had long given up, too engrossed, interested or irritated by the murmurs and buzz of gossip. Knox's entrance had shaken people up and brought lively interest to the harvesters.

'I heard it was a major theft from the caves.'

'Nah, the scouts would have spotted them. Transport were muttering 'insurgence', but they shut up quick when they saw us listening'.

'Geez that's a death warrant if that's true.'

'Sure is.'

'Nothing so juicy I reckon. Be a case of root corrosion.'

'Oh yeah? And who made you a crops expert all of a second?'

'Just saying, that's all.'

'Yeah? Well keep your mouth shut. You don't know any better than I do.'

And it went on. It was almost possible to taste the electric tension in the air, so Callie wasn't surprised at all when voices rose at the lack of support for theories or for the offence taken at ridiculing a guess or suspicion.

She was, however, taken off guard when the youth sitting playing cards at a small table on her left suddenly slammed down his hand. Jumping up, he took his chair, swore violently and lobbed it at someone just out of her peripheral vision. It whistled past her ear so close she could feel its wind moving her hair as she lurched out of the way.

19

The chair missed its intended target and landed with a loud bang, skittering along the floor and stopping, legs pointing upwards. It lay still, like a shocked, shot animal and the room fell silent for a split second.

Then with a roar, the teen the chair was intended for threw himself on top of the youth, sending them both solidly to the floor. Arms reached out, hitting and punching. Callie could hear the sound of a shirt ripping and the urgent scrape of shoes trying to get purchase on the floor to stand up. Heavy breathing, cursing and the crack and slap of skin and knuckles mixed together as they tussled on the ground.

Finally, the youth who had thrown the chair got to his feet, a smear of blood running down his sweaty, red face. His chest rose quickly, adrenaline and oxygen clearly pumping round his body. A knock from his adversary, now also on his feet, sent him hurtling backwards into the pack. This time people were not so lucky to make it out of the way. His hands grabbing out, the boy pulled someone from the crowd down with him as his back thumped on the floor.

Shocked expletives and animalistic sounds mixed in the air as this harvester pushed himself back up and threw a punch at the boy on the ground. There were cries to leave him be, others to break it up, others still egging on the fight. These won over. Soon sides seemed to be drawn in the crowd.

'He deserved it.'

'Knock him out.'

'Go for it, get him!'

And quickly this excited banter became more territorial and bad tempered.

'Who you talking to?'

'What are you on about?'

'Say that again!'

The tension turned sour, then erupted, brawl-like.

Callie had seen enough. The entrance was blocked so she worked her way to the back of the room. Back to the wall she watched in relatively safe nervousness but also with amused interest. Soon a hand reached out and Callie turned. Ben.

'This is how things are in your dorm?' he joked. 'Nice to see what I'm missing.'

'Mmm,' Callie nodded, her eyes still watching carefully for flying objects. Or flying fists.

'Want to get out of here?' Ben asked.

'What, and miss all this excitement? Sure,' Callie shrugged. Taking her hand for the second time that day, Ben said,

'Let's go.'

Quickly and carefully, they manoeuvred through upturned stools, wrecked trinkets, ornaments, magazines and books that had been ripped off shelves. Avoiding a few legs, heads and fists till they finally reached the door.

'C'mon let's go before Security Defence get here. You don't want caught up in that,' said Ben as they headed out.

The last thing Callie saw was Bree looking straight at he, her face an obvious mixture of emotions – amused, confused and also furious.

They made it out just in time. A group of grey body armour clad defence personnel were rushing across the farm. Ominous and thick necked, it was blatantly clear why this group had been assigned to keeping the peace. They looked in no mood to mess or reason with.

'Too close,' said Ben. He and Callie sat on a mound overlooking the dorms as the security personnel dragged arms and legs out of the dorm. 'You don't want mixed up with them.'

Callie nodded as two struggling men were heaved out into the yard, still kicking out and trying to escape the restraints to continue their fight. One accidentally swung a punch connecting to a Security Defender. He was deftly pinned to the ground and quietened with a baton. Despite being out cold, Callie winced to see the men brutishly add some punches and a kick to the stomach. The other knelt, bent over, shirt ripped with blood streaming from his nose. Even from their position it was obvious he was badly hurt and would need to visit the infirmary.

'No excuses or BS: you're found in there you're in trouble, involved or not,' continued Ben.

'Yeah, thanks,' said Callie.

'So,' Ben said, looking curious and amused, 'You and your friend ready to face the North East Quadrant then?'

Callie could feel her face burning. She just hoped it didn't show. 'What of it?' she asked. 'Just trying to do my bit and be helpful to the cause, nothing wrong with that is there?'

'Yeah right,' said Ben, 'The cause.'

'What? You don't care about the cause? You don't care about helping the rest of us on Earth Moon or finding a better hope and future for the planet?'

'Sure I do,' said Ben. 'I'd be careful how you were talking, Callie. A little too enthusiastic.'

'What's that supposed to mean?'

'Well, come on, it's obvious.'

Callie felt her stomach knot and a wave of nauseous anxiety sweep over her. Did he know more than he was letting on? Should she say something? Could she say something without giving too much away? Bree's comments also clung to the back of her mind niggling away.

'What do you know about me? What is so obvious? Go on, share,' she spoke, part frowning, part uncertain, part curious.

'Well, Knox comes in, asks for volunteers. You shoot out of your chair like you've been stung on the butt as soon as you hear it's the North East Quadrant. Just after we meet. C'mon, it's so clear. It's flattering. Great. You want to get to know me better.'

Mortified took over relief and Callie squirmed. 'How arrogant are you? Actually? Screw you, Ben,' she said stomping off.

CHAPTER FOUR

Callie felt on edge, prickly and generally out of sorts the next morning. She hadn't been able to find or talk to Bree again last night, so didn't know what kind of reception she would get. Although, she kind of figured it wouldn't be positive. Plus, the conversation-confrontation, whatever it was, with Ben had made her uneasy. She had tossed and turned through the night again and felt tired this morning.

The atmosphere in the canteen wasn't any better than Callie's mood. Tired, aggravated and worried bodies sat around. Some clearly stiff from knocks and bruises, a few obvious black eyes and scratched limbs. Hushed whispers hung in the thick air as many eyed each other with snide, mean glances. It was obvious the tension from the fight was still around.

Dragging her feet Callie scanned the benches for Bree and was relieved to see a spare seat next to her. This wasn't going to be easy but the sooner it was done, the sooner they could move on. She took a deep breath and walked over, not sure what to expect.

'Hi,' she said, then waited. Bree's shoulder's stiffened slightly, the only hint she had heard anything.

Callie sat down. 'You'll need to talk to me, Bree,' 'Look, I'm sorry for what happened. It was just a moment of madness. I dunno. Put it down to my sense of adventure.'

Bree dropped her spoon in her now empty porridge bowl and stood up. With barely a glance back down at Callie she sighed, 'Fine. It's not like I can do about it anyway, is there? Just stay out of my way.'

Her exit from the canteen was cut short however by the arrival of Superintendent Knox, flanked by two Security Defence guards who certainly didn't look like they had any patience this morning. She was directed, just with a look, to quickly return to her seat.

Knox's voice commanded the group.

'As you will all no doubt be aware, yesterday evening security personnel attended a severe and worrying disturbance within one of our living quarter buildings. During this time, a large group of harvesters were involved in violent and vicious acts towards both each other and those sent to protect and preserve order.

This is a significant breach of both the principles and laws of Earth and an attack on the Cause. Let there be no doubt the maintenance of law and order is of the utmost priority. Any individuals found guilty of putting that at risk will be dealt with at the most serious levels of punishment. There will be no return to the fragile times of insubordination. I do not need to remind you of the vital service and work carried out across our lands. Of the responsibilities each one of us carry. We are part of the chosen, those who in the future will be celebrated and praised – some perhaps even immortalised – for our sacrifices.

To this effect, as investigations and subsequent trials continue there will be reduced numbers of staff harvesting. Quotas are to be maintained in all areas. Anyone not meeting quotas was in danger of being subject to reprisals.

I hope I make myself clear. That is all.'

He turned on his heels and left. Seconds later the sound of his vehicle roaring away broke the uneasy stillness.

He was quickly replaced by the head of each unit. The harvesters had five minutes to assemble for the day's work. They should prepare for continual production inspection throughout the day. Those that had volunteered were to make their way to the correct boarding station.

'I guess that includes us,' said Callie.

'Let's just get it over and done with, shall we?' Bree retorted.

'Is this how it's going to be from now on?'

'Now. Yep, this is how it is going to be now. At least for now.'

Bree deliberately squeezed on to the end of a row on the journey to the North East Quadrant. Callie had no chance of sitting next to her or trying to talk to her again. Instead, she sat quietly, watching the farm disappear in the dust and the tracks lead in front of them. Callie wondered what she would find in the North East. If anything. What she would do if she discovered something. She was angry at Bree's reaction, angry at Ben and angry at herself. Her thoughts were jolted and confused, like the transport tyres on the rough surface.

Arriving and unloading the vans, Callie checked out the Quadrant. Initially they seemed identical to her familiar section. Irritated disappointment reared. Rows of corn, uncomfortable heat, imposing mountains. Maybe this was futile after all.

'Name?' the female voice spoke sharply.

'Callie. Callie Rassay.'

'Volunteer?'

'Yes, ma'am. That's right.'

'Section 7. Rhea, with you.'

Callie turned. Ben.

'Is there another detail?' she blurted out.

'Do we have a problem here?'

'It's not that, it's just…'

'Do I need to remind you already of Superintendent Knox's discussion this morning?'

The woman crossed her arms and drummed her fingers against her upper arms. Callie noticed the skin round her fingers was raw and scarred. It appeared this woman could not bear any loose ends, peeling back any rough sklifs of skin. Did she ever leave an open, stinging sore that scabbed over? Perhaps she needed order, to feel the smoothness, the uniformity.

'No,' said Callie, eyes down, realising it was better to keep her mouth shut. 'It's fine. My mistake.'

'Then as I said, Rhea, with you. Please do not waste any further of my time this morning Rassay.'

'Ma'am,' nodded Ben. Without a hint of recognition, he spoke to Callie, 'This way.'

Once again Ben was looking at her with that arrogant, amused expression which irritated her so much.

As soon as they were out of earshot, Callie snapped, 'What?'

'What do you mean, what?' Ben teased.

'What are you looking at? Why do you keep staring?'

'Just trying to figure you out,' Ben smiled. 'Why are you so intent on pretending you don't like me?'

'Get a grip. Just get over yourself and shut up. I'm here to work.'

'Sure you are,' he said. 'But that's fine. Let's go.' They walked in silence towards the rows of crop. Callie looked around, desperate to see something out of place, something different, something suspicious. She was disappointed to find nothing. It was all exactly the same as her section. What had she been expecting? Rows of mushy, sick crop? Panicked staff? Warning cordons? She was going to need to look deeper. Be more patient.

'Here's the corn,' said Ben. They had obviously arrived at their patch. Callie considered, if she was stuck with him all day, she might as well ply him for information. Even if talking to him did stick in her throat.

She began, as every shift, turning and twisting the corn from the stock and filling her container. They worked together in silence for a while.

'You're a quick worker,' said Ben. 'Impressive.'

'Thanks,' Callie smiled, trying to at least lie that she was being friendly. 'So how long have you been here?'

'I thought you weren't interested.'

'I'm not, but if we're going to be working together, we might as well be civil. I'm just making conversation. I don't remember seeing you since the other day. But just forget it.' Callie rubbed some stubborn hairs from a husk.

'I'm kidding. I'm kidding. Geez are you always so touchy,' Ben said. 'About eight months give or take. Transferred from the greenhouses.'

Callie felt herself physically jump. 'You worked the greenhouses?' She didn't need to feign it: she was interested now. Regardless of anything

26

else, she'd never met anyone who had worked there before. Just heard the stories and seen the pictures like everyone else.

'I did.'

'I imagine you've seen real food?' Trying to stay casual she hadn't looked up but tried to steal a glance out of the corner of her eye.

Ben twisted an inflexible husk and yanked it free, 'Yep. As real as it gets.'

'What's it like?'

'What kind?'

'You've seen different foods?' Callie knew he was showing off and trying to impress her, but she didn't care. The thought of experiencing one kind of actual, purely organic food was out of reach enough without seeing more.

'Sure. The greenhouses aren't like the fields you know. Yeah, they're huge glass warehouses, the outdoors inside. But all the glass and space in the world doesn't hide that you are indoors. I always thought I was cooped up. It never felt vast in there, more cramped despite the size. Least there was air-con though – shit I miss that,' Ben looked up at the insistent sun. 'But yeah, they've got variety going for them. They're not like here where it's corn and corn and more corn.' He threw another stock grudgingly into his basket. 'Each one had a different kind of food inside.'

'Everyone different?' Callie didn't mean to interrupt again – but the thought of harvesting, of touching, of smelling, of even seeing, anything but corn, struck an envious, fascinated chord.

Ben paused. If Callie's mind hadn't been focussed so intently on his words, she would have accused him of preening and showing off as he continued.

'I suppose. Never really thought about it when I was there, didn't appreciate the difference to here. Work is work wherever you are. The same old dull routine every day. But yeah, there were different foods. Orchards and fields and weird water plants. I dunno how they do it, but the scientists want to see how they react to equal conditions as much as possible. Had to have the same position, soil, temperature, water. A whole list of variables. Yep, there were different types of food all over.'

27

'What does it look like? Does it smell? Did you taste any?'

Ben spun, horrified. 'Of course I didn't taste it! I wouldn't be here now if I did. Don't you know what happens to people on Earth who eat EarthMoon food? Do you think I'm crazy?'

Callie's face reddened and she said nothing. She could feel her chest tighten with worry she had said too much. But moments later, Ben smiled, genuinely this time rather than his confident smirk.

'Sorry! Yeah, It's pretty cool. I gathered fruit there. Apple orchards and pears.'

'Actual orchards? Pears! I don't remember ever seeing a pear, even in bioplastic.'

'You get used to it.'

'It sounds great,' said Callie, pushing further. 'More interesting than corn.'

'At first. But honestly, food's food. Once you've seen one apple tree, harvested one day's quotas of pears, the novelty wears off. You have to be quicker and more careful than here. So the food can be frozen and transported as soon as possible. Monitoring of spoils and damage is stricter. And monitoring of staff.' There was a dull tone to his voice, final.

'Can you smell them?' asked Callie. 'What does the fruit smell like?'

'Fresh. Real. Sweet. Strong sometimes in the greenhouses in the heat of the day, blowing through the air con. That never leaves you – you never forget the scent of the heat. Are you tempted? Here was me thinking you were an outdoor girl at heart.'

Callie blushed at her obvious enthusiasm. She didn't particularly want to give Ben any reasons to start acting so conceited again, but she couldn't help her curiosity.

'I am,' she said. 'It's just it sounded interesting. Really different.'

'Well, like I said, not that different. Work is work is monotony. Shifts, targets, rations. It doesn't matter where you are, that doesn't change. And you can end resentful even. Don't tell anyone I said that, though.'

'Resentful?'

'Sure. Here we harvest but at least part of what we're working for we get to eat here. There it's for nothing. Everything sent to Earth Moon.'

'For the Cause,' said Callie weakly.

'For the Cause,' nodded Ben. 'Whatever that means?'

Callie felt uncomfortable. Could she sense Ben might feel the same way as she did, have the same questions and doubts? But she couldn't say anything or push him further. She didn't know him enough; didn't know him at all in fact. He was basically a stranger who had suddenly just appeared in her life. A stranger that was proving to be much more interesting than she had first thought, though.

They continued, working in silence. Callie felt uneasy. She had so many questions, about the section, about the greenhouses, about his doubts. But she was struggling to figure out how to ask. Every casual comment she came up with sounded too obvious. Eventually it was Ben who spoke.

'Tell me, if you really aren't obsessed with my charm and good looks, and weren't looking for a way to get closer to me, why did you volunteer?'

'Honestly?'

'It's the best way!'

Callie sighed, buying time. 'You'll think it's stupid.'

'Try me.'

'I wanted to see another part of the farm. See what it was like, experience something different.' It wasn't exactly a lie and vague enough.

Ben burst out laughing, 'Seriously?'

'I told you you'd laugh.' Callie muttered, embarrassed and annoyed.

'Sorry, sorry. You're right. But look what you've found,' Ben gestured round.

Callie looked at him confused.

'Corn. A mountain moved slightly to the right. Sun beaming down at an indeterminable different angle. I can see the attraction.'

'It was a change,' Callie said, argumentative even though her reason was a lie. 'I know, it's corn, it's hot, it's dusty. But it's here. It's still different. Just leave me alone.' She threw the corn in her hand into her basket and stomped off to the loader.

Ben followed and grabbed her arm.

'Sorry. I was only joking. I'm glad you're here,' he smiled at her and she felt that new feeling – curious, dangerous, irritating, confusing.

'Really, I am,' he said. 'Let me help you.' He put his hands out, offering.

'I can carry my own.'

'I know you can, I just want to help. To apologise. Callie, come on.'

With a sigh and shrug Callie gave in, 'Whatever.' If she was going to get any of the information she needed, Ben was her best chance. No matter how much it stuck in her throat.

At lunch Callie collected her rations and made her way to where Ben sat.

'Can I sit here?' she asked.

'Sure. You don't want to sit with your friend?' he asked, nodding towards Bree. She had just collected her lunch and was sitting with harvesters Callie assumed were from her row. As far as she could tell Bree hadn't noticed her.

'She's still mad at me for volunteering her without asking first,' Callie said. 'I figure I should give her some space. Anyway, I wanted to thank you for your help with the basket earlier and to apologise for snapping at you.'

'Don't mention it,' said Ben, wiping his bread around the sauce left in his bowl. 'Anytime.'

'So, who are your friends here?' asked Callie, trying to sound casual.

'You know better than that,' said Ben. 'We're not meant to have friends. Colleagues yes, acquaintances possibly, but friends? Now that can set alarm bells.'

'You know what I mean,' Callie pressed. 'I'd say Bree was a friend, hopefully still is. We're hardly planning the next revolt, are we?'

'Who knows? You two could be taking the farm one section at a time. Or you're trying to figure out if you have any competition for my affection.'

Callie ignored the bait and drank a long glass of lukewarm polywater. No matter how hard they had tried, the scientists had never found a way to completely cool the plastic infused liquids. It was so obvious Ben's favourite topic of conversation was himself. Eventually he wouldn't be able to resist discussing his working day. She was right. He finished his bread and sauce, collected his liquids and returned to the table.

'You know how it is,' he said after a large swallow. 'We see the same faces every day. Chatter on the transport, in the lines, at mealtimes. Some people I prefer to chat to than others, I don't know if I'd call them friends but yeah there are friendly folks and small talk. But I'd rather keep myself to myself. Safer that way.'

'Safer?' asked Callie.

'Sure. I don't know how long I'll be here. I don't want trouble or implication or suggestion of wrongdoing. Maybe it's different for a girl, but a guy spending too much time with other guys. The world is way too paranoid for that. Look at what happened last night – that was us arguing with each other. Imagine if Security Defence thought it was conspiracy.

'Must get lonely,' Callie said, with genuine empathy.

'You get used to it,' said Ben standing up. 'We'd better get back to work.'

As the sun slowly started to set and the shadows began to stretch out further in front of them, Callie and Ben made their way back to the transport. Callie was too tired to even look for Bree, or somewhere to sit. She flopped down next to Ben and rubbed her aching palms together. She was dozing, calmed by the movement of the truck and the rumbling engine when Ben spoke.

'Was nice working with you today.'

'Hmmmmm,' she replied.

'Least you were slightly easier on the eye than the last guy.'

'What do you mean? What other guy?' Callie asked, lurching awake.

'I dunno. The one usually sharing my section.'

'Where is he? What happened?' She could feel a tight lump between her throat and her chest and her head buzzing. Every word sounded loud and loaded as she struggled to remain nonchalant.

'No idea,' said Ben, more interested in rounding the corner and the farm appearing in view. He put his hands on his stomach as it growled loudly.

'Guess maybe he was in the fight yesterday,' he said, jumping down from the truck and wasting no time unloading the crop.

He disappeared quickly towards the dorms before Callie could question him anymore. But instinct told her this was the information she needed.

CHAPTER FIVE

Callie slept fitfully, constantly waking with a racing mind. Bree and their argument; Ben and the irritating, compelling way she felt around him; the snippet of detail he had left her with. Every time she closed her eyes and started to drift, her dreams were loud and full, pulling her awake. She felt like she was sleeping on the transport truck. Nothing was comfortable, everything and every part of her body seemed to have an irritating sharp edge, forcing her back alert. The more she tried, the angrier she got at herself, the less she was able to sleep.

As she lay awake, blinking in the darkness and giving in to consciousness, the image of Ben's face bobbed in front of Callie's eyes. She could see him smiling, frowning, laughing. See the way he had so easily pretended not to know her when they were given their directions that morning. His arrogance and sureness riled her so much, yet Callie felt equally engrossed by him. He had worked in the greenhouses; he knew someone who had disappeared; there was something about his confidence and how his eyes looked at her that was so annoyingly fascinating.

And he had information. Information she wanted. Callie knew she would need to be careful – Ben was clever and, she thought, could see straight through her at times.

Callie avoided both Ben and Bree at breakfast – she was tired of arguing and watching every word. She wanted a clear, alert mind for the day ahead.

She deliberately took different transport to the Quadrant but, once equipped, worked her way to Ben's row in section 7.

'Back for more?' Ben grinned. 'You just can't stay away from me, can you?'

'Volunteer, remember?' Callie retorted. 'Get over yourself.'

'You do know, the more you deny it the more likely it seems?' Ben continued.

'Yeah, right,' said Callie. 'I mean, what's not to like.'

'Exactly,' said Ben. 'Tall, handsome, skilled…'

'Arrogant, irritating, self-important, full of his own crap.' Callie jumped in. 'Yeah, you sure are a catch.'

'You're the one that keeps initiating the conversation, though.'

Callie did her best to remind herself she needed to keep calm and keep him onside. However much he was riling her inside. But she couldn't bear the thought of him winning.

'Do you know what, you're absolutely right? How about I just end it too. In fact, how about I just put us both out of our misery and go and ask work a different section.' Callie stomped off, basket under one arm.

As she got to the end of the row a woman suddenly rounded the top of the row of corn and blocked her path.

'Name?' The Superintendent's voice was abrupt, clipped.

'Rassay,' Callie said, cursing inwardly.

'Rassay …. Rassay…' The stylus tapped down the electronic pad as the woman searched. After a moment she looked up and eyed Callie suspiciously. 'You're not on the list. Number?'

'11231975. I'm a volunteer ma'am.'

'Superintendent.'

'Superintendent.'

'Going?' the woman asked, looking pointedly at Callie's basket, not even a quarter full.

Callie stumbled for an answer.

'Well?'

'I…um…I'

'I thought we might have missed some stalks from this end of the row,' a voice behind Callie said. 'Rassay was just checking for me.'

Ben.

The Superintendent glared at Callie expectantly. Callie could see her tongue cross the top row of her teeth from the inside, moistening them in readiness of her reply.'

'That's right, ma'am,' Callie finally spoke, cheeks burning in rage and relief, 'Ben asked me to check back we had cropped all the corn in this area.'

Long seconds passed as the Superintendent stared at both Ben and Callie. A wayward midge passed in front of the woman's face, momentarily interested in her scent. Her gaze did not flinch.

'And?'

'And?' asked Callie, apprehensively.

'Have you been careless enough to miss any precious corn? You do realise the importance of your work and standards expected at all times? There will be a cargo ship leaving for EarthMoon in four days' time and it must be carrying all necessary supplies'

'None missed. My mistake,' Ben replied quickly.

'Very good,' said the superintendent. 'I expect you to ensure it stays that way, Rhea.' She turned to leave before pausing again. 'Oh, and Rassay.'

'Yes,' said Callie.

'Do not call me ma'am again. I have no idea what occurs in your Quadrant, but in mine you will refer to me as Superintendent.'

'Of course. I apologise. It won't happen again.' Callie turned quickly to go.

'And Rassay.'

Callie turned.

'I was obviously clearly mistaken when I imagined you spoke of Rhea by his childhood name. If I were to hear that again I will have you removed from this Quadrant and sent to the Chancellor's Guard for interrogation. You well know the position The Founding has of personal relationships and the problems they can cause. I will not find one in this Quadrant.' As quickly as she appeared, the Superintendent was gone.

Callie exhaled deeply and spun round, red faced. Embarrassed, shaken and angry.

'What the hell do you think you were doing?'

'Eh. You're welcome,' answered Ben. 'Saving you from Superintendent Prane. I didn't realise you were just about to deliver some great excuse of your own.'

'You know nothing about me.'

'I know you don't want to get on the wrong side of her,' Ben said, nodding towards the direction Prane had left in.

'I'm not stupid. I can see that for myself.'

'Fine,' said Ben. 'I'm actually tired of this, Callie. I've tried being nice, being funny, being helpful. Thrown back at me every time. Just forget it. You get on with your work and I'll get on with mine. And that's it. Just stay away from me from now on and I'll happily do what you want and stay away from you.' With that he turned, shaking his head as he walked quickly back down the row.

'Shit,' Callie thought. She was more than slightly taken aback; she hadn't realised he had enough real feelings to get angry and care what she thought. The guilt she was beginning to feel was accompanied by worry at going too far. She'd never find out anything now, she needed him, no matter how pissed off that made her.

'Why can I not control myself for once?' she thought to herself. 'I need this guy, irritating and infuriating he seems to be, but I need him. And his face. He was really hurt by me.'

Callie remained where she was until after they returned from lunch. She glanced surreptitiously in Ben's direction as often as she could without making it too obvious. He was either ignoring her completely or doing a perfect job of pretending he was.

She sat alone at lunch, neither Ben nor Bree seemed likely to want to be in her company. Callie knew she would also need to talk to Bree and aimed to catch her that evening and make her peace. At least try to.

After she ate, Callie steeled herself and approached Ben. As he reached out to take a corn, paying no attention to the fact she had appeared at his side, she reached out and put her hand on his.

'I'm sorry,' she said, looking down at the ground.

'What?' he asked.

'Please don't make this difficult, I really am,' she said, looking up to meet his eyes. They seemed to both be twinkling at her and unnerved by her apology. 'I shouldn't have yelled at you. I know you were only trying to help.'

Ben continued to look deep into her eyes, his mouth twitching slightly at the corner. Callie noticed neither of them had moved their hands away. Feeling the heat from his fingers she removed hers and rubbed it carelessly on her thigh.

'Are we cool?' she asked.

'Sure,' said Ben, shrugging. 'Don't think you're forgiven though.'

'I am trying here you know,' Callie said.

'Sticking in your throat, is it?'

'What?'

'I'd have thought with that temper you'd be used to apologising.'

'What's that supposed to mean?' Callie stood, her arms folded, feeling the anger start to boil up inside her again. She swallowed hard to keep it down. 'Look, I'm sorry for shouting at you. I appreciate what you were trying to do, but I can look after myself. Do we really have to go through all this again?'

'What not even one more time?' Ben smirked. Callie started to turn but he put a hand on her shoulder. 'Kidding. Cool, let's just let it go. You just shouldn't get on the wrong side of her anyway.'

'Prane?'

Ben nodded and spoken quietly, 'She's a real hard-nosed bitch. Proper old school callous. Definitely got a chip on her shoulder about being here with us scumbags. How she dealt with you, that's nothing. Those eyes are dead, man. Uncompromising. Nothing gets past her. If you ask me, she's looking for a ticket out of this dump. Head down, say nothing, admit defeat, that's what I say to get you through.'

Ben paused and his eyes cleared and relaxed again, 'Besides, it's way easier to get along with you than it is to argue with you anyway.'

'Guess you must be missing the last guy then,' Callie suggested, seeing an opportunity.

'Mmmm. Something like that.'

She pressed on. 'So, was he a better worker than me then?'

'Who?'

'Your old partner.'

'I'd hardly call him that, didn't get to know him that well. But he was ok. Asked less questions and was less fiery that's for sure.'

'He wasn't here for long then?'

'What makes you say that?'

'Just you didn't get to know him that well.'

'Well, I said to you before that can be dangerous, remember. I mean, look at you.'

'Me?'

'Sure. I've known you, what, two days and you're biting my head off already!'

Callie tried and failed to stifle a smile.

Ben continued, 'He was ok. Surprised he got mixed up in that fight though.'

'How come?'

'Dunno, just didn't seem the type. He was kind of a weedy guy. Quiet. Didn't say much, just kept himself to himself. I couldn't decide if he was naturally quiet or naturally dull.'

Callie tried to joke, hoping to keep the topic going, 'You lucked out when I arrived then.'

'I thought that at first too,' Ben said. 'Slightly easier on the eye, but that attitude, man! That's going to get you in trouble.'

'I have apologised,' Callie emphasised. 'Come on, I'm trying my best here. Small talk isn't exactly my thing.' She hoped making light of the conversation might ease any awkwardness.

'Yeah, fair enough, maybe you won't be so bad after all,' said Ben.

'Least I'm not boring.'

'That's for sure.'

'You don't regret having to work with a girl?'

'What do you mean?'

'Well,' started Callie, ready to probe again, 'you don't think girls are weaklings compared to guys and I'm slower and less tough than what's-his-name?'

'Sol. I used to work with Sol. And no, I don't think that. Let's face it, I wouldn't dare tell you if I did anyway.'

'Good answer,' smiled Callie.

'And it's not that bad anyway.'

'What?' asked Callie.

'Your small talk. At least it passes the day. All Sol did the last few days before the fight was sniff and complain. I couldn't stand it.'

'Complain?'

'I mean, none of us would choose to be here, let's be honest. But we've all got aches and pains, sore heads, lack of sleep. I don't need to be constantly reminded of someone else's. At least your chosen topic of complaint is me!'

Callie had frozen. Staring. An ear of corn half in her hand, half twisted from its stalk. She only realised when Ben looked at her, forehead wrinkling in confusion.

'What? What did I say?'

Realising her error Callie stammered, 'Nnnn, no, um, nothing. Just thinking that's all.'

'Bull' retorted Ben, turning to face her full on. 'Spill. What did I say?'

'Nothing. Honestly.'

'Honestly? Yeah, heard it. You looked like you saw a ghost. I thought we were getting somewhere and over this trust shit.'

'Trust? Why would I trust you?' Callie asked, desperate to change the subject.

'Well around here there's not much choice.'

'Around here? Have you forgotten what happened earlier? How dangerous the rules are? When do any of us even have time or opportunity to trust?'

'Here. Now,' said Ben. 'Do you think I'm stupid?'

'I don't know what you're talking about.'

'All this small talk garbage. None of it was innocent. I don't know why, but you've been desperate for info on Sol from the start. What I want to find out, is why.'

'What?' Callie tried to sneer but it came out empty, weak.

'I can see it in your eyes,' said Ben, 'you're lying now, not annoyed.'

'Fuck off,' said Callie weakly, turning back to the corn. She felt a hand on her shoulder, not forcing her round, but warm, reassuring even.

'Callie, just tell me,' said Ben.

'I can't,' she said, quietly, 'I'm sorry.'

This time Ben did turn her around, a hand on both shoulders.

'Yes, you can. I think you have to.'

CHAPTER SIX

He stared at her, scratched his arm absentmindedly and sighed out a huge breath. His lips pushed out, expelling some stress and disbelief.

Callie didn't know how she felt. Relief at talking to someone. Fear at what would happen now. Embarrassment to hear the words come out of her mouth; some of them did sound stupid when they were spoken out loud.

'Say something,' she said finally.

'This could be nothing. Callie. You should leave it alone.'

'But it could be everything, don't you see?'

'Of course I do. Everything. Nothing. Either way I don't like it, but I can't un-hear it either.'

'What, and I can?'

'Maybe you should. This is dangerous. If there is anything in it, this is way out of our league. Even us talking for this long is risky.'

'But I need to know, don't you get it?' Callie pushed.

'Why?' Ben asked, 'Why do you need to do this? Why can't you just get on with harvesting, studying and stay out of trouble?'

'I just can't. I'm not stupid, Ben. I know what could happen. But I need to know. I want to know. Don't you get sick of working here, day after day? Taking medicines to survive? Not knowing what happened to your friend or if it could happen to you?'

'If anything happened to him.'

Callie shook her head. 'You pushed me, so I told you. Everything I know. You don't need to tell me it's not much. But it's something.'

When Ben didn't respond she continued, 'You know what. Forget it. Ignore me. I wasn't asking for your help anyway.'

'I will help you,' said Ben quietly.

'What?'

'You heard me, I will help you. I just don't know with what.'

'What's made you change your mind?'

Ben's voice was gentle, trying to reassure. 'I haven't changed my mind, Callie. I've been trying to help you since the second I met you. Whatever this is. Whatever you want to find, you can't do it on your own.'

'So you'll help me? We can find out what's going on?'

Ben nodded. Callie's uncertain nerves dissolved into excitement. 'Ok, what do you think we should do? Where should we start?'

'Here,' Ben said, pulling her in towards him and kissing her.

She gasped and pulled back slightly, before wrapping her arms around him and greedily kissing him back. His lips were eager. There was a rush through Callie's body as his tongue pushed against her teeth and explored her mouth. Ben smelled musty and warm, encompassing all her thoughts. Desire, fear, and confusion washed over Calle as his hands crossed heavily across her back and pulled her in closer. Her heart thumped against both their chests, pounding adrenaline and curious yearning through her.

When they finally separated, breathing heavily and flushed, Ben looked around nervously. They both knew the penalties if they were caught.

'Sorry,' he said. 'I wanted to do that for so long. Ever since I set eyes on you.'

'Don't be sorry,' Callie said. 'I'm not. But you were the one warning me about danger and recklessness, so what was that?'

'Worth it,' he grinned and they both giggled. 'Meet me after evening rations?'

Callie itched to agree but checked herself with a shake of the head and a sigh. 'I can't.'

Ben reached out again and brushed his thumb over the back of her hand briefly,

'Oh, ok. I just thought. No, ok, fair enough. Maybe tomorrow. Or, whenever.'

'No really,' Callie was flattered, reassuring. She tried not to giggle. 'I really do. There is someone else I need to speak to tonight. I've got to clear the air with Bree.' She scanned around and tucked her hair back over her ears before kissing him quickly, her lips no more than passing over his momentarily.

'Can I sit here?' Callie asked Bree as she stood next to her bench after collecting her evening rations.

'On one condition,' Bree replied, not looking up.'

'Anything.'

'Tell me what the heck this is we're eating!' Bree smiled, raising a forkful of food up, letting it slop back into her bowl. She gestured Callie to sit down.

'Cyber stew, of course,' Callie said as she sat. Lifting out a spoon of gravy and meat she chewed slightly, swallowed, and sarcastically smacked her lips.

'I can tell that,' Bree replied. 'It's the ingredients I'm struggling with.' The girls smiled at each other and sniggered quietly, alert to avoiding raising any attention.

'So does this mean I'm finally forgiven?' Callie tested the water.

Bree stared, 'You did a stupid, shitty thing Callie. But I don't suppose I can stay mad at you forever. What would that prove? I'm as stubborn as you.'

'Thanks,' Callie said, relieved. 'I missed you, you know.'

'Yeah?'

'Of course.'

'What, even with your new boyfriend,' Bree raised her eyebrows, wide-eyed.

'Funny. He's not my boyfriend. Far from it.'

'Really?' Bree, playing with her fork, was unconvinced. 'Is that why he rescued you before a brawl broke out?'

'Bree, I hardly even know him. And any *rescue* was totally on him. Pissed me off if you must know, I can look after myself. Anyway, I don't want to talk about him.' Callie waved her fork, batting the topic away. 'How was the quadrant?'

'The same as ours. Not sure your plan for adventure paid off.' Bree stared at Callie, eyes softening. 'What was it all about anyway? What were you trying to do?'

'Hmmmm, me neither. Just a stupid idea,' said Callie, shrugging. She didn't feel safe talking to Bree about what had happened. It didn't seem fair to drag someone else into this, whatever this was, right now. Especially someone as conscientious and adoring of the cause as Bree was. It wouldn't be fair to put her in a position where she would more than feel uncomfortable.

'A stupid idea about what? Come on, you can tell me, Cal.'

Callie was firm, 'Nothing, Bree. Just, nothing.' She wanted to give some sort of explanation, owed her that much. Even if it was a blatant lie it would hopefully stop her stressing. 'I dunno. Wanting to see the world, get out. A change of scene which turned out to be exactly the same. I get it, ok, you were right, I was wrong. Let's just leave it, ok?'

Bree smiled and nodded. 'I'm only glad we're back at our section tomorrow.'

'Tomorrow,' Callie exclaimed. 'School. I forgot!'

'Lucky you, don't rub it in,' Bree teased. 'I'd love a day back at the books out of the heat and dust.'

'Sorry,' Callie muttered, distracted. She would need to let Ben know whatever they decided to do would have to wait.

'Your haemo check has been brought forward this month,' Teacher Mitez informed Callie and her classmates the following morning. Murmurs and sighs of annoyance stirred around the group. 'I'm sorry,' Mitez responded, the sarcasm dripping off his moustached lips, 'Is the command displeasing to anyone? I'm sure the authorities in Salthea would be happy to discuss it further with you. Would anyone like to discuss this further?' his small, black eyes scanned the room, unblinking.

All the students faced forward, quiet now. All looked down at desks, books, or the floor. Callie also gazed forward, nothing in focus except her thoughts. It was all linked, she knew. The conversation, the missing people and now this. Early bloods. She needed to find out what was going on, why the early testing was necessary.

'As usual, bloods will be taken alphabetically. Aber, please report to the medical section,' Mitez gestured. 'Everyone else, we will return to out studies. Without hesitation a dark-haired youth rose from his seat slightly in front of Callie and strode towards the door. No-one looked forward to the monthly checks, but no-one wanted to appear weak or scared either.

Callie cursed her surname as student after student returned to the class and another left for their check. After what seemed like an age she was called forward. Sitting quickly in the stark, bright white booth she tried to smile at the medic and read their expression. Blank of course. Callie winced slightly as the needle entered her arm, looked quickly then away as the blood ran into the vial. As the needle was withdrawn, she moved her hand to rub the red spot, waiting for a tiny gauze to stop the flow.

'Move your hand please, I am not finished,' the nurse told her.

'Oh, sorry,' said Callie. 'I thought it was just one vial.'

'Two,' snapped back the nurse, without explanation.

'Oh? Why two?' Callie braved, risking reprimand for questioning authority.

As the second needle pricked her skin, slightly more painfully than the last Callie thought she noticed, the nurse stated,

'Two have been requested.'

Callie nodded, 'Ok,' and smiled to try to defuse any tension. This time she pretended to casually watch the vial filling. She desperately tried to read the label on the filled capsule lying on the desk. But there was nothing, numbers and a bar code. Any writing faced away from her towards the nurse.

The nurse finished filling the second container and handed Callie a round ball of gauze. She wrapped the label with Callie's name securely round the first vial and swapped them over. In that split second Callie made it out – one word she knew would tell her what she needed.

Larejax.

She could feel her face redden with excitement as she was dismissed and returned to class. Her head begin to spin and there was a high-pitched buzzing in her ears. A flurry of anxious, excited thoughts filled her brain. Larejax. Larejax. Callie repeated the word over and over as she walked swiftly back to class down the stark, ordered corridors. As with everything else on Earth, lifespace was always to be orderly, a purpose for everything and no hints of extravagance or frivolity. At least amongst those like Callie – the harvesters.

Returning to her seat she quickly scribbled the word down in case she forgot it. As if she would. Stuffing the paper deep within her tunic, Callie could almost feel it burning through onto her skin.

Earth History meant nothing to her that afternoon. She faltered over questions, infuriating Mitez. He threatened her with a second demerit after she failed to recall the name Agneti – one of the first Vice Chancellors to renew the Earth after the famine and drought. Of course, she knew it; the names of the original Founders were a basic rote lesson when children began school. But this afternoon her head was way beyond the past. When Mitez loomed over her desk and caustically suggested she might want to spend some time that evening in the library, Callie wondered if he could see straight through her and read her mind.

Usually a top student, he had clearly become irritated with her disconnected, vacant answers.

'Your lack of concentration is both unsettling and infuriating. If not also verging on impertinent. If you have anything more pressing to share or do, feel free to share with the group.'

Callie looked down, panicked. She couldn't afford any unwanted attention or extra study. Mitez stared intently, lips pursed, for a few more seconds before leaving her desk and tapping his papers nonchalantly on the edge. This was no casual tap, Callie knew. Her card was marked and Mitez would be watching her.

Eyes front she did her best to keep her face feign interest as she stared on as images, graphs, text appeared and disappeared on the screen.

Nodding, noting and commenting as her brain refocussed on class from time to time, Callie made it through the lesson.

There was little improvement in Survival, but at least she was outdoors and under less scrutiny. Callie loved Survival – tracking in particular – but the irony of the class wasn't lost to her. A large part of school, especially the physical aspects, involved hunting, defence, combat skills. For people traced everywhere. Kept 'free' on Earth working in compounds. With nothing beyond apart from the Wilds. Where none of these skills would help them much. For long.

Tracking, that was this afternoon's task. Callie was grateful she was the tracker and not sitting in a bush somewhere, trying to elude discovery. Her skills and talent could kick into action and hopefully stop Mitez watching her. She was ready to try to focus, uncover the clues and solve the mystery where she would find her classmate.

It was easy to follow the tracks in the beginning – her classmate had obviously been slightly careless and hurried. Half a footprint had been left in the soft earth, only partially covered by leaves and debris. It pointed west towards low shrubbery, so Callie headed that way. She knew this could, of course, be a deliberate ploy to send her in the wrong direction, it was quite an obvious sign, but she was certain it wasn't. Approaching the shrubbery Callie looked for any recognisable clues. Her head filled with fascination and fear of what she was heading towards, instead of being absorbed on this task. There were no immediately clues but when she saw a few tiny petals had been disturbed from a flowering shrub and now lay on the ground, Callie knew she was following the right path.

Stepping carefully through the tightly packed, low plants she scanned the ground inch by inch, side to side. Irritated by evasive thoughts she shook her head from time to time, trying to shake out the thoughts.

Another plant attracted her. It had been slightly disturbed, minutely if a person hadn't been focussed, but indented very, very slightly.

Callie jumped as a high-pitched alarm blared out. The time was up. Failure. Anger and frustration rose inside her, riled at herself for her lack of concentration and disappointment. It didn't help when no more than five metres away Callie's 'prey' stood up and punched the air clearly ecstatic.

'Not like you, Callie,' Zinnia grinned as she walked towards her. 'I didn't think I'd ever be able to away from someone as good as you.'

'Well done,' Callie muttered, turning and following her back towards the school building. Zinnia didn't exactly flourish at outdoor activities. The girls had been at school together since they were young, and Zinnia had always been heavy handed and clumsy. At any other times Callie would have been mortified she had caught her out.

'I honestly didn't realise I'd got so good at that,' Zinnia continued, 'Pretty pleased with myself. You didn't go easy, did you?' she added, a hint of worry in her voice.

She could have been catty and spiteful, full of excuses about her mind being somewhere else and the footprint being a big initial mistake, but Callie didn't. It was her fault, let Zinnia take the win and man up.

Forcing a smile Callie tried to convince her,

'You did great. The practise must be paying off.' Zinnia almost skipped ahead and the happiness exuding from her made Callie chuckle inside and turn her mood.

Callie's meal tasted blander and more artificial than ever that evening as she raced to finish to get to the library.

'What is with you? You can't actually be enjoying that,' Bree watched on as Callie shovelled in what she assumed was slightly stringy mashed potato as fast as she could. Callie, her mind racing, didn't hear. 'Cal? Hello?'

'Sorry, what?' Callie scooped up another forkful.

'I said, what's the rush? What's up?'

'Nothing. Nothing's up. I've just got something I need to take care of in the library.'

Bree didn't hide her disbelief, 'The library? You. Thought you were Miss A student. Top five. Naturally talented. Since when have you rushed off to go to the library? I thought you didn't even know where it was.'

Swallowing her last mouthful, Callie lied,

'Mitez was on the warpath. Forgot Agneti didn't I.' Bree looked stunned. 'I know, I know.' Callie continued. 'I don't know how.'

'I've got some idea,' Bree teased.

'How?'

Bree cocked her head to one side and pulled a face.

'Oh, come on. Not because of him. Shut up.'

'Uh uh. Tell yourself that, Callie.'

'Anyway, I'm not going through that again, so I want to get an hour's study in.' Risking her plan, but confident of Bree's response she added, 'Join me if you like.' Bree shook her head quickly and pointed her cutlery towards her half-finished plate.

'Thanks, but how could I pass up relishing all this.'

Callie deliberately passed Ben's table on the way out, dropping her tumbler with a hollow, plastic clatter. It landed at his feet and rolled slightly under the table. He bent down, seemingly innocuously and picked it up. As she reached out Callie told him,

'Thanks so much. In too much of a rush to get to the library I guess.'

He nodded, clearly understanding the message.

The door to the library hissed open almost silently and the thick calm air contrasted with Callie's tense nerves. It had been too long since she had been in here; she had almost forgotten how much it used to mean to her. Callie was herself a paradox. She loved learning, soaking up knowledge of Earth before, of Earth Moon and Earth now. Yet this knowledge just led her to more frustration with unanswered questions and a restlessness to know and understand more. She struggled between concentration and thirst to question further.

2522. The year everything changed. Perhaps it should have been called Year Zero, Callie often thought. This world may as well be another planet; it was so unrecognisable to what had gone before.

2522. The year the planet had finally fought back against humankind. Ravaged, poisoned, destroyed to the tip of annihilation, the tide finally turned. Centuries after centuries of arguing, dishonest governments, plundered resources and warnings after warnings ignored meant when it happened it was too late to turn back and make a difference. Inevitable.

The centuries of human pioneering, of progression and enlightenment had long ago turned to profiteering and plundering resources for economic gain. Technology advanced, but there had to be a casualty. Animals, plants, forests, seas, the atmosphere were all abused and betrayed. Each paid the price for 'development' and the evolution of progress. The natural environment dwindled into concrete and plastics and clouds of fossils fuels.

Nature finally drew a line in the sand.

Drought drove across the planet – slow at first – then gaining momentum and taking over continents. It was made all the easier after the years of global warming. Beginning at the equator then surging out across the globe, rivers dried, crops and animals died. Temperatures grew. The entire planet was altered irreversibly. Drastically. Fires raged across countries, reducing vast areas of forests and grasslands to skeletal ghosts and cinders. Millions of people and animals either perished or abandoned their homes and homelands in search of survival.

Sea temperatures rose beyond even the most pessimistic of statistics. Icecaps melted and sunk vast areas of land. Entire islands and coastal areas were drowned. Swamped and ruined, they too lay forgotten and abandoned under the water. Others eventually dried, bare and ruined on land.

Earth Famine followed of course. More and more species lay decimated. Stores mankind had so carefully hoarded finally dwindled and foraging tailed off. Animals and humans alike faced malnutrition and hunger. The mass starvation of nearly every species. Everything and everyone.

Of course, it hadn't been unexpected. Scientists had pinpointed the exact year. Plans had been put in place. The planet was beyond repair, time was spent blueprinting EarthMoon instead. Trillions upon trillions from all nations, from benefactors across the globe, was spent on contingencies and prototypes. The most gifted scientists from across the planet united, too late to save the Earth, but not too late to save the chosen. The important. Rulers, great minds, great thinkers, the powerful. And the rich. They made it. Before near extinction they were in place – ruling from above. Funny, the centuries of fighting, distrust and scheming was suddenly forgotten as they scrabbled to survive and leave the brutalised, hardened Earth behind.

Callie knew all this – they all knew this as soon as they were old enough to understand. The gifted lived above, supported by those below. That's how things worked now as they planned and prepared to return. She had spent hours in this room soaking up knowledge of the past, her imagination running with images of creatures long extinct, of countries long left barren.

As she stroked the spine of a large, heavy reference book she felt someone behind her.

Ben.

'Hi,' he whispered, 'I thought I'd find you here.' Glancing around to see if anyone was watching or in earshot, Ben leaned over her shoulder and pushed the book back in place. Pulling her close he kissed her tenderly, then with more fire. Once again Callie felt the heat inside her body, all her nerves singing in unison within the kiss. All too quickly it was over. She could feel the warm imprint of his mouth on hers, taste his unfamiliar, provoking smell.

Callie pulled out the book and moved towards a table. In the corner and slightly shadowed by two vast bookshelves it seemed the most secluded space.

Quickly she filled Ben in on what had happened that afternoon. Barely taking a breath, she finished.

Ben nodded, processing the new information. Impatient, wringing her hands, Callie pressed.

'So, don't you see what this means Ben?'

He looked at her blankly.

'They tested our blood today. Weeks early. This isn't killing the plants. This disease is on us.'

CHAPTER SEVEN

'You have to put this out of your head, Callie,' Ben warned her the next morning. 'If you're right…' she cut him off.

'If?'

'If you're right this is dangerous. Too dangerous for us. We shouldn't even be talking, remember. Do you really want to risk more? Can't you just be happy here? Safe?'

'Safe?' she spat, hushed, as they spoke quickly, the same argument they had had leaving the library last night. Not risking being seen or heard together at breakfast, they now arranged their packs and fiddled with buttons, laces, and uniforms as they prepared for the transportation to the corn. 'How is any of this safe, Ben? We are getting sick. People are dying, your friend died.'

'We don't have friends,' Ben said.

'You know exactly what I mean,' Callie said, 'Or have you forgotten Sol already?'

'You know I haven't, but what the hell do you want us to do? I've just got to know you, this, us, whatever that means is dangerous enough. I don't want to risk losing you when I've just found you.' Ben touched Callie's fingers gently – they interlaced them for a second and then let go.

Callie looked at him, tenderly but not wavering in her determination, 'We have to get on that cargo transport the day after tomorrow.'

Ben, now feigning nonchalance and fiddling with his laces, looked up disbelieving.

'Callie. No! How exactly do we do that? Let's just walk up casual, say hi, we fancied a jaunt and climb aboard.'

'I don't know how, yet. All I know is we need to find out what is going on. I need to.'

'Say we do get on the transport. Then what? What do we do when we get to Salthea?' Harvesters were moving around, throwing packs and themselves onto the back of the transports. It was time to head to the fields.

'I don't know how, Ben,' Callie whispered quickly, urgently. 'But we have to. We have to get to Salthea. Find out what happens when they take samples. What if this isn't just here? What if it's not quarantine? Don't you want to find out?'

Ben shook his head, walking away.

Callie threw herself onto the back of her transport, crossed her arms in to hug her body and sulked. Childish and petulant, she didn't care. She couldn't believe Ben had reacted like that. Or, as she saw it, hardly reacted at all. After trusting him, opening up to him, she was now vulnerable, angry and alone.

She was distracted and caught off-guard when the truck came to a sudden, early stop. It wasn't until she saw an unwelcome, familiar face coming towards her that Callie realised something very out of the ordinary was going on and her interest was sparked. Superintendent Prane from North East, Section 7, Ben's section, was approaching the back of the truck. Strides upright, assured. Her direction fixed on Callie.

'Rassay, isn't it?' she asked, removing her sunglasses and folding them one-handed into her palm. She did not even seem to squint against the glare and change in light as she stood, waiting for a response.

Callie looked around, confused. She could feel the colour rise into her cheeks and her head fizz with uncertainty.

'Well?'

'Yes, I'm Callie Rassay.'

'With me,' the woman said. Her tone made clear this was not a suggestion, but an order.

'I don't understand. What's this about?' asked Callie.

'I said, with me,' the Superintendent ordered, staring at Callie with piercing, cold eyes, 'I did not give permission for a conversation.' She turned and began striding towards her vehicle. Callie could see clearly the two guards already there – one in the front driver seat, one in the back. Weapons obvious. Prane moved her head slightly down and to the side, checking her request was being followed.

Callie's mouth dried as she climbed off the transport and did her best to catch up. As she got closer to the vehicle the two guards got out, guns held across their armoured bodies and watched her approach. The back door was left open, and she climbed inside. Immediately she felt cool from the air conditioning breezing through the inside. She sat back and could also feel the cold leather against her back and thighs. For all that Callie would have relished some respite from the heat, this was not a welcome cold. It was stark and fearful.

Moments later Prane was in the seat alongside her. Close enough that Callie noticed the base of her neck, where her bobbed hair ended, had become red from the sun. Callie was confused; she had expected the guard to get back in the rear of the vehicle, not the boss, yet the two guards now sat in front. She didn't know what to do, where should she look, what should she say? She said nothing, trying to find comfort and focus on picking at dried, sandy mud on the edges of her overalls.

The guards drove in silence for what seemed an unbearable foreverness whilst Prane, face pinched and stanch, stared straight ahead. Whatever this was, it wasn't good. Callie felt sweat gather along her collar bone and trickle down her chest, despite the relative cool of the car.

Finally, Prane sniffed, contemptuously, turned and looked at Callie. Her long neck was thin and serpentine, a deep hollow ran down from below her chin to beyond her collar line.

'I think we have things to discuss, Rassay, don't you?'

Callie hesitated. 'I'm not sure,' she replied.

'Sure, you are. I hear you have lots to say for yourself. It certainly seemed that way when I spoke to you in my quadrant.'

'Yes, ma'am.' Callie spoke quietly. What was happening? Was it Ben? Had someone seen them or heard them? Did they know about the Larejax? Was there something in Callie's blood?

'So. Is there anything you would like to talk to me about? Any wisdom you would like to share?'

'Ma'am?'

'Come, on Rassay. You've had so much to say. To Crossan. To Rhea. Why are you being so coy and reluctant now?' The woman almost purred as she spoke, threats and sarcasm oozing from every word.

'I really haven't said anything important.' Bree? Ben? She couldn't get them involved in this, whatever this was.

'How do you know?' the woman smirked.

'Know what? Ma'am, I'm really sorry but I don't know anything.' Taking Callie's hand, the woman tapped it gently, then ran her nails up and down. Nails that were clear and highly polished, each tapering to a point beyond the end of the fingers. The thumb of her hand carried a think hangnail, stubby and red where she had picked and pulled trying to remove it.

'We'll see,' she purred, before squeezing Callie's wrist tight, digging her nails far into the flesh. Callie gasped in pain as her hand was returned to her lap. She nursed it gently, rubbing it with her left hand, white lines outlined in red clear where the nails had dug in.

'Where are we going?' she whispered.

'I would have thought someone of your intelligence could figure it out. You don't want to talk to me, that's fine. A little disappointing, I thought we could get somewhere, help each other. That's not to be. But, if you're not talking with me, can't talk with me, you might feel more relaxed with Knox and the Security Defence.'

'No, please,' Callie called. 'I can help if you just tell me what I've done.' She knew she couldn't face Knox, but nor could she admit anything, put Ben in danger, until she knew what they wanted.

The Superintendent had clearly had the effect she wanted on Callie. The edges of her tight, red lips raised slightly in a tiny, triumphant smile.

'Tell me about Rhea,' she said, turning to face Callie and folding her arms.

'Rhea? I, um. I don't understand. What do you want to know?'

'Come, come,' the woman teased, nudging Callie on the arm playfully. 'You don't need to be coy with me. Such a pretty thing you are.' She pushed a strand of hair back behind Callie's ear and stroked her cheek slightly. 'I remember what it feels like to be a teenaged girl. Do you like him? Like Ben?'

'He was helpful to me when I volunteered in your quadrant.'

'Yes, yes he was,' she agreed, nodding.

Callie paused.

'And.'

'And nothing really.'

'Enough,' Prane erupted. 'Enough of this game and charade. Cage.'

The guard in the passenger seat up front, reached out and picked up an envelope. Callie felt fear and desperation rise as he passed it over and handed it to her.

'Go on,' the Superintendent teased, as if it was a gift, 'Open it.'

Callie's hands shook. There was nothing else she could do, she was helpless. Opening the envelope, she slid out an almost paper-thin Memory Screen.

'Well, switch it on. Let's see what's inside.'

Seconds later, staring back at her was a clear, undeniable image. Callie, Ben, in the library. Kissing

'Now. I think we have a clear point to discuss, don't you?'

CHAPTER EIGHT

'It…it was nothing,' Callie said, her hands visibly shaking as she stared at the image looking back. 'A teenage accident, I'm sorry, I…'.

'So, you admit to taking part in forbidden personal activity with Rhea?'

She nodded, 'You know I have, it's there.'

'Indeed it is,' said Prane. 'A clear violation.' Every word was tinged with meaning and threat.

'What's going to happen to me?' asked Callie.

'That depends.' Prane was giving nothing away.

'Depends?' Callie was uncertain, 'Depends on what?'

'On what Rhea says,' she replied.

'Ben? Where are you taking me? This really doesn't have anything to do with him.' Callie realised they were speeding past the farm out onto the road and spun round from left to right in her seat as far as she could, trying to get some sense of where she was being taken. She felt even more anxiety and guilt now that Ben was in as much trouble, possibly danger, as she was. She felt an urge and longing inside her chest to be next to him.

'Salthea, of course. Why Crossan, come now, don't look so shocked. Isn't that where you always wanted to go?' Disdain dripped out of Prane as she spoke. 'Don't you dream of seeing our celebrated capital, finding out more of life beyond Thorrach?'

'What? No? Who told you that? I mean,' Callie floundered, 'If it supported the cause then of course.'

Prane pierced her with those eyes again. 'My dear girl, don't you understand yet? I know you know something. Too much. And subsequently trusted Rhea.' Prane rubbed her fingers over the image of Ben and Callie, as if tenderly caressing the dangerous scene. She set it down next to Callie. 'Invited him in to share this information. Maybe even have a plan. What I don't know is what exactly. But that's what we're going to find out.'

'Ma'am, I am really sorry, I don't know anything. There must have been some kind of error. Mistake. I'm just a harvester.'

Prane's eye twitched slightly as she turned and took Callie's arm again, this time digging her nails slightly uncomfortably in to her wrist.

Her tone became colder, menacing. 'I'm not sure you're *just* anything, Rassay. So, let's cut the bullshit. Pick up the Memory Screen.'

Callie picked it up and offered it to Prane who shook her head and gestured for Callie to activate the dulling screen. As it flickered back into life, another picture from last night filled the screen.

Callie entering the library.

Ben following.

'Tap it,' Prane ordered.

Each time she did, a string of shots from inside the library, clearly images from the library surveillance filled the screen. Callie with the random book she was pretending to read. Callie and Ben together at the table. Callie's face determined and intense.

The two of them leaving independently, Callie first, then Ben shortly after.

The final incriminating images. Together in the corn. Kissing.

And finally, muffled video from when she'd unburdened and emptied her heart in the corn. Callie winced, her eyes widening then squeezing together in frustration when she saw the footage. She knew what she had said of course, so she knew beyond doubt even this barely audible scene would be evidence enough for some sort of questioning:

'Some kind of problem…came here to find out…Sol…don't you think it's strange? … something is happening…contam…team…need to know'.

It was over. Callie blinked back the tears biting in her eyes. It was so clear where this had come from. She didn't want to admit it, but she didn't believe there could be any other source.

Bree.

'Crossan has done her Earthly duty.' Callie didn't realise she must have said her name out loud. Resentment, fear and confusion rose inside her throat as she choked back waves of nausea. The words seemed to come from far away while she tried to piece all this together.

Bree had told the Superintendent about her and Ben. Someone she thought was her closest friend had deceived and betrayed her. Callie flicked back through the conversations she had had with Bree recently. 'What did she know? What had they discussed? How much jeopardy had Bree put her and Ben in?

And, why? Prane's cocked head was teasing, ominously.

'Her Earthly duty,' Callie said woodenly, finally speaking.

Prane nodded and patted Callie on the knee. The gesture was void of compassion and dripped of sarcastic sympathy. 'Her Earthly duty, to protect all of us here, and those fighting for us on Earth Moon. You would do well to remember your lessons and the rules, Rassay.'

'Bree was my friend. Is my friend. I can't believe she's done this to me.' Resentment was beginning to bubble in Callie. 'And for what?' Turning to face the woman she sputtered out, 'What did you promise her? Or threaten her with?'

Prane smiled at Callie, a glare behind the polished teeth. 'Irritation, anger, rage, good. I was told of your resolve. It's refreshing to finally see some in action. But a 'friend'? Surely you understand the basic principles of our society, our directives. Juvenile co-workers maybe; adolescent team mates whose converses stray into unsolicited giddiness or silliness from time to time perhaps. But friends! I would take care you do not falsely accuse Crossan of this conduct.'

'I suppose Bree told you all about me, then?' Callie spat back. Caution gone, she knew she was giving in to impatience and her temper, but at this moment felt there was nothing else to lose.

'Only what was necessary.'

'Necessary, necessary for what?' Callie knew she was treading dangerously but didn't care. One of the guards turned to look at the Superintendent. She nodded and he faced front again. 'Necessary to lie to people? To have them live in fear. Every move watched. Questions unanswered. School taught on rote, the heroes of the Founding.'

'The Founding that fund and provide the home, food, work, equipment to keep us all alive? The medicine to keep us safe? It is indeed very interesting to hear your resentment, Rassay. Very interesting indeed. Does Rhea share your feelings and intentions I wonder?'

'Ben, no he wanted me to forget it all,' Callie pleaded. 'He said I should just be content. Safe. Harvest and learn.'

'Did he now. We shall see. Stop.'

The vehicle pulled up, a cloud of red, dusty sand rising from the tyres then resting back on the land. Callie looked out of the window and tried to make sense of where she was. The desert still, but this was built up. There was a huddle of low, metallic buildings, industrial looking. A few strange looking squat vehicles ran this way and that, driverless and clearly programmed to a routine.

It wasn't until she fully turned, searching out the other window, that she saw the helicopter.

The guard from the front opened the door. Prane stepped out and the guard gestured with his gun for Callie to follow. She stepped out, squinting as her eyes adjusted to the strong sunlight again. She felt a prod in her spine pushing her to move towards the helicopter. As they approached and the sun stopped glaring on the windscreen she saw inside. Two more guards, heavily armoured, no doubt carrying weapons. She felt her head jerk back slightly as she inhaled sharply when she saw Ben in between them. Wrists bound.

Feeling another sharp shove, she followed the Superintendent on to the craft and took off for Salthea.

As they veered sharp left Callie felt her stomach bounce inside and narrowly managed to avoid throwing up. All her life she had dreamed of flying, of getting out of the mundane, but not like this. She wondered if, given a second chance and hindsight, if she would prefer harvesting to what lay ahead.

Ben refused to look at her – staring straight ahead and unreadable. Of course, there was no opportunity to talk to him, or even sign. They were now under continual close surveillance, who knew how dangerous any interaction could be.

She could see the expanses of dusty fields, burned dry by the sun, unfolding below her and disappearing. The mountains, blue and dark, loomed ahead. As they rose upwards her ears popped and her head became slightly cloudy. Despite her fears, awe at the world below still pushed into her thoughts and she searched for signs of creatures or animals. Of water. None of course. The mountains remained a mystery, cloaked in low lying mist so that only the peaks were visible, with occasional flashes to the dark ground below. Dark, craggy and ominous she would find nothing there, no matter how hard she looked. The hum of the engine and dull vibrations soon had her succumbing to uncomfortable, restless sleep.

With a jolt and a sharp, unfriendly shove, Callie woke up to the barrel of a gun pointing in her face. The dangerous, sarcastic smile of Prane left her in no doubt, they had arrived in Salthea. As she got off the craft she was hit by the smell. Mechanical, oily, dirty. Wrinkling her nose against it, the city hung thick in the air. Looking around she could see they had landed in some sort of bleak courtyard, a tall, grey, soul-less building looming in front of them. Her hands were cuffed, the cold metal felt alien and oppressive against her skin. Slightly unnecessary, Callie thought, where the hell was she likely to go?

As Ben stepped off the craft, she once again tried to catch his eye. He also recoiled slightly to the change in atmosphere. In that moment there was a flicker towards her. Empty. It was less than a glance, but Callie could see it was void and emotionless. Not knowing what it meant her heart sank as they were ushered inside.

The sterile atmosphere continued inside, although at least here cleaner air was pumping through the vented building. They had entered a huge hall, heavily guarded by cameras and security staff. Identical corridors ran off the stark, bleak walls which rose up to a vast ceiling. There was little sound except the hum of the air. Callie tried again to reach Ben's attention, but he was turned away from her.

Prane's radio crackled, and she moved to one side, turning her back completely from Callie and Ben so there was no hope of overhearing or lip reading.

'Understood,' she said when she returned, clipping the walkie-talkie back on to her trousers. 'Take Rhea to 75923,' she ordered the guards who had flown in with them. They nodded and Ben disappeared slowly down one of the identical corridors.

Callie turned to the guards, 'Where are they taking him?', but there was no reply. One of them sniffed in disgust and sarcasm. As if anyone was going to tell her anything. Looking at Prane she asked again.

'That is of no concern to you know. You are to be processed and will accompany me for questioning. This way.'

'Wait, no, I don't understand. Why are we being separated? I want to go with Ben.'

Glowering, Prane spoke slowly, sourly. 'What you want does not count here, does not matter. You have both made a grave mistake. We are here to find out why. Guards.'

Two arms reached for Callie, one on each shoulder. Spinning around she was led away in the opposite direction. She turned as far as she could looking over her shoulder, but Ben had disappeared. Elevator doors opened in the wall and one of the guards pushed the keypad for the 14th floor. They shot upwards with an electronic hiss; no-one interrupted their ride. Seconds later the door opened again, and Callie stepped out.

She was in another unambiguous corridor, lifeless and hostile. A member of staff, suited in a thinly striped, grey suit stood before her, waiting. Slicked back hair with a long, thin nose and beady, eager eyes. When he put his hand out it, it wasn't until he spoke that Callie realised it was for her and not Prane.

'Rassay, at last we meet. I hope you had a pleasant flight', he said, toneless. Empty politeness Callie realised. 'We are very eager to get started and talk to you.'

'I'm not sure why I'm here.' Callie stated, steeling her jaw and feigning bravery. 'I don't have anything to tell you.'

Moving in, until they were almost nose to nose, the unnamed suited man replied, 'You will.'

CHAPTER NINE

'I'll ask you again, what is your relationship with Ben Rhea.'

Callie was tired, drained by thoughts and panic. Her head ached from worry and dehydration. Her throat was rasping, and she felt cramped from so long sitting behind this desk. Her initial panic and sticky sweat had cooled and left her feeling chilled. She had long since lost track of time. There was no window to give her any sense of daylight or dark, only a cold, yellowing glow from the lights above which gave off an electric hum in the silence.

'Grey Suit', as Callie has named him in her mind, had left her yesterday, his body disappearing behind the solid, ominous door of a small cell she had been forced into. The bare, grey stone walls gave her no signal or clue as to where she was or what she should expect. Nor did she have any idea about Ben; assuming he was in another similar cell. Callie didn't want to acknowledge any worse alternatives.

She had spent the hours locked in the cell first pounding the door, shouting for attention, for help, for any acknowledgement she was there at all. None came. She sat on the thin, narrow bed for a while, sobbing and kneading the fine blanket, which was supposed to stave off the chill in the room, between her hands. Hours past as she tried to regain composure and logical thought, standing, sitting, pacing round the small space. Accusations and questions that could be raised swirled in her mind and she tried to develop and rehearse answers.

But Callie knew this was useless. They had been split up to ensure they could not concoct any lies. She had gazed at the ceiling for inspiration and any clues. Wondering if she was being watched by the man in the grey suit, smug in an office somewhere smirking at her tears and cries. Laughing at her silent pleas for the gap in the doorway to open and a face appear.

No-one did and somewhere amongst the hours Callie, lying face up, one hand behind her head, the other rolling the edge of the blanket between her fingers back and forth, back and forth, fell into a light, dream-filled sleep.

In her dream she was back at Thorrach amongst the corn. It waved around her in the wind, the plants soaring above her head so she could not get her bearings and the sun only broke the shade of the plants in sporadic brush strokes. The wind blew through the corn, rustling and calling to her as she ran towards the end. When she reached it, it just opened up again, a never-ending row. Callie heard people calling her through the corn, Ben, Bree, Prane and began to panic. She came off the track and ploughed through plants, pulling them back and shoving through. They whipped out at her, scratching her face, arms and legs, pinging back roughly against her body. She began to call out towards the voices as they dipped in and out, sometimes so close it seemed they were over her shoulder, other times distant. Suddenly, with a jolt she pulled herself awake, the corn finally giving way as she almost collided with a soaring wall, charcoal and windowless rising up like a monolith in front of her.

Callie was not certain if this change in dream was coincidental, or if it coincided with the abrasive peeling back of the shutter on the door and the key ticking in the lock. She bolted upright, her eyes scrunching to adapt to the light quickly. A medic, flanked by an armed guard, handed her a glass of water and her pill. Callie looked up mulish, but snatched both away quickly, knowing better than to reject either the medicine or the welcome liquid. As she finished the glass the medic moved aside, and it was quicky taken from her by the guard who indicated for her to rise.

Callie knew Grey Suit's patience wouldn't last. So far it had just been questions, questions after questions, rephrased and re-asked. Looking for any clues and any way of catching her out. What she didn't know was how many she had already inadvertently given or what would happen next. Callie couldn't take that chance. She had no idea where Ben was or what they were asking him. All she knew was she had to try to protect them, say nothing, give nothing away. Anything she could to keep them out of danger.

'I've already told you; I don't know what else to say. It was a stupid, stupid mistake and I realise that now. I forgot my vows and my purpose. But I promise it was only for a second. One kiss. I don't even like him. I hardly even know him, we only met when I went as a volunteer in his section. I don't know why I did it. He means nothing to me, he's worthless. Useless. If you give me another chance, I'll prove…'

Grey Suit cut her off with an incredulous sniff.

'What exactly would you like me to do? Who exactly do you think I am?' he asked her, raising his right eyebrow and sitting back dramatically in his chair. He clasped his hands together and waited.

'I mean, I, um, I just want to go back to harvesting. To work for the Cause. I realise what I've done is wrong.'

'And you would like me to return you to the farm?' he asked, his nasal voice seeming to push against the roof of his mouth.

Callie nodded, figuring this was just another game.

'Very well,' Grey Suit rose, tugging and smoothing the sides of his immaculate, sharp suit.

Her head snapped up, giving away her hope.

Uncertain, she pushed, 'What?'

'You would like me to return you to the farm,' he repeated. 'We've been here long enough. You clearly have no information for me.'

'So, I can go home?'

The man looked like he was considering something. He turned towards the door. 'As I said, you have no information for me. Time is short. Perhaps you're right. Perhaps you should just go back. If you are no use to us.' An ominous thickness hung in the air. Callie sensed danger but couldn't see where.

He turned and pressed the door release. There was a loud, dull click and it unlocked. She had a fleeting thought to try to rush through it. But then what? She was in one of the most heavily guarded buildings on Earth, perhaps *the* most guarded. And if by some miracle she did manage to get out, where would she go in Salthea? What would she do?

Grey Suit stood in the doorway with a faceless guard; all security in here wore helmets and heavy, full body armour. 'We require holding until Miss Rassay is able to leave Salthea.' The guard looked slightly confused. 'She is sadly of no more use but has been co-operative and compliant and therefore can be returned. *She* is not to be harmed.' A chill ran through Callie at the emphasis on the word. The guard nodded, lifeless, worn eyes looking Callie up and down in contempt.

Grey Suit continued 'Are you listening? My orders are clear. Rassay is to be detained until she can be returned. Should I hear of her being harmed in any way I will deal with the offender myself.' Clearly, despite his weasely face and thin build, the man held authority here. He stood aside and motioned for Callie to stand and leave.

She stood up. 'And Ben?'

'I'm sorry?'

'Ben Rhea, will he be going back? Returning with me?'

'Ah, yes. The boy. Should it matter? What of him? You've already told me he meant nothing to you; it was all a mistake.'

'Of course, but...'

'Sadly, no,' he spoke, almost apologetically, shaking his head, despondent at the thought. 'Your opinion and revelation were clear.'

'I don't understand,' Callie said.

'Well, there really is nothing to understand. You have cleared up the situation. Surely a misunderstanding as you've said. He knows nothing. Is meaningless. I'm only trying to help the cause: speaking to him won't do any use either.'

'But, I.. What? I don't know...'

Grey Suit put his hand up, waving her voice away.

'Oh, I know, I know. You don't need to worry yourself now. You will be heading back to Thorrach. Back to work as you have asked. But fret not, you have been most helpful to the cause. Useless. Worthless. You were very clear and very concise. Thanks to you I have realised we have no need to resource Rhea any longer.'

'What does that mean? What will happen to him?' Callie raised her voice, confused with the horrible realisation she was heading towards a trap.

'Why, what always happens to those who have reached the end of their service to the cause. To supporting Earth and EarthMoon.'

The bile rose in her throat as he spoke, the words brutal and thick as they curled off the roof of his mouth and through his nose. 'Immediate Eradication.'

Callie screamed. 'No, please! No. You can't.' She clawed out her hands towards Grey Suit, whipping her head between him and the guard, begging for support. 'He hasn't done anything. Please. He doesn't know anything. You have to let him go. Please. I'll do anything.'

He shook his head and put out his hands, open palmed.

'I wish I could, I really do. Such a waste of a young man. But you said yourself it was a waste of time. He knows nothing, caught up in this unnecessarily. No, in fact I would go so far as to say it was fortuitous for us that you brought his weaknesses to our attention. Resources and time are limited enough. We cannot waste them.'

'Please, I'm begging you,' Callie pleaded. 'Don't let him die. Tell me what I can do. What you need.'

Grey Suit looked towards the door. Callie's head whipped round, but all she saw was it closing behind her with a deadened hiss. She twisted back to face him, but his blank face gave nothing away.

'What will happen to him,' Callie pleaded.

'That depends entirely on you.' He walked back behind the desk and sat, elbows on the desk, his fingertips together as if in prayer. They began to tap on and off each other gently.

Callie nodded her head, defeated. 'What do you want me to do?'

The fingers stopped tapping. Grey Suit looked at Callie, looked at the chair and she sat. He folded his hands together and leaned across the desk. Slowly he spoke, enunciating each word as it spat out.

'Enough games. Start talking.'

'You admit you entered into an illegal, unauthorised relationship with Ben Rhea?'

'Yes,' Callie nodded, 'I've already told you.'

'You admit to untoward feelings?' he pressed on.

'Untoward?'

'That's what I said.'

'Why? Why are they untoward? Why is it not ok to like someone, to want to spend time with another person?'

Grey Suit sat back in his chair and stared. 'You know exactly why. Are you doubting your lessons? Your place in the progress of Earth and the rejuvenation of humankind? That would be very ill-advised should it be proven true.'

'Someone else to disappear I suppose.' Callie tried to bite her lip but her pounding head and the feeling she was going round, drowning in a whirlpool had combined her panic, fear and brazenness. Before he slammed the desk, she already knew she had gone too far.

'The truth!' he roared. 'This is getting us nowhere.' His cheeks, each lined with a long etch. flushed as he regained his composure, sniffed and wiped a stray strand of slicked hair back over his forehead. 'You begun a relationship with Rhea and that will be dealt with. It is the information you shared I am more concerned with.'

The wall behind him seemed to flicker and suddenly glow into life. Callie was once again faced with the images Prane had showed her. The details Bree had betrayed her with. These pictures, however, were life sized, perhaps slightly more. Her stomach flipped as she saw herself kissing Ben, their arms around each other, pulling closer.

Her eyes darted back from the screen as he spoke again, 'It is the discussions you had we are interested in. The information you think you know.'

'I told the Superintendent. Stories, rumours, supposition,' Callie said, knowing the words sounded pleading and hollow.

'Explain to me, what exactly is the problem you think you found? This urban myth?' the sarcasm rolled off his tongue. Callie struggled for an answer.

'Come, come. You had plenty to say in the fields. In the library.'

'Rumours, that's all. Stupid girls talking. Stories in the transport, in the canteen, the dorm. That's all. Honestly. After that fight I wanted to forget all about it.'

'Yet you are here,' he said, standing up and gesturing around. 'Whisked here to our capital city, important enough to warrant such special treatment. Such patience. So much of my time.'

A hum began and the wall opposite Callie seemed to disintegrate and give way to a huge window. Grey Suit beckoned her to join him as he looked out to Salthea.

'From here you can almost see the entire city,' he said, looking out across the fog at a sea of dark and shadow, broken up only by flashes of neon. 'Ah, look,' he smiled, moving to the side and standing behind Callie so as not to block her view, 'perfect timing. This could be interesting, how amusing.'

Standing at the left corner of the window, Callie could just see along the length of the building. Confused, she could make out something happening at the far corner, some kind of movement along the side of the building. As she looked longer, she could see the window ledge was in fact widening, not by much, perhaps a foot or two, but definitely moving.

Her whole body became paralysed as Ben appeared, struggling and in panic, forced on to the ledge. He was wearing some kind of flimsy harness around his shoulders and upper arms and looked to be trying hard to press his body firmly against the wall. But his wall was gone to; replaced by a glassless space. Callie could see him struggle to stay upright on the ledge against the wind that battered and howled this high up. When he wobbled, tipped and fell to his knees she let out a scream of despair and reached out, starfished against the glass.

'Alright, let him go,' Callie whimpered like a broken animal. 'It's not his fault. It was me that heard them talking. Five in the North Field, that's what they said. The contamination team were being sent. That's when they needed volunteers for the other Quadrant. To make up the workload for the ones that got sick.'

'Sick?' he moved his gaze from Ben back to Callie, 'Who said anything about a sickness.'

'No-one. I just thought, I assumed,' her heart felt like it was going to explode out of her chest as she desperately kept eyes on Ben. As long as she could see him, Callie felt reassured. Somehow safer.

Grey Suit nodded, acceptingly.

'Please. I'm begging you. Let him go.'

'Continue,' he said.

'I, um. Well, I volunteered. Myself and Bree. Crossan. Just to find out.'

'And curiosity brought you all this,' he smirked with a sneer.

Callie wiped a tear, her vision directed entirely on Ben, and nodded her head pathetically.

'Go on,' he commanded.

'I met Ben. Please, please let him go!'

'Go on,' he urged more forcefully.

'I met Ben. Found out his friend had gone missing too.'

'Friend?' he teased, 'So Rhea had altercations and relationships with other harvesters.'

Callie garbled, terrified this was another trap, 'No, I, I mean colleague. Not friend. Someone he worked the line with. I needed to know. Our medical obs were early. Larejax was on the label. We've been tested for something. I needed to know what.'

Grey Suit pressed a button along the side of the window, spoke brusquely 'Bring him in.'

Ben disappeared from view and Callie began to sob. Huge, heart wrenching gasps and gulps of relief and anguish.

'Thank you,' she whispered.

Grey Suit leaned in closer. 'Did you speak?'

Looking up through watery, red eyes she repeated, 'Thank you.'

'My dear. Please, don't thank me. You have no idea what comes now.'

'What do you mean?'

'Think of what you've told me. What you know. We can't just send you back.

The door opened once more, and three guards entered.

'Take her away, she's ready.' A guard took each of Callie's arms.

'Wait, no, where are you taking me?'

CHAPTER TEN

The first thing Callie was aware of was the blinding light, so intense, even with painful squinting, that she felt her eyes would burn. The second was the coldness; there was an ice-cold blast pouring in from the ceiling. Her shoeless feet felt icy against the floor and her arms started to prick with goosebumps. Callie forgot about both of these things when she became aware of the third thing. Ben. Here. Shackled to a stark, stainless steel bench. His face was swollen, lumpy and red, with a dark, painful black eye. He looked uncomfortable and Callie could tell each movement left him wincing in pain. He too was shoeless. She wondered if this was to prevent them attempting to escape. Or if it was to lessen the blows from any kicking. Looking at him, Callie thought these would be the last things Ben would be able to do, even if he wanted to.

He raised his head and looked at her. One eye was ringed with purple and red, pained and delicate. Ben looked at her, glowering; his expression matching the temperature in the room. Callie rushed forward.

'Ben thank Earth. How are you? What happened to you? I'm so sorry.'

He recoiled away from her, the shackles hitting against the side of the bench with a metallic scrape.

'Stay away from me, Callie,' he spat. 'Just stay away.'

'Ben, I, I'm so sorry. I never meant this to happen,' she sobbed, reaching a comforting hand out towards his face.

Ben batted it away weakly. 'I warned you. Told you to keep your nose out. But no. You had to keep poking and prodding and meddling. Now look.' He tugged his chains angrily and sat back, glaring at her. His dead eyes now lit with anger and rage.

Tears ran again down Callie's already tired, aching cheeks.

'Please. I didn't know, I didn't mean any of this to happen. I'm so, so sorry. I've told them it wasn't your fault; I'll tell them again. I..'

'Then what?' Ben spoke, his voice clearly seething. 'What do you think, Callie? They'll say fine, back you go young man. Apologies for the mistake. Don't you get it? We're done.'

'But..'

'Sit down please,' a body-less voice broke the atmosphere. A crackle from a microphone sounded from somewhere in the room. Both Callie and Ben looked towards the ceiling for clues to where the voice had come from, but there were none.

'Sit down,' more aggressive this time. Callie took a seat across from Ben who shuffled down the bench as far as he could, away from her. She sniffed and smiled a tight smile, shaking her head in disgust.

'Fine. Just fine.'

They sat in silence, no more interruptions, for another few minutes, till the crackle from the microphone entered the room again.

'Roll up your sleeves.'

Callie glanced at Ben, he too looked confused. 'What?' she said.

'Roll up your sleeves.'

'Yes, but what for?'

Ben hissed, 'When will you learn? Just do it!' he muttered, stumbling with his buttons as he twisted his hands unnaturally in their handcuffs in an attempt to roll up his sleeves.

The door opened and two medics, flanked by guards, entered. They held white dishes with empty syringes, their faces covered with blue surgical mouth masks, wrapping around each ear and covering from their chins to the tops of their noses.

'What is this?' Callie said, recoiling. 'What are you doing? What do you want?'

Wordlessly, a medic held out their hand. When Callie did not respond they roughly grabbed her left arm and pulled her sleeve up higher. Callie squirmed and pulled back in protest, but a guard was immediately at her back, restraining her upper body.

'No protesting,' the faceless voice was back. 'Testing will be taking place.'

'Testing for what?' she cried, teeth grimacing at the guards and medics. Callie watched helplessly as two vials quickly filled with her blood. 'Answer me! Testing for what?'

This time the voice hinted at amusement. 'Why, by now we would have assumed you would know. After all, you appear to be the expert on all hearsay and intelligence. Larejax of course.'

Vials filled, Callie pressed hard against her arm and slumped back onto the bench as the medics left. Ben rolled his sleeve down, rubbing at his arm where his blood had also been taken.

'Who knew you would turn out to be a human pin cushion?' Ben remarked. Callie screwed up her eyes into her cheeks and smiled sarcastically, inside silently relieved and happy he had actually made the effort to speak to her. 'Well, it didn't help us, did it?'

'What?'

'You and the Lanky jazz conspiracy. Or whatever you call it.'

'Larejax,' Callie corrected quietly, nervous she would be heard by someone, somewhere in the wall.

'Larejax then.'

'I'm not sure that would've made any difference anyway,' she said, biting back but keen to keep any communication going. 'Seems like that bitch Bree, my so-called friend, was waiting for any chance to improve her chances.'

'And look where it got her and us? Who was the mug, Cal?'

A door snapped shut behind them.

'Go on,' pressed an amused voice, 'Don't let me interrupt'. This time the voice did not have a metallic crack; it came from inside the room. Callie and Ben both turned.

The man was dressed dark: so dark his blue suit appeared almost black. A pin – two intertwined globes, one silver, one gold – the symbol of EarthMoon glinted against his lapel. His pale shirt buttoned tight against his neck. He moved towards them with cold, amused eyes. Whoever this was had a definite air, an aura of importance and authority. Those six words were loaded with threat and menace. Any speech, any retort, was immediately sucked out of Callie, the atmosphere out of the room. She and Ben both watched as this man walked slowly towards them before standing at the top of the table.

'Please, continue,' he motioned. Ben scowled at Callie, neither willing to say anything. Instead, the man carried on. 'Very well. I am Takot'.

Callie inhaled sharply as Ben spoke, 'I know who you are.'

'Good, very good. Then there can be no doubt to the significance and severity of my being here today. To the dissatisfaction caused so far. I am here to end the aggravation.'

Takot was the Regulator for the entire Security Defence. Ruthless, pitiless and brutal, children grew up fearing him in and out of school. He was an infamous, looming threat. Stories, infamous stories, of cruel interrogation techniques authorised by Takot were rife in classroom gossip, some even coming as stark warnings from teaching staff. People being held naked in tiny, dark, cramped spaces for days on end, only able to stand or sit in one position. Incarceration in disorientation rooms where everything was designed to unnerve the senses, confuse and sicken the mind: patterns on floors and walls that hurt to look at, strange, ugly sounds emanating awkwardly, putrid smells – all designed to upset and weaken the prisoner. And of course, stories of hurt and pain which Takot was said to enjoy watching - or inflict himself in the worst of cases.

He went on, 'There will no longer be obstruction. No games. We are aware of lapses in security. We are conscious of what you think you know, Rassay. And we know you have informed Rhea of your so-called knowledge. Resistance and denial are both fruitless. Your usefulness will be decided. Here. Now.'

'They said I was ready. I've already been through everything with Grey Suit. Ready for what?' questioned Callie.

'That will be apparent. No more interruptions are required,' Takot said. 'Grey Suit?' he sounded amused.

'He didn't give his name,' said Callie. 'But he was here, before, in the other room. Getting ready to throw us out of the windows.' Callie steeled herself, uncertain if her last comment would have overstepped the mark.

'Yes, yes, he was' Takot carried on, staring at Callie until she was forced to look away. 'But Felix did warn you, you were to be readied. Now look,' he gestured round the room with his arms, 'we are here. I will continue. You are generally a high achieving academic student. Correct?'

'What? You want to know how school is going? What is this?'

Takot raised his voice, his skeletal knuckles clenched and showed hints of bone, 'Correct?'

Callie nodded. 'Yet you have an affinity with the outdoors. Impertinence to staff. A continual issue with asking questions.' She nodded again.

'It is unusual to find someone with an attraction to both academia and the outdoors. Perhaps you are simply better than your peers, but actually mediocre at both.'

Callie could feel her shoulders tighten, but she would not speak out.

'Still,' he conceded, 'Your percentages cannot be denied, and they are regularly impressive. Disrespect is your most obvious weakness. Are you in fact, ungovernable. That is what remains to be seen. Rhea, on the other hand.'

Takot cut off and strolled round the room as if deciding on his next words. 'No academic prowess to speak of. Braun. Brute force. A temper that has found you trouble.'

Ben spoke, strongly, 'My temper is fine. My harvester record is clear. My quotas are always reached and surpassed. There haven't been any problems.'

Takot glared, 'Yet you find yourself here. Perhaps you should reconsider your idea there has been no trouble.'

'There has been no trouble,' Ben pressed, staring at Takot. 'Every error, every mistake was caused by your staff.' Callie could feel tension rise in the room. Ben was obviously angry.

'I can assure you; any errors were not made by *my* staff. You would not like to discuss this further with *my* staff, although that could be arranged.' The threat hung solidly in the air.

'I think I got close enough to them earlier when they were threatening to throw me out of a window,' Ben spat.

'Ben,' Callie put her hand out and covered his, 'Calm down.'

'Excellent advice,' Takot said. 'Perhaps you should listen to her, Rhea. Although she may not be so sympathetic and understanding if she knew the real you.'

Ben's eyes shot to Takot and his whole body seemed to tighten on high alert.

'Did you ever tell her why you left the greenhouses for the land?'

Callie looked from Takot to Ben, uncertain. 'I don't understand, what happened?'

'Go on,' Takot gestured, clearly amused. When Ben said nothing, Takot's voice became bitter and threatening, 'I said, go on. Unless you would like me to make you talk.'

Ben looked straight ahead, his words regimented and practised. 'It wasn't my fault. It was an accident.'

'What was? What happened?' Callie asked.

Takot's eyes lit up as he deliberately delved further. 'Tell her. Tell her why you were moved.'

Ben's face was deathly now, Callie was shocked to hear him almost whimper as he began to crumple.

'Please,' Ben pleaded. 'Just leave this. It doesn't matter now. What will this do?'

'Tell her.' Takot demanded, 'Tell her, or you may find yourself on the edge of another window.'

Callie was shocked as tears sprouted in Ben's eyes. 'It was an accident, there was a theft.'

'Ok,' Callie said, gently, tipping her head in agreement while she lay her hands flat on the table to steady her own feelings. 'That doesn't seem so bad. What did you steal?'

'An apple,' sighed Ben, 'I stole an apple.'

'That's it?' Callie almost laughed in relief with an exhale. 'You stole food. Well lock you up and throw away the key. I don't care about that, for Earth's sake, why would I?'

'An apple from a greenhouse, Callie,' Ben added.

'Well duh, I didn't think it was from a corn field. You stole and apple, got relocated to harvesting. Big deal.' Turning to Takot, Callie kept on, 'I think you'll need to do a lot better if you expect that to worry or frighten me.'

Takot ignored her, eyes still steady on Ben, 'And?' His voice continued to bite.

'And I was caught,' Ben spoke lowly, his voice full of pain. 'Someone caught me.'

Callie still couldn't understand, Confused and worried she began to press, 'What did they do to you? I don't understand, why is this so bad?' She looked at Ben closely, 'What is it? Are you sick?'

Ben shook his head, 'No, no I'm not sick. I stole an apple from the greenhouse. A real one. No synthetic materials, a natural apple meant for EarthMoon.'

'And got caught,' Callie continued, reaching for Ben's hands again, but not finding them. 'You've said. He's made you tell me. But you're here. You got transferred to the farm.'

'That was not why he was transferred,' Takot interrupted.

Ben was sniffing now, a clue he was still wavering in holding back tears. His voice broke and he began to bluster. 'No, it's not. There was a fight. I panicked. You know how serious theft can be. Especially in the greenhouses. There was a fight. I hurt a boy.'

Callie sat back in her seat, pulling her hands back to the table edge. 'Why?' she asked Callie, an ugly doubt beginning to crawl within her chest.

'Yes, why?' added Takot, his cruel eyes dancing and amused now.

Ben's face was hate mixed with misery and regret. 'Panic, terror. He caught me and was going to report me. I asked him not to, begged him to, but he was clear. I was so angry. I lashed out in panic. Understand now it was just his preservation. Scared himself I guess, if they found out he knew what I'd done he'd be punished too.'

'There was a fight,' is that so terrible? Look at Bree. If I saw her again, I'd do the same for what she's done to us.' Callie worried where this conversation was going to end but had to turn it. She didn't want to hear the unsettling now churning inside her.'

'Yes, it was that bad. He got hurt. Fell. Callie, you have to understand, believe me, I didn't mean any of it to happen.' The tears were falling freely now, Ben was heartbroken in distress. 'If I could take it back I could. I'd swap places with him if it was possible.'

'I still don't understand, what happened? What did you do?' Callie asked each word carefully, dreading the answer.

Takot ordered, 'Tell her. Finish this!'

The words flooded through the sobs, 'He died, Callie. I hit him. He fell. Hit his head. There was nothing I could do. Please. Please understand. It was an accident. I panicked. I'm sorry, Callie, so, so sorry. He's in my head every day. When I saw you, I wanted to help you. To ty to make some of it better.'

Callie felt nauseous, dizzy, 'Who was it? Who was it, Ben?' She knew there was no way out now. Desperate to hear and flee the answer at the same time.

'Tell her,' Takot shouted, both his fists coming down hard on the table.

Ben moaned, 'Tax. It was your brother Tax.'

Callie's head rang as she vomited.

CHAPTER ELEVEN

Takot looked sanctimonious. Revelling in his satisfaction, his eyes glistened at the situation; Callie, sobbing violently, her whole body convulsing in pain and disbelief. A string of snot, untouched, rolled from her nose towards her mouth which still had tiny signs of vomit crusting round the edges. Ben was silent, his head in his hands with his fingers threading through his hair, shoulders clearly defeated. His pleas and appeals for Callie to listen had gone ignored.

Takot broke the silence, 'And there we have it. Shall we continue?'

Ben dragged his fingers through his hair once more, massaging his scalp back to steady thought and sat up. 'Continue with what? What else is there now?'

'You have so much more to do, Rhea. So very much more. You both do.'

Callie sniffed loudly and wiped her damp face on the back of a sleeve. Her eyelashes glistened thick with tears.

Her voice was broken, empty as she spoke. 'Nothing, I'm doing nothing for you. You can do what you like to me, I don't care now. What's the point? What's the point of anything anymore?'

'Yet this is only the beginning,' Takot said, 'You two need to prepare.'

'For what?' asked Ben, 'Can you cut out the bullshit riddles and tell us. What exactly are you expecting me to do now?'

Takot turned and walked towards the opposite side of the room. As he did the wall seemed to anticipate and reveal a window in front of him. Callie assumed someone watching, somewhere else, had released a key which allowed it to happen. He ignored Callie and Ben for a few, long minutes, staring out at the fog and grey city before him.

Ben clearly could not take the unease and insecurity and asked again, subdued, 'What do you want, Takot?'

'What do I want? What do we all want? Rassay, can you enlighten us?'

Callie sighed, 'To support, supply and sustain the survival of the human race.'

'Anything else?'

'We support EarthMoon, they provide for us.' Monotone and rote, these were almost the first sentences children learned; drilled into them from well before they could fully understand what they meant.

'Quite,' Takot said drily, 'and you believe the declaration and vow?' Callie could feel him watching, waiting for an error, the slightest slip of the tongue.

'Would it matter if I didn't,' Callie asked.

'I think we both know it could have grievous results if an individual did not,' he said, grimly.

Swiping at a random tear ready to drip from her chin Callie's mood was dark.

'Do what you want, Takot. I'm done. Do I believe in the promises? No.' Ben looked at her, warning her with his eyes, but she wouldn't, couldn't look at him and stood up now, glaring at Takot. 'My parents are dead. My brother, dead. No friends. No future except corn after, corn after corn and you ask me what? If I'm loyal to the Chancellor? To you?' Her voice was raised, 'I. Hate. You. Hate all of you.'

She looked at Ben deliberately straight in the eye, 'Hate him. What has EarthMoon done for me? Slaved me to a job. Taken my family from me. Turned my friends against me,' Callie shook her head in frustration as the tears began once more and sat down quickly with a thump, fixed on not giving Takot the satisfaction of seeing her tears again.

'Very dramatic,' Takot almost purred with sarcasm. 'Your bravery cannot be denied. You will need it. Let's hope your partner can match your courage.'

'Partner?' Callie was wary and eyed Ben with disgust.

Takot nodded, 'Your closeness cannot be denied. The evidence is here. Your honesty is appreciated and will now be used.'

Ben and Callie were both highly alert now, muscles tense and straining.

'Used for what?' Ben spoke slowly.

Callie hissed, 'It doesn't matter what. I'm not doing anything with you.'

'Indeed you are.' Takot's voice was hard and severe, his double chin wobbling with each word. 'You wished for Salthea. You wanted a mystery, to discover the truth about Larejax. You drew Rhea eagerly into your plan. You will now reap the rewards.'

Callie's blood seethed. 'You think I wanted this? Interrogation. To find out my brother was dead because of him? Killed, because of him.' The way she spoke the word left no doubt there was nothing but hate for Ben now.

'It is beyond what you want. That doesn't matter now. Here we have decided what will become of you. What needs to be done as recompense for the failings at the farm.'

'Decided what?' she demanded.

'You have a use. Together, Tomorrow your practise will start. I would advise you do not fail. That could have,' Takot paused as if choosing the right word, '*adverse* consequences.'

'Practising for what?' Callie and Ben almost spoke in unison, both nervous and puzzled.

'For the Wilds,' smiled Takot. 'You will be entering the Wilds to bring us back the cure. That is the price for your freedom. Your survival'.

'What? No! Wait,' Callie was rattled and flustered as Takot turned, nodded towards some invisible camera and left. Ben, the colour completely drained from his face, shook his head with a tight, disgusted smile. Takot was replaced by brawny guards in no mood to waste time who escorted Ben and Callie back to the holding rooms.

The effect was startling, Callie had to admit. It didn't feel like outside: there was no breeze or hot sun bearing down, but the visual effect was near perfect. She was in a sprawling 360-degree virtual forest, an illusion created for the training project. Ben was somewhere in the same room. All she had to do was find him.

They had had no contact with each other in almost 24 hours – since Takot had revealed they were to be sent to the Wild's together. She hadn't rested, had barely eaten or drank the tiny ration portions shoved at her through the door of her cell. Instead, she continued to reel from grief at Ben's confession. Hate, disgust, betrayal all seethed inside her. She had kissed him, ardently kissed the very person who had taken her brother. Callie wished she could rip the lips from her body, peel back the skin that had met his – she felt she would almost deserve the pain.

Mixed in with the chaos was her confusion why he had tried to get so close to her. Was it some kind of sick joke? Would he ever have told her if he hadn't been forced into it by Takot? That he had murdered her brother. Taken the one person she had left. Callie had dreamt and imagined so often they would see each other again. Now nothing. Penance, she wondered. Did he have some kind of warped mind that if he won her over, convinced her to love him, saw himself as some kind of protector and supporter, that it would make amends for Tax's death.

She would never forgive him; Callie had made that very clear and felt it deep down. They were both here now, part of Takot's sick joke, but she would never forgive him. She didn't care if he was alive or dead. Although that was a lie, she thought, she would prefer him dead. She had to be here now, ensuring her own survival, but when she could, Callie would be gone. This was all a means to an end, she had decided in the long hours of darkness last night; focus, concentrate, look. For clues, for weaknesses. Then when the knowledge and skill was complete, she would make her escape.

She would certainly take her time in here. Callie imagined Ben crouching, hot and cramped in the artificial, humid heat, trying to stay deathly still. She willed itchiness, hot fiery cramp, nausea from the temperature. She didn't care if it was childish; she didn't care if she was reprimanded by whoever was watching for clearly taking her time and stalling. It would be obvious, from what they already knew, that Callie was skilled and adept at tracking and should be well into the hunt by now. But why should she care about their irritation? They had all played a part in doing far worse to her. Still, the stubbornness within her also wanted to ensure Ben was found and didn't outsmart her tracking skills.

Methodically, Callie scanned the area. As usual she divided it into three sections in her mind: the horizon, the mid ground and the immediate ground at her feet. Her eyes swept left and right, taking in everything and waiting for anomalies to appear. It didn't take her long to find another, a slightly flattened patch of grass, Ben had clearly stood here just with the toe of his shoe, but it was enough. A few paces later a synthetic spider's web, which must have been spun between two spindly tree trunks, was broken and hanging. An obvious textbook error, Callie thought, wondering if Ben had broken it without realising, pushing on in anger at leaving the toe print. It made no difference to her; she would win although she knew it would give her little pleasure.

Tracking was also made easier if you knew your target. Callie considered hers. Ben had spent a lot of time in the greenhouses, less outdoors. She knew his skills were in science and muscle, not deception. He would be somewhere obvious: thick undergrowth, a caved area, fallen trunk, rather than trying to conceal himself in a tiny, challenging space.

She headed west, still deliberately taking her time, but stopping here and there to act as if she was considering a sign or looking closely at something on the ground. Perhaps less than five minutes later she discovered him. Crouched in the end of a huge trunk, the disturbed moss on top, indented with fingerprints, was sign enough.

'Surprise,' he joked shallowly as she moved back the weeds and bent to look inside. Turning without recognising his comment Callie tuned towards the door.

A clammy arm caught her, 'C'mon, don't you think it would be easier to get through this together? I can help. I need to help. Need to talk to you and explain.'

'Explain what? How you cold-heartedly murdered my brother? Took away the only family I had? I don't want to talk to you, don't even want to breathe the same air as you. And you think you can help?' Callie gulped out the last few words, afraid she was going to lose composure. Her tone became lower, darker, 'Don't you think you've done enough?'

She turned and walked back to the entrance. Somewhere above them the cameras turned from red to black. As she reached the door Callie turned to face the camera, staring. 'Well? I tracked him. Let me out.' There was a brief delay before the mechanism in the door clicked in to life and it hissed open. Takot stood before her. 'Satisfied?' Callie asked and was ignored. She could sense Ben approaching alongside her and her shoulders tightened involuntarily.

Takot frowned, the furrows between his eyes deep and shadowed. He was obviously slightly irritated.

'You repressed your tracking skills from us there. I'm certain you won't hold back in the next task.'

'Next? I'm done, thanks. I've had enough of this bullshit. Just tell me what you meant about the Wilds and a cure and get me anywhere away from here. The less time I spend with him,' Callie spat out this word, 'the better.'

'In that case I suggest you will enjoy the continuation of today's training. Give the next part much more of your care and attention.'

'And what would that be?' Callie asked.

Takot paused, clasping his perfectly manicured chubby hands behind his back. 'Hand to hand combat.'

Ben rushed in, stumbling over his words, 'I won't fight her. I won't. What are these sick games?'

'We'll see if you *both* feel these are games,' Takot didn't look Ben's way, his glinting eyes instead staring intently at Callie.

Ben had been taken out first, Callie assumed to some other room where they would be expected to fight. She sat on the floor, surrounded by the fake forest, picking in turn at the skin around one of her fingers and at blades of grass nearby. She had no clear idea where all this was leading up to, but she didn't like it. Takot had said they were going to the Wild's to find the cure, but no more had been spoken of it. The few adults she had seen before being frogmarched to the tracking test had completely blanked her questions. Food had been brought, medicine of course and their temperature and bloods taken, all silently.

Whatever Takot meant, whatever was in store, Callie felt it was ominous. And now she was expected to fight Ben as part of some sick preparation.

Khalto was one area where Callie did truly outshine the rest of her class. Her athletic, gymnastic build meant she was naturally dispositioned to do well in the ancient art. The Founding's laws meant there was little chance of anyone using the skills in fighting, given the consequences, but it was a lesson still taught in school. Callie and her classmates assumed this was for fear of anything happening with the Wilds. Or for anyone finding their way into the grasp of Security Defence.

She enjoyed the power of having the polished, wooden staff in her hands and challenging her energy through it in defence. She saw it as a thing of beauty: handcrafted with carefully to ensure an equal balance throughout; made to match the height and weight of the owner. The methodical learning of stances and holds, becoming emotionless and concentrating only on the challenge and attack slowed down her mind and gave her focus and energy combined. During an exercise Callie was both graceful and strong, her muscles often ached, satisfied, after throwing and manipulating her body in uncommon movements and ways.

She was also, with some trepidation, prepared to fight Ben and hurt him. Callie wasn't stupid, she knew this was what Takot wanted. That part of her wanted to deny him this satisfaction, but she wanted Ben to feel some of the pain she was suffering knowing he had taken Tax from her.

At last the door was opened, and guards once again stood to escort her. The courtyard she was taken to was fully enclosed by the Founding's building; an outdoor atrium bordered on each side by the soaring walls. The air was stifling and thick, the clogged city hung in every breath. Callie was aware of faces watching from the windows as she faced Ben in the middle of the square. Like Callie, he too was holding a staff, knocking it methodically from hand to hand.

'I'm not going to fight you Callie,' Ben spoke quietly, peacefully. 'We don't have to do this.'

Callie ignored him, 'I want this over, done. Over, then I never have to see your face again,' she replied. Tightening her jaw and lifting her chin she added, 'Not fighting? That's up to you.' Callie spun the staff up and around her head, darted towards Ben and, channelling all her strength and energy through the weapon, brought it down lengthways in front of her body, hands at each end. She shoved into Ben, sending him flying back onto the ground with a scuffling scrape.

Circling an injured wrist with his other hand, Ben looked up,

'Enough, Callie. Don't do this.' He dodged out of the way before the end of Callie's staff struck him in the stomach, took his own stick in hand again and took back to his feet.

'I don't want to hurt you,' he said.

'Don't you get it,' Callie taunted, 'This isn't about what you want.' She came at him again, this time spinning the staff around in front of her body before swinging at his shoulders. The movement hissed through the still air. Ben reared back to dodge the blow, as she swung to the other side. Just in time he reached up with his own staff to block the blow. The strength sent Callie back, stumbling to stay upright.

She used the pole to steady herself and swung back round, aiming another thrust, this time catching Ben in the side. He cried out, the wind partly taken out of him and stumbled, reaching to the dusty ground to stop himself falling and rising to his feet again. Looking up he saw Takot appear on a balcony behind Callie. This distracted Ben and Callie slammed her stick down sharply on his shoulder.

This time Ben did raise his staff and swipe towards Callie – fighting not defending. She snarled her teeth in defiance. He couldn't say for sure, but Ben knew inside that Takot would be enjoying, relishing this rupture of their relationship. They were broken now, no longer stronger together. Worse, she had become his enemy.

As Ben spun again, he did catch Callie in the side, and she gasped out in pain when the stick stabbed in to her waist. Dropping her weapon instead she spun and kicked him hard in the hip, giving her the momentum and seconds to reach for her defence. Callie wanted this done. They almost danced together, sticks knocking, sending them one way, then back, forward, then retreating. Ben swung high, Callie ducked away, she spun her staff forward, her circled around. They both waited for the opening, the tiring. Ready for the final hit.

Eventually it came. Ben stumbled back and Callie spun low, bringing the staff down hard behind his knees and sending Ben starfished back onto the ground. Raising her staff lengthways in the air she brought it down fast, as if to plunge through, then stopped with a jolt just as it was about to reach his stomach. The staff clattered and echoed on the ground as Callie threw it to one side with disgust, turned her back and dropped to her knees on the dusty courtyard.

A single, slow clap entered the ground from the balcony above.

'Remove them,' ordered Takot. 'Get them ready for final preparation.'

Ben turned, muscles aching as he rose, panting. 'Final preparation? Not enough for one day yet? What exactly are we going to be forced into doing now?'

Takot spoke coldly, 'What you've always wanted. Freedom and Knowledge.'

CHAPTER TWELVE

Callie stared at the reflection glaring back at her – unsure whether to feel terrified, dazed or bewildered. She would never admit to anyone else, only daring to even whisper in her head, but she also felt faintly satisfied. The person she was looking at was a version of herself she'd never seen before. One she would only have admitted to the deepest part of herself as imagining just days ago.

She was dressed entirely in a smooth, dark coloured outfit that clung close to her skin, moving with her body, very different from the baggier uniform she wore in the field. The material seemed to change shade and tone in the light and shadows: here grey, here midnight blue, becoming black depending on the crease and how she turned. Despite how it hugged her skin it didn't feel restrictive or limiting, even though it ran from collar to wrist and hip to ankle, strengthened and protected further at the knees and elbows. On her feet were thick, laced boots. Given their appearance they should have been heavy and cumbersome, but like the clothes were light, warm and completely shaped to her feet and calves.

At her waist was a belt which hung low on her hip. It was weighted down with a collection of pockets containing equipment and tools. Some reminders of back when, others from this world. Catapult, knife, compass, shock pellets, sense disruptor. A haemo blocker should she face an injury. No gun of course, Callie laughed, hollowly to herself, not so naïve then. Neither she nor Ben would be shooting their way out of here. Still, since she had been given these new clothes and kit at least one guard had been with her at all times, closely watching her every move. Takot was obviously not one for taking too many chances.

She wondered how far she would get if she managed to somehow overpower the guard – confuse his senses perhaps – and rush through the corridors. It was doubtful there was a door in this place that wasn't wired, never mind manned. The likelihood was if she attempted it, she would find herself in a far worse place than the holding cell.

Callie tucked a strand behind her ear, the braid down her nape, the only common feature from the person who stood here now and the one harvesting. Only a few days, but they seemed a lifetime away now, another life. Was she the same? She wasn't sure. She didn't know if she felt as self-assured, confident and spirited as before. Too many questions swirled in her head, adding to her confusion, fear and frustration. She hated the riddles, Takot's smug attempt at mind games. She hated seeing Ben's face, hated listening to him try and talk to her, begging for vindication.

A piercing, high pitched alarm burst into life and brought Callie back into focus. The door to the room opened and Superintendent Prane entered, taking Callie completely by surprise. She let out an audible gasp.

'Not who you were expecting?' Prane asked Callie, her hands clasped behind her back.

There was no point in her holding back her shock, 'What are you doing here?'

The woman wasn't about to engage in niceties. 'You are to accompany me to medical'.

'Medical? I'm fine. Haven't they had enough of my blood already? Or do you want the soul now?'

Prane eyed Callie up and down. 'I can guarantee they are satisfied with any results so far. Otherwise, you would have no doubt been declared surplus and there would have been no more use of you.'

'Then what do they want me for.'

'I am not privy to that information.'

Callie couldn't help it, the retort came too easily off her tongue, 'And I bet that really pisses you off.'

Prane's lips tightened and thinned. 'I have little interest in reports on your health, only that the tests are completed before we continue. That stage concerns me much, much more.' She had a chilled, admonitory tone.

'When will that be?' Callie continued to try to find any details she could.

'Once medical is concluded we will proceed with final checks. You are obviously more than concerned with moving on to the next stage so if there is nothing else?' When Callie remained silent, Prane continued, 'Good. After you,' raising her hand she signalled towards the door. As

Callie approached the waiting guard, Prane called her back, 'And Rassay,' Callie turned,

'Yes?'

'Don't attempt to uncover information or stall for time with me. The effort would be totally futile, understood?'

Callie gripped her jaw and teeth tightly and said nothing, returning to face the guard who motioned her forward.

The three of them passed into an elevator, lined on all three sides with mirrored glass. As the door closed, they jolted slightly before shooting downwards, how many floors Callie had no idea. After only a few seconds they opened out into another artificially lit, stark corridor, this one tainted with the lingering odour of cleaning fluids. The chemical trail climbed into Callie's nostrils and clung there as she was marched along the slate grey tiled floor, the only sound other than their feet striking the tiles was the murmuring whirr of the lift as it shot away.

A glass panelled room appeared, the staff inside all robed in white gowns. All wore face mask and poly gloves. In the centre of the room was a large, looming chair, padded at the head, elbows and knee. Around the chest, waist, wrist and ankle areas thick brown straps hung down.

The faces in the room turned and eyed Callie as she appeared in view, their eyes nondescript. Before she could protest the guard was close behind, she could feel his body heat, hear his breathing through his mask. There was nowhere else to go other than forward. She fixed her mind, under no illusion that in a matter of moments she would be strapped to that chair.

With no other explanation a voice from behind a medical mask commanded 'Sit.' Scanning each person in the room, Callie perched herself in the chair, hands on her lap. The voice in her head told her they needed her, wanted her and Ben for some plan, so surely this could not be evasive, tortuous.

'Hands,' a voice at her side said, at the same time taking her right wrist and strapping the band around it. As they tugged on the strap really tightly around her wrist to align it with the gold pin Callie gave a small audible wince.

A soft, gentle voice on her left whispered, 'Don't worry. IT's just a precaution. For us not you.' Callie could see the sides of her eyes crinkle above the mask in a smile.

'That's enough. We do not engage with subjects,' the first medic snapped.

The smile disappeared,

'Sorry,' she muttered, tightening the strap around Callie's left wrist. 'Ankles?' she asked, looking at Prane.

Prane shook her head,

'That won't be necessary. Miss Rassay will always have the pleasure of a monitor while she is with us. Stay here,' Prane indicated to the guard before leaving. No doubt to ogle from behind another mirror or camera, Callie thought. She scanned the room, noticing a red light flashing from a box in each corner. Whatever went on in here they liked to see it from every angle.

'Ah!' Callie turned as the medic began pulling the syringe. 'More blood? You know you might want to leave me with a little, thanks very much.'

The voice that came back was dry, 'Plasma. Poly level checks.'

'Don't suppose you could have done them with some of what you've already got, no?'

'Place your finger in here,' the medic at her left side said, her eyes calming and reassuring. Callie looked down and placed her index finger in the measurement clamp.

'What are the readings for?' she asked. The woman glanced warily at her superior who nodded in approval.

'Basic measurements. Height, weight, body mass, body temperature.'

'For?'

'Physical Status determiners.'

'Great,' Callie replied, tapping the clamp on the edge of the chair. 'Like they would release me, free to skip off into the sunset if I was shorter.'

'Read this.' A board emerged from the ceiling, travelling down slowly. First letters, then words, then complete sentences, getting smaller and smaller each line. The black and white was replaced by colours, some with garish contrasts so the letters seemed to bounce and merge out of their usual shapes.

This was replaced by images which appeared at different points on the board and at different time intervals: testing reflexes as Callie pushed buttons as soon as she saw them.

Later sounds of different pitches and tones piped in from around the room. Again, she was to indicate when she heard them and from which direction.

Finally, sore from the time in the chair; hungry for anything they would spare for her to eat and too tired to feel more than flustered by the poking and the prodding and the questions and the checks. The straps were taken off and Callie was once more returned to her cell.

'You are to accompany me to the Hunting Pool.'

'The what?' Callie was sitting on the edge of the cot, worn out by another erratic sleep but also cautiously alert in anticipation at Takot's next move. Her neck ached from the flustered sleep and the pointlessly thin pillow: she rolled her head around trying to ease off any muscles.

Prane, the authoritative body once again, stared, her jaw clenched. 'If you are going to interrupt with these questions, I will have no choice but to have you sedated until arrival. Believe me, it would be a pleasure.'

Callie was silent.

'Enough?'

Callie nodded. Although she now despised her, Callie couldn't help admiring Prane's authoritative aura and presence, perhaps enhanced by her tall, willowy frame.

'Excellent. Charming as this whole catch up has been, I suggest we don't waste any more valuable time. Hunting Pool. Now.' Her outstretched arm pointed towards the door and Callie rose to follow. Silently the two walked closely together down the corridor and left the building. If there had been any civilian strangers outside, they could have mistaken the two for a mother and daughter silent after an argument. The same frame, similar stubborn jaws, deep, mysterious eyes.

They weren't without similarities. Neither accepted their positions, both wanting more, better, different. Although that could be where the similarities ended. Prane lived and breathed her supervising work. That was not to say she wasn't ambitious; in fact, it was entirely due to her ambition. She didn't want to spend her career on a forsaken corn farm, surrounded by harvesters, she often wondered if there were even too many, believed some could become natural collateral as part of an improvement plan for the planet. After all, that would reduce pressures on the rest of the population and free up resources. She had long had her sights set on Salthea, government control. EarthMoon, at her age and with her specific skills, she had to grudgingly accept was out of touch, but Salthea was a real possibility that had suddenly fallen into her lap. She wasn't about to miss ensuring it became a certain reality. She knew she was ruthless and ambitious enough to succeed and find her place there.

When they reached the high, thick glassed, imposing front doors Callie hesitated.

'I thought we were going to the Hunting Room?'

'Hunting *Pool*,' Prane corrected.

'Hunting Pool? I don't understand, isn't it a pseudo-room?'

'You've been moved on to the pure realism stage. The transport is prepared and ready to take us. I suggest you spend time conserving energy instead of irritating me with incessant questions.' Prane gestured to Callie who saw no option but to climb into the vehicle parked outside, one of its doors open but not welcoming in the dim, dawn light.

As they approached it became clear why this was known as a Hunting 'pool'. They were passing down an uneven track towards an empty, bean shaped loch bed. Parched, cracked land lay below; Callie wondered in awe what it must have looked like before the Drought. Tried to imagine it full of water, teeming with movement and life. To her it seemed impossible there was ever enough water here, in one point, to fill the space. Callie's imagination almost couldn't compute the picture in her mind.

Now barely anything existed. Ragged, rough rocks and boulders grew from the ground, long revealed from underneath the surface, punctuating the scene. Callie was being driven down into a valley, steep slopes surrounding the destination below. It appeared there were only two ways in and out: the track they were currently on and a faint line almost directly across, winding steeply through a dip in the hills. There were few plants, dried, thin, skeletal branches, hanging useless. A reminder of past richness and life.

Callie stepped out as the vehicle stopped, marked closely by Prane. There was no sign of Ben, she assumed she had arrived first. She squinted against the morning sun glare on the bleached, sandy surroundings. It was already hot even at this morning hour and the temperature would only soar as midday got closer. Faint puffs of sand from above signalled that Ben was approaching. She tracked the dark shape as it turned into a vehicle and came closer and closer into view. Not small like the one Callie had arrived in: this was a large, military style truck with blacked out windows and bashed, armoured sides. Callie was sure she would find Ben inside; she just wasn't sure what else might be in there.

She didn't have long to wait.

Rather than anyone exit the truck, the door swung open, and Callie was asked to step inside. No longer squinting from the sun glare, her eyes quickly adjusted to the duller interior. Callie, stared around at the interior, eventually stopping on Ben. Despite her hate, she could feel the colour rise in her cheeks when he looked at her. Just as she had been, he was dressed in similar dark clothing. Callie noted the identical belt hanging from his waist.

'So what?' Ben asked, turning to one of the guards who flanked him, 'I hunt her here? Surprise, there she is. Game over.' Ben tried to move towards Callie, reaching out as if to grab for her arm in capture. Instantly he was boxed in by the guards and stopped. They were so close they were almost skin to skin, making sure Ben had nowhere to move. Callie was forced to sit opposite Ben, within another seated alcove moulded into the inner décor of the truck.

'No?' Ben continued, 'What then? Is one of us getting a head start? I'm not sure if anyone has noticed but you've not exactly picked a great place for hunting. Where do we hide? Behind one of those boulders out there?' Callie could see he was clearly irate and in danger of at least a stick in the ribs from Prane or the security. Still, the more stupid and angry he felt, the more she knew if she focused and kept her composure she would come out on top. Whatever that meant. Whatever this was.

'My dear boy, where did you get such a mundane idea?' Takot spoke as he revealed himself from the front of the armoured truck. Callie understood perfectly now why the journey had angered Ben so much.

'But you said,' Callie jumped in.

'Said what? That you would hunt each other?' Takot smiled, 'Now where would the fun be in that? We have a long way to go before we are at that stage.'

'Who are we hunting?'

Prane came alongside Takot and crossed her arms in front of her body, smiling as he continued. 'I'm not sure who would be the correct terminology anymore. I'd prefer to think in terms of what.'

Silenced, Ben and Callie listened on, joined together again, at least for now.

Prane began the briefing. 'You are aware of course, there was a security breach at Thorrach. Clearly that has been dealt with and is why we have all found our way here today. What is equally clear is how little you know of what you assume you know.' Prane's eyes shot over Ben and Callie, then back again as she spoke, clearly enjoying their attention and helpless innocence.

She continued. 'Rassay was under the impression, gung-ho in her summation, that people were victim to a Blight outbreak, quickly covered up to avoid panic and investigation from contamination officers. Those affected disappearing right under everyone's noses and dealt with before anyone noticed or was suspicious.' Prane's eyes stopped and lingered on Callie, who nodded her agreement.

'Only, there was an explanation,' Prane began again, 'and they did vanish overnight.'

'They were shot.' Takot interrupted, matter of fact. 'Shot and killed. Each one. Then burned and the ashes contained to avoid any more outbreak.' The words were blunt, each one emotionless as if he was rhyming off details of damaged crop or ration details.

Callie glanced at Ben, who met her gaze with the same shocked expression. This level of openness was as frightening as it was compelling.

'Shot?' she felt disgusted and weak. 'Not even their fault. Was the suffering not enough for you? Did you not even want to waste resources or time on treatment?'

Ben spoke, 'Easier to shot and remove and install other workers. That way no precious quotas are missed, or resources used unnecessarily.'

Prane looked at Takot, who nodded for her to continue.

'You two are so passionate, so fired up. But the truth is not that easy. The decisions we make are not that simple, or so black and white. The reality of Larejax is much darker.'

Callie could feel her skin prickle at the sound of the word. Written on the test tube at school. She heard herself whisper the name as Prane continued.

'One element Rassay did uncover was the name, Larejax.'

A rush of questions bombarded in from Ben. 'What is it? Are you going to tell us we have it? What happened at Thorrach?

Takot took over. 'Larejax is a strain of new polyvirus. So far immune to our science and our treatments. A virus we have known about for some time, but which we believed was being successfully controlled.'

'Until now,' said Ben.

'Until now,' Takot mimicked. 'Five months ago, there was a breach at one of the scientific facilities. A raid for medical supplies.'

'By whom?' Callie asked, guessing the answer before he told her.

'The Wilds. One of them was caught. Interrogation proved our fears.'

'Interrogation? Ben's voice was droll, 'I take it that was of the tortuous type?'

Takot stepped to Ben, faced him nose to nose and continued.

'Those apprehended told us Larejax has begun to spread into the Wilds. We have lost our hold on the virus. We can't tell if there have been any further mutations, how much it has multiplied or how many are infected.'

The fight had left Callie, she was left with worry and intrigue and spoke quietly, 'What will it do?'

Clearly Takot and Prane had come prepared for these questions and for sharing more information. From the centre table separating Callie and Ben a tall, thin obelisk shaped screen emerged and flickered into life.

'At first it causes distracting skin irritation. Itching so severe it will feel like relief will only come from ripping your own skin from your body.

'Sol!' Ben exclaimed. 'Sol was going on about itching and a rash. On and on for a couple of days. Wondering what the hell he had a reaction to. It was this, wasn't it?' He received no answer. 'You bastards. And what? Where is he now?' Ben fell silent as he felt the draught of a guard's breath on the nape of his neck and the muzzle of a gun slightly press into the base of his spine.'

Takot went on, 'You are not privy to classified details. I have no awareness of this, Sol. He will have been processed accordingly. Fever follows. In many cases this will cause death. In others the fever leaves the body and takes over the brain.'

'Then what?' Callie asked, appalled.

'Then uncontrollable thirst and hunger. The nervous system takes over sense and thought. The body is led by compulsion to feed.'

A picture appeared on the obelisk screen, then merged into a collage of moving images. Youths, males and females shrieking, wide eyed as they clawed at themselves, pawing at their faces, unaware or undeterred by the scratches and wounds they created. Callie stared, disgusted and awed by footage of emaciated people, clothing hanging in ripped rags from skeletal frames with red, blistered skin and dark rimmed fish eyes, unblinking. At times they clawed at the camera, grabbing out at whoever stood filming.

'And there is too little in the Wilds to feed on. The poisoned start heading in to farms. Greenhouses. Labs. Anywhere they can find something to eat.'

Takot nodded. 'True. Yet you still don't get it. They are not breaching security to attack the crops. They do not want to feed on them.'

'What do they want?' Ben pressed.

It was Callie who spoke, just as Takot opened his mouth to speak the same word. 'Us. They want to eat us. That's what we're here to hunt.'

Gesturing towards the screen the words were proved correct. Callie and Ben watched, terrified to look, yet scared to look away at a crazed, incomprehensible youth, bleeding from open, pus filled, deep scratches. In a sudden, unexpected move he lunged towards the person behind the camera and there was a tussle to the ground. The camera was knocked over, onto its side but once it steadied the images were undeniable. The man who had been filming was now floored onto the ground. His face was out of shot but his legs were kicking out as he tried at the same time to scramble to his feet. He struck and struck at the undeterred attacker, the same youth who had been in the shot before, who was now clawing and trying to grip the legs of the scrabbling film maker. The shrieking sounds of pain and madness had been replaced almost by growling; the hands which had seemed to be scrabbling for support in anguish, were now trying to grab and tear. Callie and Ben could clearly see dirty, receding gums through the snarl.

The film came to an abrupt end and Ben swung around.

'And if we refuse?'

'Again, not that simple,' Prane spoke. 'You are not here to hunt them. Only be aware of them and face them if you have no other options. You are hunting the cure. You two are bringing back the cure. If you refuse you die.'

'You've told us so much already,' Callie faced her. 'Do you expect us to believe you will just let us go?'

'Clever girl,' nodded Prane. 'But yes. I don't see anyone else here to believe, do you?'

Takot took up the discussion. I can guarantee that, yes. Returning with the cure will be the price for your freedom,' he nodded.

Ben unbuckled and threw down his belt and began to wrestle with the hunting suit. 'We go, we die. We come back, we die. I don't believe your worthless promises. We stay, you kill us. Or the disease does. Any which way I don't like the odds. How about you do your own dirty work? I'll gladly take death now rather than scrabble for you.'

'Conviction,' Takot clapped, 'I knew that would be your final ploy. But there is one part in the puzzle that I feel has the potential to sway your mind.'

'Really,' Ben folded his arms, 'and what might that be?'

'Larejax itself. The virus is not airborne.'

'Then where is it?' Callie asked.

'It is not spread through contact or contamination. If one of the infested attack and harm you, their infection will not transfer. If you somehow managed to even survive their frenzy. Larejax doesn't transfer through human contact. This fire and rage is fatal because of the fury, not any contamination.

You have to bring back the cure because the poison is in everything. Our bodies are rejecting the plastics, despite the antibodies in the medicines. Everything we eat. Everything we drink. Our daily medication? Every week that passes reduces the potency and effectiveness. It is weakening, simply holding back the time now, days for some, a few months for others. We can almost render it useless. A basic placebo to avoid panic and mass hysteria. A panacea to prevent revolt.'

Callie felt her stomach lurch in shock.

'You're lying.'

'Why should we believe this? How do we know it isn't bullshit?' Ben broke in.

'Why else would you be here and not dead? If this were lies you would not have made it off the ledge,' Takot glanced at Callie, 'neither of you.'

'You have been prepared and equipped,' Prane eyed them both up and down. 'Studied and the best of both of you combined will succeed in bringing the cure to us. You can refuse, face the penalties. As will your colleagues, your families. Each and every one of us.'

Callie shook her head and spat the words in disgust, 'Unless we find the cure.'

Prane and Takot nodded in unison.

'Our scientists believe it is within the Dealga root. The plant is one of the few to have survived EarthDrought and EarthFamine and rejects all bio enhancements. It has the ability to propel them out or disintegrate them.'

'So why not just make some, grow some?' asked Ben.

'We can't. The biology of the plant is so unique, so elemental, the bio mechanics fail every time. The intricacies are too many. It rejects all manufactured soil, all enhanced light and nourishment. Everything except nature and where it chooses to grow. What we create is perfect in every way, except in nature.'

'You make it sound like it can think. A plant that's smarter than Salthea, isn't that just great,' Ben quipped.

'It seems it almost can,' retorted Prane. 'That's why we need natural collection. A real, natural harvest. Once we find it, *you* find it, we can study it, extract what we need, develop a vaccine. Begin mass production.'

'So just go ahead and send harvesters, trucks. Security. Why send us? Look at us. This is just a game to trick us, extend the process till we die out here anyway.'

Prane toyed with Ben further, 'Entertaining as watching you both suffer might be, racing in gung-ho would be far too risky. Let's call this task you are doing an important errand. A confidential, highly classified errand which falls out with the remit of most at Salthea. The background to it is clearly highly sensitive and delicate; we can't risk any leaks or hearsay which a bigger operation would most certainly bring. Delicate times called for delicate action, particularly at this stage. We cannot have any unwanted attention.'

A look passed between Prane and Takot, both nodding gently towards each other almost in time. She continued,

'Those who inhabit the Wilds may believe they have ownership over the Dealga. It is doubtful they have the resources to know the preciousness of it, or, given their state of mind, care. We cannot have a harvesting party being tracked and traced leading to the deliberate destruction of the Dealga. Not before we are 100% sure it will provide the cure. Therefore, something stealthier was required.'

As she continued, Callie exploded as rage boiled into her throat. 'And you brought us here. Dragged us to this deserted wasteland before you told us the truth. For what? Because you knew if you told us back there we'd refuse? Try and escape?' Both were silent. 'Of course you did,' the tears - of fear and anger – fell freely now as she continued, 'If we refuse here we die anyway. There's nothing. We don't even know where we are!'

'Ah, there it is,' smiled Takot, almost clapping.

'There's what? I'm sick of these bullshit riddles.'

'The fire, the hate. The determination. That is why you're here. Why you are both still alive.'

Callie shook her head, sniffing loudly. 'That's where you're wrong. I don't care anymore if I live or not. My family is dead,' her eyes lingering on Ben as she forced out the word. 'There is nothing left for me. Get someone else to do your dirty work. We're here because we're expendable. Necessary casualties. Disposable. I might as well just sit here and die. Let the insects take my body. I'd rather they had it than give it to you.'

Takot ignored her and continued, 'But you won't. We know you better than yourself. You think this is just a coincidence? That you in particular are here because of some kiss with a boy? Because of some gossip and chitter-chatter you heard outside your window by a less-than-careful guard? Oh, how naïve you are.'

'What are you talking about?' asked Ben, 'What else is there?'

'Scores,' Prane began.

Callie and Ben looked blankly at each other, then back at Takot and Prane.

'I don't understand,' said Ben, 'What scores?'

'Admittedly, individually you have impressive, very impressive, but not exceptional skills and talents.'

'Thanks for the vote of confidence,' Callie muttered sarcastically. 'Maybe you should have looked further for someone to do your dirty work in that case.'

Takot ignored her and went on, 'You think you are here to do our 'dirty work' as you called it. Dear girl, there is so much more to it than that. You two are not here by some accident and coincidence. We have been researching, watching, collecting data. Selecting our contenders. You yourself provided us with the perfect opportunity, so innocently put yourself forward.

Crossan your record and the reports received show you are undoubtedly one of the finest trackers we have. Your propensity to retain and recall knowledge of our history and planet also does not go unnoticed. It is a pity your temper and self-control leave so much to be desired.' Callie simply glared, unwilling to speak for the moment.

'Rhea, your tracking and hunting skills are sadly less impressive. However, your brute strength is clear for everyone to see, and your athleticism is equally obvious. You both also showed your aptitude and dedication to the battle arts, Khalto.'

'Perhaps you should have embraced the stillness of mind more, Rassay,' Prane interrupted wryly.

'Fuck you,' Callie replied. In one swift, sudden moment Prane raised her hand and brought it down to slap her. Just as it was about to reach Callie's face Takot caught it.

'Enough,' he said firmly, placing Prane's hand back on her lap. The look of hate which left her eyes was almost audible.

'That's why you were both the almost faultless selection,' Prane redirecting her gaze to Callie and Ben. 'Your scores, personality, aptitudes balance each other completely.'

'Well didn't she just play innocently into your hands, volunteering, then,' said Ben icily.

Prane sat back, 'Oh there was no coincidence. You don't think it was some kind of romantic quirk of fate that Rassay ended up on your lane, do you?'

'But I volunteered me and Bree,' Callie could feel the sadness and bitter regret when she said her name.

'Granted, that's true. But as soon as you volunteered, as soon as Crossan raised her concerns about your impulsiveness, questioning and comments about Rhea, it was apparent information security protocols had been breached. You appeared to be the ideal choices to support our efforts to stop the spread.'

Prane paused, sitting back smugly with her arms folded and Takot continued. 'Together you are quite a skilled, formidable pair. Perfect for the collection of the cure. Young, without suspicion. Those few who may still be sane in the Wilds will, hopefully, not kill two teenagers on sight as they most definitely would any adults they came across. You can bring back the Dealga. We can ensure our ideas and inspections so far have been correct. Then we can execute details for further long term, more widespread reaping and limit the collateral damage. Hopefully any being you meet will believe your story.'

Ben interrupted, 'Story?'

'Of two wayward, lucky runaways, escaping the harvest for being caught in forbidden romantic liaisons. Plus, of course, you are both completely dispensable should you sadly need replaced on incompletion.'

'You mean death. Then why tell her what I did?' Ben asked. 'Why tell her about Tax?'

Callie forgot herself, 'Don't you dare say his name,' she cried, turning on Ben. 'You don't get to mention him.'

Takot raised his hand, nodding. 'Simple. Together you can plot and conspire negatively against our cause. But hate. Hate means you will comply. Do what we ask to gain your freedom. And quickly. Now, pleasantries over, are you both ready to be briefed and begin?'

CHAPTER THIRTEEN

The final Briefing had been straight and uninterrupted. Callie had no idea from his expression how Ben felt or what he was thinking, but she was certain. Find the cure and disappear. She knew not to trust Takot, despite what he said. Callie and Ben both knew too much. The situation on her return would be hopeless. Unsustainable. The government couldn't risk what she and Ben knew. Couldn't risk them living the rest of their lives without letting something slip. No, she knew she had to find the cure and disappear. Find someone, somewhere who could help her.

They had been given maps within their packs and pointed to a location further north, deep within the Wilds. The hike would take them to where it was presumed almost certainly, an abundance of Dealga grew. This she assumed, was her domain. Ben had basic scientific testing equipment and biological charts to enable him to find the plant. A ploy, Callie realised, to keep them together. A need for them to stay close to each other.

From the crass, unclear satellite footage it appeared to be heavily forested, dank and thickly dense. There was no intelligence about what they may encounter or what they should expect.

Alongside the map and Dealga apparatus they both had their camouflage clothing and belt plus basic rations, Khalto sticks and a light, self-expanding shelter.

Prane stood before them. Callie realised she looked almost proud of what she saw. In her hand Prane thoughtfully rolled around two small, greyish circular containers. Eventually she stopped and held one out each to Callie and Ben.

'Your final requirement.' she said, 'Daily medicine.'

Callie took it and slipped it securely into a pocket. Ben looked closely at the opaque sphere and shook it gently. 'How many days?' he asked.

Realising the implication, Callie stood frozen.

Prane smiled, once again the look was ominous and detached. 'Six.'

'That's it?'

She shrugged, 'That is all we have. All we need. The data shows clearly you can make it to the Dealga in just over two days. Collect the samples and return. Six days is therefore a more than generous allowance.'

'And if there is a problem?' Ben continued, 'What then?'

'Then you solve it.' Prane held his stare until he looked away, nodding.

'Great, just great. A death sentence. That's what you're sending us to. Do you even know what could be there? What we could find, what could find us?'

Nothing.

As if on cue they all turned as the sand began to twist and turn and the sound of a helicopter approaching grew louder and clearer. They shielded their eyes from the mini storm it created on landing, which subsided slightly as the rotors slowed. Through the clearing air Takot sat inside, with a guard on each side. Prane gestured towards the helicopter. Callie and Ben climbed inside as the rotors started up again, churning and spinning the ground as it flew low towards the drop off point – the indistinct track through the hills on the opposite track of the lake bed.

The pair dismounted, their sticks and packs followed, tipped out by the guards on board. Then the helicopter rose once more, dipped to the side before straightening, as if it was nodding good luck to Callie and Ben, before heading back across the empty loch. Callie stood and watched it as it turned from an ugly, bloated insect to a smudge on the otherwise empty sky then disappeared altogether. Realising there was nothing else to distract her, she breathed deep and turned to face Ben. He was perched on an uneven boulder and steeled his shoulders as she turned.

Callie broke the silence. 'Let's get one thing clear. We go, get the Dealga, get back. We talk about what we need to do, where we're going and that's it. I don't need your help. I don't need your excuses or empathy or some gesture of guilt and self-retribution. I need you to find the Dealga, you need me to get you there. End of.'

'Understood', Ben murmured. 'I understand how you feel. Know how much you hate me right now.'

'Right now?' the words were careful, slow and cold. 'There is no right now. I loathe you with every pulse in my body. I'm here for one reason only, I get us there, you find the Dealga. After that this is done. I don't care if you live or die.' She stared with burning eyes until he nodded silently, stood and picked up his pack.

'Let's go,' he said.

Callie adjusted a shoulder strap and twisted her belt which had moved round her body and ordered, 'This way.' Without looking to see if Ben was behind her, she began following the track before stopping and, without turning round, spoke flatly. 'Actually, I lied.'

'About what?'

'I do care…If you live.' In silence they set off again. The track was only wide enough for one person, abandoned, broken and overgrown. In places it was defined only by the faintest indent appearing in shadows. It was also littered, precariously, with loose stones and roots. The pair had to walk carefully; a twisted ankle (or worse) out here would be disastrous. It was also deviously steep.

They spent a slow, uncomfortable two and a half hours climbing slowly to the bridge of the peak, rearranging their new clothing, packs and belts as they discovered and learned what was comfortable. Regular, deliberate footsteps which heavied quite quickly. Deep, concentrated breathing, long and full. Not a word had passed between them. The blaring silence highlighted the tension between the two teenagers.

Once Ben had stumbled over a root and brought his weight down on one knee with a thump. Callie had turned, checked flippantly to see if he was alright and merely continued again. She still led the pair. She thought it was bad enough she could sense and hear him behind her, but she didn't want to have to watch his back plod up the hill in front of her. Stubbornly she was also afraid she would not be able to keep up, the last thing she wanted was to have him slow for her.

From this point they could not yet see what lay beyond the hills, but they could look back at the valley. Green and yellowing jagged pinpricks of shrubs and bushes dotted the valley floor, the slight, wispy shadows the morning sun drew off the boulders created optically illusive shapes. At times the shadows flickered and caught Callie's eye, tricking her into believing someone, or something, was moving. She could feel sweat underneath her pack and her new boots. It didn't bother her, she was used to this from the field, but the sky dazzled down and here there was no respite in corn. Callie hadn't realised how sheltered they could be in the fields, the shadows never seemed long enough, the crop never high enough to give any shelter or respite. Until now. The top was nearing, and she was determined to get there before taking a welcome stop and fluids. She wouldn't stop until then, not give Ben any satisfaction that she was showing weakness.

Finally, a little after lunchtime, Callie stopped, shook off her pack and, bent over with hands on knees, bent her aching back and breathed deeply. The air felt warm but sweet and clear. There was no dust here, at least right now it was pure and welcoming. Unbuckling the strap from his pack and taking out his water tank Ben took a long drink, his throat rising and falling greedily. He wiped his mouth then sucked the last drops off the back of his hand, wasting nothing, before offering the flask to Callie.

She ignored the gesture and drank, equally as welcome and greedily, from her own, before sitting, cross-legged on the ground and removing her left boot. She shook it out, removed some wayward pebbles that had been irritating her sole for a time, re-laced them, stretched out and looked at what was ahead.

It seemed to Callie beyond them lay the whole of the world, it felt like she could see everything. The peak they were resting on was wide and flat. The welcome breeze hummed in her ears and caused her eyes to run as she turned 360 to look around. Behind her lay the empty loch where they had begun. Callie pushed the worry of returning there in time to the back of her mind – focus was what they needed, not uneasiness.

In front and on her left was uneven, bumpy looking land, similar to where they had left, rocky, cracked and dry. From her position Callie could see dark, thin veins running and crisscrossing along the land, stopped in their journeys from time to time by rocky outcrops, squat scrubs or hoodoos that had somehow stubbornly exploded from the cracks and shaped themselves defiantly in gravity resisting ways. She wasn't sure if the occasional movements that flickered at the very edges of her peripheral vision was real, a lizard perhaps, or a trick of the light and shadows.

To her right was another slope, arcing round to the left in a sort of crescent shape, from this position it seemed shorter and gentler than the one they had trekked up. Again, they would need to find their feet, there was no obvious path, why would there be? They would follow this crescent then dip down towards a wilderness on the unseen far side. The inside, shadowed side of this slope had a sheer, cliff drop, the rich, golden sides smoothed and eroded by years of winds and sands battering against them.

Prane had warned them of caves at the foot of the curve. It was unknown if they were inhabited now, but there was evidence they had been used in the past. Callie knew to be aware of signs of life as she tracked them to the Dealga. As much as she was curious about the caves, the legends she had heard, the ones they had all been brought up on, she felt her skin prickle with thoughts of having to face an enemy and hoped they were abandoned.

Past the crescent was the wilderness, one of the rare ancient forests that had withstood decimation and still remained here now. It wasn't visible from this standpoint, but Callie knew from the map that was where they would find shelter for the night – kilometres of land just safe, simple centimetres on her map. Trees had, of course been thoughtlessly and relentlessly savaged by man before Drought and Famine. In the centuries following, carbon dioxide levels grew and polluted the atmosphere along with other toxic contaminants. Trees were no longer the air filters for the world. There were not enough of them left, perhaps less than 20% of the already ruined figures from the year 2,500. Most of these were sickly or young, still to fight against mankind to mature and flourish. Now oxygen levels were maintained in the enormous, town sized factories. Factories pumping out pseudo-oxygen solutions across the globe through giant, stories high, droning fans.

Even though she was trapped in this situation, in this moment Callie felt free, freer than she had ever been in her life. She realised this was who she was. Alive. Every cell in her body triggered, activated and alert. She was aware of the dangers, they sat in her stomach like a low warning rumble. But as she breathed in the air and her eyes darted around, soaking up the atmosphere greedily in case it was suddenly snatched away, Callie couldn't deny this excitement and passion.

A forest, they would be inside a natural forest. Experience life that had stood far, far longer than anything else existing on Earth now. Life that was far wiser, adaptable and indestructible in its silence than much left here. the cooling shade of real branches, the smell of real leaves, and the feel of the dank, dark earth under their feet. Whatever happened after that, Callie didn't know. She did know she had no trust or faith in Prane or Takot; knew she and Ben just couldn't simply return with the Dealga and be free. Callie had steeled herself to acceptance of imprisonment or worse after this. Perhaps it was this knowledge of the future that led her to this sense of immersion and absorbing the time and experience she had left.

'We should probably go.' Ben broke Callie's thoughts, she hadn't noticed him come alongside. She turned, barely looking at him as she grudgingly nodded, took another grateful drink and started loading up her pack again. 'Just to stay on target,' he tried to explain.

'Okay,' Callie snapped, 'I'm getting ready.'

'Do you know where we need to head to reach camp?'

Callie heaved her rucksack on her shoulders and tied her pack round her waist. 'Cal, do you know where we should be headed?' he asked again.

She shrugged, 'It's Callie, and yes, I know. Don't worry, I'll get you there safe.' Her sarcasm was obvious, and they set off, following the curve of the ridge. It was a softer, kinder incline which was welcome after the tough hike. Unconsciously both of them kept to the left side, avoiding the sheer drop. At times vague depressions in the land led close to the edge and they glanced down. Callie's stomach had lurched and rolled, and her limbs turned weak and jelly-like. It was as if her legs had their own thoughts and emotions and were escaping a fall, trying to climb up inside her body for safety. The woozy circling in her head steered her away off the hinted track, following the arc around the steadier, wider left side.

Eventually they reached the point where the map showed it was safest to start the descent to ground level; far enough away they would not be ending their journey down immediately where the caves sat and where the gradient appeared easy enough. Callie turned to Ben and spoke, without intonation. 'We need to start going down from here. The caves are at the bottom, but over that way,' she pointed to the left. 'Once we get down, we will be completely in the open and vulnerable. We head Northeast for a few kilometres to reach the wood and the communications post. All being well, we can camp there.'

'All being well,' agreed Ben.

Silence returned, both youths realising that was the most interaction between them in days. And both realising if they were to get through the situation that would have to change.

There was little or no sign of a track or path leading down this side of the hill. Steep areas meant Callie's lower back began to ache as she battled tripping if she leant forward too much with leaning back and feeling the pull of her pack dragging her back.

Ben this time, was striding out in front, checking back from time to time to check they were still in alignment. Suddenly, during one of these checks he slipped, falling awkwardly on his left, without time to put his hands out. Loose stones flew up and the sound of his body thumping and scraping the ground was clear. When he lay for longer than he should have, Callie realised something was wrong and broke into a light jog. As she approached, Ben was shrugging off his pack and sitting up, wincing and grabbing his left knee.

'You ok?' Callie spoke coldly. Ben winced, looked up at her with a grimace and shook his head. Callie sighed and held out a hand. Ben shook his head again,

'I can't. I can't get up.' She realised he was in difficulty and dropped to the ground.

'We need to see it.' Ben looked through slanted, tightened eyes and nodded. Callie unlaced his boot and slowly they rolled up his trouser leg. As they reached the knee Ben cried out in pain. His knee was already red and swelling. Callie felt bile rise in her throat when she saw the kneecap bulging out, painful and squint.

'I heard it pop when I landed,' Ben spoke through snarling teeth. 'Think the kneecap is dislocated.' Callie nodded in agreement.

'Can you bend it? Put any weight on it?'

'I don't think so.' He reached up and Callie lurched back as he tried to put a hand on her shoulder. 'Please,' he whispered, looking her straight in the eye. She sighed and nodded. Ben reached out and tried to right himself onto his knee. Crying out he shook his head and returned to the ground.

'Can you straighten it?'

Easing his leg down slowly bit by bit, Ben tried to stretch out, but it was clear this wasn't going to happen.

'You'll need to pop it back for me.'

Callie was shocked and put her hands up fingers splayed out, 'Me? No! I'm not doing that. You're on your own.'

'Callie, you have to. I can straighten it, but you need to push it back in place.'

She creased her nose in disdain. Ben went on, 'Well what else are we going to do? Sit here? Wait and hope it gets better? I thought you'd enjoy seeing me in pain.'

'I didn't say I wasn't enjoying it. Fine. What do you want me to do?'

Ben rolled slightly onto his right hip.

'I'll straighten out my leg, you manipulate the kneecap back into place. Ok?' Callie nodded, unconvinced.

Slowly, hissing and contorting his face in obvious discomfort, Ben straightened his leg as much as he could, gently massaging his thigh to try to help the movement. When it was as clear he had moved as far as possible, he nodded to Callie. 'Ok?'

In reply she gingerly put her hands on his knee and began to massage the kneecap. Mouth shut, Ben moaned. Callie stopped but he eyed her to continue. She pushed again.

'It's not working,' she said.

'Once, hard,' Ben said to her. 'Just do it, one time, as hard as you can. Promise, it'll work.'

'Sure?'

'Sure, go for it.' Callie took a deep inhale and shoved. She felt and heard the crack as the kneecap bumpily slid back into place and Ben yelled out in agony. Immediately she rubbed her hands on her trousers, as if she was removing every trace of touching him and backed off slightly.

Ben sat up, beads of sweat bursting on his forehead and warily straightened his leg. Bending it back. Straightening again.

'Can you get up?'

'I think so,' he said.

Callie's hand appeared in front of his face, holding a silver foil.

'Here, take this. Painkiller.'

Ben took it, continued to get to his feet, ripped the packet open and drank the thick, sweet, syrupy liquid. 'Thanks.'

'If you can walk, we need to move,' was Callie's reply. She was already taking another drink and preparing to leave.

His gait was slightly limping, and charges of pain surrounded his knee every time his foot met the ground, but Ben knew it could have been much worse. He hoped it would wear off soon and besides, it wasn't really holding him back, so for that we was grateful.

Together they were more than halfway down the mountain, a few more hours and they should be able to set up camp for the night. By tomorrow they would have found and gathered the Dealga. Ben, like Callie, was in no mood to believe this could or would not happen, the consequences were too severe.

He caught up with Callie, she wouldn't admit it but she did seem to be keeping a slower pace, was it to help him keep up? Ben wasn't sure but he wanted to think so.

'We need to talk about happens when we get down there,' he said. 'Be prepared.'

'For?'

'For anything. Something in the caves. Something else. We need a plan.'

Callie's shoulders relaxed in agreement.

'Fine' she said.

Callie unzipped a compartment of her belt and took out the map Takot had given her. She had only needed to look at it for few minutes to absorb the details they needed to reach camp successfully today. Successfully meaning without danger or obstacles. Other than Ben's fall their progress was good, but the rest hinged on whether or not the caves were occupied. She had to hope, if not fully believe, that they were. There were a few precious hours of daylight left but the sun was beginning to tire and hang lower in the sky. Callie and Ben cast longer shadows on the hillside and the light was clearly starting to cast an amber glow. Anyone, anything they met going forward would be much more aware of the landscape, the geography of where they walked. Equipped as they were, Callie and Ben were still strangers here.

Ben pointed to the map; grateful she was such an experienced tracker. He could not say it to her, knew it would not be a welcome comment, but in his mind their success lay solely in her hands. 'Do you know where we are?' He could sense her muscles tighten and bristle at the comment, 'I mean, where are we?'

Callie bent and placed the map on the ground, a corner unsettled in the breeze was retained with a spiky rock.

'Here,' she pointed to a location nowhere near where Ben expected. Once again, he realised Takot and Prane had been correct in their pairing. He glanced at her, then back to the map and nodded.

'So?'

Callie continued, 'If we can get down directly from here, we should be just under a kilometre from the caves. According to the map out of the safety of the hill we'll be more or less totally exposed – barren plain and hoodoos all the way to the communications post. There should be an indistinct road we can follow, but it's probably as good as this one.'

'But you can track and get us there?'

'I'm pretty sure.'

'That's good enough for me,' Ben reassured – uncertain if it was for her benefit or his own.

'What other option do I have?'

CHAPTER FOURTEEN

Delicately and as silently as possible they had made their way to the foot of the hill and now rested, briefly on the edge of a boulder which had long since collapsed down the side and embedded in the ground below. Rough and lumpy, it was hardly restful, but it shielded them as much as possible from view and provided some relief. Ben rubbed his knee and fiddled with the wrap around it, luckily the pain was bearable and despite some sharp jarring on the joint as they walked downhill, it wasn't holding him back.

Callie, irritated, waved away a flying insect as she looked from the map to the distances in front of her. She looked unsettled, tense. Certainly, the details were right – flat blandness lay in front of them, now clearly lined and shadowed with the brassy, glowing sun as it shifted through the hours. Instead of warm and optimistic it just added a gloomy haze to the horizon. But they had seen the wood on the way down. Both of them had stolen precious minutes to regard the colours, shapes and textures with awe through the binoculars they held in their packs. They now knew it definitely did lie ahead, they just needed to make their way there.

'Something up?' Ben asked lightly, moving slightly closer along the rock. Callie instantly leaned away and reorganised herself so there was still a distance between them.

'Nothing. I'm fine,' she said, without looking at him.

'It's just you seem on edge.'

'She pursed her lips, 'I said I'm fine. It's just, I don't know.'

'What?'

Callie sighed. She hated this feeling of being trapped, stuck in a situation she couldn't change, had no control over. Didn't want to deal with. Every word she spoke to him stuck in her throat, jagged at her heart, in her mind betraying Tax. Trying to drive it deep down inside she fixated on what she needed to do.

'Something doesn't feel right. And before you ask, I don't know. There's an atmosphere. A wrongness. We need to go.'

Ben could tell she was on edge, feeling the pressure of what was ahead of them, 'Maybe we could rest? Should we wait till it's darker?'

Callie considered, then shook her head. 'Maybe, but it's harder to track, harder to move in the stillness. And besides,' she snapped, 'your wittering will drive anyone, anything towards us. No, we need to go. Now.'

Ben took a deep breath between his teeth and rose to his feet.

'Ready.'

She pointed and nodded, 'This way. We agree now, we don't talk unless we absolutely have to. If we go directly Northeast it's quickest but there's less cover. We should try and follow the stacks for as long as we can, at least heading North, then cut over as late as possible. By the time we reach the wood it'll be twilight, we can't stop before then.'

Ben was comforted at the clarity of her thought process, 'Okay.'

'Just keep alert.'

'Anything in particular I need to look out for?'

'This isn't a tracking lesson, Ben. Prane couldn't tell us for definite the caves were empty; those things weren't out here.'

'I didn't mean…'

'If we're out here, jumping from rock to rock, sneaking around and hiding, so is everything else.'

These words hung ominously in the air, unchallenged. They set off, silently.

Callie couldn't figure out or decide if it was the sensation something was wrong, the unknown terrain, the burden of what they were trying to do, but her whole body felt an amplified sharpness. They didn't speak, no longer had laboured uphill breathing, but the stillness that encircled them heavily intensified every sound either of them made. Every footstep seemed to last and echo, it was like the ground was trying to expose them and reveal where they were.

They wove their way forward, stack to stack, the comfort of the hill now a memory behind them. They couldn't dawdle, but equally trying to hurry or run could be dangerous – they needed to remain as quiet as they possibly could and be aware and receptive to their surroundings and any hidden obstacles. The clothing Takot had issued did at least offer some protection, the tone of their clothing had invisibly and undetected changed to the arid, sandy tone of their surroundings, scattered as they walked with shadowy shades of brown and grey. If nothing else, Ben thought, at least we're camouflaged.

It seemed like they were making good progress when Callie pulled up, put out her arm in a warning and crouched down, one knee on the ground. Carefully she picked something up and turned it over in her hands.

'What is it?' Ben asked quietly, squatting down to join her.

Callie offered him her open hand. In the palm sat a small flat stone, somewhat triangular but bashed and misshapen. Dull, dark grey and scratched it filled most of her palm. To Ben it was innocuous. In fact, he thought, he would most likely have walked over it without even noticing.

'I'm not certain,' Callie answered. 'But it didn't come from here.'

'How can you be so sure?' Ben was curious.

'Look around. There isn't any other stone like this. The colour, the texture. These rocks are soft, relatively easy to break. This is dark, solid. No, this was brought here.'

'By whom?'

'That's what worries me,' Callie spoke slowly. 'How do we know? It was embedded in slightly, but not overgrown. Not new. But not old.'

'What do you think it is?'

Callie held it out and Ben took it gingerly, 'Look at the shape Ben, the raised, snapped middle just there', she pointed to where something seemed to have snapped off and splintered an edge. 'I think it's a flint.'

'An arrowhead?' Ben was shocked. 'Shit,' he looked around, turning an almost 180 to his right, then back to his left.

Callie nodded. 'I can't be certain but that's what I think. We need to find the outpost soon. I might be right, and this has been here a while, but it doesn't take away the fact it's here in the first place.'

Ben handed it back to Callie who turned it over and over between her fingers as they continued their tramp to the site. Callie had been clearly scanning and examining their way before she found the arrowhead, but she seemed even more meticulous and careful now. Her shoulders were raised and tight, her gait long and controlled, peripheral vision ensuring nothing went unseen; everything was of equal importance.

Finally, just as they couldn't deny it anymore and the luminous sunset gave way to the shadowy mystery of twilight, Callie and Ben reached the trees. Excited tension had risen in both of them as they got closer and closer – colours and textures revealing themselves out of the distant blur and smudge – but nothing could prepare them for the senses overload that exploded when they finally found the edge of the wood.

Without saying anything to the other they both reached out and explored; their senses overwhelmed with extraordinary new sensations. Two sets of eyes darted here and there and up and down, trying to take everything in, every tiny detail. They rubbed their hands over the trunks and branches, the wood both solid yet delicate under their fingernails. Callie traced along the intricate, strange bark, entranced by the cold, comforting feel as the trees wrapped them in foliage. She didn't think she had ever seen anything more entrancing than this rough, grooved skin. She moved her fingers over lime-yellowy patches of lichen, explored deep cracks in the bark and followed the patterns of hollows. She wrapped her arms around solid, stretching trunks, awestruck at how vast they were: her arms having no hope of reaching each other.

They both soaked in the deep, still smell of the wood: warm and dense and earthy. It encircled them, hanging almost solid in the air. Sounds were heightened, held longer in the arms of the trees. Callie and Ben were used to the occasional contrary mite or stray flying biter invading their space in the fields with their low, repetitive buzzing. But here it was obvious how adaptable and resilient insects were; they had not diminished over the centuries and their strident wings and drones were in abundancy here.

As Callie and Ben walked deeper inside, they were both aware of the sensations underfoot. No matter how careful they were, the forest seemed to be alive with sound. The thought both excited and worried them, it was almost impossible to be stealthy – they were as much in the open here to trackers as they were in the plains. Leaves and lichen teased them. Dry it snapped and scrunched underfoot; damp it squelched with sucking delight. Longer grasses and brush rippled and swished as they passed through, occasionally gripping out and pinging back from their clothes or hair or packs.

The last long rays of orange and crimson sunlight specked through gaps in the leaves onto the forest floor, highlighting the skeletal veins running through the leaves. Callie couldn't bear to pick one from a tree so took one from the ground and, as she rose, saw Ben had done the same and was examining one, entranced.

'I thought you would have seen all this before?' she remarked. 'In the greenhouses.' The word was loaded with memories.

Ben flinched and shook his head, speaking gently. 'Not like this. Not like these. These trees are, I don't know what the right word is. I don't know what they are.'

Looking up, a branch held before her eyes, Callie answered for him. 'Beautiful.'

'Not only beautiful,' he continued. 'These are free. Alive.' Ben paused, 'Like you. Callie, can we talk?'

'We need to move.' She had cut the atmosphere, the invisible knife so sharp and fatal. 'I need to get back on track, shit, ok.' Callie spun 360, both getting her bearings and, Ben knew, throwing off the moment. When she spoke, he didn't answer at first, unsure if she was muttering to herself or to him. 'When we moved inside there was a fallen tree. Mostly dead. Where was that? Which way?'

'I think there,' Ben pointed to the right and headed a few steps in that direction. 'Yeah, is that not it, I think it might be, see just through there?' He turned to see if Callie had heard. She was following, her face thunder. As she passed him she turned to look him in the eye. The pain and disgust remained brutally obvious, then she swept on and was away.

'No more distractions', she announced once they had righted their course, Ben picking up on the accusation and wondering if she remembered she was as in awe of the nature as he was. Maybe even more so. 'We move quickly, silently, precisely. Now.' Watching the back of her head disappear into the shadowy forest Ben followed, wordlessly. There would be a time and place for the confrontation they needed to have, but not here and not now.

True to her word and skill, Callie found the derelict communication post seamlessly. Squat and rectangular it stood nondescript in a small clearing in the forest. One door, one window, it was bleak and austere but would be a welcome hide for the night. Ben carefully approached the bare window and strained to see as far in as he could before, satisfied it was empty, he threw off his pack relieved and rolled his aching shoulders.

The building had been painted in a deep green shade, though the paint now flaked severely. There was no denying the walls were solid, tribute to how it had managed to stand for so long but was now covered in random gouges which allowed cracking, powdery concrete to spill out on to the forest floor.

Gingerly Callie entered the shelter, the doorway now just a gaping hole, finding Ben already inside. The flat roof was partially destroyed, a flap fell inwards and swung against a corner of the one room. Parts of the outside world: leaves, roots, branches encroached inside, but it was solid, and it was dry. Callie shook off her pack and leaned it up against a wall. Sitting next to it, knees bent in front she took a long, relaxed drink from her flask and unlaced her thick boots. She sighed as she pulled them off and massaged her feet grimacing from time to time. Across the room Ben chewed something grey and dried from his pack. The rations Prane and Takot had given them must be on a par with the food at the farm Callie thought wryly.

'Thank you,' Ben broke the silence with a gently smile.

'For what?'

'For getting us here. Safe.'

'It's not like I had many other options,' Callie sighed, turning her head left to right as she massaged her neck.

'You could have left me to manage myself,' Ben tried.

Callie finished massaging her neck. 'Tempting as that was, you bumbling around erratically would only have drawn more attention to us. I'd really rather not risk death any more than we already are, if that's ok with you?' She loosened the straps on her pack and began searching for her own meal. Or what would pass for it.

'Bumbling is a bit harsh,' Ben tried to joke, 'I'd accept shambling clumsily.'

'We're done talking,' Callie was abrupt and clipped.

Both sat in silence, chewing at tasteless rations and adapting to the creaks and moans of the building. Slowly they stopped jumping at every crack and rustle as they listened, intently, to the sounds of the resting, darkening forest. Thin branches teased the open roof with whispers and scratches, but that's all they were. Dust and leaves swirled and swished along the floor or roof, sometimes escaping through the window space.

Eventually, before it was too dark to move confidently and quietly, Callie began unwrapping her bedroll. She wasn't expecting a peaceful or comfortable sleep, but they both new they had to at least try to rest their muscles and try to snatch some energy for the day ahead.

Ben, standing at the open doorway, looking into the forest, turned. 'We should take turns keeping watch. What do you think?'

Callie looked up and nodded. 'I'll stay here. Please don't get too close.'

'There's not exactly tons of room in here, Callie.'

She stared. 'Just keep your distance. It's going to be hard enough getting rest without sharing air or space with you.'

'We're sharing it anyway you know.'

'You know exactly what I mean. First or second watch?'

'What?'

'Your great sentry idea.' That was unfair, and she knew it. It was much safer if one of them kept watch. Still, she wasn't going to concede that.

'Um, I don't mind. You choose.'

'No, no. It was your plan. You decide.'

Ben didn't know if this was a trap or not, but he knew either way he was going to mess it up.

'Fine, I'll go first. You look ready to settle down anyway.'

'Oh, so I'm lazy?'

'What, no?'

'I'm lazy, weak, ready to sleep without even thinking about what could happen in the dark. Is that it?'

Ben shook his head, whispering angrily. 'No, Callie. You told me to pick. I'll go first, I don't mind. But, fine. You stay up, I'll sleep.'

'Is it because you're a guy then? I'm too weak to stay up? Too feeble to stand guard. Don't forget who got us here in the first place?'

'What is your problem?' Ben knew he was in danger of raising his voice too much, but she was beginning to push his buttons.

Callie's face twisted into a sneer, and she spoke slowly and steadily. 'My problem? Are you actually serious? What's my problem? With you? I don't think I'll even dignify that with an answer.' She looked him up and down in disgust. 'I don't even care. Take it. Be the hero and keep watch. Four hours? Just make sure you wake me. I don't want to owe you a thing.'

Ben stared at her, saying nothing. She wasn't going to move her glare, he realised, so eventually he shook his head, turned and sat on his pack in the doorway.

Callie punched and thumped her pack, trying to smooth it into some kind of pillow, threw her sleeping bag over her and turned away. Ben doubted there was any danger of him falling asleep. Not with the way adrenaline and anger were rushing through his body. His head was roaring. He doubted she would get any sleep either, which gave some reluctant comfort.

Ben was wrong, the lingering heat; staring into the dark; the subsidence of adrenaline or the events of the day: one of them took its toll. His head jerked back with a jolt, twisting his neck as it did. He winced and simultaneously rubbed his neck and shook his head awake. He didn't know if he'd slept for five minutes or five hours and anxiously groped his wrist for his watch. Twenty minutes. Well, twenty minutes since he had last checked the time, so it was somewhere in between. He was relieved. He knew, of course, what could have happened in that time. Still, it could have been worse.

Ben stood, gingerly and quietly. He wasn't trying to save Callie's sleep: more he wanted some more solo calmness without her. Standing in the doorway he stretched deeply, arms raised above his head, which nodded from side to side. Rolling his shoulders, he started to pace round the shelter. As he reached each corner, he gingerly peeked round before continuing. First one way. Then the other. Even in that couple of minutes he felt more awake and settled back down. Fifty minutes. Fifty minutes till he could sleep.

'Nice walk?'

He physically jumped and felt the wave of electricity fire his body. Turning, Ben was aggravated to see from her expression that was exactly the impact Callie had been going for. He didn't answer. He did hope she hadn't seen him sleep. It looked like he was in luck or saving the knowledge to throw at him later.

Callie got up and stood looking out the black window. She moved her face left and right in the slight breeze, soaking the smells of the static forest. She had never realised before how loud silence could be. How impossible it was. How beautiful.

'I'm done. You can sleep, I'll start now,' she said.

Ben was uncertain. 'Is this a trick?'

'Why?'

'I say ok, you fly off the handle, accuse me of not pulling my weight. I say no, you explode and accuse me of sexism, not trusting you, not thinking you can handle it.'

The edges of Callie's mouth twitched upward for an instant, then she took control of the smile.

'No trick. I can't sleep anymore. I'll swap.' Ben looked her straight in the face, after a second or two she nodded almost imperceptibly.

'Ok, thanks,' he conceded. Callie turned and brought over her kit: sitting on her pack and wrapping her sleeping bag around her shoulders. She shivered in the changed position and night air. Ben thought better of asking her if she was ok. As he tried to find a bearable position in his own corner he heard her whisper, 'See you on the other side.' He smiled. And slept.

Ben was in a field of corn, not working this time, but walking. His hands gently rubbed carelessly along the plants as he turned his face to the sun and took in warm, dusty air. He continued down the path, his muscles relaxed and under no stress for once, simply baking comfortably in the afternoon heat. Suddenly he was choking, sand was filling his lungs and he struggled to catch a breath. Pulling himself out of his dream he felt a weight pushing down on him, forcing him immediately to heightened consciousness. Callie, inches from his face was holding her hand over his mouth and shook her head, a warning to stay silent, her eyes wide and sparkling in the tiny glow of wakening dawn. Ben nodded, understanding, and she carefully took her hand away. He, as carefully as he could so as not to make a sound, sat up.

Callie spoke in less than a murmur, 'Someone, something is outside. Watching.'

'Where?' Ben mouthed.

'Through the trees. Not far, but no stationary. It's moving around.'

'You sure? Did you see it?'

She shook her head. 'I can feel it. Sense a change, shadows where there shouldn't be. An awareness in the silence it's still too early for.'

'You're certain?' Ben whispered and her nod was good enough for him.

'I just know. Trust me. It's out there, and it's watching.' Ben noticed Callie had packed their kit up, clearly ready to leave. Both Khalto sticks sat at her side, ready to grab in an instant.

'Why doesn't it attack?'

'I don't know. Want to go and ask it?' there was a slight hiss to her tone. 'I don't know that it's human, it could be an animal, but it knows we're here. I can feel it watching, waiting.'

'An animal!' Ben peered, trying to find the shape. 'Maybe we can scare it.'

'Just wait. I can't be sure of the size. And neither of us have any idea what the hell lives out here. What animals have you seen, because I'm limited. If we go out there shouting and hollering and it charges, where does that leave us? No, if it's an animal it might just be curious. If it was hungry, dangerous it would have attacked by now.'

'But it's not one of them,' Ben said, mostly to himself. Callie nodded,

'One of the blistered, the sick? No. If it was, we would know all about it.'

'Assuming there is only one? What do you want to do? Run? Fight?'

'Wait.'

'Wait?'

Callie snarled, 'What do you suggest? Run off now in the pitch black? There's not even enough light from the stars out here. Where will we go Ben, which direction will you bravely lead us in?' He said nothing.

'Exactly. First light isn't far off. We have to wait until there's more light. I can't track us safely in the dark, not in terrain I don't understand. For now, we're stuck. Believe me, there's one and it's not one of them. I think if there were more, they wouldn't be so cautious. To me it feels like just one, looks like just one.' Callie paused and Ben nodded. 'It hasn't done anything yet. There's a reason for that. We need to prepare, then go as soon as we can. Quickly.'

'Ok, I guess so. Agreed,' he said, 'But in the meantime be ready.' Ben was already reaching for his belt. The edge of his knife felt reassuring as he ran his thumb down it, before locating his shock pellets and sense disruptor. Little comfort against an ambush, he figured, but they might at least give them a head start.

Callie focused on her compass and the map which she had unfolded silently. One hand on her Khalto stick which lay in her lap, she tracked their journey. They needed to head further into the woods, the Wilds. It would be slow moving through the thick, dense terrain. Unknown and untracked she hoped Ben would show at least some basic tracking skills. Providing shelter and concealment as well as unknown hazards and threats the trees and undergrowth would both be a blessing and a curse.

'Cal, Callie,' Ben's tiny, muffled voice found her, and she turned. 'It's right there' he mouthed from his position crouching beside the doorway. He slid his shoulder along the wall and looked out briefly with one eye, before pulling his revealed face back behind the wall. 'It's there. It's right behind that tree straight opposite the door, I'm sure of it. The shapes have changed in the dark'. Callie nodded and moved herself to the other side of the door, her back pinned tight against the wall.

Peeking out she saw Ben was right. They were in a forest surrounded by trees; some were taking over the hutch they sheltered in. But there was something different in the gloom directly in front. A thicker, straighter trunk, less warped and beautifully twisted compared to those nearby. As her eyes adjusted to the outside the trunk moved, narrowed and widened. She caught Ben's eye and nodded once.

Despite the danger of the night, they needed to go. Now. Whatever was out there was closer. It had decided it had waited long enough. Callie and Ben were trapped, but at least for now it seemed to Callie they had one slight advantage – there were two of them and definitely only one of 'it'.

She knew what to do. Whispering, gesturing, she explained it to Ben.

They would run, now, together. But not towards it to attack, as Ben had suggested. There was no way of telling for certain that this individual was actually on their own. They would run apart, in opposite directions and regroup. This way whatever it was had to make a choice, had to follow one of them. A theory Callie very much hoped they wouldn't have figured Callie and Ben would do.

Taking a different direction from the shelter, heading out and round in a semi-circle, whatever was observing wouldn't know which of them to follow. The confusion and indecision in deciding would give them a head start. That's what Callie hoped anyway. And, as long as Ben didn't mess up and managed to follow his compass north, always heading slightly uphill, she would be able to backtrack and track him. After that she wasn't sure, but any unwelcome visitors would at least be more on their terms. And hopefully shocked to find them united.

They helped each other on with their packs, Ben noticing the abhorrence and aversion she had for him was momentarily gone.

'Ready?' Callie asked, stick in hand.

Ben nodded.

'Try to head in a semicircle. Once you're pretty sure there's nothing following head north. There will be light by then. I'll find you.'

'Stay safe.'

Callie bobbed her head. Once.

Padding the end of her stick in her left hand she took a deep breath.

'Let's go'.

They ran.

CHAPTER FIFTEEN

The blood was cursing through her head and her veins, every part of her body was alert and ready. Callie battled with fear, apprehension and elation as she tried to focus, not easy at speed. This was proving to be much harder than she appreciated. It wasn't just having to judge flailing, hazardous branches in the pre-dawn shadowy dullness, it was also being mindful of the roots, ditches and uneven ground underfoot, often rooty and covered in leaves and grasses that hid protruding obstacles.

She did feel alone, checking behind her constantly and trying to listen beyond the rushing in hear ears to the forest and sounds that were irregular. Yet everything seemed gloriously irregular out here. She could never be sure what was simply the wood and what could be something else. However, Callie believed in trusting her instincts and felt certain she had not been followed. What she couldn't tell was if that meant Ben had been.

Pausing at a greying, fallen trunk Callie regrouped and assessed the area. She knew for sure she had headed exactly where she had wanted. She had roughly followed a semi-circular share out and was now rounding to come back inwards. Her compass told her soon she would be directly north of where she had left. From there she should be able to find Ben. Taking stock of the area she crouched and looked deeply into the woods behind her, looking for clues she wasn't alone. There was nothing. Nothing paused. Nothing shook out of place or crackled oddly.

Satisfied, Callie stood again and still staring intently, gulped water from her pack before continuing.

Was this the right way. I don't have a bloody clue, Ben thought. As soon as they had darted from the communications post he only concentrated on power and speed. Get away from whatever was watching them, put as much distance between them as he could. After that he could afford to look and find where he was. He thought he was heading in a rough semi-circle shape. Not that he had particularly concentrated on trying to, but it seemed like he had; he was definitely heading uphill so knew at least that was right. Just a slight constant incline, but that was what Callie had said, wasn't it?

At first, he had been certain he was followed. Why wouldn't they follow him, he thought. To anyone he would seem the strongest, most threatening of the pair. It would make sense to the naïve eye, he thought. Anyway, he had been sure he could hear laboured breathing behind him, hear the distorted air as a body trying to keep up. He didn't know if it was terror, or uncertainty or just blood minded stubbornness but he ran and ran, feeling like he could almost fly and run forever. Hands protecting him from wayward branches, luck supporting his legs and ankles from whatever lay on the forest floor, he had made it.

One thing he was grateful for was the painkillers he had crunched just before they left. His knee was tingling now, agitated in pain. Ben knew he would suffer later when the muscles cooled.

He wasn't sure now if he was in fact alone. He thought he'd either lost them or they'd given up. Certainly, he had slowed down, so maybe they had too and were careful again, sneaking closer silently and unexpectedly. As Callie had done across the forest, Ben tried to watch, his eyes more accustomed to the dimness, to see if he could see anyone approaching. Before anyone discovered him. Gingerly he decided no-one was there and concentrated on figuring out where the hell he was and how off target he had gone.

'Shit' he cursed out loud. He tapped the compass hopelessly, knowing it wasn't suddenly going to swing and reveal he had actually, miraculously, found north in a perfect swoop.

'Could have been worse,' he continued to mutter to himself, wondering if the sound made him feel more secure or more alone. North was going to take some getting back on track. Why hadn't he stopped earlier? Clown.

Twisting the dial on his compass Ben examined the situation. More east than anything else but turning to the left directed him back on track. At least in the right direction for sure. The clinometer was perfect, he was right, he had been climbing, just off on a diagonal. With any luck, his reset and Callie's tracking skills would kick in and they would find each other soon.

Taking one last survey of the area, Ben raised and lowered his shoulders a couple of times and, compass in his right palm, set off.

Heck I'm hot, Callie thought, wiping her forearm across her clammy forehead. Hopefully they would spend a lot of time in the shade of the forest today if she felt like this already. The yellowy, morning rays mottled the wood, the sharp light penetrating right to the floor and highlighting the beautifully asymmetrical patterns and shapes. The branches and leaves seemed to dance in their shadows on the forest floor, carefree and teasing. Callie felt nettled; she didn't particularly care that she was alone, the angst came from wondering how the hell she would find Ben quickly if he turned out to be lost.

Was he injured? Heading North at all? She shook the question out of her head, returning to her task. Ensure she was on course so if Ben couldn't get to her at least she could find him. She had been so certain of her plan before, but doubts were colliding and growing inside.

The limited details on the map showed they should head north, through the forest, on a slow, gentle incline. This would eventually even out onto a flatter area where they would continue north and breach the edge of the forest. After that details were even sparser.

Callie, not realising her instinct was so lucky this time, suspected Ben would not have headed in as clear or correct a direction as she had. She knew he had headed roughly north east at first, but wanted to track east as well as north, not trusting him to have kept completely on course.

It was much more difficult to track here. Callie had little experience of thick vegetation – tiny signs would be much less obvious. She tried to stay positive: perhaps bigger signs would be obvious and quickly noticeable. She had to remember she was here for her tracking; she could do this. Eyes down, scanning, peripheral vision absorbed, she reformed her thinking and continued.

Twenty minutes, half an hour later Callie was disheartened. Ben couldn't be this off track. Couldn't be this stupid. But there were no signs. Another thought rose in her throat. Callie battled to beat it away, but it swam in her consciousness. What if he had been caught? And by who, or what? Was she now out her on her own, not even really sure what it was they were looking for? Should she not be grateful if that happened? Callie battled with herself. She hated him, didn't she? No matter, she didn't want to be out here alone. Could she say she truly wanted him dead? Well, why shouldn't she after what he had done.

Infuriated, she shook her head and ground her palm into the side of her water bottle as she opened the tightly wound lid. Tipping her head back she took a warm gulp, relieving yet irritating her dry, sore throat as she swallowed. What she would give for a cool drink: one she could feel trickle down her throat all the way to her stomach. Who knew when, or if, she would ever have one of them again?

It was while her head was thrown back, drinking, that she noticed it. Straight in front of her. Bringing her head down slowly, so as not to miss it, she screwed the lid back on her precious water without looking. Wiped her mouth with her hand and stepped forward. Smiled.

Callie traced her fingers over the trunk of the tree. Just below her eye level there were still crumbs of torn, disturbed bark hanging. The scratching had left vibrant green bark exposed. This was recent. The messy but definite 'B' meant one thing. Ben had gone this way. Ben was alive.

'Shit'. Ben groped on the ground to find his knife which had landed in some damp, decomposing leaves just to the right of his foot. Currently he had a basic 'P' sliced into the tree and needed to complete the second bowl stroke. Retrieving the knife and brushing off the dirt and tree already stuck in it, he dug in, round and completed the letter. Not perfect by any means but it would do. Callie wouldn't miss these, he thought, reassuring himself. He was almost guaranteed she wouldn't, this was beyond even the most rudimental tracking. But, how would she know which way he had gone? He hoped she would head north from the 'B', figuring he was actually on track now, following the sparse trail. Yet maybe that only made sense to him, he thought.

Ben tried to put his doubts to one side; the whole thing was risky anyway. If anyone was out here, they would see the same thing. He had hoped they would miss it, be so used to the terrain and the area they wouldn't be looking for such obvious clues, but it was risky. Still, this whole bloody scenario was risky, and he'd blown the rendezvous so much he had to something. Plus, if there was someone, he wanted tracking him down, he knew it was Callie. He just had to hope if she wasn't the only one looking that she'd at least find him first.

Continuing north, obsessed with the compass point now, Ben marked out his paces before finding another trunk. He had wondered if he should stay and wait, backtrack even, try and find Callie instead of putting his faith in her finding him. But it all seemed to waste precious time and energy. He had to go on. They had to go on, even individually. There was too much at stake.

Reluctantly he realised how clever Takot and Prane had actually been. It was so obvious now how right they had been about their pairing. Together they were, if not quite formidable, undeniably impressive, reinforcing the other. Apart they were two teenagers on a goose chase, one of them roughly lost in the woods. Lost and hungry. Or at least he was. There was no doubt about it now and he punished himself with the certainty. No more self-denial. Ben had made a deal with himself. He was not stopping to eat until they were back together. As if reading his mind, his stomach gave a long, complaining grumble. Ignoring it, he continued on.

He was taking a chance, but not the worse idea ever, Callie thought as she found a third primitive 'B' in the woodwork. The letters did stand out to anyone giving more than a passing glance, but what else could he do. Callie conceded she would have done similar had the shoe been on the other foot. Plus, she supposed, he's definitely heading north now.

Standing back from the tree Callie noticed disturbed leaves at the roots. Running her fingers over them and having a closer look confirmed the clammy, rotten leaves had definitely been shifted and spoiled. She rubbed her hands on her jeans and screwed up her nose at the musty, stale smell that rose up from them.

'Closer', she spoke out loud, satisfied and reassured. There could still be a way to go but she would find him.

Fortunately, it didn't take much longer. The fifth 'B' she found was pretty rough and not as clearly embedded as the others – the stem of the letter barely cut – only the two arcs breaking the greying bark attracted her. Callie knew it wasn't the fault of the knife – those were Security issued, developed for any scenario the computers could generate and un-bluntable to any known force. No, she thought, he was just getting fed up with carving. Becoming irritated.

Pressing on, her tired legs revived and determined for now, Callie upped her pace.

It didn't take long either. Now she was obviously making up the distance between them, tracking became simpler. Perhaps she had a newfound confidence in reading the forest. She found his, at least hoping it belonged to him, footprint in drying leaves, abandoned from the trees. An indentation, perhaps where he had bent to tie a lace or set his pack down to take a drink, was squashed, lightly but clearly in a bush. And finally, a thin, juvenile branch swung more forcibly than it should. He was close.

A rustle and gentle snapping confirmed it. Running the last few metres Ben turned as she saw him ahead. His grin radiated and, forgetting himself in the moment, he approached arms wide.

'Am I glad to see you?' Realising what he was doing he swiftly put his arms down. Yet there was no doubt from her eyes as she came closer, she felt some warmth and the iciness had vanished.

'Well done with the letters,' Callie conceded.

Ben nodded, 'I knew you'd see them. I was just worried who else would,' he shrugged, 'But I couldn't think of anything else to do. Knew you could track me as soon as you found a trail, but we're against the clock so I didn't want to waste any time.'

'Agreed. It was a good idea. Hopefully we'll be out of here before anyone picks up on it.'

'Or anything.'

Callie stared. 'Yeah, or anything. Mind you, I'm not sure those things can think of anything except rage and hunger.' She shivered as she finished.

'You hungry? I didn't want to eat until you found me.'

Callie looked confused, 'Why?'

Embarrassed Ben admitted, 'Kind of a pact I made with myself. My fault I got lost so the punishment was I wouldn't eat until we were together.'

Callie smiled for an instant, before regaining her composure. Ben could almost see the veneer cooling, hear the ice cracking as it formed again. 'We shouldn't hang around. I'd rather walk and eat,' she said.

'Fine by me,' Ben agreed, shoving a hand deep into his pack to feel for a silver, foil wrapped ration pack. 'Cold stew. Brilliant,' he muttered to himself. 'Didn't think there was actually something worse than lukewarm stew.' He raised the pack to Callie in a reluctant toast, ripped the top and dug in with his spoon as they continued into the wood.

The ground slowly began to level out and feel softer underfoot. The earth began to change. Where it had been hard, dry and covered in leaves, with mulchy, muddy patches, it was becoming increasingly spongy and supple – at times Callie and Ben could hear the soft squelch of liquid as they stepped. The plants were changing too, the surface was littered with lime coloured moss spreading out between the trees and patchy fungi grew on roots and dead branches. There was a definite mildewed, vegetation smell becoming thicker.

'Can you smell that?' Ben nodded.

'We must be further than I thought.' Callie said, hopeful. 'It shouldn't be long till we reach the loch. Actual, real water!'

'How wide do you think it'll be?' Ben asked, not really expecting an answer but trying to fill the conversation.

'Can't tell, it's barely on the map at all. My guess is they weren't sure if it had even dried up or not. But I'm not worried how wide, just how deep!' Callie answered. 'It should be pretty stagnant, but I don't fancy losing my footing. Or kit. I take it you can swim?'

Ben shrugged, 'I guess so.'

'You guess so?'

'Well, can you? For real I mean?'

Callie exhaled, 'I hope so.'

'Simulation booth too?'

135

She nodded, 'Unfortunately wasn't lucky enough to nip down to the nearest reality pool. But, yeah, I think I'll be ok. With any luck there will be so little water we can just wade across anyway.'

Ben stopped, 'Well, we're about to find out.' Callie looked from him to the small clearing in the woods they were nearing and gasped loudly. Both of them hurried to get alongside.

They stopped.

'It's…it's…pure.' Callie exclaimed.

In front of them lay the loch. Virtually motionless, smooth and effortless. The trees and sky reflected perfectly off the sparkling surface, only a breeze broke the illusion of solidity.

Ben approached the edge, trees and land gave way to a miniscule, pebbly shoreline, and bent down. His fingers caused ripples in the surface, moving out and disappearing not far from the shore.

'Real,' he said turning, not caring about the little boy voice rising from his throat, 'It's real Callie. Real, bona fide water! Shit, I thought the trees were something, but this? This is something else.'

Callie joined him, bent and rubbed water up and down her arms, enthralled by the way it beaded and shone.

'How did they get the synthetic stuff so wrong?'

'Seems a shame to ruffle it up crossing over,' said Ben, picking up a stone and throwing it as far towards the middle as he could reach.

'What was that for?'

'Trying to figure out how deep it is, that's all. Any other ideas?'

Callie shook her head. 'Didn't help though, did it?'

'Nope, guess we'll just have to find out when we get in, won't we?'

Apprehensively she answered, 'I guess so. So, how do you think we should do this?'

'Wow!' Ben exclaimed.

'What?'

'I think that's the first time since we left you've asked my advice. Or opinion.'

'Don't start with me, I'm serious. How wide do you think it is?'

'Hard to say. Five, six hundred metres, maybe. Not much more, could be a little less. I suppose we won't be able to tell for sure till we're further in. Ok?'

Callie didn't look convinced, 'What do you think we should do?'

Ben curled his lips upwards, thinking and staring, before he answered. 'Packs on tight, they're waterproof anyway. Fingers crossed the suits don't let us down either and the water soaks off instantly.'

Callie interrupted, 'Sure, but that's on the other side, we've got to get across first.'

'You mean should we cross here or go round?'

'Yeah,' she answered, quietly. Annoyed at her scepticism and indecisiveness.

Ben considered, staring out into the water. He'd seen Callie stubborn, furious, bossy, hell he'd seen her desire for him relishing as they kissed, but he didn't think he'd seen her like this. Uncertain. Mutedly frightened.

'We could go round,' he said, his voice empathetic but logical. 'But it could take us a lot longer, look at the distance.' The loch was at least two or three times as long as it was wide, it was hard to tell from the shoreline, they just looked at its span reaching out to their left and right. 'I'm not sure if we should spare the time. We don't know what the ground will be like. And...'

'And?'

'And I've already wasted us hours,' Ben said, launching another pebble out into the water.

Before the rippling circles faded, Callie had made up her mind and stepped on.

'Let's do this.'

'Okay. Well, we wade. Slowly. Close. Take our time testing each step. Swim if it gets too deep. Just make sure you keep your chin up, mouth out. I'm not sure how much of this we could take before it would make us sick from the contamination.'

'Ok. Straight across?'

'Straight over. There's no tide. Should be ok. You sure you're ready?'

Taking a deep, noticeable breath, Callie answered,

'Ready.'

CHAPTER SIXTEEN

The first thing Callie was aware of when she stepped into the water was the temperature. She hadn't expected such an extreme difference between the hot, humid forest and the loch. A shiver shot visibly through her body, goosebumps bursting out. When Ben gave a shocked gasp, she realised he was experiencing exactly the same. The suits did adjust but the coolness did still lap around the edges, making them feel slightly cool: too cool to be comfortable.

The second thing was, despite the still, inertness of the water, there was still a pull and current which was strong and unexpected enough to tease them it would knock them over if they didn't pay close attention to each step. The movement of the water around their bodies, slowly getting deeper and deeper into the river – now hip deep – felt strange and alien, as if unseen hands were circling and trying to drag them down.

'Ok?' Ben was looking over at Callie.

She nodded, 'Yeah, it's weird. Stronger than I thought. Do you really think we can swim in this?'

'If we're lucky we won't have to find out,' Ben said.

'Hope so,' she cried before letting out another gasping sigh as the water reached her belly button. Ben let out a snort in laughter.

'It wasn't this cold in the reality tank.'

'Yeah, but there wasn't actual water in the tank,' Ben shook his head. 'Even under my feet it's wrong. Nothing's solid. I don't know if I'm going to sink in or fall over. My balance is shot to hell.'

'Let's just go as fast as we can. I'd rather slide around on the bottom than actually attempt to swim in this!'

'Agreed. Stay close.'

Callie winced, then nodded, moving to within arm's length should anything happen to either of them.

Carefully they pressed on, both awestruck and timid of the water, eager to leave it behind but entranced by the patterns and qualities of it. It was somehow smoother than the poly water then were used to and didn't cling. When they lifted a limb out of the loch, they could watch the drops run off their arm or fingers, leaving tendrils pathing out and disappearing rather than blobbing and pooling as their water did.

Callie let out a shout,

'There! Look! See it?'

Ben whirled, almost losing his footing and splashing down.

'What? Where? What it is?'

'I don't know,' Callie's eyes were wide. She pointed and scanned the water, 'It was right there.'

'What was it? Was it alive?' Ben was directly alongside her now, 'Are you ok?' He glanced anxiously, checking her over.

'Yeah, I'm fine, there was definitely something there, though.' She scanned again, exclaiming once more after a few seconds, 'There. See?'

Again, Ben was too slow and shook his head. He turned in a slow circle, scanning below and around them. Almost in unison they both called,

'There!'

'I see it!' Ben splashed around to try and follow it, full of animation.

'There's another one!' Callie pointed a few metres out in front. 'Fish, I think it's a fish.'

They stepped cautiously forward, a few more metres. Suddenly Callie let out a scream, 'Ben, look!'

It swam round the front of her body and made its path through in-between them. Callie grabbed on to Ben instinctively as helplessly they tracked it on its journey.

The fish was huge, much longer in length than either Ben or Callie in height. Long and flat faced its head was etched with hieroglyphic type markings, telling the story of its evolution.

'Beautiful, look at the scales,' Callie began reaching down before Ben grabbed her hand away. Deep, midnight blue and red, the roughly hexagonal, iridescent scales flashed as the body flexed and curved effortlessly through the water.

'That was it! That's what I saw,' Callie said as it disappeared on, continuing its journey through the river.

'Wow!' Ben said. 'I don't know what to say. That was alive, Cal, actual life. Real and living.'

She nodded and when she looked at him, he realised her eyes were cloudy with tears. She nodded again and looked away, pretending to track the journey of the fish, scared she wouldn't actually be able to speak.

'Do you think there are more?'

'I guess,' she managed to say, inhaling at the same time. 'Maybe even different ones.' Callie looked around, carefully, slightly disappointed when nothing else materialised as they continued their crossing. They were approaching the centre of the river now and the water had crept up to their chests. The inch or so height difference was making moving slightly easier for Ben; Callie was instinctively holding her head back, thrusting her chin up and out making certain she would not go under, despite the clear space between her head and the surface.

'Do you think they have water, rivers and lakes and streams like this on EarthMoon?' Ben tried to relax the tension he could see appearing in her face and gait, Callie did seem to be swinging her shoulders more to cut through the loch.

'They ship it up, obviously,' she said. 'But real, natural water like this.' Callie shook her head, 'How could they ever make so much? How far do you think this goes o...'

Callie stopped abruptly and both her shoulders dunked violently under for a second.

Ben lurched to the side and reached for her just as she righted herself and let out a nervous giggle.

'What was that?' he asked, 'You ok?'

'Yeah, fine,' Callie was breathless. 'I think I just missed my footing, that's all.'

'You sure?'

'Yeah. Sorry. I dunno what happened, it felt like something changed, made me lose my balance. Must've just been a deeper bit.'

'Could be,' said Ben. 'As long as you're ok. Couldn't have been that fish again going past?'

'I'm ok. I don't think so, I never felt anything. Let's just get out of this bloody water.'

'Deal.'

Ben yelled in horror as Callie was once again yanked under the surface without warning, arms flailing momentarily before she disappeared. This time he had felt the displacement, a nudge. There was something under the water. In here with them. Ben panicked, grabbing his Khalto stick and spinning in the water, desperate to find Callie yet unable to see.

Her head surfaced for an instant, winded and panting for air, gulping at the surface.

'Help,' she tried to force out of her aching, lungs before she vanished under again.

Ben drove his stick into the water again and again, trying to focus through the mud that had been churned up. He spun round as, this time for sure, he felt something brush against his leg, catching him momentarily off balance. Something large. Something heavy. Something fast.

With a battering splash Callie broke through the surface, arms whipping out as she tried to keep afloat.

'It's got me. Ben. Help. Please.' The words floundered out of her in a hurried babble as her whole body drove towards Ben, away from the invisible terror.

She was taken under again. But as she was a body rose out of the water. Ben froze. It was huge. The one scaled piece that flipped out and then was gone as Callie was taken again was wider and thicker than the whole length of the fish that had passed. The scales were rigid, ferocious armour. Faceless, body-less, save for these few instances, Ben realised they were both facing death from a terrible creature.

Callie thrust up once more and when she did the stirred up brown water took on a new shade as her blood-soaked in.

'Callie,' he cried, reaching for her and grabbing hold.

'My arm. My arm, it's…I can't move it Ben!'

A huge, putrid, yellow head loomed out of the water. Elongated with heavy, thick jaws it stared knowingly at Callie and Ben. Gills along the back of the head opened and closed, panting in anticipation. It looked from Callie to Ben then back again, soaking them in eagerly. There was no confusion or fear of the unknown in the glazed, grey cloudy eyes. Only death and menace.

The massive jaws opened in a foul grin, revealing two rows of razor-sharp teeth that seemed to go on and on back and back into its mouth. It flicked a thick, fetid tongue, tasting the air – the fear – and plunged again. Callie again struggled as the monster circled its body around her, teasing its prey.

This time Ben was quick, terror giving way to anger and hate, plunging his stick into the water. He didn't miss the target this time and felt the ricochet up his arm to the shoulder when the blow made contact. The creature rose out of the surface again, letting out an ear-splitting cry of fury. Callie was forgotten as it lunged for Ben who tried to bring his stick down in its eye. Missing, he gave a heavy blow to the snout, the creature shook its head, stunned, then dove down again.

Ben grabbed Callie. 'Can you move?'

She nodded, 'My arm. I don't know.' It hung lose at her shoulder, now a dragging, useless limb. Blood ran from teeth marks above her elbow.

'Do you still have your belt? Your stick.' She nodded.

'There's something in me, Ben. I can feel it moving through my arm.'

'Ok,' he said, his mind focusing on Callie, the water, survival. Adrenaline flooded his body; he could feel his heart almost bursting through his suit. 'We need to get you out of here. Can you get to your belt, take it off?' Callie nodded and fumbled in the water. With effort and a pined sigh, she lurched round, her belt plopped up with a bounce.

'Ok,' Ben said, letting go of her momentarily and tucking her belt over his shoulder. 'I just need to get the pellets and sense disruptor.' He scrambled and fumbled with the fasteners on the belt but finally released the catch. He strung the disruptor round his neck, refusing to even contemplate whether it was waterproof or not and stuck three pellets tightly in the neck of his suit. 'Hold on round my neck as best you can, yes?' She nodded with a lurching bob. 'Callie, stay with me, stay awake,' Ben moved her head up, pushed her chin so they were eye to eye. 'You need to stay awake.'

'Okay,' she said, then louder, 'Okay. I'm ok.'

At that moment they both felt a heave underneath them and looked down. Nothing.

'It's coming back and it's mad. The only chance we have is to be ready. And to fight.'

Ben began to move forward again through the water – leaning awkwardly to one side as he took the full weight of Callie and her pack, journeying in an awkward swim, paddle, wade. His stick was firmly in his right hand, Callie's trailed in the water as she battled consciousness. There was nothing he could do about that, he thought, they had worse problems than Callie losing it. Much worse.

With a swift surge the beast rose once more out of the water, only metres from Ben and Callie. It opened its jaws and screamed in hate and determination before heading straight towards them, glazed eyes pinned, unblinking on attacking. As it approached it seemed to smirk its lethal smile again and showed off its jagged fangs. It was close enough for Callie to gag, her stomach heaving from the rotten stench of whatever lay within its dense, heavy body.

As it reeled towards them Ben aimed a shock pellet at the back of the beast's throat, cursing loudly when he missed, and it sunk just beyond reach. The movement meant the creature's strike was futile, however, and it splashed through, leaving a wobbling flux behind.

'Next time,' Ben muttered to himself, 'got to get it next time.' He held a pellet tightly in his clenched fist. Callie's head bumped against his shoulder, waking her from the poison. Ben splashed her face and pushed her hair out of her eyes. 'You still with me?' he asked, nervously. 'C'mon, we're nearly there. Don't give up now. You can do this.'

'She nodded weakly, then looked up.

'Don't let go.'

'I won't,' he said tenderly.

The beast climbed once more out of the water, snarling and grinding its jaws. It shook its head furiously and crashed towards them. Wait, just wait thought Ben. Time seemed to slow down. There was no sound. No smell. Nothing except him and this monster. He watched from somewhere else as he stood, standing, standing as the creature swept closer, lustful and resolute. When it was almost upon them Ben made his move, his knuckles white from clenching the capsule so tightly. Instinctively within he knew the time was now. As it opened its mouth he aimed and threw. The pellet fell deep within the throat.

In those split seconds everything and nothing happened. Ben had time to think it was done. They were going to die. It hadn't worked. There would be no forgiveness for the past.

Then the creature stopped short.

Callie must have sensed a change in atmosphere as she too raised her head and watched.

The best pulled its head back into its neck, as if in confusion, before shaking it and releasing an almighty bellowing screech that deafened Callie and Ben. The sound still ringing in his ears Ben yelled, 'Now!' and threw the sense disruptor directly at it. The device landed short, but only just. It would still work, it has to, he thought.

'We need to go, get far away so the sensor doesn't get us,' he urged Callie, dragging her through the water now. Behind him he could hear furious splashing and roaring, but didn't dare turn, yet. There was still too much distance between them and the shore.

The water was getting slowly shallower once more, below chest height now, but still dangerous. Curiosity and tiredness took over and Ben took a moment to turn and watch. The creature was writhing, squirming it seemed, trying to get away from some force. The ripples on the water were violent now and tinged with waves. There was no gentle, symmetrical pattern; that had given away to signs of twisting and struggling.

Got you, you bastard, he thought, but at the same time the creature met his eyes. It sneered, the wetness on the piercing teeth glistening. Once more it came for them. In the seconds he had, Ben shook Callie into galvanised consciousness,

'You need to get to the shore, understand?'

Nothing.

'Callie, can you hear me?' He threw her head back and shook her shoulders. 'You have to go. Look.' Pointing to the shore he pushed her on, hoping there was enough sense inside to get her to safety, then turned to face the monster.

Ben raised his stick out in front, ready to drive it forward into the creature. It was under the water now, but he hoped he had the advantage as the shallower side meant his footing was more certain, what was under the surface easier to see. He was right. The creature curved towards him, but he saw it just before it rose up and this time was ready. He raised his arms up overhead and drove the stick down with all his might on the blunt snout. It shook then rose again.

This time the giant sea creature was quicker, leaping up and baring down. Ben grabbed the stick horizontally in defence, holding it out in vague hope it would protect him from a torturous bite. Teeth snapped through the stick, sending one end down into the river bed.

The force set Ben back, splashing down onto his back, water flooding his lungs. Barrelling back to the surface he gulped air into his burning, choking lungs and looked for Callie. Whatever happened now, he had to know she was safe.

Callie was thigh deep now. Bent double, swaying and staggering drunkenly to the shore. She fell to her knees but righted herself and pressed on. She was going to make it to shore. That was all that mattered.

A penetrating call. The creature was there, bearing down on him once more. The cavernous mouth yawned open in triumph, ready to crash through. With the last energy he had, Ben stepped to the side as the creature lunged and brought the splintered, jagged end of his stick down, burying it deep in the monster's eye. With a revolting pop the eyeball burst, puss, jelly and fluid mixing into the river or floating on the surface. Ben pulled, raised the stick once more and drove it again within the empty eye socket. Floundering back, he pitched forward, splashing, half swimming, half running towards the shore.

Behind him the water churned frantically.

Ben shouldn't have turned, the motion caught him off balance and he fell to his knees, inhaling the loch in shock. Blinded by water and coughing he scrambled up, bent over, hands trailing. Behind him he could hear fury, ire and torment. Closer.

But he was in the shallows now, the water reaching little over his knees. He could hear the angry waves and desperate splashing closer, imagined he could almost feel the rank breath of the monster on his neck, but he knew he was safe.

Floundering the last few steps he collapsed on the shore, panting. The pebbles and sharp, stubby grasses dug in, but at least for these few seconds he didn't care. Getting his breath back he sat up gingerly – there was a dull but clear throbbing in his knee now – and faced the water. All was still again, calm and inviting. Nothing gave away the danger they had been in just moments ago. The water teased, invitingly, minute waves glittering in the sunlight.

Callie.

She lay a few feet up the banking. Motionless.

Rushing towards her, Ben called her name. He reached out and moved her damp hair out of her face: her suit and boots had of course dried themselves perfectly. She didn't respond. Ben put his ear close to her mouth and looked down the length of her body. There! Her chest slowly rose and fell. It was slight, laborious. But she was alive.

'Callie, Cal. Can you hear me? Callie, come on.' Her eyes remained shut, but there was a flicker of recognition in her head.

'Alright. We need to get you up. You understand?' Another movement. Ben took it as agreement and dragged Callie to a sitting position, her back to his chest in his lap. As he pulled her upwards, she let out a short, painful gasp.

'Sorry. But we need to see the damage. Can you get your arm out of your suit?' Callie opened her eyes and looked at him blankly.

'Callie. I need you to focus and stay with me,' she stared again, a little more light returning to her eyes. 'I think you might have been poisoned; we need to see your arm.'

With a weak whisper she seemed to realise, 'Poisoned?'

'Poisoned, that's right. We need to get inside your suit. Ben began undoing the fastenings. Callie batting his hands away feebly. 'I'm sorry,' he continues, ignoring her, 'we need to do this.'

'Poisoned,' she repeated, her voice slurring slightly. 'By the water. By the thing in the water.'

'Yes, yes Callie. Talk to me. Keep talking. Poisoned. We need to see how hurt you are.' Then, more uncertain, Ben added, 'And what we can do.' Callie stopped trying to flick his hands away and instead tried to help. Her hands had lost power, couldn't feel her brain sending signals to them to work and she struggled, uselessly over the suit.

Finally, Ben leant her forward slightly and pulled down the top of her suit. Callie let out a painful cry. It was clear why.

Her left bicep was an angry red, tiny, powerful finger of infection starting to reach out from the bite mark where the poison had entered her body. This centre was black, purple, an evil bullseye trying to pump venom on through her veins.

'Hot,' Callie garbled, 'too hot'. Reaching for his pack, Ben opened his flask and put it to her lips.

'Here, drink, take some of this.' He poured gently into her mouth, almost immediately causing a coughing fit.

Callie buckled forward pushing the flask away, 'Can't swallow,' she forced out, before lurching into another coughing fit.

'Ok, take this.' Ben clasped her hands around the flask, his own pushing them together. She looked and nodded in understanding.

'You've been bitten. I need to find something to stop the spread.' Shaking he unbuckled his belt and searched the pockets. For what he wasn't sure. 'Can you crunch this down,' he asked, handing Callie painkillers.

'Try,' she muddled, putting two in her mouth and chewing awkwardly. She began to wretch.

Ben held her tight, 'Keep them in, Callie, try to keep them in. Here, take another drink.' He lifted the flask to her mouth; she batted it away shaking her head.

'Ok, I'm ok. Will swallow.'

'Yeah? Promise'

She nodded, before wincing as she tried to swallow the bitter fragments.

Satisfied, Ben took a deep inhale, clasped his hands together tightly to try to regain composure and searched again.

'Useless, this is all useless,' he muttered in increasing frustration before, three pockets left, he pulled out a thumb sized metal tube. 'What the hell? Why is this in here?'

Callie looked, 'What is it?' she forced.

'I think an infection extractor. Compressed gases draw out any poison.'

'Good?'

Ben looked at Callie's swollen, burning arm uncertain. The arm was fiery, raw and already the redness was stretching out. Was it too late? Was too much of the toxin already surging through her? Ben didn't know, but he knew he had to try. Faking a smile he nodded, 'Yes, good.'

Holding Callie tightly in his lap again he spoke, he hoped, reassuringly. 'This is going to hurt, I'm really sorry. But you'll be ok after'.

'Just do it.' Beads of sweat were gathering on her forehead now, her cheeks were flushed, eyelids drooping. Clearly, she didn't have much time.

'Ok,' Ben hesitated. He held the metal tool over the black centre of the wound and pushed gently into the skin.

Callie convulsed and yelled out in pain. He snatched his arm away. Shaking her head, Callie found the strength to reach for his arm and grab his hand. She shook her head,

'No, do it now.'

Galvanised, Ben once more pushed the instrument into her arm. Callie gritted her teeth, shoulders braced even in their exhausted semi-consciousness. There was a loud hiss as he clicked the top, drowned out by an excruciating scream. Callie spasmed and he had to tighten his grip to stop her jerking free. He tried to soothe her,

'You're ok now, that's it. I'm sorry, so sorry.' She shuddered and then folded still in his arms. Ben counted, finally reaching 25 and pulled the tool away. A nasty trickle of blood began to flow from the puncture wound. He wiped it away, found the bandages and wrapped one tightly around the wound. The black eye now lay hidden, the reddened swelling now contrasting against the pure white bandage. Staring at the edges, Ben wished and prayed he would see signs of them subsiding.

'Draw,' Callie murmured.

'What?' he put his face down, close to hers, to hear her whispers.

'Pen. Draw,' she repeated.

'I don't know what you…' then it hit him. Scrabbling for a pen, Ben drew lightly round the edge of the infection. He could track it, see how long it took to heal. If it didn't? He pushed the thought away, refusing to accept the intrusive possibility.

Gently, he settled Callie back on the earth momentarily. Hoping the packs were as secure and waterproof as their suits – they were – he unrolled a bed pack and manoeuvred Callie as lightly as possible onto it, covering her up softly.

'Rest, now,' he said tenderly. 'You need to rest now.'

Grudging even the slightest blink, he watched over her.

CHAPTER SEVENTEEN

Ben flew awake with a gasping inhale and shot up, wide, worried eyes immediately searching all around to check they were awake. In front the loch was clear and still, nothing caught his eye on the opposite shore. The banking around was pebbly and deserted; he was no tracker, but he couldn't see any signs of footprints or anyone watching. He listened intently, straining his ears as if that would help him hear further. There was nothing except his own breath, the panic subsiding. He swore at himself under his breath and checked the time, not having an idea if he had been asleep for five seconds, minutes or hours. He'd slept for most of the afternoon. Stupid, stupid, stupid he thought to himself, shaking his head.

Fully conscious and satisfied there was no-one there, at least for now, he moved swiftly over to Callie. Her face was still drawn and pale, but the colour was returning to her cheeks and the flushed sweating looked to have stopped. She was still sleeping deeply. Ben touched her face with the back of his hand. Cool and clammy. He hoped that was better than fever ridden. As gently as he could, Ben checked her wound. The bandage was stained with crusted, dried blood. He lifted her arm slowly, her unconscious only recognising the movement slightly as she furrowed her brow and then relaxed. Underneath the bite her arm was a hot, raging crimson, the hard, dark centre staring like the cold, dead eye of the beast. But it did appear to have subsided. Slightly. The infection was drawing back from the lines Callie had told him to draw.

As he changed the bandage, Callie woke with a loud, watery gasp. In the split seconds before she came into consciousness and understood her surroundings, she tried to jerk her arm away and sit up, before memory, pain and reality hit and she winced back down.

'Sorry, I didn't mean to wake you,' Ben said tenderly.

Sitting up, more tentatively this time, Callie searched around, no doubt looking for her own signs of hidden dangers. 'It's fine.' she replied, 'What are you doing? What happened?' She nodded to the water. 'What happened…after?'

'You remember the creature that attacked us?'

Callie nodded, 'Up close and personal,' she said with a wincing snort. 'Not sure I'll ever forget.'

'It's gone.'

'Gone? How?'

Ben nodded over to the splintered half of the Khalto stick he'd rescued from the water. 'Let's just say it was eye popping. I think you were poisoned when it bit you,' he went on, more gently.

'I remember. Stop!' she told him as he continued winding the fresh bandage, 'I want to see.'

'Sure.' Ben slowly unwound the clean dressing and let Callie investigate.

'Going to have a great scar to show off,' she mocked. Then, tracing the line with her finger added, 'Great idea about the lines. To trace the venom?'

Ben smiled, 'You don't remember? It was you that told me, it was your idea.'

'Really?' She looked shocked. 'Huh, I don't remember. Wait,' her expression suddenly changed – from a patient coming round to alert and aware, 'how long have I been out?' Ben recognised the behaviour; he'd been there just minutes ago. Scanning for unwanted company, dangers, threats. Callie had found her bearings again; her intense attitude was back. She had almost seamlessly, instinctively changed from weak, confused victim to astute, shrewd survivor.

Ben tried to calm the nervous edge, 'Just a few hours. You needed to rest. To let the treatment work.'

Callie lurched awkwardly to her feet, flinching. 'A few hours? You let me sleep for a few HOURS? What time is it?' There she was the spirit and disgust was back.

'Callie you were attacked and bitten by who knows what. Poisoned. Near death. Give yourself a break. Yeah, I let you sleep.'

Her arm bare and stinging in the warm, late afternoon air, she padded around locating their packs, trying to overcompensate with her opposite side. Ben watched as she patted down her back, presumably checking it was dry and intact. Picking up her belt she made sure all the compartments were closed before picking it up to fasten around.

'We don't have time to sleep! What time is it?'

'It's getting close to four.'

'Four! We need to go, I don't know what you were thinking,' she muttered, irritated both by her anxiety and the pain in her arm. 'Useless bloody thing!' she cried angrily as she tried to swing her bag onto her left shoulder, but the pain caused her left arm to give way and the pack thudded on to the ground.

Ben got up, frustrated, picked it up and dusted it off.

'Callie, calm down. Look, you need another dressing. Let me do it.' He reached out and took her hand, which she immediately snatched back as if he had burned her.

'I'm fine, we need to go.'

'We do, but your arm needs attention. It's still infected, could get worse.' Then he spoke more firmly, intonating and pausing after every word, 'Let me do it.'

Callie frowned, her overactive eyes already calculating the minutes wasted and danger expectant.

Raising and dropping her arms in defeat she caved in. 'Fine. Just hurry up.'

'Thank you,' Ben gestured to the ground, and she sat again tapping her feet in impatience. After a few minutes he was done. With a quick glance she was satisfied and pulled on her suit, taking only a careful second with the injured arm.

'Finally. Ready? We need to go now. Try to make up time. I don't know how we're going to do that!'

'We'll do it, Callie,' Ben tried to reassure, 'Even if we need to walk through the night.'

'The night?' she spat. 'If that is out there during the day, I don't want to know what could be out there in the night. We already have to camp out here, I'm not relishing trying to walk. Attempting to track. We're in the

Wild's Ben. In case you'd forgotten. Fuck knows what else could be out there. What or who!'

He didn't know if it was frustration at Callie perhaps being right; perhaps being ungrateful; fear or the reality of the day finally hitting home, but Ben exploded.

'Enough! You could have died out there. We both nearly died. You were unconscious, needed treatment and rest,' his voice rose and echoed slightly. Ben didn't care. 'Yes, I fell asleep. Yes, we need to make up time. But it's done. Over. We've got now. That's what we work with.'

Callie folder her arms, left awkwardly on top and looked down. He was right. They had to regroup, concentrate and go. What was done was done.

'Sorry,' she whispered, stubborn and reluctant. 'But we have to try and make up for that time somehow. We should've taken more care with how long we rested.'

'And with we you mean me? Ben messes up again! Just say it. It's fine. It's not like any of it's your fault, is it? This was all on me.' Ben picked up a stone and threw it in frustration. It arched out over the water before landing with a short, dull splash. Relocated on the loch bed.'

'You're right. I'm sorry,' Callie said, reluctant but grateful. 'And I'm glad you were there to help me. That you wanted to.' She flashed a look, brief but undeniably warm and he knew she meant it.

Once again, they set off.

Callie was scared. Bottom line. Not only had they lost time sleeping (the thought of it still disgusted her but what was the point in going round in circles discussing it), they'd lost hours this morning separating when Ben was lost. And in the loch. She wasn't ready to admit how terrified she had been, how it had heightened her energy and nerves. Every rustle was a threat, every brush of wind an as yet unseen adversary. They had left the river behind, couldn't see it now as the trees thickened and surrounded them again.

Finally, she couldn't bear it anymore and had to express her fear. 'Do you think there is anything else out here?'

'Animals?'

Callie nodded. 'At least dangerous ones. Whatever; animals, birds, insects. Evil, stinking, gnashing people-eating monsters. So stupid. I was so busy thinking about that, that sickness we saw, I forgot about everything else there could be. Look at this place. This is the whole world. There has to be so much hidden. So much waiting.'

They both felt fragile and pathetic then. This huge expanse had so many hidden secrets in its awesome beauty. It wasn't just the trees – full of life yet stationary – out here. The green, shady forest held an abundance of eerie mystery. Callie realised how ironic the situation was. Her whole life she had dreamt of this, of exploration, of the more beyond wherever she was. Now she was here her naivety stared back at her and she was embarrassed at the vulnerability she felt.

'Do you think they know? Knew?' Ben asked.

'Who?' Callie asked. 'Takot and Prane?' she spoke the word with disgust, as if saying their name was diseased and tasted vile.

Ben nodded.

Callie spat. 'Maybe *she* didn't. I don't think Prane's high enough up the food chain. And I think that sticks in her scrawny throat. All she knows is self-promotion. Take out whoever along the way as collateral damage. Him. I'm not so sure. How could he not? He's got access to every available technology, communication, science on Earth. He doesn't give a shit about us.'

'Yeah, but he needs us back with the Dealga. I'm not so sure. It doesn't make sense.' Ben shook his head.

'He knew,' Callie spat. 'I'd bet my life on it.'

'Poor choice of words,' Ben said drily.

Callie smiled, 'Guess so. He knew. Maybe not about that thing. Fair enough. But he knew.'

'How can you be so sure?'

'Why else would we have an infection extractor? That's not going to help a maul or a bite or an attack. The biters don't infect us, they eat us! Think about it. He knew.'

Ben stopped and punched out in front, his right hand in a fist.

'Bastard,' he exclaimed. 'Sleekit, sly bastard. You could have died, we both could. When I get back, I'll wring his scraggy neck.' Ben curled his fingers in front of him and clenched them tight around the imagined, invisible throat of Takot.

'Tempting,' Callie agreed. 'Think it would be better to use that energy to get us out of this. In to it. Wherever the hell we are in it.'

'Still think it's beautiful, amazing?'

Callie thought, gazing around at the forest enveloping them. How could she not? The air was heavy and fresh – the cooler late afternoon air trying to slowly brush away the heavy heat of the day. The flecked light filtering through the trees made asymmetrical shapes which altered before her eyes as she moved forward, alongside and past. Branches reached out for attention: scratching, catching, trying to hug with bare, thin fingers.

'Yeah, yeah I do,' she said happily.

Ben was not completely surprised. 'You're on your own there. I can't wait to get out of this wretched place. Bloody grim if you ask me.'

Callie sat, leaning on a fallen tree trunk, a mound of fuzzy, green moss giving it new life.

'Deep in thought? All good?' It wasn't like her to sit unannounced. Ben was concerned.

'Yeah fine, just need some water, that's all.' He stared, brow furled, and Callie caught him watching. 'Honest, I promise.'

Not completely satisfied, but aware of the clear improvement in their relationship, Ben did not argue. He sat alongside and took a long, welcome drink.

Callie wiped her mouth with the back of her hand and picked a hard remnant of rheum away from the corner. 'You were right you know. I needed to sleep. Recover. I guess you saved my life back then.'

Ben, leaning forward on his hands, looked at his fingers but said nothing.

'I mean it,' Callie nudged his side with her elbow. 'Thanks.'

He looked round, squinting slightly as beams of sun teased back and forth off Callie's face, appearing and disappearing behind a flapping branch high up in an overhanging tree.

'That's ok,' he said. 'I couldn't leave you.'

'You could've.'

'Would you?'

'What?'

Ben knew the question was dangerous, 'Have left me?'

Callie looked upwards, the heat of the sun not unwelcome on her face. There was no answer.

Ben smiled and shook his head. 'That's ok.'

Callie was thankful for the answer; she genuinely didn't know how to respond. Her feelings couldn't have changed that much in 24 hours, could they? This was the guy that had killed her brother. Accident or not he had cost Tax his life. That was something that would live, festering in her gut forever. An icy realisation she could never forget. But he had saved her, despite all the hate she had projected at him, he had saved her. Did he do it because he needed her tracking? She was sure partly yes, that was a reason. But she knew there had been more to it, she knew how he felt about her, knew he needed to atone. Would she have tried to save him, risk her own life, risk not making it back? That was something she had to figure out. What Callie did know was she was now grateful he was here. Thankful they were here together. She enjoyed a few more second of sunlight on her face, before deciding they should press on. A cloud passed over the rays and she opened her eyes with a sigh.

'Ben, look,' she said with a jolt and pointed. 'Up there.'

Ben's eyes moved from Callie to the waving branch, but he couldn't see anything. Confused his eyes looked back. Keep looking,' she urged, 'there's something up there. I swear.'

Ben took the damaged stick in his hand and reached for his belt. Callie put her hand on his, calming. 'Not like that. It's little. Whatever it is, I don't think it's a threat.'

'I'm not taking any more chances.' Ben was serious, on edge, not taking his eyes off the trees and readying himself for attack. 'There, I see it.' A white flash, long limbed, seemed to leap above him then disappear again. 'What the hell was that?'

'It's too quick,' Callie was shaking her head, she'd seen it too. 'It's not human, too small. And I've never seen a human that can jump like that.'

'Small I like,' said Ben. 'Not seeing what it is, the speed. Not knowing about claws and teeth and poison. That bothers me. Oh!' Whatever it was had jumped again – another blaze of white through the green then gone in a blink.

Ben and Callie both got up and tried to follow the direction.

'C'mon,' Ben was nervously irritated now, 'what is that?'

'My money is on a primate. You know, a monkey. Or an ape.' Callie answered.

'Yeah?'

'Makes sense. In the trees. Fast. Nimble.'

'I guess. I'd be happier if we could get a look. With any luck it's a friendly, vegetarian monkey!' Ben grinned. 'We should move you know.'

'I know.' Callie said reluctantly, eyes skyward, 'At least it's heading the same way'.

'Mmm,' said Ben, more than a little apprehensive. 'As long as it stays up there.'

As Callie and Ben walked through this part of the forest it became clear they had entered a world again different and altered, even from the one they had stepped in yesterday. Was it actually possible that was only yesterday, Callie thought to herself as they moved forward. She had no idea if it was because they were so far from the bland, burned plain or if it was related to the river, but there was more life here.

The forest floor was thicker and more varied; underneath their feet went beyond dead leaves and rough shrubs in shades of green. Flowers uncurled, enticing them with a complete spectrum of colour. Climbing vines swirled and spun around trunks and branches, reaching down to tease the back of their necks with scratches and tickles. It wasn't that they tried to keep Callie and Ben out, but nature was happily ill prepared for human contact and the need to make their own route continued.

As far as they could tell they had been joined by a curious monkey. The monkey, monkeys as it turned out, did indeed join them on their hike, from a distance high up in the top branches. A small colony, white bodied with dark brown faces and tails, leaped and acrobated across the sky, amazing Ben and Callie with their gymnastic skill. Their powerful, muscly shoulders swung long arms with ease; sharp claws tearing into and off branches nimbly and with formidable ease. It crossed both their minds that those arms and nails could just as easily rip into them. Thankfully it did seem that their instinct, passed down through millennia, meant Callie and Ben were an interesting, funny even, novelty to them, but they kept their distance.

From time to time the bravest dangled down from lower branches, observing these strange beings, before leaping back to pass on the knowledge and sights in noisily, amused screeches. But none came close.

How amazing, wonderful would it be to study these creatures, Callie day dreamed every time they came close enough to see clearly for a moment or two. Bright, almond shaped eyes stared wide at Callie as Ben as much as they stared back. Small, fur lined faces cocked their heads back and forth with interest. Mouths formed into round disbelief or open, teeth baring laughter – sometimes silent and sometimes a cackling whoop. Sometimes one almost came close enough to reach out and touch, but the times Ben or Callie did reach out the creature flew back up to the safety of the treetops.

Overnight Callie and Ben had become immersed in this world. Real water, forests, plants, trees, creatures. Callie's shoulders tensed at the memory of the river. She forced bile back down, deep inside. But despite that, this was life. These were the snapshot pictures in the textbooks she had memorised and obsessed over. She wasn't stupid – the chance of her being given her freedom was slender – but she would have the memories of here. Positive and otherwise. If they made it. They were both still injured, Ben was doing his best to hide the pain in his knee, but she could tell; the throbbing in her arm was easing but still providing a constant, burning throb. And what else was here. Deeper inside. The creature in the water would not be the only threat. Maths had never been her strong point, but Callie knew those odds weren't good.

Still, they had made it this far. Overnight. Not entirely safely but they were both still here and together. She had to concentrate now on finding a safe camp. Tracking and looking for any signs of danger. She knew Ben wasn't daft, wasn't helpless. But she could see beyond the obvious. Hoped, she could; the deeper they ventured the harder it was becoming. It wasn't just the monkeys – there was other life revealing itself out here. Hardly abundant like they had both read about and studied in school, but nevertheless it was around them now. Buzzing insects were becoming more and more irritating, especially as the cooler evening air returned. There were flies and crawling bugs in the corn of course, but they didn't swarm in clouds as they did here. They didn't bite or scratch or tickle any more than on the farm, bugs avoided people as much as possible given the percentage of pollutants in the human bodies. It was more the haze they had to walk through from time to time that was irritating. Callie and Ben flicked them away, annoyed, with the palms of their hands, blew sharp gusts towards groups floating in front of their eyes and spat when the occasional one, with the whole world to choose from, still managed to land in the back of their throat. This was all coupled with the ingrained human instinct to scratch. Insects, they both agreed, they could definitely live without.

They could make exceptions for the intermittent dragonflies that appeared, their delicate, translucent wings hovering then darting invisibly away. They were beautiful and ethereal rather than a menace. The long, slender colourful bodies in vivid greens and blues seemed too fragile to hold the huge, bulbous eyes of the insect. These were beautiful, so distracting Callie was sensibly glad they didn't appear too regularly while she was engrossed in maintaining their safety.

But there were no obvious signs of human life. Or danger. They didn't disturb any hidden lairs, find any unusual or suspicious tracks or observe and sense anything to unsettle them further. The noises of the forest became a natural melody, a beat of new, vibrant life. The clamouring monkeys didn't make either of them jump as much when it took off; the sounds of the vegetation be it whispering or creaking in wind or the muffled, crunching, snapping earth under their footsteps became comforting, enveloping them in their canopy.

It was a welcome change, a tentative compromise between calmness and being on edge at the same time. Not jumping at every sound, checking every noise or shadow or movement, meant they walked faster and preserved energy. But remained aware. Ben certainly never released his grip on his Khalto stick. It amused and also comforted Callie that, when uncertain, he would raise it to his chest ready. She had retained one end of the splintered, broken stick. Sharp and hard it could still cause some damage.

'We should stop. I'm starving and your bandage will need changed.' Ben snapped Callie out of her thoughts, and she nodded.

'Okay. How's your knee?'

'Sore, but not too bad. It'll stiffen if we rest too long but I need to eat! Let's see how you're doing.' Ben pointed his stick at Callie's arm. Dropping her equipment, she unrolled her sleeve.

There was no blood soaked through this time, a positive sign. The dressing had stained sickly yellow and purulent, but the wound had clotted and scabbed over. Callie wasn't looking forward to the tight, itchiness that would no doubt follow. While Ben was applying paste and a new dressing, she tried to pull her arm around enough to see if the infection was still regressing.

Ben notice and reassured her, 'It's receding. Look.' Gently he traced the line he had marked, now sweating off in patches, then ran his finger along the new edge. Callie shivered under the touch which despite herself she was forced to admit wasn't unpleasant. She didn't pull back. 'It's going down and I don't think it's so red. I think you'll be ok,' Ben gently held an end of binding down and began winding it round.

When he finished Callie ran her hand over it. 'Too tight?' he asked, concerned.

She shook her head, 'No, not at all. It's fine, just going to itch like hell pretty soon.'

'Yeah, it is. One step up from a phantom itch though,' he tried to put light on it.

'Do you want me to look at your knee?' she asked, figuring she should return the support.

Ben shook his head, 'Nah I'm fine.' Callie gave him one of those looks of disbelief and distain – head cocked to one side, chin down, mouth pursed. 'Honestly. It's ok. Stiff, probably going to give me jip if I make it through to old age, but it is fine. Really.'

'Let me see.'

Ben gave a useless whinge, 'Callie.'

'Just do it. I want to check. I'd like to.' She folded her arms across her chest and waited, not blinking, 'Then we can eat.'

'Well, if you put it like that, what option do I have?' he joked, rolling up his trouser leg. 'There, see. Happy?' Ben wasn't sure if she was flirting with him or not. He didn't dare hope that she was, but something was different since the water. He had sensed it but now he was more or less certain.

Callie crouched at his feet and ran her hand over his knee. Taking the leg in her hand she encouraged him to bend and straighten it.

'Satisfied,' he asked.

Callie contemplated. 'It's still a bit swollen, I've seen you limp when you need a break. But yeah, it looks ok. Lucky.' Her hand went to her arm again.' Both of us.'

'What's on your mind?' Ben wasn't sure the state of his knee was the only issue.

'Do you think we can still fight? Be ok?'

'Of course. Nothing's getting past me. You've got the speed. I'll provide the muscle.'

'I'm serious. We don't know what else is out here. Your leg, my arm. They're healing, but they're not perfect. What if, you know?'

Ben was softer now, 'I know. I know what you're saying but yeah, I think we'll be ok.'

'But you don't know. Neither of us do.'

He didn't answer straight away, when he did it was quiet. 'No, I don't. But I do know we made it this far and we probably shouldn't. Suppose we proved Takot and Prane's theory about us. That's all I know right now. And it's good enough for me.'

Callie didn't answer, just looked, still holding on to his bent knee. The word did seem to rally and revive her though. She started rolling down his trouser leg, stood and asked,

'Food?'

'Now you're talking', Ben grinned.

CHAPTER EIGHTEEN

Ben swatted another hungry fly away, drolly noticing at least something was enthusiastic to eat what almost passed as food. Still, if the pest was trying to eat this over processed, scentless and almost flavourless bar of taupe whatever-it-was, it meant they weren't landing on him and exploring. Between bites he spoke, maybe the conversation would take his mind off the nondescript taste. Who knew eating would be such a chore.

'Do you think the monkeys and the bugs are the only thing out here?' Ben looked up, waiting for a flash of black or white to leap across.

Callie considered while she chewed. 'I don't see why they wouldn't be, but it's a huge forest. Just because we've not seen anything else doesn't mean...'

'I know. That's what I'm worried about.'

'It's the not knowing that's worse. Being on edge. Stunning, enthralling as it is we don't know this place. What's here – we don't even know what plants could be deadly. Or where *they* are. I feel like we're getting used to it, not comfortable – no way – but more at ease. Distinguishing sounds and shapes and shadows. But I won't relax again. Will you?'

Ben shook his head.

'We've been lucky to get this far. Yesterday all we were concerned about were the Wildings, then those...those...Shriekers. Today I even forgot about them for a while.'

'But they're out here.'

Callie's voice was low and solemn as she agreed and repeated, 'They're out here.'

They ate in silence, the conversation leaving them both on edge, restless and becoming more irritated by the flying insects. It was as if they were taking their worry and change in mood out on them.

By the time they had finished eating the evening shadows had clearly caught up with them and were tiptoeing closer and closer. Callie rolled down her sleeves and wrapped her jacket back over her shoulders. The breeze had picked up, a welcome respite to the insects which it swept along, but there was a distinct chill with it.

'We should move,' she said, tracing something that appeared nondescript to Ben on the map. 'We can't go much further before it's too dark and too dangerous, but there should be some kind of small clearing where it will be easier to pop up the shelter.'

'How far?'

'An hour, hour and half max. Assuming...'

'Let's just go for that,' Ben smiled, 'An hour or two I can do. Get the shelter up. Sleep. Or at least rest.'

As they reattached their packs, they once again tried to remove any obvious signs they had been there. It wasn't perfect, they had to be too quick for that, but it was habitual now and could make a difference. The difference between life and death. They brushed away any crumbs; moved around squashed leaves and plants; checked for any stray hairs or footprints or scraps of wrapper. Ben hoped if anything obvious was missed the monkeys would soon make short work of it anyway. They could be as messy as they liked!

The twilight and perhaps the conversation had definitely affected the mood. The atmosphere was now melancholy, overanxious. Callie's eyes strained in the light, intent on tracking again, looking for any inkling, any suspicion. Even the animated babble of the monkeys had quietened. They no longer leaped, energetically along the trees, instead the few that still moved with them ambled and slowed, perhaps also getting ready to hanker down for the evening.

'What was this place?' Callie commented, rubbing her hands along what was left of a crumbling, shoulder height brick wall.

'Some kind of home, maybe? Or a farm building,' Ben wasn't sure either.

The clearing they had entered wasn't really a clearing at all, more an overgrown ruin where trees had yet to establish firm, deep roots. They stood examining the remnants of the disintegrating wall which ran, precariously leaning in places, around seven metres along the ground in one direction, then about three off at a right angle. At its highest point it reached Callie's shoulders, the lowest was just two or three bricks high, peeking out rebelliously from thick moss in places.

'How old do you think this is?' Callie asked, rubbing cracked remnants between her fingers and feeling the dry, solid roughness of the dents and contours.

'It must be from before,' said Ben, 'back before the Famine and Drought.'

'Must be. So old! Do you think Salthea will be standing after the same time?'

Ben shrugged, 'I dunno.' Rubbing the veiny lichen on a tumbled piece, long embedded in the earth he added, 'But I sure as hell know who I'd like to be under it if it's not.'

Sprouts of determined life had found a safe home along cracks and joins in the wall. Callie took the stem of a straggly, purple flowered plant in her hand and awed at it, then picked at dried mossy clumps which had also taken hold.

'Life always finds a way.'

'Guess so,' Ben agreed, propping their packs against the wall and unrolling the shelter, before shaking it to pop open. 'I was thinking here.' He put the shelter down against the highest part of the wall, where the corner of a mysterious, ancient room must have been. The opening looking out into the part of the forest they just left. 'If anything, anyone happens, at least that's blocking one way they can get to us.'

Callie nodded in agreement and grabbed a couple of secures to hook the shelter to the ground. Once it was set, she stored the bags inside.

'Safe as we can get' she said.

'You telling me or hoping?'

With a thin-lipped smile she answered, 'Both.'

'Want first or second watch?' asked Ben.

'First, I'm not so tired yet. And I want to get this bandage off and let some cool air in,' she finished, sitting and shrugging off her top.

'Here, let me help,' Ben said, sitting alongside at the entrance to the shelter.

'I can do it,' she shrugged him off. Ben saw a flash of the old irritation and hurt, but she continued, 'Thanks though, but I can do it. Why don't you sleep?'

'Not tired either. You sure you don't want to go first.'

She nodded, 'I'm fine here. I kinda like the noisy silence.'

Ben looked up and around. The forest was settling down for the night, but that didn't mean it was silent.

'I know what you mean,' he agreed. 'Eerie though.'

The darkening light had long faded orange, now deep blue and dark purple were giving way to grey and black. Callie and Ben sat, listening and looking, their eyes growing more accustomed to the darkness. The breeze chilled them now, slightly unpleasant and Callie wrapped her sleeping bag around her shoulders to keep warm, trying to leave only her scabbing wound in the open air.

Ben leant back, propped up on his elbows, Khalto stick once again in his lap and stared into the forest.

'What do you think will happen after?' he spoke softly.

Callie stripped bark off a dead twig and threw the pieces in front of her,

'If we make it out, you mean?'

'Yeah.'

'Oh, I dunno. Medals, glory, a one-way ticket to EarthMoon.'

'I'm serious.'

'Why you asking? To confirm the horrors you are thinking? Because I agree. Screwed over. Prison camp. Death.' She threw the twig in disgust, but it's almost imperceptible weight meant it fell straight, landing weakly.

'Pretty much. Thanks. Put's my mind at rest.'

'Anytime,' Callie reached out and patted Ben's thigh. Their eyes met for a fraction of a second before she swiftly looked away.

Awkwardness began to hang in the air.

'Would you go?' he asked.

'Where?', Callie kept her gaze on the forest.

'Up there. EarthMoon.'

Her eyes moved to the sky, mystical and vast. She searched for the moon, out of sight from where she sat. Standing she answered, 'Of course, wouldn't you?'

'In a shot. Real food. Safety. The best of everything. Why would I stay here?'

Callie was outside the shelter now, staring at the sky. Her eyes fixed on a mottled white star. It didn't shine. It didn't flicker. But it imposed. Hanging defiant and proud at its infancy up there with the ancients. EarthMoon. Adding more secrets and questions and riddles to the skies. Alien yet familiar. Venerated yet loathed.

'You'd go for good?' she was curious now.

'In a heartbeat.' Ben was shocked, 'Wouldn't you?'

'Maybe. I mean, yeah of course.' Callie turned from the sky and returned to the shelter, climbing inside her sleeping bag this time. 'But leave Earth? I dunno.'

'You'd rather harvest forever, stay at that miserable dump, eating that crappy food?'

'I didn't mean that. I don't care if I never see a husk of corn again. But Earth. I could stay here. Explore. Discover. Look at it. Why go there, why need to go there when there is already so much here with us.'

Ben shook his head. 'You're crazy. Nuts! All that today and you still don't give up.' The criticism was marked with pride in his eyes. Slapping his hands on his thighs he straightened up. 'You sure you're not tired.'

Callie shook her head, 'Nope, knock yourself out.'

'Poor choice of words,' he said, getting to his feet and into his bag at the back of the shelter. 'See you in four.'

'In four,' she said.

For someone who insisted they weren't tired, Callie was amused by how quickly Ben fell asleep. She could hear the gentle rise and fall of his tired breathing, the occasional movement of his body adjusting to the cold and numbness of the ground. As she watched the increasing darkness, he was forefront of her mind. Ben. The thought of him still forced bile to churn in her stomach, her chest to tighten at the thought of what he had done to Tax. And to her. Lied to her, knowing who she was. Drawing her in, into what, some kind of mournful relationship of retribution? She knew he had tried to talk to her about it since they had been dumped out her, but she couldn't bear it. Couldn't face hearing it.

And Callie knew that wasn't just because she didn't want to think of Tax and hear what happened.

She knew it was because part of her wanted him. There, she had admitted her darkest most horrific and awful truth to herself. He had destroyed the family she had left; smashed her hope of finding her brother. But something inside her still wanted him. Callie wrestled with this as she sat in the darkness. She didn't even know if she wanted this part unrooted and ripped from her psyche. And to her that was worse. Wanting to want him.

Shaking her head, hoping the thoughts would dissipate she pulled her bag tighter around her, tucked her knees deeper in to her chest and sighed. Watching into the woods again the darkness she didn't notice the darkness redirect her thoughts. If she had realised, no doubt she would have been grateful. The dark erased her thoughts and left nothing but calm.

It seemed only moments later she felt the cold at her throat, before catching the glint of the knife from the corner of her eye. A face, fierce and warped pressed up against her, a finger pressed against fat, wet lips warning her it needed silence. Without moving Callie nodded - only with her eyes.

Ben woke with a start, thinking for an instant he was somehow suffocating. His eyes sprung open, wide and confused in the pre- dawn gloom. A hand was clamped down tightly on his mouth. His confusion changed quickly to fear and anger when he saw, fuzzy and without edges, what was above him.

169

Callie stood frozen. A sickly sliver of light was casting from a torch or lantern somewhere and in the dimness, he could see the swelling across her face. A large bruise was starting to rise on her right cheekbone, her nerves twitched and winced against it. A figure stood behind her, stooped over in the height of the shelter, one of their arms wrapped tightly around her waist, the other holding a large, serrated hunting knife at her throat. The person holding her against them looked wild and crazed. It was hard to even define if this was a man or a woman. Assuming they were human at all.

Growling down at Ben, wicked, distrusting eyes were filled with nothing but suspicion and trouble. The hand eased its grip on his mouth, as with Callie, a knife appeared in front of his face. No words were needed. Ben nodded slightly, slowly, just as Callie had done and eased himself up to sitting. With a shove Callie was pushed towards him. She hit the wall hard, winced and sat down quickly beside him.

'Ben reached out, concerned to touch her injured cheek.

'Hands down!' a voice bayed, a warning threat more than an instruction.

She nodded, her eyes never moving from the faces of their captors.

They were easier to see now as his adrenaline fuelled eyes adjusted. Human, definitely human. Long, dark hair hung in straggly strands jutting out untamed in every direction. Their dirty skin was tanned and long dried by the sun, scraps of filthy clothes hung on sinewy limbs. They held their knives in hands lined with dirty ending in ragged nails. These were not their only weapons: strapped along one back was a bow and arrow, on the other a pair of sticks criss-crossed down.

'Who are you? What do you want?' Ben asked.

The two looked at each other and grinned. Maniacal smiles that showed off chipped, decaying teeth. One licked their lips and spoke.

'What do we want? What do we want?' the voice was male and clearly amused. 'Why, how do you know we want anything? Look around, we're not the ones far from home.'

'Then why attack us? Why the threats?'

'Attack? Oh, we're playing nice,' grinning he turned and addressed the other intruder, 'Don't you think we're playing nice?' Running his finger along the edge of his knife his partner nodded in agreement. 'After all, you two appear to be really far from home.'

'Put the knives down and maybe we can explain.' Callie spoke with the same spirit she showed Takot and Prane in Salthea.

'Did you hear that Fly?' the male spoke again. '*Maybe* they can explain. Get her up.'

Callie was grabbed by the hair and forced to her feet, crying out in pain and her eyes watering. She rubbed her head carefully, checking her fingers for blood. Her assailant, this Fly, dusted his hands, smiling satisfied as strands of her hair fell off his palm and floated to the ground. It was clear now, that he too was male. Younger, a youth like Callie and Ben. Eager to take instructions from the older man, perhaps not as smart. 'There is no 'maybe' here. You tell us what we want to know, everything we want to know and perhaps you won't find out how sharp these knives are. Do you understand?'

Callie said nothing.

'What is it you want?' Ben asked.

'That's better,' the man said, 'Sit her down.' With a hollow thump Callie found herself on the floor next to Ben once more.

'We going to slice them, Ankor?' Fly asked, licking his lips and tossing his knife from one hand to the next. He stopped and rubbed a sweaty palm on his torn, fading trousers, tongue still lolling ridiculously from his mouth. Suddenly his head flung back as a loud slap rocked him. With a gasp his hand flew to his cheek. Ben and Callie glanced at each other in shock.

'No, we're not going to slice them,' the one called Ankor hissed between gritted teeth. 'Why would we cut them when they have information we need?' Dramatically his demeanour changed, he dropped to the floor in front of them, crossed legged. He placed his knife on a thigh and smiled, almost warmly, gesturing his arms out as if inviting Callie and Ben into a hug. 'We're going to chat with our visitors. Welcome them to the Wilds.' He patted the ground next to him and looked up at Fly who, confused, sat down next to him, crossing and uncrossing his legs, shuffling from one side of his butt to the other trying to get comfortable. Ankor glared touching his front teeth with his tongue.

'Sorry,' Fly mumbled, becoming still.

'Now we're all comfortable, let's begin, shall we?'

Callie and Ben said nothing. She rubbed her head where she had no doubt lost a lump of hair and tucked her knees round under her right side, shuffling to find some comfort on the hard ground. Ben glared, his eyes never wavering from watching Ankor and Fly, looking for both threat and freedom.

'What finds the two of you out here so far from home?' Ankor asked.

'How do you know we're far from anywhere?' Ben retorted.

'Smart arse, eh?' Ankor nodded.

Fly giggled, 'Yeah, smart arse. Cut him now?' he was clearly restless.

Ankor raised a hand, clearly enough for Fly to quieten down, his vicious lust once again on hold.

'I'll ask again. Why the hell are you two here?'

Ben leaned forward and casually scratched the side of his mouth before speaking. 'For shits and giggles.'

Ankor's eyes flashed with irritation. He nodded. In an instant Fly was next to Callie, bent forward and panting, bouncing from foot to foot. Ankor pointed the end of his knife towards Callie and with another grab of her hair Fly yanked her closer towards her. He licked the side of her face, leaving a dripping sheen on her cheek. She could see the beads of moisture on his skin: from the humid, tense air in the shelter and his grossly excited sweat. The relish and desperation to commit more obscene violence on her was clear. The knuckles that held his knife were rigid and white.

'I'd say you need some persuasion to answer, wouldn't you? Fly as you can see needs no persuasion. Not even a word. One nod from me and you can watch his eagerness on your friend. Still unsure?'

Ben's eyes flew from Callie to Ankor, back and forth. She looked at him, wide-eyed, grimacing at the pain coming from where he held her, tugging at her hair. Ben wasn't sure if there was any message coming from her, but he conceded he had lost this round.

'We ran away,' he muttered. 'Now let her go'.

Ankor looked at Fly and shook his head. Fly remained where he was, Callie still in his grasp, trying to drag her head as far away from his maniacal face as was possible.

'Go on.'

Ben continued the plan, the cover story they had constructed with Takot and Prane.

'We ran away. That's it. Hated working as harvesters. We ran.'

'From where?'

'Thorrach. We harvested at Thorrach.'

'Harvested what?'

'Corn', Callie and Ben said in unison.

'I see. I hear you. We have two simple, mere corn harvesters. From a farm known as Thorrach. Jobs, food, shelter. Yet you find yourselves here.'

Callie, grappled with Fly, trying to push him away, get away from his grasp and his knife.

'Like he said,' her voice was breathless, 'we hated it. We ran. Escaped.'

'Escaped? Now things are getting interesting. Here was I thinking you were workers, able to come and go as you please. Yet you had to escape, make your way to the Wilds. Find yourself here. Why, what was your plan?' He looked from Ben to Callie, expectantly. They exchanged glances, as if figuring out who would speak next.

'We didn't have one,' Ben sighed, hoping he sounded as pathetic and stupid as he wanted. 'We just away, didn't think past getting out of there.'

Ankor looked sympathetic.

'Perhaps we've misjudged you. Fly, put down the knife, step back. These souls are searching for a new start. New beginning. We've scared and startled them while they're trying to regroup and gather their thoughts. Their big plan worked and they're free.'

173

Fly looked confused and disgusted; a dog being faced with a treat but not allowed to have it.

'Stand up,' Ankor gestured to Ben. 'Please. I want to shake the hand of someone who has clearly made such a sacrifice and journey.'

Ben didn't move. Like Callie he could feel an uncertain tension in the air, uncertainty as to what his next move should be. Ankor nodded expectantly, put out his hands in an embracing gesture. Ben got to his feet. Like Ankor, he couldn't stand straight in the shelter and had to stoop over slightly.

'There,' Ankor purred. He put out his hand expectantly. Ben took it in a firm, solid handshake.

'How did you find us?' Ben dared to ask.

'Monkeys,' Fly screeched. 'We followed the monkeys'. He whooped and pointed up, the dark sky of course peaceful and still now while the forest slept.

Ankor smiled and released Ben from the hand shake. In the next split-second Ben buckled, winded under the force of the blow to his stomach. He stumbled back against the wall, arms on his abdomen, retching for air. The disbelief on his face came from a mixture of pain, confusion and the stars that pierced in and out in front of his face.

Callie cried out and grabbed out to him, steading his stance to stop him falling on to the floor. She was again wrenched away, this time by Ankor who pushed her up against the wall, his hand tight round her neck. Eyeball to eyeball he glared, she could feel his chest rising and falling impatiently against her. He squeezed her neck slightly and sneered at her, his upper lip curling towards his nose, clearly showing his teeth.

'Enough of this,' he threatened. 'I know exactly where Thorrach is. You two didn't come from there. You didn't cover that distance. So perhaps you can tell me this time. Where did you come from?'

As Callie said nothing, he tightened his grip again. She gasped, in fright and in attempt to breathe freely.

Almost inaudible she answered, 'Salthea.' The hand relaxed slightly. 'We came from Salthea.' The hand disappeared and she fell to the floor, searching noisily for breath on her hands and knees. The handprint on her neck stood out distinctly.

'And now we're getting something,' Ankor said, scrutinising them both. 'Why were you two in Salthea?'

Callie kneeled back, still filling her lungs.

'You hurt?' whispered Ben? She shook her head.

'I said,'

'We were arrested,' Callie jumped in.

Ankor looked bemused, perhaps pondering whether to believe them or if they were brave enough to lie again.

'For what?'

Callie looked at Ben, his eyes and the steel in his face told her she should continue with the cover.

'For being in a relationship.'

Ankor looked at Fly who took his lead to sit down.

'I think we might finally be getting somewhere.' Ankor folded his tanned, scarred arms across his chest in anticipation. The position outlined the muscles in his biceps and shoulders.

Ben sniffed and continued, seeing the opportunity to defuse the situation and lead away from the reality.

'Callie and I were caught. Arrested and taken to Salthea for punishment. We should have been more careful.' He reached out and took her hand, trying to play his part. Fuelling the anger inside, he redirected it in his tale. 'Why shouldn't we be allowed to choose a partner? We work hard. I've toiled and bled and ached for that place and they deny us a little happiness. It's bullshit. So yeah, we were taken to Salthea. They tried to brainwash us again with their crap about the purpose, our meaning. Our defiling Earth and risking lives by wanting to be together.'

Ben paused to draw breath and regroup. Ankor spoke,

'So how did you escape?'

Callie looked at Ben, frightened. This wasn't exactly detailed. He had to make it real. Convince them.

'We um, well we.'

'We accepted what they said.' Callie jumped in. 'Agreed we hated each other. Even went hand to hand fighting with those,' she pointed to the Khalto sticks. 'Took our vows again. Knew the consequences. Then when they processed us to ship back to the farm we got out.'

'Got out?'

She nodded, 'Stole a truck and drove. Just drove till the gas ran out.'

'And where would that be?' Ankor pressed.

'Some plain,' Ben took over. 'It was hot, no shelter. We headed for the hills. We needed to hide. To eat. Water.'

'And we find you here,' Ankor smiled but his eyes remained cold and callous.

Callie and Ben nodded.

'Bloody monkeys,' Ben muttered almost to himself, holding his guts, his face scarlet.

'Helpful, they were very helpful. Far more curious and animated than usual. So easy to follow, just think of the result of their innocence.' Ankor paused, as if philosophising. 'Well, now that's sorted out we should make a move. Be going.' Ankor cracked his neck from side to side and stretched out his arms through interlaced fingers. 'Ready Fly?'

Fly, looking despondent nodded.

'Well come on,' Ankor spoke as he swept his arm along, taking in Callie, Ben and their belongings.

'I, I don't understand,' stammered Ben.

'We can't just leave you here,' Ankor explained. 'That just won't do.'

'Where are you taking us,' Callie asked.

All pretence, all niceties gone from his voice the answer chilled her.

'To Them'.

CHAPTER NINETEEN

Fly shoved Ben forward again, the stumble as he maintained his balance sent a shooting pain through his knee and up his thigh. A hot, angry pain that pushed forward and throbbed. Ben embraced it; it added to the hate he felt in his stomach and the buzzing rage swarming in his head. Ben had no idea how they would get out of this, but he knew what he was going to do if he did. Another name written on the hit list.

Ankor and Fly had stripped them of their weapons and belts, they now hung smugly around their waists, their packs over their shoulders. Fly had grown bored of threatening them, of showing off the edge of his knife. Instead, he pushed Ben and Callie sharply in the back with a Khalto stick every now and again. Since they left neither Callie nor Ben had spoken, communicating rudimentally only with their eyes. Mostly this 'conversation' was passing glances of panic, confusion and fear. Both Callie and Ben knew they had to get out of this situation. Out of it fast.

Callie was disorientated. In the wrenching out of the shelter she had lost any real sense of direction. The darkness in the forest didn't help; she couldn't focus for long enough on any stars to right herself. Any flickers of early dawn she did have time to glimpse at were too quickly obscured by treetops or one of their captors pushing them along. What was clear to her was they were two full nights in, they only had four days left. And it would already be dawn soon. She couldn't even be sure how long they had been walking for. Certainly, there were, so far, no hints of life or stopping, but time was ticking by. The best she could hope for was that they were moving nearer towards where she and Ben wanted to be and not backtracking.

After a particularly rough prod in the back, Callie snapped.

'Where are you taking us?'

Fly jumped in from behind her, his word mixed with eager, heavy breaths.

'That's for us to know, us to know.'

Callie turned slightly, aware if she slowed down she would find another bruise emerging along her spine.

'I wasn't talking to you,' she snapped back at Fly.

He lolloped round to face her, now moving backwards which made him appear even more ungainly.

'But I was talking to you,' he snarled, his thin neck bobbing his face in and out of Callie's space, threatening.

'Leave her,' Ankor commanded, and Fly scuttled back behind, spitting at her feet as he did.

'Where are you taking us,' she asked again.

'To Them. If you are refusing to explain yourselves to me, perhaps they will loosen your tongues.'

'And who are they?' Callie asked. Ben shut his mouth, clearly simultaneously about to ask the same thing.

'You'll see.' Ankor was clearly not going to share any information.

Callie glanced over at Ben and met his eyes. They said the same. Feared the same. Them meant the crazed – the hungry.

'Why can't you just leave us? We're no threat,' she went on, rubbing her already sore hands back and forth uselessly against the bindings on her wrist.

'That remains to be seen,' Ankor said.

Ben snorted, 'Doesn't really seem like much of a threat to me. You've our packs, our weapons, our food. We're tied up. What do you think we're going to do? Grapple you to the ground.'

'I'd like to see you try,' Fly sneered, jabbing Ben painfully between the shoulder blades with a splintered end of the Khalto stick. He raised the stick again, but hurriedly dropped it to his side, innocently, after a warning glance from Ankor.

'Look, we've told you. We're no threat. Look at us. A couple of teenagers out here trying to run away and start again. Can't you please just let us go? What good are we to you? We're just wasting your time.'

179

'Yet we have all the time in the world. You two? I'm not so sure.'

Callie darted a look at Ben.

'What makes you say that?' she asked.

'Food for a start. You've got enough for, oh, I'd say three or four more days.' Ankor looked Ben up and down, 'Although I'm not too sure this guy will be happy with the portions.'

Ben glared, deep down satisfied with the acknowledgement of his size. Five minutes alone with this guy, he thought, just five minutes.

'That's all we could snatch before we left,' Callie tried to convince him.

'Sure it was.'

The high-pitched panicked anxiety in her voice wasn't completely contrived as she continued, 'It's not like we could carry much. All we wanted to do was get away and be together. We didn't care where we ended up.'

Ankor smiled and nodded. 'Yet you ended up here. Rations, medicine, weapons,' there was extra emphasis on the word, 'sighters, compass, map. Not exactly ill prepared. Not exactly scrabbling to throw things in a pack, is it?'

Callie did not reply.

'Is it?' he asked a bit more firmly. When he was satisfied, she was not going to answer he snarled, 'Your silence won't last. Answers will follow. You have no idea. Taught to fear the madness of the Wilds, the brutal savageness. But you will find out.'

Callie's eyes dropped and she continued to march and stumble forward. As she tried to orientate herself, she prayed Ben was trying to figure out a way for them to escape. It seemed they were heading the way they needed, but it was really only instinct guiding her. The forest had become more crowded. Dank, humid air surrounded them and held them in. It appeared darker than ever. The plants on the ground were no longer squat and rough, burnt growths interspersing the trees. Here some were knee high or higher on Callie; reaching out in curiosity to touch this stranger as she swept through them. She was thankful for the protection of the suit against those more thorny and sharp. Still, despite the unknown, despite the threat, Callie tried her best to keep one positive at the forefront of her thinking. Deeper into the forest was where the Dealga grew.

Ankor and Fly clearly knew every inch of the terrain. They looked to be following an almost invisible trail. Other than tiny depressions or disturbed greenery she made out in fleeting light, Callie could not see any clear trace of a path. Another sign they were now firmly in the Wilds and in their territory. Ankor, still leading, pushed aside condensed branches and swinging vines, at times hacking at them with his knife to make the path easier to traverse. Tears jumped up and stung her eyes when one swung back and slapped her smartly across the right cheek. Hands bound, Callie and Ben had to lean forward, headfirst and try to use their shoulders to barge on and move through behind. She took small pleasure in the occasional hiss or complain from Fly as a wayward branch disturbed by Ben, caught him unawares.

They could tell they were approaching their destination before there were any signs. Fly couldn't hide his excitement of arriving. His breathing became faster and shallower, each breath noticeably audible, his gait even more lolloping. He was bent forward, arms trailing chimp like, gurgling with excitement and chattering to himself. A number of times he caught the heel of Callie and Ben as he tried to shuffle forward more quickly to reach their target.

Callie almost did the same, catching her step and pulling up short just before bulldozing into Ankor. He had abruptly stopped, sighed and put his hands on his hips with dramatic relish. There hadn't seemed to be any sign of life: no break in the forest or change in the tense, uncertain atmosphere. He breathed deep, Callie could see his back arch as his chest raised up, and exhaled with exaggerated appreciation, then turned.

'So, my friends, we are here. Welcome to the Wilds. Now we will find out the truth about our guests.'

Callie and Ben moved forward, feeling a mixture of trepidation and dark curiosity.

Before them, secluded by the edge of the forest, was a perfect hidden clearing housing this community. The sun was still rising, casting soft, early rays which merged into the contours of ramshackle buildings of various sizes. They were created from thatch, stone and the remnants of the past and looked as if they had accidentally sprung up and now hung together. Half a dozen or so single level constructions that had somehow stubbornly stood all this time, in one state or another, filled the area in a rough three-sided rectangle. All were in shifting states of disrepair. Some had caved in roofs or patchy, crumbling walls; others had walls which had completely disintegrated in places. Others lay insecure: doorless or windowless, metal and wood hanging down unsteadily as makeshift random shelter. A few had clouded plastic sheeting or stacked poly packaging tied together to let light inside. Behind these buildings even fewer sturdy canvasses stretched over tented shelters.

Although at first glance the settlement appeared deserted and abandoned, the abundancy of life was clear. The ground over the whole area had been partly cleared and flattened. It was worn and scattered with circular patterns of scorched earth from fires or piles of debris which appeared to have been arranged into some kind of order.

There were metal mounds that might have been vehicles, equipment or machinery before they had been stripped and reused in other ways. Various sized and shaped pieces and chunks of wood also lay piled up: what looked like window frames, pallets, furniture.

And hills of plastics grew out of the ground, the morning rays catching and bouncing off a giant collection of colours and shapes and moulds. The edges of thinner pieces flapped up and down, back and forth gently, the pile holding itself together somehow like one enormous, fused object.

The entire complex appeared like an ancient scrap yard where everything was catalogued, useful and had a purpose – or was stripped and altered until it did.

Beyond this area the forest began again. But it was what lay in between the camp and the forest that caught Callie's breath. Caused a trickle of fear to begin down her spine then spread through her arms and into her brain. Where the last edge of the rectangle should have been, slightly centred within the space, was a circle of tall, thick trunks, sharpened into intimidating spikes and bound tightly to each other. Inside was a metal cage, large enough for a couple of grown adults to stand in and move around. The floor of the cage was earth, stained dark brown in places.

This wasn't the only foreign body on the ground. Callie could also see stripped, dirty rags. And, as far as she could tell from where she stood. a single boot. Ripped from a foot.

Unexpectedly, a dull, echoing horn sounded, Callie and Ben both shrank back in fright. The camp fearlessly erupted into life: chattering and indistinguishable noise rose as dirty, suspicious and calculating faces appeared from the buildings and the forest. Here were men, woman and youths ready to examine these intruders.

These prisoners.

The word suddenly ripped through Callie. That's what they were. Prisoners. Ankor bent and with a hiss of putrid breath announced, 'Let me show you around' before forcing her forward. Ben was at her side.

They stepped forward, walking towards the gathering crowd. Every pair of eyes was on them, Voices gained momentum, louder and louder as they approached. There was too much excitement, too many conversations to focus on what exactly was being said, but Callie and Ben snatched words and phrases here and there:

'…returned with captives…'

'…sent from Salthea as spies…'

'Maya will sort them…'

'… so young…'

'…make them pay for what's been done to us…'

'…won't be so confident for long…'

What was certain was the tone. Wary, harsh and unforgiving in its curiosity.

The cluster parted as Callie and Ben moved further on, forming a rough semi-circle around them, not wanting to miss a second of whatever this was. Callie noticed that Ankor was clearly revelling in the celebrity he was stirring up. Fly too was leaping around, panting excitedly and commenting on their 'catch' with those close enough to stop him with an outstretched arm or grab on the shoulder.

They all had the same wild, unkempt look of Ankor and Fly: grimy, weathered faces, making their eyes appear even whiter and larger, although not their chipped, yellowing teeth. Eyes that, at often stared through long, wild hair that had most likely never been tamed. Their clothing matched this place – fragmented and thrown together.

Ankor eventually stopped, clearly satisfied he was deep enough in his audience to address them and pulled Ben, who had continued to step on, roughly back. He spoke loudly, proudly and with authority. A hush fell over the gathering.

'As you can see, our scouting has produced something much more interesting and unexpected from what we set out to find. Perhaps much more valuable.' He paused, letting the crowd murmur and soak up his words. 'We have the monkeys to thank. Deep within our lands we found the camp of these traitors, resting in our lands in the dead of night.' As if on cue, Fly dropped a pack and began unloading the contents on the grass in front of him. Eyes darted from Ankor to the treasures it could perhaps contain. He went on, proudly. 'They alluded us the first time, but the monkeys guided us to them, and they were not so fortuitous.'

There were short bursts of congratulatory comments,

'…protecting our safety.'

'…dangers from out there…'

'…could have been hurt.' Ankor raised his hand, calling for silence again. This time his voice was firm, sombre.

'Unfortunately, after questioning, they were unable to explain why they find themselves in our lands, so we had no choice but to bring them here for further interrogation.' His voice now rose, inciting excited agreement. 'We have to look after our people. We have already lost so much, had so much ripped from us. Forced to live here. In the shadows. Yet our way of life is free. Liberty. We will not be chained to Salthea again.'

The crowd nodded, cheered 'Yes' and 'No', 'down with Salthea', 'lock them up' as Ankor spun round, Khalto stick raised above his head. Ben and Callie stared at them, then at each other. Aware to the bone what this could mean. One word, one name was muttered more than once, becoming clearer and clearer.

'Maya'

'Where is Maya?'

'Take them to Maya'

'Maya will know what to do.'

The prisoners were pushed forward, towards the cage. The crowd jeered, those they had already passed now followed on, not wanting to miss anything of the incarceration. Fly bounded ahead, so eager to undo the locks on the cage his hands were shaking, and he dropped the keys and bolts more than once. As Callie and Ben came level the door was flung open, and she was pushed inside.

The change in level caused her to stumble to her knees in the straw. Ben whirled round, eye to eye with Ankor.

'Anything you would like to say?' Ankor sneered.

'Plenty' growled Ben, spitting on the ground inches from Ankor's feet. 'But I can wait. Till we're alone.'

Ankor roared with amused laughter, throwing his head back. Some in the crowd looked at each other, confused as to what was going on.

'I look forward to it,' he snarled, taking Ben by the shoulder. Ben struggled,

'Leave me alone. Get your hands off me,' he threw himself sideways, shot Ankor another hateful look them stepped into the cage himself. Fly, with a flourish, slammed the door shut and locked it dramatically. Callie and Ben, red faced, moved together. Ben dropped behind her and started struggling to undo her ties, his own grip restricted by rope. They surveyed their new surroundings, both looking for any possibilities to help them escape.

The crowd began to goad, as if the closed gate gave them free reign and security to threaten more. Some came close up to the railings, leering in at the pair. Finally, Ben eased a weakness in the knot holding Callie's wrists tight and worked it back and forth until it was loose. He winced when he began easing the ties out and bent a nail back away from its bed, but there was no time. Scrabbling blind eventually he loosened the bonds enough for Callie to wiggle her hands loose and tackle his bonds.

Ankor stood at the door, amused, and once again addressed his crowd.

'Maya. Where is Maya? She needs to be here now.'

The name Callie had heard again reverberated around the camp in revered, venerated tones.

After a few moments there was movement and silence fell. From a corner of the compound Maya appeared.

CHAPTER TWENTY

The woman who had emerged reminded Callie of Autumn. She held a regal air as she walked, almost floated through the crowd. Even the air seemed to freeze still in anticipation at her aura; the warmth that was finally beginning to creep into the morning was stunned and driven back for the moment, like the heat driven off at the end of the summer. Tall and slim she had a long, thick blonde plait running down her back, tousled with loose wayward strands. Her robes, Callie could think of no other word for the calf length open tunic she wore was flecked with orange and red, hints of purple and shades of brown and red. Even with its faded, worn material, it stood out easily against the rags worn by the others.

Callie and Ben rose and stood side by side, both with trepidation and subconscious, instinctive veneration. Maya approached the cage and passed around it, all four sides. A predator teasing its prey. The crowd automatically as one took a step back to allow her room, as if they feared her brushing against them or having her view obstructed. Close it was easier to examine her face. Sunbeaten, as the rest of her group, Callie placed her in her mid-40's. Slight lines were emerging on her face, each one full of tales and wisdom. Her cheekbones lay high and sharp, giving her a long, pointed expression. Her hazel eyes were liquid and thoughtful, by no means warm, but intelligent rather than instantly perilous. The woman was both severe and stunningly beautiful.

Twice she circled the cage, paying no attention to the crowd. Still, they remained silent, clearly waiting for some sign, some command or judgement. She spent little time examining the prisoners either, Callie noticed. Her eyes hadn't left them as she floated from her hut, now she walked, hands clasped, eyes down, appearing to consider and ponder deeply. Finally, she stopped, directly in front of Callie and Ben and their eyes met.

Unblinking, iridescent eyes soaked in Callie; she could almost feel them seeping into her. Flashes of hazel, sand and dying embers, battling to maintain existence, watched her, measuring her.

When Maya spoke her voice was everywhere, hypnotic, like thick smoke over a fire. Her words seemed to echo from the crowd and bounce back towards them.

'I trust you were not harmed as you were being delivered to me?'

Ben snapped, approaching the bars and reaching out to hold one in each hand, 'Harmed? Look at us. Beaten, bound, strangled. Knives held at our throats. I'd say we were plenty harmed.'

Maya looked slightly amused; Callie doubted the people here had ever spoken to her in this way.

'For that I am sincerely saddened and sorry.' She turned and scanned the crowd for Ankor and Fly. When her eyes fell on them the colour drained from Fly's face and he managed to stand stock still, at least his version of it. 'That is very disappointing and no way to treat visitors from the Norm' Her eyes met Ben's again, 'That is something I will investigate personally.'

Taken aback with this response Ben spoke no further. He met her gaze until he could bare it no more and his eyes fell to his red wrists which he rubbed timidly.

'The Norm?' Callie didn't understand, seeking further. Maya finally broke her gaze on Ben and smiled, a genuine smile from deep within her eyes.

'Why yes. The Norm is everything outside the Wilds. Greenhouses, farms, Salthea.' Callie noted a miniscule hint of animosity at the mention of the capital city, as if she did not want the word circling her mouth a second longer than it had to.

'I didn't realise,' Callie stopped. It sounded so stupid; she didn't even know what she didn't think.

The silken voice was soothing and encouraging. 'I understand. You didn't think about us. You live out there, organised, regimented, ruled. You call us the Wilds believing us feral savages. Yet you have names for us, surely it makes sense that we too, our people, our communities, have names for you?'

Callie nodded.

Maya smiled at Callie again – warm, open and encouraging. Although she was captured, mortified to be encased in this cage surrounded by these people, Callie felt the first hope she had in hours. This woman seemed intelligent, reasonable, kind.

'And just as your people have routines, structure, law, so too do we. Is that not fair? I'm sure you would love to hear of our ways, our survival. How it is out here. I don't blame you. I'm sure back where you harvest, we are an exotic unknown, dangerous and unusual. Feared. But in so many ways that is how we feel about your life. Can't you see that?' She cocked her head to one side, waiting.

Callie nodded again, wanting to listen to the silken voice filling her head with new information. Not only attracting and drawing her in with its undiscovered knowledge but perhaps providing them with a way out. Of course, she was suspicious of her – her people had beaten and thrown her in here – but what she said seemed real and true. More open than anything Prane or Takot had shared with them.

Callie's voice was small, guilty even. 'Yes, yes I suppose so.'

That smile again, fingers joining in a prayer gesture and brought to Maya's lips where there was a faint smile.

'Now, I offer a heartfelt apology to what happened to both of you and assure you any impropriety will be dealt with most severely. You have my word on that.'

Ben did not seem so drawn in. As Maya spoke, he had felt a change in the crowd. Something had changed in the atmosphere, infinitesimal, indefinable. But different. The breath of the horde seemed to hang in the air waiting. Not for the first time he felt like prey just as the first prickling of instinct warned a predator was nearby.

Maya saddened. 'We could have learned so much from each other, shared, developed and evolved in harmony together. Co-existing with understanding and truce. But that time has passed.' She sympathetically patted Callie's fist, wrapped round one of the cell posts. 'A little mutual collaboration and support was all we asked. Co-operation from those with so much more power, more resources than us.' Her voice was pained, a feeling of burden ladening it.

Ben realised what was happening, just as Callie's face changed as, she too, saw the snare she had been sucked into.

Maya's eyes, strong and remorseful, left Ben and Callie and she spoke to them while now looking at the crowd, her voice instantly staunch and intent. 'You chose not to help us. To support us in our meagre community.' There were murmurs, nods from the group as they looked around each other in agreement. 'All we needed was reassurance you were not looking to damage our ways, our peaceful lives. Instead, you gave us stubborn lies.'

Callie pushed herself against the bars, appealing to the woman with the voice, the eyes, the smile, fighting the knowledge she had been sucked in, tricked. 'No, wait, it's not like that…' Maya raised her hand to silence her. The face that now turned was a face of painful, treacherous beauty. The fluid eyes still drew Callie to their intensity, their depth, but this was now cold, hidden, midnight light from the bottom of the ocean.

'The time for negotiation, for tolerance, for benevolence is gone. Spent when you dared broach our lands and sully this space with your lies. I will know why you were sent from Salthea. I will have the truth. Or you will face my justice.'

A cacophony of sounds rose – jeers, shouts, chants, screeches from disturbed animals, as Maya returned to her hut.

'No, wait, please! The tablets. Please! We have our ration in our packs. Please!'

Callie's cries to come back and to wait were drowned out or ignored. After a few moments the obscene, maniacal grin of Fly appeared at the cell door and scraps of something were pushed inside.

'Our medicine?' Callie asked. Fly shrugged, noncommittal.

'Who knows, maybe it's in there, maybes it's not,' he chuckled, clearly entertained by this sense of power and importance.

'We need the tablets.' Callie commanded. 'Don't you understand? Or we'll,' Callie stopped abruptly, the suddenness of the truth slapping her.

'Or you'll what?' Fly asked, acutely gleeful of the power he was holding, however short.

'Or we'll die.' The words were insincere, flat. The weight of the reality thickened Callie's tongue, but the truth was information she would not exude. Her head still couldn't comprehend or verbalise it to herself even if she could.

Fly stood, akimbo, soaking every iota from this pretence of power. He said nothing, simply continued to watch them, entertained.

'It could've been ground in there,' he said, pointing to the food. 'I didn't ask. But I suppose that would mean there could be anything mixed in, don't it?'

Neither Ben nor Callie would give him the satisfaction of seeing them devour this food and so the trio waited each other out until Fly grew bored. He scratched his back with seeming great joy, picked whatever dirt and grime he amassed through doing so from his fingers pinged it in the direction of the cage and left.

Once he was no longer watching them, at least from where they could see, Callie and Ben approached the food. They had no way of knowing of course if it was safe to eat or not but would have to take the chance. They were both ravenous after walking through the night and had no choice but to accept what had been left.

Ben, meanwhile, had been examining the food. Large, stale chunks of bread smeared lightly with sticky, yellow honey, partial honeycombs sticking up from the surface. He also took care, ripping off a tiny piece of edge, smelling and chewing long and carefully before swallowing. Neither of them spoke until Ben, satisfied there was no danger from the food, handed Callie a piece.

'Thanks.'

'It seems alright'

'We really fucked up.'

'Do you think it's in there?'

'I dunno, but we need to eat at least.' Callie examined the bread for any signs of powder. She found none.

'We don't need it you know, remember what Takot and Prane said? It's useless.'

'Do you trust them? Truly believe that? Besides, they said it still staves off the turning. Holds it back. The longer that takes the better.'

'I don't know what to believe anymore.'

Callie turned the bread over and over in her hands. 'Me neither. But old habits. What if they're wrong? Take it die, don't take it still die. I'd rather hedge my bets and live a little longer.'

Ben nodded, there was no point trying to hide or soften the blow of the reality facing them. They sat, gratefully chewing the bread and honey, hungrily enjoying the sickly sweetness, not leaving a crumb behind. Callie wiped her licked clean fingers on her thighs and stood up again, walking around the cage, examining every corner and every post. She shook the lock then, unhappy in the realisation there did not seem to be any immediate way out, surveyed the township instead, then spun round. 'What the hell do you think we should do now?'

'Your guess is as good as mine.' Grabbing a post, Ben pulled himself up, rattling a few to see if there were any weaknesses. 'Didn't think so,' he muttered to himself in disgust.

Callie had crossed the cell and picked up the torn, battered boot that was left. The sole was almost completely ripped off, the person wearing them would as well have been barefoot, she thought, before the more ominous idea that something had ripped it off while the wearer was in her crossed her mind. There did not seem to be any obvious signs of teeth or nails; putting it back she picked up the cloth and ran it between her fingers. Nondescript canvas, engrained with dirt and more or less shredded, it offered no clues. Except, of course, that someone else had been here.

'What do you think their plan is?'

'You don't want to know.'

'Try me,' Callie pushed on, not sure if she wanted to hear the reality she already knew.

Ben's face was serious, gloomy and his voice forced and lifeless, 'Well it's not good, is it? Find us once, bother to follow, attack and assault us,' he gestured to the bruises sprouting proudly across both their bodies, 'then throw us in here.'

'What do you think that speech was all about?'

'Bullshit. Bullshit you fell for.'

Callie's face clouded and her body stiffened,

'Thanks a lot Ben, as if I need reminded. I bet you just couldn't wait to hit me with that nugget of opinion, could you? I suppose it's my fault we're here too, is it?'

'I didn't say that.'

Callie eyeballed him. 'You don't need to come on just spit it out. It's written all over your face. I mean, why not, I was on watch so I should have seen them coming. Known they were tracking us. Isn't that right?'

'Quit trying to put words in my mouth and pick a fight. I thought we were over all that?'

'Really? And you'd love that wouldn't you? Get a wee happy every after for yourself? No more guilt. No more wishing you could change the past.'

'Callie, come on!' he was losing patience now, 'You're just pissed because she sucked you in and we're stuck in here. Why don't you just quit it with the pity party will you? We don't have time for all this b.s.'

'This bullshit?' she was angry now, not caring if anyone was watching or listening, the boiling words inside were taking control. 'How dare you call my brother's death, all that happened in Salthea, all this bullshit. 'No, Ben, I don't think I will quit it with my pity party. In fact…' Callie curled her fingers, crossed her arms under her armpits and let out a frustrated screeching groan. Anger, frustration, exhaustion and pain all release at once. Then, crumbling to the floor Ben was taken aback more than by anything over the last few days as she began to cry loud, wailing tears.

Ben stood stunned and helpless as Callie sobbed into her arms, folded over across her bruised, scraped knees. Her head and shoulders rose and fell in jerky, spasms. For the first time Ben thought she looked slight and fragile; all the guile and fight seemed to have left her, coming out of her through her tears.

Uncertain, he sat next to her, wrapped his arm across her back and pulled her towards him. She looked up, leant against his side, her head resting on her shoulder and said nothing, clean trails of tears forming winding pathways down her cheeks. Translucent salty beads formed droplets as they reached the edges of her face and fell silently. Her back continued to lurch awkwardly through her sobs while she sniffed and worked to regain composure. All the while, Ben rubbed her back, occasionally pushing her damp hair back from her eyes and tucking it behind her ears.

Eventually she snuffled loudly, cursing down all the snot gathering in her nose and throat, ran her hand across her nose, taking care of excess moisture and leaned up, Ben's arm remaining comfortingly across her back.

'Better?' he whispered gently.

Callie nodded, looking at him with floating eyes and a tiny awkward smile.

'Sorry,' she said.

'Don't be daft, there's nothing to be sorry for. I wish I could take it away.'

'What?'

'All this,' Ben broke his arm away and wrapped his arms around his knees. Callie shivered slightly, her back instantly cold after the heat from his body. 'This mess, Salthea, all of it. I wish we could just go back to the farm. Harvest corn. Not know any better.'

'Yeah,' Callie mumbled, wiping dried mud from her trouser legs.

'Never thought I'd here you say that.'

She shrugged, not able to give in to Ben's attempt to lighten the mood. 'I mean it, though. Look where we've ended up. If we hadn't tried so hard to get caught up in all this. Maybe I should have tried harder to persuade you just to let it go, forget it. We should've left them to clean up their own mess. If Bree hadn't seen us. Or even after, if we could have got away. Maybe we could even have got out of Salthea, escaped.'

Callie rubbed the end of her nose, checking it wasn't still running.

'And gone where?' she asked.

Ben sighed and shook his head.

'I dunno. Stayed on the farm even.'

'Stayed on the farm?'

'Sure, why not?'

'Kept in the dark. Cheated on. Lied to.'

'Fed. Safe. Better than this, isn't it?'

Callie moved out of Ben's arm, turning to face him better. The bright, afternoon light shining on her emphasised the clean streaks the tears had made through the grime on her face. Her cheeks were flushed, with crying, the increasing heat of the day but also the animation Ben could see coming back inside of her.

'Is it?' she asked. 'Is it really? At least here we know where we stand. Know we're in danger. People tell it like it is.'

'You'd rather be a prisoner?'

'We were prisoners before, Ben. Trapped in that place. But no, no I wouldn't. I'd rather get the bloody Dealga and get the hell out of her, away from Salthea, away from the farm, away from,' she stopped short.

'Away from me?'

Callie was silent.

'Just say it. Away from me.'

'Yes, away from you,' Callie stared deep into his face, her eyes pierced and focused now, no longer tinged with tears. 'Of course, away from you. I want this done. Give them what they want. Get my life back or whatever the hell they decide to do.'

'And that's what it all comes down to. What it always comes back to.'

'Sure it does. What? You think I'm going to forget what you did? How you killed the only family I have left?'

'Tax…'

Callie jumped in, rising to her feet,

'Don't you dare say his name. Don't you ever. He's gone because of you; you don't get that privilege.' She moved in an attempt to get as far away from Ben as she could, facing a so-far shaded corner. She could hear him get up and come up behind her.

Ben touched her shoulders, and she spun round,

'Get off me.'

His voice was gentle, steadied into a monotone.

'Callie, let me try, let me talk. I don't want to hurt you anymore.' Inches from her face, looking into him Callie could see the hurt and regret, clear and honest. Yet all his pain was nothing like hers. She felt blood rise into her face, clenched her hand white into a fist, then relaxed as if to slap out. In a frantic instant her mind muddled, emotions tumbling, and Ben was lost for words and dumbfounded for the second time as her lips met his.

Callie's mouth was hot, forceful, alive. She tasted of salt from her tears, the cracked edges of both their lips at first rough and dry, then disappearing wet and oily as they gave way into each other. Her mind thankfully, restfully went blank – all the turbulence and trauma and dread and exhaustion disappeared. That was all she wanted, all she needed. Longingly she explored Ben's mouth with her tongue, remembering how this had felt, how this had been before. She ran her tongue over the edges of his teeth, teasing the end of his as she encouraged him further into their embrace. Right here, right now this was right, this took her away from everything else. She needed these arms wrapped around her, tighter now, his uncertainty gone as he craved for her too. She pushed her body up against him and knew from the heat between them he felt the same.

In these moments neither cared where they were, who could be watching or what the consequences of this were. It was beyond rationality – was an elemental release neither of them wanted to deny.

Finally, Ben broke away, panting, feeling the imprint of her hands and lips still on him. He kept her close, hands on her shoulders, the heat between them still trapped for a few moments.

'Cal', he said softly, lifting her chin so she looked him in the eye. The grief and childlikeness were gone, replaced once again with her searing audacity.

Her words were soft, but sure, 'Don't Ben, just don't. Please!' However, she didn't move, didn't try to leave his arms. He pulled her back into his chest, wrapped his arms around her one last time and buried his head into her hair. It smelled lightly of grass and sweat and sunlight.

'Okay Callie, ok,' he said, kissing her gently and releasing both of them from whatever it was.

The powerful heat cast narrow shadows in the cage. They provided little relief for Callie and Ben as they baked uncomfortably. Nothing had been said between them since they had kissed. An awkward silence had been an unwelcome guest between them for a time but had thankfully dissipated into an understated nerviness.

There did not seem to be much activity going on within the camp. At least nothing clear. Young, inquisitive faces peered out from tents, some even walking past, from a safe distance, on some contrived chore. Occasionally irate voiced geed them back with strong warnings. The smell of cooking rose up from time to time, as did the oily, sharp smell of mechanical work and the grinding, squeal of some kind of tools. But from their vantage point Callie and Ben could see little. Callie realised this was probably not accidental. The position of the cage more or less in the centre of this settlement was beneficial for the wild ones- they could see Callie and Ben perfectly but position their tents to keep them strategically secret.

A young member of Maya's tribe as Callie had come to think of them, had brought them a welcome jug of water a few hours ago. In Callie's estimations she couldn't have been more than 11 or 12, petite and dark. Like Callie she had a long, loose braid running down her back. The girl had approached warily with curiosity, jumped from foot to foot perhaps desperate to speak but fighting an urge after warnings not to talk to these prisoners. She had watched suspiciously then placed the jug right on the edge, as far away from Callie and Ben as she could.

As she stepped back from the jug the girl stood back, a little more confident now. There was a little hesitation then she reached forward again and solemnly placed two white capsules next to the liquid, clearly aware of the importance of this offering.

The girl had been taking no chances, no doubt after warning, in case they had reached out and grabbed her. From a safe distance she stood watching, smiling proudly when Callie took the jug and looked into the cloudy water. Sediment had settled on the bottom, but it was still not clear by any stretch of the imagination. She dipped a finger in, sucked the liquid, covering her lips and, after no immediate ill effects, took a long sip.

'It seems alright,' she said, offering him the jug and Ben drank deeply, thankfully. Callie lifted one of the capsules, rolled it between her fingers

That had been a couple of hours ago and they were now left with a deep thirst again. Not before time another elected character approached, took the empty jug and replaced it with another. This was slammed down with disgust, some valuable liquid slopping over the side and leaving a damp ring wastefully on the bottom of the cage. Clearly not everyone was simply inquisitive about the captives, animosity was also prevalent all around them.

Callie reached first for the jug, quickly checking for suspicious and offensive additions to the water before taking a heavy, greedy mouthful, her throat moving eagerly as it sucked down the precious liquid. Moving the jug from her lips she wiped the rim then offered it to Ben with an outstretched arm. Leaning over he took it and also enjoyed a long, relished swig.

'Thanks,' Ben said, wiping his mouth slightly breathless as the last of the water went down.

'Do you think it's real?'

'What?'

'The water. Do you think it's real?'

Ben looked into the jug, as if that would somehow reveal the answer. A light sediment was settling again on the bottom.

'I hadn't thought about it,' he said, 'I'm just glad they gave us some more.'

'Tastes different.'

'Huh, maybe. Or maybe we're just so desperate we'd drink anything.'

'Maybe.'

'Is that where we're at now?'

'What do you mean?'

'Discussing the water, skirting round things. Bloody awkward silence. We need to get a way out of here.'

Callie couldn't hide her irritation or push the sarcasm back down her throat,

'Really, I hadn't noticed. What do you want me to say? I told you I didn't want to talk about it.'

'It isn't all about you Callie. This has nothing to do with you kissing me…'

Snapping, she jumped straight in, 'You kissed me back.'

Ben paused, sighed, then began again. 'As I said, this had nothing to do with the kiss. All I want to do is get our heads together,' Callie threw him a dirty look, 'and figure out a way out of here.'

Callie, seemingly galvanised into the reality of the situation, stood up. 'Me too. Any ideas?'

'Snap these bars with our bare hand; sneak through the camp without anyone noticing; make for the woods; head straight on till we find the Dealga then turn left.'

Callie's voice was slow, low, but not without humour, 'Great, let's get started. Least your optimism and sense of humour haven't disappeared.'

'Sorry, I missed the week we covered escapism from a cage surrounded by wild mentalists as quickly as possible so we can find a plant to help avoid everyone dying in school.'

'Me too,' Callie agreed, staring out beyond the camp into the trees. Despairingly she groaned loudly in frustration and slammed her hands against the cage posts. 'If we could just get in there, away and hide I could figure out where we are.'

'If only. Not sure how much help that would be anyway. There are too many of them.'

'How many of them do you think live here?'

'I'm not talking about just here, Callie, don't' you get it? She said 'communities', not 'community'. They're not the only ones out here. They are not the whole Wild.'

Callie's face flickered in realisation, and she swallowed hard, the moisture beginning to leave her throat. She shook her head, battering on.

'I'm trying to stay upbeat here Ben, figure this out. We need to refocus, do something. Or end up like that, whatever that was.' Callie picked up the destroyed boot and turned it over in her hands again, not really sure what she was looking for. Any clues of anything.

'Who.'

'What?'

'Who it was,' Ben corrected, pointing at the boot.

The fear and frustrated despair were back on the edge of her voice,

'Exactly. Who. A person, Ben. We don't even know why the hell they were chucked in here, what happened. But I'm damn sure it wasn't for anything as dodgy as suddenly appearing in the forest, tooled up and apparently escaped from Salthea.' Perhaps to restore her composure, perhaps in fear and anger at losing her emotions again Callie hurled the boot at the wall of the cage. It battered off it with a dull, metallic thump before landing uselessly again on the dusty floor. 'Shit,' she mumbled under her breath. 'What time do you think it is?'

'Dunno, getting to mid-afternoon?'

'A whole day wasted.'

Ben didn't reply. There seemed to be some kind of commotion coming from behind them, back where Ankor and Fly had forced them into the camp. A little distant but voices were rising and there were definite sounds of increased rustling and stirring life.

Callie turned too, as she realised something was happening. 'What is it?'

'Dunno yet, something's going on over there'.

They stood together and waited.

Heads, accompanied by their bodies, began to appear from tents and mingle around, forming a small swarm. Eager chatter rose, nothing comprehensible that Callie or Ben could pick out other than the body language. Enlivened uncertainty. Ben noticed all the children stuck close to the adults, some even staying behind, peeking round as they held on to their backs.

He realised he was holding his breath, his voice taut. 'Whatever this is, it ain't good,' he cautioned.

They appeared at the same time as Maya, Callie's eyes diverted from them momentarily as she saw the flicker of movement in her peripheral vision and Maya emerged, flanked on one side by Ankor and on the other by an immense, physically astonishing woman. She was close to the tallest person Callie had ever seen, with hair shorn right down to the quick. A deep, jagged scar ran down from her right eye to just underneath her mouth, so thick Callie could see it even from the cage. The sight of Maya bordered by this woman and Ankor would have kept Callie's gaze intently, if it hadn't been for those that were also approaching. Instinctively she took a step back and stared.

Chained at the ankles and wrists and led by thick chains clamped round the neck, three of the biters were being led straight towards the cage.

CHAPTER TWENTY-ONE

Maya stood, grandly, at the front of the cage, passively watching as the crowd circled the cage again, impatiently watching the biters approach. Her whole being seemed to be alive and burn with energy and verve as her people watched, rivetted. Someone passed close to the edge, leaned in frenzied and spat with glee,

You're for it now,' their battered teeth grinning through chipped, burst lips. Callie and Ben scarcely noticed, scarcely blinked. What was approaching was far, far worse than what they had seen on the screen. The produced, flat image was unreal, fictitious, mythical. The panting, screeching, glazed, demented eyes of the recording had not been able to truly represent what was in front of them now.

The three creatures nearing the cage were nearly void of humanity except in shape alone. All of them were haggard and emaciated, skin hanging scabbed, lose and useless from their arms; cheekbones jutting sharply high on the sides of their faces where their faded eyes focussed only on their two targets, eyes finished with human existence and motivated solely by bitter survival. Whatever that was for them. Callie and Ben both realised this was probably not be the first time the biters had been brought before the cage.

The hands that reached out from the shackles had torn skin pulled tight and taut over bulging, pulsing, iridescent veins. Their blue tint was a sharp contrast against their clammy, deadened skin. Jagged, reaching fingers swiped at the air, swooping forward in futile attempts to grab and tear. Through a large hole in the filthy material (somehow still holding on to their bodies) crossing one of their torsos, Ben could see every rib pushing roughly through pusey, infected skin.

For a few fleeting seconds Callie considered how, in other circumstances, it would have been possible to pity these monsters, feel natural empathy towards them. Their life had been stripped from them, polluted by human error and turned into a horrific, tortuous presence. But these thoughts were brief, replaced by awestruck terror.

The closer they hobbled towards the cage, the louder and more passionate the biters became, straining now to fight against their manacles. Their teeth chattered up and down, biting and grinding, desperate to eat. They whipped their heads around, first growling lowly then howling piercing screeches as their throats strained out.

Without even realising, Callie and Ben had now reached the side of the cage, their backs now pressed back against the wall. They looked at each other with dread-filled eyes, Ben reaching for Callie's hand. Looking down she took it, squeezed it lightly before they both raised their chins, staring forward as Maya stood before them, still guarded on each side, the biters behind her.

Callie could feel the cold heat emanating from Ben now, his grip on her hand tightening slowly. Pressed so hard against the side of the cage it rubbed harshly against her shoulder blades. All her senses were fired, the adrenaline of horror pulsing through a body tight and fighting to stay calm. Her brain felt swarmed with flickering, transient thoughts that were in reality useless. She could not see a way out, no escape, negotiation or plea. She looked up, close enough to see a tiny twitch had taken hold under Ben's right eye. Quivering sporadically, as if parts of him were slowly starting to burst through, break away from the whole to exodus from him. Her focus stayed on this tic, a scrap of pure human mortality within the horror forcing down on them. When he spoke, she hardly registered it was him, her ears fearful to listen at first, any sounds now could not be welcome, only littered with pain and the futility of what they had tried to do.

The voice was naïve, hopeful and pitiable, yet stubborn enough to need heard. 'You can't do this. Look at yourselves. How can you do this?'

It made no difference. The crowd, the biters still bayed. They were at the door now, a freak, distorted entertainment designed to display the power of the Wilds and act as a reminder of what could face those who disobey.

With a nod the three biters were yanked back a few feet, their throats rasping angrily at the tug on the shackles. One turned sharply, gnashing at the guard who held him, trying to grab for their arm. With a shriek he shook and fell spasming to the ground, convulsing, as he was shocked with an electrified baton. The grinning guard kicked him hard in the stomach as he clawed the ground, whimpering.

Standing in the foreground, her voice smooth and hushed as calm dusk, Maya enraptured everything once more.

'Here, we stand at another Covenant. The bonds of the Wild will never be broken, cannot be sullied or challenged. Our people and those like us have worked tirelessly, selflessly to create our communities. That cannot be risked from the outside.' Maya's words hung heavy within the clearing. The grating and crunching of the biters and leaves careless in the light breeze were now the only sounds.

'What risk are we to you? You dragged us here, remember?' Ben's voice sounded weak, pathetic, childlike.

'Do they not teach you of us in school? Teach you of our dangers, our badness, our crimes against the Earth and Earth Moon?' Maya waited for a response which did not come. 'Well? Do they not?' A few shouts rose from the crowd.

'Outcast.'

'Thieves and scum.'

'Come in nightmares.'

Maya nodded in agreement. 'Yes. Children are warned of us in ancient tales. Teens are taught to fear life beyond their compounds. Threatened with savage brutality, torture and rape. Adults subjugated so they are bound, thoughtless to the cause.'

'And what is different here?' Ben shouted. 'It looks like we were taught right. You're going to let them rip us apart.'

Maya's voice was deep, toneless and regretful. 'You have made your fate. Your choice. There is no force here. The Wilds is freedom.'

'Free? How is this free? Look at her face,' he pointed to Callie, 'Beaten by your men. Thrown here. This is not free.'

'Laggan, bring her to me.' The cage door swung open, heavy and ominous. The woman accompanying Maya, the colossal Laggan, filled the door, so tall there was only a sliver of light between her head and the roof. She walked, her head slightly bent forward, towards them, covering the distance in a few strides. Wrenching Callie easily from Ben's grasp she dragged her from the cage.

Callie struggled. Screamed and tried to grab out.

'No wait, you can't do this. What are you going to do? It was me,' Ben lurched behind them, babbling in panic. He grabbed at the woman's tunic and was knocked back and off balance with a shrugged throw of her arm. The cell door slammed closed. Ben threw himself against it in useless anger, screaming for this to stop, to let Callie go, to take him instead. The cries succeeded only in stimulating the crowd to more agitated bile and excitement.

Callie, locked in a tight grip, stood small and helpless between Maya and Laggan, this epic mountain of a woman. The hate rippled off her like heat rays in the height of summer and she glared through rage filled eyes. Her fury distracted her from all other senses, fear or rationality.

It was Ben who spoke. 'What are you going to do with her?'

'She cannot tell the truth in words; therefore we will reveal her truth through actions. Perhaps pain and hate will reveal themselves to be the focus, the only truly honest certainty. We must have our Covenant now, a binding promise of security for our people.'

'Actions, what actions? What does she have to do?' Ben gripped the sides of the cage as if willing them to absorb him and let him through.

'Fight. She must stand and fight. You were brought to make peace but have refused, putting our existence in jeopardy. Now, she needs to atone and earn your freedom.'

Ben felt icy fear grip his nerves and goosebumps crawl into life across his body at her words. The freezing cheer drove deep inside, and his muscles tensed even further to try to combat it. His voice was both that of youthful defiance at the pathetic-ness of is sound and that of someone becoming confident and assured enough to be teetering on the cusp of adulthood.

'How can she fight her?' he signalled uselessly at Laggan. 'She'll be killed. How is that a match? Let me. Let me do it. I'll take her place.'

Maya nodded, 'Indeed you would. A brave, valiant sacrifice. And yet I'm not so sure it would be reciprocated,' she looked pointedly at Callie who held her gaze, not reacting. 'Exactly why she was chosen instead of you.

She might yet win. Might in fact prove to have strength in character you lack.'

Ben's cries came in disgusted anger, fear had gone – replaced with loathing and abhorrence.

'You talk of fear and weakness in your people, yet you are happy to do this. Watch her tortured at the hands of this...this warrior. Clearly no match, clearly persecuting and oppressive. And you,' he spun around, a disgusted tirade at the boding pack, 'will stand and watch her ripped apart for entertainment.' Useless, exhausted his shoulders gave and he turned back, his head bobbing, shaking as adrenaline cursed through his body.

'Ben,' he heard Callie's voice ringing loud, assertive and clear through the taunting mob. 'Enough, Ben. Enough. You're wrong, so wrong. They don't want me to fight her.'

'Then wh..' the word disintegrated into the ether as she pointed.

'I'm here to fight them.'

'No! NO!' he roared, throwing his shoulder against the cage bars in desperation. Thrashing against the unyielding bars in uncontrollable fury. Maya stepped aside and the gnashing, scrabbling biters come back into view.

Maya nodded and the mountain woman moved back, casting Callie the undamaged Khalto stick.

She held it to her body, running her hands along its shaft, feeling momentarily powerful. It spun round in her grasp, a few gasping people taking a step back in the crowd and looking around, uncertain. Maya remained unflinching; her eyes rooted on the girl before her. Callie examined the scratches the stick had picked up, gouges from the water and the journey through the forest.

Maya signed to Laggan who turned, arms outstretched and took a step into the crowd. As one they immediately knew what was requested, obeyed and stepped back, sensing and fearing the space that was needed. Fear that did not detract from the clamour to see, be ringside to watch this battle. There were mumbles of irritated shuffling as they pushed and jolted elbow to elbow, shoulder to shoulder for the best viewing position.

Callie was alone in the middle of the semi-circle of bobbing, staring eyes. She could feel her heart beat pulse roughly through her neck. It occurred to her perhaps it was trying to jump and run, burst through the skin. For a sick moment she hoped the biters couldn't see it, wouldn't be attracted to it even more.

She felt ridiculous. Inadequate. Laughable. Her life launched before her eyes, flickering regrets and desires, knowing there wasn't much longer. Blurred memories of her parents, dimmed ones of Tax. Bitter sweet now, knowing he too was dead, but they would be together soon. Did she actually believe that? Right now, she convinced herself yes, she did. Would try. Ben. That was a black hole of a whirlpool – could you desire, yearn for and hate at the same time? Bree. Was their friendship all lies? So many questions – betrayal, grudging understanding. The farm. Her incessant desire for knowledge, travel, more and more, nothing ever being enough. Had that ultimately got them here? All these juggled in her mind; Callie realised this was more like slow motion than flashing seconds.

All the while her subconscious sat pinned on the biters. What was left of their instinct had sensed the change, intuition acknowledged Callie was alone. Left. Waiting. They stumbled and struggled from foot to foot, lumbering on the spot, not getting anywhere while they reached out, frustrated. The sound of Ben shouting, ramming pointlessly against the bars of the cell, wailing, did not distract them. He was forgotten. Callie's silent motionless was enticing and their enchantment.

A dull clunk indicated the first manacles were now abandoned on the ground.

The biter was on her in a hulking, hungry second. It moved with swift, twisted jerks like some kind of horrific mechanical insect with damaged limbs. There was no sense of mercy or recognition of another human – Callie was cure for the rage, a need for the bite. Unhinged it reached for her face, clawing widely with long, sharp fingernails. Callie snapped her head and shoulders back quickly, sidestepping out of reach, Khalto stick up as a barrier. A bawl came from the creature as it snarled, lips curled back and drove for Callie once more. She could smell the death, the rancid, decomposing peel of it, make out the tracks of dead veins below.

As it flew at her she stabbed, blunt and hard into its saggy stomach, knocking it back onto the dusty ground. A shocked shriek rose from its throat while it scrabbled upright and reached towards her again. The grotesque, angular movements were inhuman, the biter flailed forward limbs searching almost without restraint, intent on finding her. Jumping forward once more it was able to grab a handful of Callie's hair. She gasped loudly and whipped her head round, dropping her stick.

The movement worked and her hair was free, but not before the lost grip found her forearm. The biter snapped excitedly and pulled her towards him, Callie wrenching and hauling as she tried to release herself. Its black, dripping mouth was open, a rank tongue eagerly searching for a taste. It found her arm just above the elbow and bit down.

This time it was Callie who called out in furious agony as the skin broke and blood began to trickle down her arm in sticky red threads. She slammed her body against it, neck stretched out of the way, trying to release herself or knock it off balance but it held fast. She felt the teeth rip further, deeper and pushed her arm fast into the mouth, trying to choke it and stop the teeth finding more flesh, more of her. Shoving herself against the brute again and again, it finally relented, keeping its clasp tight but breaking its mouth away.

The greedy mouth was relished with her blood and Callie staggered instantaneously as a wave of nausea washed over her. Spiteful, harsh tasting vomit rose in her throat. She swallowed it away and shook her head, casting it off. The biter was chewing loudly. Mouth open on a piece ripped from her arm. She could see the pink torn muscle crush down between its teeth, a strip of skin teasing as it swung from the side of its mouth and continued to try to twist and turn out of the grip. Callie could not look at the wound, instead feeling the warm air begin to sting and nip. Thankful of it being a flesh would she prepared to fight again as, grinning at the taste of her, the biter tightened its grip and came again.

Keen, brutal teeth moved towards her as she took a reckless chance and fell deliberately to the ground, pulling the creature with her. The biter was on top, still holding the upper hand, but the confusion of the fall

208

gave Callie a precious moment. Kicking her legs for any kind of grip on the empty ground she kicked backwards with her heels and, finding traction, scuffled back a few precious inches. Enough to reach back and, with a lounge, grab the stick. Driving it overhead she slammed it into the shoulder of the biter, hearing bone grind on impact, the biter squawking in shock.

This gave Callie the space she needed to push forward and not quite on her knees, thrust forward again, awkwardly and with less strength. This didn't matter, it was enough to make the biter howl, scrabbling out for her as Callie got back to her feet, dust and sand sticking to the sweat on her face. Her wounded arm screamed now, dust and dirt violating the wound, the air rasping and rough rather than soothing.

From the cell Ben watched, helpless and silent now. His eyes were strong, shoulders rolled forward, as if all of him was trying to reach out to Callie – bore his own strength and abilities into her. He bounced from foot to foot, too apprehensive, too much adrenaline racing for him to stand still.

The biter came again, upright too now – racing towards her arms outstretched and gnawing, its mouth a gaping sore of hate and death, greyed eyes circled with wrecked, despised desire. The screech coming from it was pained and desperate, bursting from a void soul. Every tendon moved towards her with the goal of ripping and tearing.

Callie had one chance to strike – defence was futile. The Khalto stick raised high on her arm she waited a long, painful moment, the creature closer now, bearing down. So close its vile stench roamed inside Callie and she wondered if it would ever leave. As it forgot all injuries, all weapons and thought only of her meat she drove the stick hard, fast, her shoulders ringing in pain, into its face.

The nose exploded.

A shocked gasp ran round the crowd, replaced almost instantaneously by a piercing, animalistic squall which echoed throughout the camp. Ben exclaimed, unable to contain himself, punching the air.

The biter twisted and reeled on the ground. Flat on its back it thrusted it's hips up and down, flailing arms and legs in frustrated agony and a surging, uncontrollable frenzy. Where its nose had been was now a crushed dark space, a globulous mess of pus and ooze erupting from it.

Panting, leaning on the stick, now slippery with blood and sweat, Callie got to her feet. He wiped her face on the side of her good arm and looked. A three-inch gap was missing from her arm between the elbow and shoulder. She could see where it was starting to clot and harden, getting tight and restricted. Orange nobules of fat sat jelly-like over the deep crimson dark in the centre. Callie searched quickly for severed veins but found none. At least for this she was grateful.

She returned her attention to the biter. Callie lifted the stick high overhead, ignoring the cries from her arm.

'Do it Callie! Now!' shouted Ben and she drove the stick down once more into the biters face. It gurgled, kicked out and lay still.

There was a slow, sarcastic clap. Maya. The woman's face was unreadable, impassive. For a few long, meandering seconds there was nothing.

'Impressive child. Impressive. I can see why you made it here. No matter. This is where you will remain.' She turned and approached the two shackled biters. Reaching out she tenderly stroked the thin, lanky hair of one of them as it sniffed the air and rolled its eyes back, trying to bring her into view.

'Release them. Now we will see.'

The two men holding the surviving biters moved quickly, glad to be released from guarding the fetid beasts. As they arranged keys to unlock and set them on Callie a shout rose, clear and fresh.

Ben

'Wait! No! Wait! I'll tell you. I'll tell you everything!'

The hint of a smile twitched in the left corner of Maya's mouth. Her hand rose, the men stopped, retracted the keys irritated.

'I thought you would.'

CHAPTER TWENTY-TWO

Maya smiled a calculated, unreadable smile as the canvas curtain that stood as a doorway pulled back and she entered with Ben. 'Thank you, Laggan. That will be all.'

The woman named Laggan looked doubtful, concerned, 'Are you sure? I don't know if I should leave you here alone with him,' she said, staring at Ben full of angry disgust.

'Do you doubt my judgment?' There was the slightest hint of bitter suggestion in Maya's tone.

'No, Maya, of course not, it's just...' She was cut off as Maya raised her index finger to her lips and shook her head.

'We will be fine, won't we Ben?' More a statement than an answer Ben did not respond, standing, cuffed before her. 'And besides, you will be right outside, will you not?'

'Of course. As you like,' Laggan gave Ben a lingering sneer before exiting.

'Please, sit.' Maya gestured to the array of large, thick, mounded cushions layered on the ground like ridiculous, giant toadstools.

Ben was short, blunt, taking great care not to get sucked in to relaxed hospitality. 'I'll stand.'

The lines running from the either side of Maya's nose, down towards her mouth, twitched slightly, the only sign she was irritated at his words and actions. She grabbed either side of her long, draped robe and wrapped the sides across her, holding them to her body as she sat down, leaning back, relaxed as she sank slightly on a grand, thick, maroon cushion almost the size of a mattress. Clearly making a nonchalant show of her comfort she laid her gown out before her, smoothing the long, trailing edges against the cushion, running her hands across the warm, soft material, very slightly worn in places but still dense and indulgent. Carelessly she ran her hand across an edge, finding a silver tassel, pleated and knotted at the bottom, tassels hanging from it like slivers of icicles. She played with it in her palm, enjoying the glossy, silken material soft between her fingers and tickling her hand.

Ben stood, aware of the extended silence and her deliberate ignoring. He too could be obvious; with an exaggerated sigh he dropped opposite her, sinking immediately into a deep, forest shaded pillow fashioned in waving lines of greens and fawns.

'I'm sitting, happy now?' he asked.

'Much more amenable. More agreeable. Much more friendly.' The last word was tinted again, a warning or a threat, Ben wasn't sure. He had the information but knew Maya held all the power. And Callie.

Straightening up, aware of the comfort his joints and muscles could easy fall into, he leaned forward.

'Where is she?'

'Safe.'

'I didn't ask how she was, I asked where she was.'

'Clearly. Although I find it strange. If I was in your position, I would much rather be interested in how my dear, damaged friend was, rather than simply *where*.'

'You know exactly what I meant,' Ben said, 'Why don't we just cut the shit and the small talk.'

Maya tapped her teeth with the nail of her index finger,

'As you like. Callie,' she purred the word slowly, relishing the effect it had on Ben. He could not hide the flush that sprung on his neck or the gaze that crossed his eyes, 'is safe. Her wounds are being treated, there will be no permanent damage other than a scar. Sadly, unavoidable. She is a formidable fighter. You should be proud to have her affection. Grateful even.'

'I don't believe you,' his voice was cool.

'Of course you don't. I wouldn't expect anything else. But you will have to. And should you want a reunion, want to make sure she gets all the help she needs and deserves; you and I are going to have to trust each other.' With a start Maya sprung up and gestured for Ben to stand. As he did, she reached out for his hands, nodding to ease his reluctance. 'Please. Trust. You would be more comfortable with your hands free would you not?'

Hesitantly he nodded, surely if this was a trap, he would be better off with free hands. Maya took a key from her pocket, and, with a tiny click, he was free. She secured the key back deep within her pocket and casually flung the cuffs on cushions next to her before reclining again. Ben rubbed his wrists, noticing the damp, reddened ridges caused by the tightness of the cuffs. He flexed his fingers and clenched his palms into fists a few times before sitting again.

'What have you done with her? Is she ok? You going to tell me now?'

'As I've said, she is safe, rested with our medical team. I can assure you she is in good hands and will make a full recovery.'

'You have a medical area?' Ben did not try to hide the surprise.

'Why of course, we are not savages you know. How would you expect us to survive without medical support?'

'Stolen from us, from farms and greenhouses and the compounds and the cities I suppose.' Ben's contempt and disgust was clear.

'My boy, you have so much to learn. Re-learn. You know nothing of what was stolen from us, the losses we have suffered and sacrifices we have made. Continue to make.'

'Like what?' he sneered.

Maya pursed her lips to hush him and flapped the question away like an irritating midge,

'That is not for now.' Cocking her head to one side she considered and continued, 'Later, perhaps. Now, you and I have business to discuss. Would you like a drink?'

From behind a cushion, she took an elaborate bottle, shaped like a giant teardrop. Carved with sharp angles when the light hit a spectrum of colours bounced off, illuminating the light, creamy liquid inside. Maya poured a glass and offered it to Ben. He refused. Drinking deeply from it herself she sat back, luxuriously,

'Now, where to begin? I'm curious, after you two found yourselves unfortunate enough to be captured in Salthea, what did they offer you in return for your release?'

213

'We weren't…They…How did you…' he stopped short. All too late. If there had been a way back, there was none now.

'Now, now Ben, you offered me the truth. Promised it. Until now I only have the bare bones passed on so inarticulately by Ankor and Fly. What they offer us here is far removed from logic or cogency. I would rather not return there again.' Her eyes flashed their warning flames. 'Now, please, continue. Start at the beginning if it helps your memory.' Maya sat back further, gazing him on.

He began to explain it all. Bree. The kiss. The information, half information really, Callie had heard. What they had pieced together and tried to do. How he was ashamed he hadn't tried to stop her from pushing further, could have tried harder. Their separation after they arrived in Salthea. Grey Suit's interrogation. Takot.

Here she stopped him.

'You were questioned by Takot?' Ben nodded. 'The head of the Security Defence?'

'Yes.'

'You're sure it was him?'

'Positive, why?'

'How did you know?'

'Pictures, articles, school. It was him, ok? Definitely. Unequivocally.'

'Interesting,' Maya said, more to herself than to Ben, 'please, continue.'

'Questioned. Basically tortured.' The words brought the memory back: Ben hurt from the thought, could feel his breath quicken and his body tighten. 'Hung from a window out of the building. Denigrated.'

'You poor soul. Takot,' she sounded disgusted at the name, 'treating loyal workers like that. Horrific.' Maya's voice was soft, it seemed hurt by the knowledge.

Ben snorted, 'No better or worse than you have. At least they didn't set biters on us.'

Her words were slow, each exaggerated slightly, 'No, they just left you to them.' Taking another sip from her glass she nodded for Ben to continue.

'Callie and I fought each other. Trained. They wanted to see our Khalto, see if we matched – my science and her tracking. They needed to find out if her tracking skills were as good as they thought.'

'And were they?'

Despite himself, the pride was clear. 'Better. She's the best tracker I've ever known. No-one at Thorrach comes close.'

Maya adjusted her position, leaning forward and resting her chin on her upturned hands, elbows on knees. She looked deeply at Ben,

'And is that why you love her?' she teased.

He was taken aback, his head physically snatching back as if punched.

'W…w…what?'

'Is that why you love her, because she is such a good tracker?'

'No, it's, it's,' regaining his composure he continued, 'That's none of your fucking business.'

'Dear boy,' she breathed, reclining back on her cushion once more, 'don't forget why you are here. What I require. I will decide what is my business. Or not. Now I will ask again, is that why you love her?'

His voice was small, embarrassed, answering with his face down towards the floor. 'No.'

'No?'

'No, it's not.'

Maya continued to tease, bending down towards the ground to catch Ben's eye and force his head up.

'First love. It feels like the sun's rays on your face. A hunger that nothing is good enough to satiate. An urge that could pull organs from your body. Pain that stabs and strikes deep within your soul. I remember. So, tell me, why do you love her?'

Ben shook his head, 'I don't know.'

Maya's instructions were simple. The consequences clear. 'Try.'

Ben looked at her then, his face cloudy with hate and humiliation but yielding with adoration. A flush rose on his neck, like a petal uncurling, as he spoke.

'I love her because of what she is. Intelligent. Brave. Passionate. Real. Because of her tenacity and power and self-belief. Because even when she could have dumped me, ran, left all of this to someone else, she didn't.'

'And yet there is a darkness between you.'

He shook his head, 'I don't know what you're talking about.'

'Ben, Ben. You should know me better by now. I have read her. And I can read you. There is a darkness. Tell me why.' She cocked her head to one side and raised her glass two handed to her lips, her eyes dancing eagerly.

'There is nothing. I could tell you something, but I'd have to make it up.'

'OK,' Maya nodded. She put the glass down and stretched out, yawning and twisting her neck from side to side. Standing she moved silently towards a cupboard, once more all swishes and folds and swirls of colours merging together. Turning to face Ben he saw a small circular object in one hand, a knife in the other. Maya stood, throwing the purple plum up and down, casually in the air. Finally, she caught it swiftly in her hand.

Cutting into it and licking the oozing sweet juice from her palm before it could drip, she asked, 'Would you like a piece?'

Ben shook his head, lying.

She cut deeper into the fruit, breaking it in half and discarding the stone. She continued with her show, quartering a piece, the orange flesh bursting open enticingly. Maya returned to her seat opposite Ben and again offered him a quarter. He shook his head, looking away so he was not tempted. Maya swallowed the fruit down in a few simple bites then used the very edges of her sleeve to dab the corners of her mouth.

'Shame, you would have enjoyed that. Fruit. *Real* fruit. No matter.' Slumping to the floor, Maya sat on her knees in front of Ben and turned his head, holding it in her hand so he stared deep into her eyes.

'Now, I thought we were building trust, getting somewhere.' She licked her lips, tasting the last of the plum juice as it dried in, then smiled and ran her tongue slowly across her teeth. For a horrible second Ben thought she was going to kiss him. Then he saw the sharp, slightly serrated edge of the knife, felt it press against his right cheekbone.

'I really did. I thought you and I were becoming friends. But still, you don't trust me. Don't tell me the truth.' Maya tutted, 'I am very disappointed in you.' She turned the edge of the knife slightly into Ben's skin, enough to hurt but not enough to draw blood, holding his face tighter now as he began to pull back and twist. 'It would be such a travesty if you had to lose an eye. Over one meagre, easy-peasy question.' When she spoke her voice became sarcastic, sing song, as if teasing a baby child.

'Please,' he whispered as the knife flashed closer and dug deeper.

'Yes?' she purred.

'Please. Don't.'

'Don't you understand? My hands are tied. What would they think of me if I didn't find what we need?' Maya nodded towards the door. 'They would kill you. They might believe I am weak and think they could find another leader. Battle with each other. End our civilisation, a civilisation that has stood all this time. I have no say. You see, you have all the power, Ben. You can stop this right now with peace. Just with your words.'

He nodded.

'Yes?'

'Yes, yes, please,' he said, frustrated, scared tears threatening to erupt. Removing the knife, Maya held his face, twisting his chin in her hand, a white pressure mark where she held fast.

'What is the darkness between you?'

The words were mumbled, ashamed, forced through his mouth for the second time, 'I killed him.'

'Who?'

With a wretch Ben pulled back, catching Maya unaware. As he lurched back and grabbed his chin she reached for her knife, but he had no fight, just hate and despair in his eyes,

'I killed her brother. Callie hates me because I killed her brother'.

Maya raised herself up and sat back with a flourish. She seemed to be almost glistening, radiating wickedly at Ben's words.

'Her brother?' she was breathless, truly clearly taken aback. 'At Thorrach?' Ben shook his head. He was drained, felt debilitated.

'In the greenhouses.' The ghost of his voice seemed to come from somewhere else. It rang loud, echoing in his head.

Maya was alight, curiosity surging and pressing,

'How? Why?'

Ben looked up, eyes red and useless, life drained out. She knew she had won; he had finally relented and would spill his secrets.

'Does it really matter?' He was cold, spat out the words but with no real life, just acceptance he would have to stand here and explain. His body began to crumble, sway. Swallowing hard he rooted to the floor. When Maya didn't answer, instead stabbing him with her fixed gaze, he continued. 'I killed him in the greenhouses. In a fight. He caught me stealing fruit. It was one punch,' Ben opened and closed his fist, willing the past out of it, seeing the force, the accident pass over his palm. 'One stupid punch. He fell. There was nothing I could do.'

Maya reached out, took his hands. Ben was too weak to resist. She had stripped him of everything; for the second time his worst had been thrown forth, his shame announced for everyone to see. He had no idea if she had a modicum of compassion or was compelling him to continue with the painful, beautiful graphic details. No matter.

'There's nothing you can say', Ben said to her. 'You've ripped me open. That's all, I swear that's all.'

'And there we have it. Perhaps the greatest mystery. Now, what did they leave you together for? What did they need from you?'

'That's why they left us together. They knew she would never leave with me, never help me unless she had to. Why would she? How could she? Unless it was all at risk. Everything we know and everyone. They knew we wouldn't escape. Half the time she can barely look at me. Every day I have to see the disgust in her face, see him over and over. Relentless guilt.'

Maya nodded, her persistence listening, rapt.

'Then they sent us to get the cure. Saw the strength Callie has, the urge, compassion. How could she say no and let people die? She had to try, was born to. They knew I loved her, would follow, watch over her, try to atone for what I did.' He gave a sick, empty laugh. 'How the hell did I think I could do that?'

She stood before him now, glancing up and down at his face, still ashamed and turned to the floor. She brushed her palm gently across his cheek. Ben pulled away.

'Larejax?' Ben stared through glistening eyes at her awareness of the word, then nodded. His whole neck and shoulders bobbing, lurching in exhaustion and relief. 'They wanted you to find a cure for what you call Larejax. For what turns us into those lost beings? Oh, you poor, poor boy.' Maya swept his cheek again; this time Ben did not withdraw. 'And what did they tell you was the cure? What have they sent you for, risked your lives for?'

'Dealga'.

At the sound of the word Maya's eyes flashed with familiarity and heightened interest.

Ben burst to his feet as Callie entered. He encircled her in a deep hug, only pulling back, apologetic, when she winced under his touch. His eyes darted all over, taking her in and taking in the injuries.

'What happened?'

'It's fine, I'm ok. What did you tell them?' Callie was acutely aware of Maya watching them from her seat.

'It doesn't matter right now, what happened? What did they do to you?' Ben held her back gently, clasping her elbows so it was possible to take in every inch. 'How's your arm?' He touched the bandage suspiciously, turning her arm slightly back and forth.

'Least they're more even,' Callie joked. 'It's fine. They took me to a centre: Ben they've basically created a hospital, you should see what they've got in there. What they've made and stolen. What they've fashioned out of waste and junk and just, just nothing! Equipment, cabinets of medicines, supports for rehabilitation. Shelves of medical journals from times ago.'

'I don't care,' his voice was monotone. 'Did they give you anything?'

'Poison me you mean? No, I'm fine. They stopped the bleeding, patched it up really good. It'll scar, maybe some nerve damage. And the muscle will never be as big, but at least I won't lose my arm.'

'You're sure they didn't give you anything?'

Callie moved her arms and took his hands.

'Yes, I'm sure. They took me to the medical centre, dealt with this and patched up my scratches and stings. I slept a bit. They brought me here. I wish you could see this,' Callie lifted her newly dressed arm towards Ben. 'It's fixed better than anything back home. Even this one got checked over,' she added, indicating the wound inflicted back in the river.

'Cal, you don't trust them, do you? Remember what they did, how you ended up there in the first place.' She was shaking her head as Maya interjected.

'I'm glad you appreciated our hospitality and treatment.' Maya's voice made Callie jump. 'What a lovely reunion. It's so sad to break it up but I think we have important business to discuss, don't you?'

'I'm not telling you anything after what you did to me,' Callie bounded forward, Ben grabbing her round the waist.

'It's too late Cal.'

'What are you talking about?'

'Larejax. Dealga.' Maya's voice was firm. 'That's what he's talking about.'

Callie glared at him, 'What did you do?'

'What I had to, to make sure you were safe. To make sure they didn't hurt you even more. I had to Callie, it's over.'

'Oh no, no, no!' Maya was exuberant. 'It is very, very far from over.'

Callie stood; arms folded. 'It sounds like you've got what you wanted. What you going to do with us now?'

Maya's reply was shocking, Callie and Ben looked at each other dumfounded.

'You are free to go?'

'What?' Callie could not hide the incredulity from her voice.

'Free. You can leave as you wish.' Raising her voice lightly she called, 'Laggan.' The woman filled the door instantly.

'Yes Maya.'

'Our guests would like to leave.'

Laggan looked bemused, disheartened. The woman clearly enjoyed throwing her weight around, intimidating and threatening. Callie and Ben stood stock still, unsure what was happening, acutely aware this could be another snare.

'We can leave?' Callie asked, clear disbelief and misgiving in her voice.

'If that is what you wish. Laggan, please have their possessions brought to me.' The woman paused too long, and Maya's voice was both commanding and aggravated, 'Now!' Laggan nodded quickly and left.

'So what?' Ben returned to Maya. 'We can just walk out of here now. No tricks. No-one following us, nobody guarding over the Dealga, no tracking bloody monkeys, waiting to slaughter us in the middle of the night?'

Maya nodded. 'You gave me what I wanted. The truth. Here we pay our debts, live by honest rules of society. You are free to go.'

Callie could sense her breath quickening as liberty, anticipation and uncertain nerves began to course through her. Still neither she nor Ben were willing to make another move. Her skin pricked as Laggan re-entered carrying both their packs and Khalto sticks. Clearly still baffled herself she reluctantly placed them beside Maya then stood to attention at her side.

'Thank you, Laggan. That will be all.' With a worried look towards the packs she slowly left, her eyes casting a chilled, warning look to Callie and Ben as she left.

Maya kept the staff at her side but held the packs out to Callie and Ben. 'Please, check them to make sure your things are intact'. Ben grabbed and unfasted his quickly, dropping to a squat back on his knees as he scrabbled through, greedily. 'Please,' Maya offered the bag to Callie again.

'Callie, come on. Take it!' Ben pressed. Her lips tight together, eyes gripping her temples in doubt, Callie took it. She unzipped it, looking quickly from the bag back to Maya as she took inventory of her things.

'They are all there?' Ben asked. She nodded slowly.

'Belt, medicine, shelter...'

She cut him off, monosyllabic, 'It's all there.' As Ben hurriedly zipped up his pack, Callie asked, 'Why are you doing this?'

'For liberty. Freedom. Your choices are yours.'

Ben was breathless now, anxious to leave before Maya changed her mind.

'C'mon, Cal. Let's get out of here.'

Again, she didn't move, staring at Maya as if caught in a spell. Ben stood in front of her and put his hands on her shoulders. 'Callie, come on. Let's go!'

Blinking, shaking her head slightly as if wakening, she nodded and shrugged her bag over her shoulders.

'Stick, please,' Ben put his hand out for the Khalto staff. Maya handed it to him, still drawing Callie with her eyes.

'Of course. Here. I wish you well. In another time, in different circumstances,' she shrugged, 'who knows.' Pressing her palms together as if in prayer she tapped her front teeth against them.

Ben turned to leave, Callie following, half turned, half expecting the trick to be revealed and attack to unfold.

'Yes. It is unfortunate you feel the desire to leave.' Ben flung back the curtain and a beam of sunlight exploded into the room. Maya became engulfed in its flame, almost fully a silhouette.

'You could have stayed. Learned the truth. Left with true knowledge. Power.'

'Wait!' Callie called, towards Ben, yearning.

CHAPTER TWENTY-THREE

'This is bullshit,' we need to leave Callie'. The concern, spite and urgency in Ben's voice was clear, he was in no mood to spend a second longer than needed here. 'We're running out of time.'

Maya pressured. 'The question isn't whether you can afford to give up the time, Ben, but whether you can afford not to listen.'

'I think we've afforded quite enough from you,' Ben retorted sarcastically, putting a guiding palm on Callie's back. 'Let's go.'

'Callie?' Maya spoke directly, her voice a waterfall rushing through Callie's senses, insistent and entrancing. Maya's head tilted down and she smiled, part motherly, part wise woman. A sorceress spinning her spell once more.

'I want to hear her,' Callie spoke faintly, ashamed of her admittance after everything that had been forced on them.

'You can't be serious?' Ben, on the other hand, did not care who heard. 'We can go. We have to go. You can't actually want to hear anymore crap from these people, do you?'

'I don't know,' she mumbled softly.

'What?' This wasn't even a question, the word tinged with disgust.

'I said I don't know.'

'I heard what you said, I just can't believe I did. Look at you. Look at what they did to you. How can you forget all that, expect her,' he sneered on the word, 'to tell you some truth. Fill your head with fantastic nonsense.'

'Please do not harass my guest,' Maya's tone was icy.

'You can't be serious?'

'You are free to leave. You are both free to leave. And to make up your minds which you prefer. Callie can choose for herself.'

'We go together.'

'Then stay together.'

'Unlikely,' Ben threw her the glimpse of a sulky smile.

'Ben, please,' Callie hissed. 'I need to do this.'

'Let me speak, allow her to listen and I promise you I will have people take you to the Dealga much quicker than you could on foot'.

Callie turned, her eyes burning deep into his soul, pressurising him to concede.

'Please. I have to stay. You go if you need to, I won't stop you. I'll find you.'

'No way.' His words were definite. Final. 'I won't leave you here alone.'

'Overnight. Just give me till the morning.' Callie looked to Maya, for reassurance. The woman nodded.

Ben's eyes burned and his voice was clear. 'The morning, First thing. Not a second more. Or I'll carry you out of here myself.'

'Agreed,' Callie said.

The room was hot, not unbearably so but the heat hung in the walls, lounged on the cushions and embraced the thick curtains. A soft breeze wafted them lazily from time to time when it snuck into Maya's space as it waved through the camp. Callie was grateful for it cooling her skin. She compared the trapped atmosphere to that of the field and decided she was grateful to be out of the heat, like the breeze, needed to fly outside, be beyond the confines of walls, however thin.

Maya's words flowed like a stream after a storm; rushing powerfully over rocks, swirling and discarding debris as it passed, curling and spiralling close to the edges. Callie had barely spoken, listening intently for hours except to ask for Maya to repeat something or with a question. Ben saw in her face the same desire and awe he had seen when they had first met Maya and it scared him. How could they trust her? How could her words be true? Was so much about their way of life, education, hell their human history just a lie? What bewildered him equally was how Callie with all her sense of independence, lust for facts and adventure seemed to be taking this all in without doubt.

Maya had exploded their truth shattered it into shards of glass which now bound together in a semi-conscious reality cracked in a misshapen, piercing bond of truth and lies.

'Larejax is devastating for humanity, which is true enough,' she had confirmed. 'It could be the vicious, violent end for many, many people, perhaps even most of those left on Earth. Centuries of poly-food, poly-liquids have brought us here. Nature is not dead. Nature was brought to near extinction by mankind. Yet in her strength, beauty and spirit she has found a way to fight back. This was all only a matter of time.'

'But the capsules keep us alive. Kept us alive,' Ben said.

Maya agreed, 'Indeed, they did. Decades of necessary science, defeats, deaths. Of children, families, brilliant minds.' Callie's mind envisioned her own parents, finally taken by sickness when the last drugs failed, and she felt a stabbing in her heart. 'Some worked for years as the science improved. This time,' Maya held out a capsule in her hand, spun it in front of her eyes delicately, 'they thought they had a final cure. Solved the biology. Found a way to save mankind.' With more gravitas she added, 'And control'.

'And how are you so sure?' Ben didn't try to keep the doubt or sarcasm from his voice, his face still tense and clouded. Callie glanced at him, annoyed and warning. She needed to hear this out.

'What changed?' Callie asked.

'I am no scientist. We have no real labs here, little scientific equipment past what we need for medical treatment. But the body, the persevering, self-assured human body is still rejecting the plastics. Nature is too strong. And she will prevail. She may stay quiet, dormant even for a while. But her beautiful brutality rises again. We continue to disrespect, to see ourselves as better, more intelligent. More advanced. Perhaps finally we need to stop, accept and change.'

'Or we will all die,' Callie spoke out loud but to herself.

Maya nodded, but with grief in place of hate, sadness in place of triumph. 'Yes, many, many will die. A herd might be immune. Lucky, or not, depending on your thought process. But yes, it appears our fragile humanity will be ripped apart as easily as petals torn off a flower in the wind.'

'Unless we find Dealga.'

'What did they tell you about the Dealga?' Maya asked.

It was Ben who spoke. Ben who wanted control over this moment. After all, he thought, it was he who had been sent as the scientist.

'We know it is likely to be the cure. The complicated biology of the plant means it cannot grow abundantly in the fields or the greenhouses.'

'True,' Maya interjected.

'We know it is ancient, from the time before. It survived. It cannot be modified or altered. Somehow it has the make-up to reject all enhancements.'

'Impressive,' Maya nodded, once again tapping her pressed palms against her teeth. 'Perhaps I have underestimated the intelligence and study of the Salthea labs. For once. So, tell me, why do they not order mass poly-production?'

Ben clearly understood Maya knew more than he had anticipated, seemed to be toying with him, questioning to find out what they knew, rather than divulging further. His mistrust had not diminished and was now coupled with a hostility and twitchiness he was being toyed with.

'Something tells me you already know.'

'Who knows, humour me. Please.'

'Ben, go on,' Callie urged. 'Unless you want me to do it?'

He shook his head and continued, quicker now and with less faked gravitas.

'They can't manufacture Dealga. Its genetics are too complicated. They need real plants to study and use and extract from.'

'They sent you to harvest?'

Callie and Ben nodded.

'And what happens after that?'

They looked at each other, then at Maya, silent and confused.

'What do you mean?' Ben asked.

Maya paced, the edges of her tunic billowing slightly in the strengthening breeze towards the entrance. She clasped her hand together and stretched her arms up above her head, a shoulder cracking slightly in the welcome effort.

'You collect Dealga. Take it back to them. Then what?'

'Then they extract the essence or the protein or some bloody thing, make the cure.'

'Yes. Yes, they do,' Maya agreed. 'Then what?'

Nothing?

She stood, firmer, 'Then what?'

'Then they come,' Callie jolted.

'Then they come,' Maya agreed. 'Trample. Build. Pollute. Destroy. Eke out every drop of the world that they can. And then it goes on. Dealga will cure for now, that is certain. But what next?'

'How do you know? And why should we care?' Ben folded his arms defensively. 'We can only do what we've been asked. Do our bit for now. We're just two kids among the world.'

Maya seemed incredulous at his words. 'Kids? You are not just anything. You have the future. You are the future. You have the power to learn, lead, shape what is coming.'

'And what is that?' Callie spoke with fervour, intent once more on soaking up available knowledge, desiring to draw herself closer to the truths.

The word came like a sudden, distant clap of thunder on a cloudless day – ominous and hanging in the air.

'Rebellion.'

Callie felt a course of adrenaline move through her body, the hair at her nape prickle. Her ears flooded and rushed and for a moment it was as if she could only hear a dull echo. Ben too was hit with a power and clinging dread at the intensity and meaning the word held.

Breathless, she repeated the word, turning Maya's statement back at her into a question.

'Rebellion? What do you mean rebellion?' Her urge for an answer hung in the air, crackling silently.

Maya smiled, tilted her head back and breathed deeply. She rolled her shoulders as if they were stiff and sore, taking her time with each second she used.

'What do they teach you about us in school? Warn you of?'

Callie looked embarrassed, remembering the lessons involving the Wilds. The late-night chats amongst the children, telling horror stories of people being captured or wandering so far or disappearing forever into the distance. Tales designed to set you racing under the covers, shrieking and laughing at once. She thought of how the Wilds had been built up as tribal and primitive, almost de-evolving in their squalor and animalistic ways. She wanted to keep this conversation amiable, more than anything to find out about the rebellion. Callie could not explain these lessons or warnings to Maya.

It was Ben who spoke.

'What do you expect them to tell us? The Wilds are beautiful; you don't need to work or go to school or eat rations; you can steal the medicines you need; live lazy; no laws or rules. And by the way don't worry if you decide to kidnap and half torture people that turn up nearby. Oh, and there are huge, ghastly monsters that will most likely catch you and eat you'.

Callie, her eyes piercing him with their heat, cheeks flushed, hissed.

'Ben, stop it. Shut up!'

'Well, am I right or am I right, Callie?' he muttered angrily, exhaling deeply and loudly.

Maya had folded her arms across her body, listening but more amused than shocked or angry.

'And here was me thinking you wouldn't have listened in History lessons, Ben,' she smirked.

'Sorry. We…they…' Callie stammered, trying to find the words but knowing Ben was more than partly right. Maya shushed her to quiet.

'I know what they teach you. I went to school back there. Back then.' Callie and Ben exchanged a shocked look, Maya continuing before they could ask her anything further. 'Yes, like you I was born in the farms. Many of us were. Children are born here now, but many, many of us came from farms, labs, greenhouses. Salthea. I sat the same lessons, heard the same things. The Wilds and their people are savages. Crazed. Full of hate, not only for Salthea but for everyone working on Earth. We want people to run, flee and be ripped apart when we find them. We sneak into greenhouses, medical centres pillage and loot, ruin crops and destroy civilised lands.'

'But why? Why tell us this?' Callie asked.

'Because it's not all lies,' Ben mumbled, Callie casting him a hateful look again.

'Fear. Fear breeds fear, creates legends, myths. Once established who can tell whether they are true or not? Who can even remember?'

'To keep us working,' Callie nodded, a bitter edge to her voice. 'To keep us working and to keep us there. Under control.'

'Or to keep us safe? Don't forget what they did to us, Cal. What she sanctioned,' Ben spoke strong this time, the silence leaving his voice.

Maya's voice was serious, there was no apology or explanation, merely statement. 'I did what was right for my people, my community. Ben, open your eyes. You are letting you prejudice, distrust and hate of me cloud your judgement. You need to open yourself to see, to hear. Then you will believe.'

Callie turned to face him, took his hands and gazed up into his eyes. He could see the craving and need in them and their fragility. They looked at him helpless, she needed him to help her hear.

'Ok,' he said softly. 'I'll listen, but only for you.' Looking sideways at Maya he went on, 'I'll consider everything she says. Then judge. But only for you, Callie.'

When she replied he could see something else in her eyes, something alive and tender and sweet. 'Thank you,' she said, smiling a deep, real smile.

Callie was sniffing quietly, trying to hold back the signs of tears and fear, the frustration that Maya didn't dispute the unconceivable ferocity and filthy destructive power of Larejax. Her mind and body were crying for sleep and acutely awake at the same time, almost consumed by knowledge. She picked at a thread in the side of a cushion, again finding some kind of childlike comfort and distraction in rolling, tightening and relaxing the soft threads, then releasing and doing it again.

The two biters dragged to torment Callie had, it was now confirmed, been carriers, riddled with the pollutants. Their stinking, pus filled bodies were contaminated, their brains transformed, little better than the mushy centre of soft fruit. But with a clawing fever to scrape and scratch skin and flesh from their own selves. And the hunger.

Maya had expected pillaging of Dealga; she told Ben and Callie they had long been assessing and researching its healing properties. Callie's thoughts drifted, Ben more alert, as Maya spoke of the resilience and success of the plant. It grew impressively, prolifically in the wild, solid and tough. Her people had also tried to farm and control the plant, with varying degrees of success. It did seem at least to grow on their farms: whether that was related to the proximity to its natural habitat they did not know. But the plants were weaker, even in appearance. Too much support, too much interference however and it stubbornly shrivelled and died, its secrets releasing back into the soil. Although slightly mundane and boring to Callie, she was amused by the intensity and interest in Ben's eyes, how he nodded silently, no stubborn, rude questions or comments.

They had deliberately been taken by Ankor and Fly as suspected spies. The two had been shocked and confused by their youth but had followed orders to the letter in taking them to Maya. Callie considered this to be recognition of the authority and gravitas of the woman.

Finally, she asked a question of Callie and Ben again.

'Your capsules. They are included in your daily rations.'

They nodded.

'Once a day,' Callie spoke.

'Every day?'

'Of course, every day. The pills keep us alive, quash our natural reactions to the polys. Or at least they did until now. But even now I'd rather take them and hold off the turning.' Callie felt slightly as if she was talking to a small child, rote learning or reassuring a lesson.

Ben's brow was furrowed lightly, two lines creasing between his eyes.

'Why are you asking that? The Wilds attack and ruin medical resources searching for valuables such as the pills.'

Maya admired a pattern on her tunic, flashing and unflashing the gold thread in the light. She spoke nonchalant, offhand, without looking at Ben.

'You've seen this?'

'Well, no, but…'

'You?' interrupting and pausing with the material in her hand, this time looking up at Callie. She too shook her head.

'Then how do you know?'

'Well, from books,' Ben felt he was floundering, 'from school, the Superintendents.' As the words left his mouth, he felt they sounded immature, weak.

Maya exhaled, nodding almost sadly, sympathetically. 'Stories. All stories.'

'But they show us pictures, footage.' Callie felt she needed to support Ben.

'Oh, I have no doubt, I'm sure they do.'

'You're telling us they're fake?' Ben folded his arms across his body, a sign he was shutting down, unwilling again.

'Fabricated. All of them. Well, perhaps not all but anything we take we take peacefully. The rebellion means we have less use for raids now, we can gather anything necessary from supply chains within.'

'Prove it.'

Maya's mouth rose at one side in a wry smile, her eyes flashing irritated for a split second.

'Ben. Ben. Still so suspicious, distrusting. It must be exhausting.'

There was more than a hint of exasperation in his voice. 'Not as exhausting as listening to nonsense. Prove it.'

Maya almost purred, 'I think we know I can't do that. You will have to trust me a little longer.' Ben and Maya kept each other's gaze. Anxious to continue, keep the generally amiable mood, Callie jumped in.

'Look, we all know how vital the capsules are. Stolen, rationed, this is all a little futile right now. We all take them, need them. Maybe that's one thing, the only thing we have in common.'

'That's just it, dear child, we don't.' Maya's peaceful, enchanting tone had returned, laden with mystery and knowledge.

'We don't what?'

'We don't take them. We don't need them. None of us do.'

CHAPTER TWENTY-FOUR

A thick, lumbering silence hung almost visible in the air. Callie could feel it compress around her, pushing down on her head as if it was caught in a clamp. She felt her throat restrict against the pressure, tasted the metalness of it on her tongue. It stole the words from her mouth, the flying, rambling thoughts now sparking and burning in her head suffocating, drowning in incoherence. The silence bore down, shallow breathing the only sound filling the void for endless seconds.

Maya's words still echoed in the room, repeating and teasing over and over, waving in and out in a torturous, relentless mocking.

'We don't need them. None of us do.'

Eight short, simple syllables that had just crumbled the very world Ben and Callie knew. The world they both hated but understood. Belonged to. What was a reply? What could they say? What should they say? For the first time she was willing to admit in her life, Callie felt like an innocent child. Felt naked standing before a divine authority. Helpless and meek. The questions, the thirst to know and understand had been sucked out of her like the air in the room. She now feared the answers, didn't know if she wanted the reality.

It was Ben who spoke. His voice too was that of a chided child, scared, uncertain and repentant. His words were more of a quiet, reluctant, useless question than assertive surety.

'Horseshit.'

Maya shook her head slowly, in sympathy and understanding rather than anger.

'I know it is too much. But look deep within yourself. You know it must be true. You've seen it here. My words are real. It is true.'

'But how…?' He did not know how to finish the sentence, didn't know what he wanted to know. If this was true their world, the world of generations before them was a terrible, beautiful dishonesty. If Maya was lying, they were being trapped and played with again. The bubbling in his mind couldn't decide which it would prefer.

Maya was patient, allowing the comprehension and magnitude cling to each breath, long and slow. Callie sliced through it, jumping to her feet.

'I need some air, I have to get out of here,' she spluttered, wringing her hands and shaking her head. 'I can't, I just can't.' She strode towards the door, desperate.

Ben started up, 'Wait, I'll come with you.'

'Let her be,' Maya spoke silkily, motherly. 'Let her be.'

He sighed and nodded; this time frantic eyes appealed to Maya for help. She reached forward and took his hands in hers. Ben winced and tried to recoil. Maya held fast, only for a moment till he relaxed, and ran her thumbs over the back of his hands. She nodded, encouragingly. 'It's ok. I promise. I will show you both the truth. Let you see.'

Callie had burst through the door and started Laggan who immediately reached for her weapon and stood, ready to give chase or fight. Callie barely noticed, bent double, hands on low thighs and breathed deeply, panting in the air. She stood like that for twenty, thirty seconds before retching violently and vomiting on the ground. As she gulped down and wiped any strands from her mouth Laggan wrinkled her nose in disgust. Callie heaved emptily a couple of times before sighing and standing up. She started when she saw Laggan.

'Sorry' she mumbled, staggering slightly before walking aimlessly into the settlement. Laggan seemed uncertain whether to follow, looking to see if Maya would appear at the door. When she didn't the woman stood and, realising Callie was not posing any risk, watched her from her post.

Callie now leaned on the outside of the cage, clearly still shaken and dazed. She didn't trust herself to walk confidently, purposefully. Her whole body was somewhere else: her legs felt like weak, waving twigs, ready to bring her crashing down. Her balance was woozy and unsteady. Every instinct in her body was now redirected to supporting her mind – comprehending what Maya had told them and realigning everything she thought she knew.

Part of her wanted to run, escape from all of this into the darkness. Return empty handed and see what they did. She didn't care, lock her in a grey, dim cell away from stimulus and learning. Safe and comfortable with whatever she knew. Or punish her, make her confirm and return her to a farm. She could dutifully spend her life cropping corn, silent and meek. She thought on the alternative. Listen to Maya, see the world she knew crumble and die in the air while she spoke. Face a reality which could be even more terrifying. After everything she didn't know if she could take any more.

Feeling momentarily weak she turned and sagged, like a bag of corn, onto the ground in front of the cage. Her hand rubbed over the sharp, stubbly grass, back and forth, back and forth, a sensory need trying to detract from the spinning overload in her mind. Her breathing did calm, her mind settled and soon she shivered in the air as the adrenaline started to wear off.

She stared up at the sky. Stars flickered above her, teasing as they winked down. Mesmerising and enchanting they calmed her as she traced some of their paths, found the familiar patterns, just as she had done so many times in Thorrach. They flashed their power and influence, breaking through the darkness of the sky with ease. Callie wondered what truths they carried, what wisdom. She turned searching over her shoulders, for the moon or EarthMoon, but neither was visible from here. Only the stars. She wished she could have their effortlessness, their quietude. Callie wasn't sure she could ever have that again.

She knew she had to go back.

As she approached the door Laggan's shoulders braced but soon subsided as she could see the girl posed no threat.

'Can I see her?'

Laggan said nothing, considering for a moment, more out of control than real need. Slowly she looked Callie up and down, turned and pulled back the heavy curtain.

Callie once again took a few seconds to adjust her eyes to the light. Maya stood as she entered, rolled her sleeves and put out her hands and smiled.

'You're back,' she welcomed. 'Just in time, Ben is gathering his strength and having some refreshment.' She looked over to Ben, sat on one of the large, plush cushions. Callie's eyes followed.

'You look cosy,' Callie commented, not really knowing if she was being cheeky or jealous. Ben sat with a bowl of what appeared to be steaming vegetables in a thick stew held between his hands. There was around a third of the volume of the bowl left, so it looked like he had had his fill.

He smiled, nervously.

'What has she told you?' Callie asked.

'Not much, reiterating what she said before. She wanted to wait for you.'

'It's true.' Maya appeared at her right shoulder and handed Callie her own bowl of the stew. She could smell it, herby and earthy, the spices inviting her warmly. Reluctantly she took the bowl, trying to convince her inner voice that she would not eat it but at the same time the pangs in her suddenly awakened stomach telling her she would do just that.

'Please,' Maya gestured. Callie sat. She toyed with the spoon, running it through and looking at the shapes and colours it stirred up. The meal was certainly more flavoursome, more abundant in content than anything at the farm. The dully muddy colour hid vibrant green and cream and yellow chunks of vegetables which rose and fell as she stirred.

'It's good,' Ben whispered. 'Try it.'

Maya also spoke, encouraging her. 'You will need your strength. Eat. I give you my word you will be safe.'

It was as mouth-watering as she had smelled. The soft vegetables burst between her teeth, sweet and bitter together. The stock was littered with aromatic spices and herbs she had never tasted before. The tastebuds in her mouth were drawn to them, soft and sour and sharp. It wasn't long before she was finished. Placing the spoon carefully back in the bowl and the bowl at her feet, Callie sat straight and matched Maya's eye.

'Now tell us.'

Maya stood and lit a lamp between them. The gravity once again began to return to the air.

'Dealga is the cure, which was true. They didn't lie, not then. Now we know it is only the cure for now. Both of you, all of you, are already slowly dying. Poisoned by the polys in everything.'

'But the tablets counteract the effects. Or they did. All they need is Dealga'

Maya shook her head slowly.

'No, no they don't. The tablets keep you shackled, keep you bound to the regime, terrified of the Chancellor, Security Defence, the Regulators, even your Superintendents.'

'But years of research. My parents died…' Callie couldn't find the sentences.

'I know, I know. We have all lost people.' Maya was sympathetic. 'This was the panacea, the final freedom. Empty promises. There is no cure, there cannot be a cure while your bodies are corrupted, possessed with the polys. The polys in *everything*.'

Her emphasis on the word was obvious.

'Even the medicine' Callie whispered.

Maya smiled, a grim, knowing smile in agreement. 'In some form, even trace, yes.'

Ben spoke, his voice grave, 'And Larejax?'

'The result of rejection. The most extreme, brutal rejection yet. Virulent in its spread. I am not even sure Dealga could do much more than hold back symptoms, disguise them for a time.'

'So we are here for nothing? Here so what? So that we can return with a lie that will lead to millions dying anyway?'

'Not nothing,' Maya spoke. 'They want the Dealga. Want to both salvage something and retain commitment through terror. They cannot risk the truth. Risk freedom. The Rebellion is starting to reach ears in Salthea, in other cities. They need to fight it with allegiance and affirmation. Remind people of their power to heal and support the loyal and faithful. Dealga could provide that and buy them time.

Callie asked just as the words reached Ben's lips.

'And what is the truth?'

'Purge from the medicine. You have the power to live poly free. Start again. The process is long, excruciating, takes you to the verge of life, but after it you can be cleansed.'

'But how, where?' Callie's voice was eager.

'Here. In the Wilds.'

Callie spluttered, hearing how dazed and stupid her voice sounded,

'But why? Why let us live like this? How can we be free? Basically, everything is poly. There is hardly any real food left.'

'In the camps, the cities and the farms. But here, in the Wilds all is natural. Any polys are remnants, dregs. We have almost eradicated them all.'

It was Ben's turn to push, 'So what, they let us work for nothing, knowing we could be poly free? Natural. Fuck, if this was true, we could rebuild. Relocate. Start over.'

'Exactly. The Earth could be liberated. After the pain. But why would they want that?'

'Who?' Ben asked.

'And this is the glory of youth,' Maya's arms went out towards Callie and Ben, her voice mixed with sadness, sarcasm and hope. 'Innocence, naivety. You have yet to fully realise the depth of corruption.'

'I don't understand.'

'Of course you don't. To you it is good and evil. Fair and unfair. Right or wrong. But life is grey, contaminated. Earth Moon was created pure, a new beginning not only for the championed and the best, but for the powerful and rich. Those that could ensure their survival through wealth. Their society is not hard, not dangerous, not polluted. They are provided for. They are the elite. Finally luxuriating in what they have always wanted, their own exclusive society.

'You're telling us they lie to us to keep us here- what - slaving for them?'

Maya nodded,

'The greatest secret of all. The truth behind everything.'

Ben was agitated, he rose up, opening and closing his fists, trying to find something to say that would prove her wrong. But in his head, it all sounded pleading and pathetic.

'How can this be true? Why would Prane, Takot, all of them in Salthea stay? They wouldn't put up with this bullshit if they could be on EarthMoon.'

'They're scrabbling for scraps. Failed intellectuals, not rich enough, not enough clout. All of them missing out and left with Salthea. It beats harvesting, the greenhouses, teaching, labs. Gives them power, misguided, hopeful power. But it isn't EarthMoon. And for most it won't be. They sit, plotting, backstabbing, waiting for an opportunity to rise. You have no idea of the corruption. Do you really believe all this control, reign of terror, Security Defence, is just to ensure you remain subjugated? To fix workers to the fields and the greenhouses and the labs?

Imagine the revolt, rebellion, uprising if the truth was discovered. An uproar throughout. EarthMoon could be starved, left depleted. How could they risk these great minds, great thinkers, the richest? They would never allow it. They stay and subdue and govern with fear and force. Hoping to usurp each other, garner favour and earn their own selfish tickets out.'

'But if Earth could be renewed?' Callie's words hung in the air, bringing a chill as Maya spoke. Her tone, given the immensity of the news, still gentle and supportive was turning cold and grave.

'Why would they want to renew?' she answered with a question of her own, leaving it circling for a moment before she continued. 'Do you really believe they give a shit about Earth? Look what they and millions like them, billions even, did to the planet. Why would they come back, struggle and face intense, fierce hardship when they can sit up there? Up in their steel, barricaded fortress. No pollutants, no disease.'

'And they leave us here for what?' said Ben. 'To live and work a pointless life, slaving for them when we will die anyway? No hope for ourselves or our future or our children's future?' In spite of the situation Callie felt her cheeks redded and her neck and shoulders quiver at Ben's mention of a future with his own family. She was glad it was a passing, glib comment as she fixed her eyes on the floor until it passed.

'And that is finally your fulfilment of reality,' Maya said, almost victorious. 'Thank you, Ben. You are tied, we are all tied, to this glorious, brutal planet, chained to work for those who ravaged and destroyed it. There is no master plan for future repopulation. They live a blessed, limitless existence. We conform, work, die, our entire being created and sanctioned to make theirs certain.

But shifts are coming. Change will fight. The Wilds are expanding, populating and rebuilding nature. We were too weak in the past; even if we could have shown people the truth there were not enough poly free resources, enough safe space. There is more now, every season, every year it grows and strengthens. Soon we will be ready.'

'What is the pain?'

'Pain?' Maya was uncertain what Callie meant.

'You said we could be ploy free but there was pain.'

'Do you believe in the Wilds, mark my words of truth about the Founding?'

'I believe you believe,' Callie answered. 'And I believe I need to see, need to know.'

Maya's smile was deep, her eyes twinkling at Callie's reaction.

'Distrusting trust. That is how you will survive, fight, perhaps even lead. That I have thought of you since Ankor and Fly brought you to me.'

'Lead? I don't know what you're talking about.'

'No, of course you don't. That path hasn't happened yet. But I am curious to know...' Maya's words faded and died as she spoke, Callie frowning, confused. What was she to lead? How? She had no idea, only knew her voice and words sounded more trustworthy than anything Prane, Takot or Grey Suit had told them in the days following their arrest.

Ben was standing, one arm folded, the other leaning on it, his hand grasped across his mouth in thought.

'Lead? Pain?' he asked, uncovering his mouth. 'It's still more hints and riddles. You've asked us to disregard, dispute everything. Told us our whole lives are a sham. For a bowl of stew. Well, we need more. Proof.'

241

Nodding and slapping her hands on her lap, Maya stood up abruptly.

'Undeniably. And that is what you shall have. Then finally you will both trust me.' Her eyes lingered on Ben, sparkling and amused as she stepped towards them. 'But first you need to rest.'

'We don't have…' Ben started.

'Time?' Maya sighed and crossed her arms, her long sleeves hanging down in front of her like a shield. 'We shall have to see, won't we? But what would the alternative be for Takot if he did not wait a few hours? You have time. That is my guess. What they desire will be worth the wait will it not? Perhaps you have the power, the clout to pause and stall just a little longer'. She put a hand gently on a shoulder of each of them. 'Please, stay here, rest. I will return in a few hours.' Maya did not wait for a response as she exited.

Maya returned, stopping momentarily in the doorway she was little more than a dark silhouette, encircled with the burning orange and yellow rays from the sun which appeared to emanate right from her. 'You will trust me,' she pushed.

Callie and Ben followed, Ben being unable to resist giving Laggan a smug, condescending glare as they passed.

Maya led them along a path leading behind the backs of the buildings forming the rough circle of the community. The path led to the edge of the forest but did not enter. It skirted the edge, following round a well-trodden route. As they veered slightly right, the high wall of another remnant of a building appeared. The crumbling wall was littered with graffiti and the patchworked signs of repair. Callie figured whatever it held was important enough to warrant keeping it standing but had no idea what this may be. The wall was solid, no windows or entrances gave clues to what lay behind it. She felt a twinge of unsteadiness at the thought it could be more biters and swallowed the thought forcibly down, desperate to believe Maya's words. Whatever, this was clearly where they were headed.

The tenseness in Callie's jaw relaxed when they turned the corner of the building and she saw the door. Unguarded. Surely this meant there were no dangers, no creatures inside.

The double doors were dark, solid wood, uneven and worn at both ends, held fast with a vertical bar which reached across both holding them firm in two heavy brass locks. 'Please, could you help?' Maya asked Ben, her voice smooth as glass. Ben stepped forward. Was Maya deliberately asking for his support to garner favour, massage his ego? He couldn't decide, either way it made no difference, he wanted to know what was behind the door. Taking a hold under the bar with both hands he nodded at Maya,

'One, two, three.' With a sharp scrape Ben could almost feel in his teeth, the bar lifted. Maya let her end drop to the ground, Ben carrying his round away from the door before letting it fall with a useless thud. Maya pushed open the doors with both hands and stood back as they parted inwardly.

Inside was a grey, concrete courtyard. Weeds sprang up stubbornly from long created cracks and furrows in the heavy stone. Ancient marks from vehicles or heavy dragging ran across here and there like an ancient, long faded motorway map now little more than a raised, faded scar.

All around, layered and layered up and up on top and on top were piles upon piles of rubbish of any and every description. Walking in and looking up and around as she circled, Callie's head spun as she tried to make sense of the perfectly arranged mess surrounding her. The slats, cubes, shapes were like a huge, pixelated screen she was too close to. It took long moments to comprehend the colours and textures, understand some of what she was looking at. She recognised spokes from wheels poking through; cans and bottles slotted in, almost completely faded. She was tempted to pull one out just to see if the whole structure would fall. Packaging had been crushed and slotted into gaps, laid out in haphazard rows of plastics. She noticed sockets, plugs, wires trying to escape and hang down from cracks. Sheets of crushed metal, waste wood, flaps of fabric wafting bored. Glass glinted and made winking appearances. Thin, rectangular, cylindrical, sharp, smooth, gloss, matt, textured, smooth: the place was an architectural curiosity and nightmare. Everything was waste. A remnant from the horror story of the past. Piled here in what looked like a semi-order.

Maya walked along one side, running her hand carefully up and down and along, looking like she was searching in a library.

'We use what we can,' she said. 'Strip it back and reuse, reshape. Take as much back from the land as we can.' Her face was sombre, melancholy, her eyes somewhere else.

Callie's eyes still darted off, fireflies spinning around. Her attention diverted between colours, shapes, recognition of something.

'How long did this take?' she gasped in awe.

'This was begun well before me,' Maya said. 'We continued the order, what we scavenge and collect comes through here, but we didn't start this.'

'How long?'

Maya scoffed lightly, obviously unable to supress her disgust at the Founding,

'Since it all began. The Wilds were built almost as soon as Salthea, the fields, EarthMoon. They were not, are not, the reprobates, dangerous, uneducated, crazed. Well, perhaps a few,' she added with a puff of humour through her nose, 'but we built this civilisation. And be in no doubt, it is civilisation. Those that questioned, spoke out, challenged, thought independently, saw an opposing future. That's who built the Wilds. That is who they fear. But that is not for now. Now you are here for this.'

Callie and Ben had followed her across the concrete courtyard as she spoke, paying little attention to their destination. Maya raised her arm to point, and they were surprised to see they had arrived at another large, solid door. This time, this one had long, thin panelled glass windows. They were too grimy and shadowed to see much beyond, but it was clear from the haphazardly painted red crosses above them what this was. A hospital.

The silhouette of a figure appeared from nowhere on the other side, starting Callie who inhaled in fright and took an instinctual step back. Ben turned, concerned and reassuring and nodded to signal it seemed safe. Callie righted herself and smiled back, raising her chin and stepping forward again.

The figure opened the door. It was a tall, angular man, with wild hair made worse around the ears where it launched out in all directions from under the ear pieces of the face mask he wore. Greying, patchy stubble covered his cheeks and chin, thicker in some places, balding in others. Clearly this was a man who cared more about his work than his personal appearance. His lined eyes lit up in surprise, pride and pleasure when he saw Maya and he nodded his head, almost in a bow, as he addressed her,

'Maya. What a lovely surprise. We weren't expecting you. It would be an honour to be of service.'

'Thank you, Findo,' Maya smiled, reaching out and taking both his hands in a solid clasp. Findo, it appeared, didn't want this clutch to end; Callie noticed it continued into awkwardness, Maya clearly too polite, or used to it, to say. She could see how Maya was adored by these subjects.

'You have brought visitors?' Findo asked, dragging his eyes away from adoration and looking curiously at Ben and Callie. 'Or injured?'

'No, no, not injured. Findo these are my guests. We have been sharing knowledge of our community and theirs.'

'Theirs?'

'Salthea.' At the word Findo's expression changed. His cheeks tensed, his lips snarled. The curiosity of Callie and Ben being Maya's revered guests disappeared and it was almost possible to feel the chill in the air.

Maya reached out with a reassuring hand, wrapping her arm through Findo's and patting his hand.

'Don't worry. Don't worry. Callie and Ben are friends. Do you think I would be with them if not?' Findo looked trusting into her eyes, his darting from left to right in search of reassurance. 'I brought them here to show them the trouble. To show them the purging.'

Findo's head very obviously recoiled in disbelief at this, his mouth open in the turmoil of his confusion. Maya said nothing, just smiled and nodded continually, raising her eyelids and looking into him deeply. 'Really, it is fine. I will be with them the whole time.'

With a deep breath, Findo relinquished control and smiled an uncertain, forced grin that was trying very hard but still stopped at his eyes.'

'As you wish. Please, follow me.'

CHAPTER TWENTY-FIVE

Findo led them silently down a narrow, colourless corridor. Maya walked beside him and from time to time he turned his head very slightly to check Ben and Callie still followed. A tiny movement summing up his suspicion and aversion to them, as if he could not bear to look them in the eye or deem them worthy of his time. Callie couldn't decide if this was because of the mention of Salthea or if he would have preferred Maya had arrived alone, ready to be impressed by his work. But she didn't really care, all of her attention was focussed on what she could see as they passed down the corridor.

Here, at least in this part of the building was actual electric light. The first Ben and Callie had seen since they arrived. Fading strip lighting ran down the centre of the ceiling, some flickering stubbornly from time to time in a bleak, insipid glow. The well walked floor was tiled in a mild, faded mint, adding to the stark, sickly atmosphere. They passed no-one else, but Callie caught glimpses and fragments of conversation out of ajar doors which cast long rectangles across the corridor. They only had seconds to crane their necks and glance hurriedly as they passed, but both Callie and Ben caught glimpses of wiring and trays of grey, metal medical tools; of wheeled beds, some flat, some filled with the lumpy outline of a body; of people in white uniforms moving quickly, checking charts, loading syringes, deep in discussion. Eyes raised and darted attention to them as they passed, causing these dialogues to stop and brows to furrow.

At the end of the corridor was another door, this one bearing a digital lock. Findo once again turned his had slightly, checking where Ben and Callie were, before moving his body to cover the pad and entered the code. With a short, sharp beep, the door shuddered open. They entered a square vestibule, two sides lined in frosted glass, another locked door in front.

This room was noticeable chilled. Ominous. Callie shivered and grasped her arms into herself.

'Now we change,' Findo spoke for the first time since entering the building.

'Change?' Ben asked. Findo shot him an incredulous glance,

'Do they not know why they are here?' he asked Maya.

'They do,' she replied. 'They know most. They have experienced biters. I have brought them so they can see this. The Passage.'

Findo pressed a keypad in the wall, 'Very well,' he stated, 'you will need to put these on.' The walls unclouded to reveal hangers of yellow toxic contamination suits and head wear.

Callie was confused, 'But we've seen biters,' adding with a murmur of bitterness, 'up close. Too close!'

Findo looked at Maya, who was clearly not willing to waste time going over the events of the day.

'They were not bitten, you were sure?' he asked.

Maya nodded, touching his forearm in reassurance. 'I will enlighten you on events as we go, Findo,' she stated. 'For now, we need to press on to view a Passage. Please.'

His concern returned to Callie.

'The biters are not in question here. It is not you who need the protection. It is those during the Passage. They are at the extreme of existence, some teeter on life. The slightest germ from a cough or a sneeze could be fatal. An undetected infection, no matter how innocuous, could spread through our patients too rapidly to control. If you want to continue, you must change.' Findo took two suits from the hangers and passed one each to Callie and Ben, before returning and reaching for another two.

Callie struggled into the rigid, impermeable trousers, pulling them over her own. She shrugged the heavy material over her shoulders and tugged up the thick, solid zip. She could see now why this room was so chilled; inside the clothing it was almost like there was no air, just an uncomfortable heaviness. She tried the visor for curiosity while she waited, pulling it over her neck and sealing it round her throat. The constriction and feeling of claustrophobia were almost instant; Callie had a second of panic when she felt she couldn't breathe. Her hand swiftly ripped off the seal and she breathed the cold air deep into her lungs, chastising herself as she did so.

Ben's hand was on her shoulder.

'Don't worry,' she nodded. 'Just being stupid.'

'They're awful, feel so weird,' he consoled, 'but you're fine.'

'I know,' she looked at him and gave a half smile, before turning to Maya and Findo. 'Ready,' she said, sealing her visor back up.

Findo entered another code into the keypad and the door opened with a tremor. Lights blazed in to life before them. Their eyes all squinted to adjust to the brightness and, with the exception of Findo, all raised a hand to their noses as the smell hit them, smashing the visors with invisible force. Callie felt her stomach rise into her throat and try to lurch up before she managed to force it back down.

Ben's face was creased in surprised disgust, 'What is that?' he asked, lowly. 'It's like rotten death.' He's not far off, Callie thought. The smell, more of a stench in her opinion, was blistering into her nose, at times she felt she could taste it. It was an acrid mix of disinfectant and decay. There was a rancid sweetness about it, a mixture of the earthy, bitter smell of mould and meat that had been left out in the heat. The strong, sharp smell of urine mingled alongside.

Findo was clearly amused at their reaction, Callie wondered if his own nose blindness was a blessing and how long he had had to work here to achieve it. His lack of care gave him a conceited air: he knew he was not troubled as they were. He was able to court favour with Maya as he handed her a pristine handkerchief to place against her nostrils.

'The smell of death, yes. Plus the pain of the journey through the Passage. Are they ready to see?' The question was clearly aimed at Maya; Callie and Ben's opinions meant nothing to him.

'They are,' she replied. With a nod he turned towards a door in the corridor, the clouded, misty glass revealing little behind it except blurred shapes and colours.

'As you wish.' Findo released the door, 'Welcome to Block 9.'

There was a brief blast of cold air which swept the smell away for a welcome instant, before it returned. This block was clearly a medical ward, lined on both sides with beds, some open and some surrounded by curtains of assorted shades and states and patterns. Some hung well from rails, others had missing binds and tears, some so threadbare in patches you could see clear movement behind them. Round beds stood drips and stands for surgical equipment. A few monitors bleeped here and there. Halfway down the vast room was a thin dividing screen, hiding the beds from view as the corridor continued on.

In every bed was a body. All appeared to have been human at some point. To Callie and Ben, they now seemed to be in varying stages of humanity. And various stages of life, or death.

Some were still, lifeless save for a rise and fall in their chest or a rasping breath. Others were strapped to beds at wrists and ankles, mattresses shredded under their hands, sheets skewed underneath them or piling under their feet where they had scrabbled under their restraints to be freed and now lay exhausted.

But the majority writhed. Scratched. Wailed. Gnashed their teeth and clawed the air, throwing themselves wildly, desperately trying to free themselves. Deep gouges pussed orange, yellow, grey where they had scored their own skin. Sharp, broken nails reached out, full of dried blood and skin. Some mouths bubbled with spots of spit and blood as they bit at their own tongues and lips. Many cawed out, animal sounds that were nonsensical, hopeless anger, or whimpering.

Medics scuttled around quickly, here and there – responding to a screech or monitor; puzzling over charts and meters and notes; injecting; taking temperatures; tightening straps; shuffling bodies into more comfortable positions. All wore the same suits they stood in to avoid contamination.

Findo spun round – arms outstretched. 'Welcome to the Passage,' he said vehemently, further delighted by their shock, disgust and disbelief.

Ben arched his neck over towards a bed, clearly uncertain how close to get. 'What is this place? Who are these people?'

'They've got Larejax? They're dying?' Callie spoke in statements that were questions themselves.

'Yes, yes they are,' encourage Maya. 'These souls are the truth. The reality of us all. And there,' she pointed to the area beyond the partition, 'is the Passage.'

Ben's eyes were wide and glaring in compassion,

'But look at them, they're dying. How can you keep them like this? This....this inhumane torture? This is cruel, disgusting.'

Findo stretched up to full height, clearly shocked and annoyed at the outburst. As he opened his mouth with a grunt to speak, Maya raised her hand and spoke first. Her voice was understanding, but steady and stern.

'This is survival. Our survival, yours. Endurance for us all.'

'But you keep them like this, these things?'

'We are trying to treat the Larejax.' Findo was resolute. 'These things are people. Each and every one a member of our community. You, you don't even know what community means.' His voice was rising, clearly put out by Ben's response. 'You are nothing more than battery animals, working without question, for what?' His voice was rising and quickening now, there was no time for response.

'He,' Findo strode over to a bed, smiled down and gently touched the clammy forehead of a patient strapped tightly to the edges of the mattress, his mouth snapping uselessly at Findo's glove-sealed hand, 'was a curator here. Gathering history, knowledge, artifacts. Filing, cataloguing, documenting, teaching. Now look at him.' Callie's eyes did not reach the bed, she stared at the floor, the reality of this man's humanity waving through her. Ben, red faced, also hung his head.

'Look!' demanded Findo and four eyes rose. Callie met the gaze of the man on the bed; her eyes welled at the sight of these darkened, deadened globes now only set to see feast or fear.

Findo's chest was rising and falling quickly, his deep breaths audible as he tried to regain composure. 'This is why we treat them. What would you have me do? Shoot them like animals? Have we learned nothing from the past?'

'No but,' Ben began, then faltered.

'No,' Findo's voice was a calm whisper. 'We treat them best we can. Learn. Explore. And yes, if it makes you feel better, use them. When they become so entrenched there is no way back, no hope, we use them. In a vain effort to find some hope for the future. Some way to return them to us.' Maya reached out and touched his forearm. Findo looked down, stared at her arm as if confused, then followed it up to her face. She smiled and pressed her fingers, reassuring him with her grip.

'And for that we are eternally grateful,' she said. 'Their sacrifice, and yours, could save so, so many more. Look at what we can do already, what we know. Come, let's move through and show them the Passage. This way.' Maya nodded Findo on and addressed Callie and Ben.

'Our ways have faults; nobody would deny that. But we need to do what we can, use what we can to create a future for our people. Larejax is just as much a plague here as it is with you. We have not all taken the Passage. Some have only begun. Others still join us, escape to life here, poly ridden. Larejax is merely a waiting game. Should there be a miracle, some revolutionary cure that leads you all to kowtow again and revere Salthea how long for? How long before the polys grip again? That is why we aim to discover what we can.

'I understand, it's just hard,' Callie said.

'Yes, yes it is,' agreed Maya, 'but many things that are necessary are.' They had reached the dividing screens. Once again, every bed was full, men, women and youths lay prone or curled up in rows of beds. Some held their stomachs to their knees, curled tightly in foetal groans, mouths yelling out in silent agony. Others clutched pillows to their abdomens, wailing loudly in clear suffering. Faces glistened with sweat and tears which were not consoled. As Callie and Ben's eyes passed along the beds a youth further down started jerking and spasming, his body trying to leap out of the bed, chest first. Medics were instantly on him, rolling him onto his side as foam began seeping out of his mouth.

'What's wrong with him?' asked Callie.

'It is his Passage,' said Findo. 'Soon, all being well, he will be back to full strength. Purged.'

Maya nodded, 'Free. Poly neutral. There won't be any toxins left inside.'

'He won't need the medicine.'

'No, Ben, no he won't. This, all of this,' Maya's voice rose proud and noble, 'is what they don't want you to know. What they're scared of.'

'It's true,' he spoke quietly, gravely processing what he was staying – the gravity of what this meant. 'Callie, I…we…' Ben sighed not knowing how to continue, what the words were. Instead, his gaze returned to the room and all it meant.

Callie had more questions. 'After the Passage are they ok?'

'Of course. Better in fact. Findo, Laggan, many, many of those you have seen have taken the journey.'

'You?'

Maya nodded. 'Yes. I could not lead by example, play my part, unless I had travelled the route myself.'

'Everyone in the Wilds is free?'

'They are all free of mind,' said Maya. 'Not all are free of polys but that is their choice. But we nurture and care, look after our own.'

'But why steal and risk being caught when you can be free? I don't understand that,' Ben asked.

'Each person here is free to make their own decisions, their life, health, soul is theirs and theirs alone. As long as they do not endanger our ways or our people they can choose their own route.'

'But why not just take the Passage?'

'Look around Ben,' Maya turned her head to the left and right. 'It is not such an easy decision. Some take it straight away and throw themselves into the Passage. Other see the fear, hear the pain and are scared. They often take longer; they might never be truly free. But their freedom in mind and heart is enough for them to have a new belonging.'

'And after?' Ben asked.

'After?'

'Yes. What next? They have to stay here? Work for you?'

Maya shook her head, looked deep into Ben with those eyes containing a timeless season within.

'No Ben. I spoke the truth before. All are free to go. But in all my time here, they stay.'

'Why would they go back,' Callie's voice was grim, bitter. 'It's all lies, all of it. Why would they go back when they have hope here? I wouldn't.'

Ben spun, eyes wide.

'What do you mean?'

'How can we go back now? Knowing all this. Knowing what they're going to do to us?'

'But we can't stay! Callie, we have to get the Dealga. Provide them with the cure.'

'Do we?'

'Do we?' Ben was clearly shocked, stunned at her words. 'Callie, people will die without us. Have you forgotten those things? We've got two days to collect and deliver the Dealga. The camp, they could be sick already. Biters destroying their own flesh. If we're not back by tomorrow evening, then we're lost. We become the hunted'

Her eyes flashed with grief and stubbornness.

'For how long? Till the next poly formula is rejected? And what next. Larejax is the worst. But that's right now —what could come? There is no point Ben, don't you see, this is only a stop gap, giving them time to contain and control once more.'

'So what? We do nothing. Let Takot come looking for us and take our chances? Let them send someone else who may not be so lucky? We don't have a choice. We can go back. Take the Dealga. Tell people.'

'Tell who. Ben?' Callie's voice was mocking, acerbic. 'Bree? Look where that got me. Don't you see? Our whole society is set up so there is no-one to tell, no-one to trust. Say we do confide, if Takot even lets us live, who will believe us? Even if they do, how long would it be before whispers emerged? I don't want to end up back on a ledge in Salthea.'

Ben was disgusted, 'So you'd rather we stay here? Leave the world to suffer in sickness and die. Unaware?'

Callie shook her head and approached him. She took his hands, interlacing her fingers in his. When he tried to gently pull back, confused, she pushed their hands down, arms straightening. Then she

253

looked up, deep into his eyes, her own darting from left to right, appealing for him to see and understand. Her voice was level, assured,

'Tell me you don't actually think that. No Ben, we don't stay here. I do. Only me.'

The effect of the words was powerful. Ben dropped his hands, jolted back, charged.

'Callie..what..how…What are you saying? What do you mean?'

'Ben, you're right. We have to do what they've asked, of course we do. We have to take the Dealga back. Have to help save who we can or at least give them a chance. But you can do that. Just you. I need to stay.'

He shook his head, resolute.

'No, no way. Absolutely not.'

'Yes, Ben.' Callie reached for his hand again. 'I've made my mind up. I need to do this.'

CHAPTER TWENTY-SIX

Maya and Callie found Ben when they left the medical complex. He had stormed out, frustrated at her pig headedness and unwillingness to see the stupidity behind what she was suggesting. He was under no illusion as to how stubborn, reckless and single-minded Callie was, but this time she was verging on ridiculous. Has she lost her mind? His thoughts flew in anger, panic and shock. Could she even be showing the first signs of sickness? Ben's mind flooded as he stomped in the confines of the high-sided, concrete complex again. Part of him just wanted to sod her, sick of her flighty selfishness, and collect the Dealga himself, to hell with what she thought. Fuck the interrogation he would face from Prane and Takot. The other part of him wanted to rush back into the building, find Callie and embrace her, smother her with understanding but bring her to her senses.

Neither would work. Instead, he fretted, hot and irritated, waiting for Callie and Maya to re-emerge.

At the same time Callie was trying to put his actions to the back of her mind, embarrassed at his outburst and furious at the expectation he was in charge of her and her desires. He might have forgotten all that had happened in the past, their history, the revelations. She had not. She might have grappled with and accepted her feelings towards him, but that didn't mean he had any right to a hold over her. He can piss off, she thought.

After they had left Findo, Maya had walked them briefly through a small, bright ward designed for children and maternity. Babies! It seemed so basic, so obvious but the idea had never crossed Callie's mind. She had never equated the children she had seen here with babies.

There was one tiny, round, red faced infant with his mother in the ward. When Maya approached Callie noticed the reaction was similar to that of Findo – pride and a sense of accomplishment. Maya looked over and smiled, the baby looked up with wide, innocent blue eyes as she sucked, insouciant, on her mum's pinkie finger. Maya rubbed the back of her hand gently along the child's cheek.

'How is she?'

'Completely free,' the mum beamed, clearly delighted, holding her daughter out in joy. 'She's flawless. Clear.'

'Yes, yes she is. Perfect.' Maya agreed. 'Well done. Have you thought of a name?'

The woman delicately hugged her daughter to her, a gesture of absolute love and care, and nodded.

'Caitrin.'

'Pure.'

'Yes,' she nodded.

'It's lovely,' Maya smiled before nodding and leading Callie off. She too smiled awkwardly at the woman as she left.

Callie was itching with questions but waited until they were out of earshot.

'Pure?'

Maya looked at Callie and smiled proudly again, 'The baby's name. It means pure.'

'You mean the baby was born without polys? She's free?'

'Of course,' explained Maya, 'The tests are complete and distinct.'

'Wow,' Callie was lost in her own thoughts momentarily.

'It's not unusual anymore you know,' Maya's words broke her imagining. 'Most of our children have been born poly free. Depending how long beforehand their parents changed over.'

'Freedom,' whispered Callie.

'Freedom,' repeated Maya, putting a motherly arm across Callie's shoulder blades. 'You may be nearing your own readiness.' Callie turned, eyes of awe and smiled, an expression of longing, insecurity and turbulence. Maya's arm pulled Callie closer in towards her shoulder, an act of assurance and encouragement, before releasing her.

With that the two walked in silence, until they located Ben on the outside.

Callie felt a pang of compassion, guilt and something else, something she couldn't admit, when she saw his eyes - full of misery and insecurity. She was determined now, had found her destiny and belonging. But she had to find a way to make Ben see. That wasn't going to be easy.

'So,' he said, both irritated and relieved, when she walked up alongside.

'So, yourself.'

'I half expected you to leave me standing here and sneak out some secret entrance.'

'And go where?'

Ben shrugged and kicked at a pebble loose on the concrete slab. It bounced a few times before coming to rest in a crack. 'I dunno, off with your new friends somewhere.'

'I wouldn't do that.' Callie reached out and ran her hand down his arm. There was no response and she sighed. 'What do you want me to say?'

'Nothing.'

'Then what?' Callie's voice raised pitch, more forceful.

Ben moved to stand in front of her, stepping back to see her face, her expressions clearly. 'You know what, Cal. I want us to get out of here, get the Dealga, get home.'

'And then what?' Her voice was assured, certain.

'Then? Then we hope we can get on with the rest of our lives. Escape jail, or worse. Put our heads down and have some kind of future without being under constant scrutiny. Hope we don't get sick.'

Callie shook her head and scoffed, 'I can't do that. Not now. Look around, Ben. You can't expect me to leave this, pretend we haven't seen this. Knowing what we know.'

Ben interrupted, curtly, 'What we think we know.'

'We know enough. I've seen enough.' Callie was curt, resolute. 'I'm not asking you to stay. You need to go. One of us has to go back with the Dealga. Don't think I haven't forgotten. Don't try to pin that guilt on me. We need to give them it, for the short time it might be useful. For the few it might save. But not me. I'm done.'

Ben clenched his jaw; tried to direct all his frustration, disbelief and irritation there. He pushed down on his back teeth so hard he wondered if it was possible to dislocate your own jaw like this. Send it flapping, uselessly against his chin. Might as well be, for all the notice Callie was taking. This was bullshit he thought. This took reckless adventure to another level. Ok, for now they seemed to be on an even path with Maya, but had she forgotten what that woman had done? Trust? He was a long way from trusting anyone, at this stage even Callie.

'What are you suggesting?' he pushed the words out, hoping he sounded levelled, patient. The complete opposite to what he supposed his face told. 'I don't think I need to tell you what's at stake if we don't go back with the cure. Millions of people…'

'Will die. I've already said,' Callie clipped every word, her own impatience on the tip of each and just waiting to spill over, 'you can take it. I'm staying. Besides,' her voice broke off, wistful and full of regret, 'Dealga's not a cure, Ben, it's a stop gap.'

'Ben put his palms up, conciliatory, not wanting to argue.

'Okay, look. Say we get the Dealga. Take it back as a cure or a placebo or whatever spin the Chancellor wants to put on it. I take it back, you're not there. Then what? Prane and Takot mourn your disappearance no questions asked? Just lead me back to the farm, pat me on the back and say off you go? Get real. That won't happen in a million years. I actually don't fancy being quizzed, interrogated, hung out a window again lying for you.'

'And I wouldn't ask you to,' Callie was compassionate, firm. 'I need to figure it out, talk to Maya. I think I know a way. In the meantime, we have to focus on the Dealga.'

Maya approached, interjecting,

'That is taken care of.'

'What do you mean?' Callie was startled.

'The Dealga is being harvested for you. It will be here soon. Then we will secure your safe passage back to wherever you need to go.'

'For both of us,' Ben was uncertain, ascertaining exactly the situation.

Maya looked long in his eyes, then lowered her gaze to smile as she looked deeply into Callie's. 'If that is what you both decide. But the decisions are with you individually and you alone. Come back with me, take some time.'

'We don't have time. This needs done. Now,' Ben urged.

Maya put a calming hand on his arm, 'And it will be. It is being taken care of. That you don't need to worry about, relinquish control. Come, be with each other. Make your plans. The route cannot be changed once it is set.'

Ben's thoughts stung and clawed as he followed Maya and Callie's return to the camp. He lagged back, slightly, watching the two from behind. Two women now. Callie's shoulders were certain, her posture strong, mature. She kept pace with Maya, almost hip to hip, her voracity for life pulsing through every self-assured step.

She is hers now, he realised, hopeless. Was there nothing he could do to make her return with him? Ben was disgusted at his own thoughts of trying to intervene in her decisions and control; was that not one of the things he was attracted to the most? Was the life that pulsed through her, sparkled out of her eyes not a reason for loving her?

She would go. But not before she knew it all. Not before he made her listen to how he felt. Really listen. Not before he knew if she felt the same.

And then what, the spikes and jabs rolled in his head like barbed wire. What danger would she be in? Would they look for her? Realise she was with Maya. Would they care? The unknown, endless possibilities were toying with him, terrorising.

Ben's head continued to crash and clatter, disjointed and without clarity as the trio walked. Maya had taken her arm now, the two walked arm in arm, oozing closeness, succour and hope. The older woman's chatter of routines and roles; uses for this; zero wastage for that; what's stored over there; what's piled up over there fluttered in his consciousness but couldn't break through to comprehension.

Suddenly he realised they were back at Maya's home.

'Please,' Maya said, pulling back the curtain and gesturing for them to enter. Callie stepped forward without hesitating, Ben eventually joining. Callie was already sitting on a cushion, checked in shades of green, arms out, bent at the elbow, leaning forward as if eager for more conversation.

'I am not going to disturb you any further.' Maya was warm, perhaps her own voice tinted with her own hopeful aspirations of what could follow. 'You will need time to discuss, decide. I will arrange food be delivered, otherwise I will leave you both for the time being.' She smiled at Callie, nodding deeply at Ben, then turned and left. An embarrassed, awkward silence teased round.

Ben broke it sighing and sitting down opposite Callie. He picked at a callous on his palm, unable to speak, unsure of what to say.

Eventually it was too much. Callie burst through the discomfort that had blanketed them,

'So, you got me here. You obviously have things to say. Shoot.'

Ben dropped his hand, rubbed it against the cushion, the pain rubbing out of his hand replaced by the pain in his head. His heart. His voice was quiet, tired,

'I don't know what else to say.'

'You don't want me to stay, that's clear enough.'

'No.'

'Why?'

'Why? Callie, you know why. We don't know these people. Look what they tried to do to us. How can you throw your life into this hoping you can trust them?'

'How can you not?'

'I……..oh…….what's the point. You don't care what I think. What I want.'

'What you want? What about what I want? When did you suddenly become my keeper?' her voice was rising again, her stubbornness blunting her words.

'I haven't. I didn't. Look, there's no point in talking about it anymore, we're going round in circles.'

'You're just not willing to understand,' she was bolt upright in her seat now, her hands clasped down between her knees.

'No, Callie, you're not.'

'What's that supposed to mean?'

'Nothing. It doesn't matter. I...'

'I'm not abandoning you, Ben. This is my decision to make. They're bringing us Dealga. You take it back. They bullshit, find a cure for now, a placebo, whatever. I stay here. Don't you get it?' her voice was impassioned, desperate for him to see and understand, seeking his approval. 'I need this, this is it for me now. This is where I belong. All of it is what I've dreamt of, longed for.'

Ben saw it in her face then and the knife burst through into his chest. He hung his head, eyes tracing the grain in a plank on the floor.

Callie sighed and dropped to her knees in front of him. She couldn't leave it like this. Had to make him understand and see what this meant.

'Ben?' she said softly, titling her head down to try and reach up into his eye. 'You need to let me do this.'

'I don't think I can,' the voice was a whisper, and his head shook uselessly from side to side. 'I really don't think I can.'

'But why? It's what I need. Everyone gets what they want.'

She felt an instants shock as his eyes met hers. They were lost in deep oceans of tears fighting against the tipping tide, the eyes of a little boy. This instant dissolved when suddenly his mouth was on her, kissing her deep.

'Because I love you,' he said, breathlessly.

CHAPTER TWENTY-SEVEN

'I can't do this. Can't hear this! I'm sorry!' Flushed, the redness of Callie's neck was quickly rising to her cheeks where she felt the growing heat pulsing upwards.

'I'm sorry, I..'

She shook her head, put her hand up to touch his lips.

'Don't. We can't do this. I can't do this. How could I after…?'

'I know, but..' Ben sighed, 'I don't know. I just needed to say, to tell you.' The determination, surety was gone, and Ben was embarrassed, childlike.

Callie spoke quietly, a sense of pain in her small voice, careful to be respectful of his feelings. 'You know I need to stay?' Ben nodded.

'You'll stop trying to make me go?'

Ben smiled, tightly, as he spoke, trying to encourage humour into his voice. 'What choice do I have? I did my best but boy, that stubbornness, how can I compete with that?'

'Thanks.' Ben shrugged. 'No, I mean it. Thank you. I know it's not easy, it wasn't easy for me to decide. But I have. I need to do this for me.' Ben nodded.

'Yeah.'

'And we need to make things safe for you. Figure out what to say, how you can convince them.'

'You don't need to worry about me,' Ben said.

'Kind of got used to it though. And anyway, I want to.'

Ben looked into her face then.

'You do?'

'Of course. After all we've been through. You saved my life, remember?'

His voice trembled, cracked and broke, 'I didn't have an option.' It hung in the air, he had to say it, the reality was time was running out and he now had nothing to lose. 'But what about…what about Tax?'

The edges of Callie's mouth twitched; her lips pursed tightly forward for a moment as she gathered her thoughts. Her voice cracked as she spoke,

'Tax is dead.' Both of them physically reacted, it was the first time she had spoken these words out loud. Callie continued, grave and controlled. 'Neither of us can change that. I have to live with it. So do you. But he would want me to go on. To deal with what happened and not let it fester and consume me. So that's what I'm going to try to do. You and me? It's fucked up. I don't know how I feel. How can I want and hate a person at the same time? How can I feel physically sick when I'm with you and only want to be beside you? I dunno. But that's what I'm left with.'

'I'm sorry, I..'

Callie shook her head, continued before the words ran out or away. Just as Ben had taken his chance, this was her opportunity. Aware of time slipping through her fingers the words spilled, breathless, agonising, luxuriating in finally being free and speaking the truth.

'I can't forget what you did. I can't be with you, go back with you to some kind of life. Because of what you did. But I can't help loving you.'

Ben felt punched, the roaring in his head started again and he reached out. Callie stepped back from his embrace, shaking her head.

'No.' The word stung both of them.

'But I don't understand, you said you love me?'

She stared into him deeply, looking at him fully honestly for the first time, soaking him in. His face, his body, their story. She was sure.

'Yes, I love you. But that has to be your penance. Understanding what we could have been but what we have been left with.'

The heat drained from Ben and a chill replaced it, crawling unceremoniously up his back and through his nerves as Callie's words engulfed first his comprehension, then his heart. Hope seeped out through his veins, replaced with dull, numb recognition of her declaration. It was done, the finality squatted within his chest, tightening its cruel, sour grip. He forced a nod. There were no words. None he could find. None he would be able to speak. Only the cold.

Callie looked uncertain, flustered inside but resisting the tickle to move or speak. It hadn't been easy, more a release of relief, and she had her own hurt. Yet she knew his was worse, her words had been a fatal blow between them. They still needed each other to go on, to succeed in the deception they needed to convince Takot and Prane was true. She had to keep him safe, the image of him discovered, tormented, back on that ledge, murdered for her, by her, played out iridescent right in front of her. She would not allow it, intended to do everything she could to allow him to live a life. Sacrifice anything she could.

Their mutual discomfort was interrupted as Maya's promised food arrived. Two villagers, clearly gathering whatever information they could glean from their short visit brought a tray of food and jug of water. They hesitated, uncertain of where to put down the tray and wary of the two strangers unguarded in front of them. No doubt words of confusion – were they enemies, friends, something else – was sweeping around the camp with a variety of views, anecdotes and opinions galloping uncontrollably.

They appraised Callie and Ben without embarrassment, eyeing from foot to temple, trying to analyse body language, atmosphere and any snippets of conversation they could eavesdrop on. Of that they were most definitely out of luck. They left both with relief to get back to where they felt secure and understood and with a sigh.

'I need to eat.' The pain and tension in Ben had found their way into his stomach. Food might at least confuse and trick them into subsidence. He picked up a handful of small, dark coloured berries and threw them in his mouth. The juice, vibrant and sharp caught and tingled in the back of his throat, tart but enjoyable. He offered the bowl out to Callie. She shook her head, not wanting to eat. Fearing this would cause a fight she took a chunk of still-warm bread and ripped into it, chewing a small bite. At least having something in her hand was making her feel less awkward. Although her mouth was now even drier, and her throat was starting to ache. She poured a glass of water, then thought better of it and poured two. Offering one to Ben she drank deeply, washing the bread crumbs and irritation away.

'We need to…' Ben spoke softly, clearly not wanting to fight. But Callie jumped in, unwilling to start another spiralling circle of futile arguments.

'No,' she murmured, her mouth still full of water, a few drips escaping as she urged the words out. 'We can't keep going on like this. It's decided, you know it. You need to go back; you don't have a choice. I know that. I've accepted it. But I need to stay. I don't have a choice either. That's my make up. And you have to accept that.'

He couldn't speak. Couldn't bear admitting he must agree with her. Saying the words would be too cruel. He looked at her, her eyes free and already full of hope and excitement and nodded. One long, slow, consenting nod.

Callie stepped so close he could feel the heat radiating from her once more, smell her sweet, musky smell and the yeasty mouthfuls of bread. She kissed him once more. Not passionate or romantic but softly, compassionately, understanding deeply what he had just done for her.

'Now we need to make a plan,' she said. 'Will you listen to me first? Before you say anything? I mean really listen?'

'I will.'

'No matter what you'll hear me out and hear what I have to say?'

He nodded.

'It could be our only chance. The only chance for us all to be completely free.'

'I'll listen, just tell me,' he said.

Ben burst through the doorway to Maya's tent, red-faced and gasping for air. His ears burned with what he had just heard, and he gulped down mouthfuls of pure, clean air trying to get rid of the nasty taste he imagined he had in his mouth. He knew he had to hold it together but even for Callie this was stupidity personified: wild and outrageous. He had expected reckless. He hadn't expected this. He rubbed his eyes and face roughly with his hands, shook his head, braced his back and re-entered. There was no point arguing anymore. She would do it. He was wasting time.

'So?' her voice was slightly obnoxious as if prepared to fight.

'You've decided. Come up with this horseshit plan. Mutilation? Callie, this is beyond crazy even for you.'

'Got a better idea?'

'I've got a thousand ideas. None of them involve you chopping yourself up!' Ben's voice was a mixture of confusion, bewilderment and disgust.

'Don't over exaggerate. It's a hand.'

'How appropriate.'

'I don't need sarcasm.'

'No, Callie, you need help! Serious bloody help!'

'You said you'd listen. Promised.'

'And I did, didn't I?'

Callie couldn't disagree so harumphed and crossed her arms across her chest.

'You won't be able to do that comfortably for much longer.'

'Very funny. You know there's no other way, right?'

'I don't know anything. Except we're running out of time. It doesn't matter what I say anyway, does it?'

Callie shook her head, releasing relief and a bit of disappointment.

'How? Actually, don't answer that.'

Her voice was deadpan, matter of fact, 'Maya said she'll arrange it.'

'I bet she did.'

Callie snorted, 'You still don't trust her?'

'I don't know what to think anymore. I do know I don't like the thought she is more than happy to dismember the girl I love!'

Callie was struggling to keep her voice and temper in check, at the same time trying to acknowledge Ben's place and worries. If there was ever a time to focus and stay level headed and together it was now.

'Let them take me. I'll do it.' Ben was there, in front of her, his hands gently on her elbows.

She looked up into his eyes and could see immediately he meant every word. She gripped his forearms too and looked deep into his eyes.

'I know. I know you would. But this is my story. My path. And besides, if they were suspicious and wanted more, there is this.' Callie flashed her left thumb upwards, showing off the chestnut coloured, almost heart shaped birthmark that rested there. 'Fingerprints, which might have left us an option. But the polys have taken those from us.' Contemplating, Callie rubbed the smooth, even surface of her left thumb and index finger together. Imagining how different they would look or perhaps even feel with miniscule grooves and patterns embedded in them. Unique to each individual, a marker of their importance. How amazing it must have been to pinpoint one person from all there were then through something as simple as a finger. She went on. 'You know without this there will be doubt. My birthmark. My DNA. It's me. It has to be. Come with me?'

Ben nodded softly, 'When?'

'Now.'

'Now? Are you serious?'

Callie's mouth was fixed. Her eyes steeled into him, resolute and prepared. 'You said it yourself, we can't wait. How do we know they don't already have a party out looking for us. Ready to drag us back and destroy this place. Yes, now.'

Ben was silent, his insides rolling in turmoil at the truth she spoke. Callie continued. 'Maya has gone back to the medical compound to prepare. I need to ask you something. Will you come with me?'

Ben winced, knowing that was what she was going to say and dreading the answer.

His voice was drained, empty. 'I don't think I can.'

'I need you.'

He smiled and embraced Callie warmly, breathing in her energy as he buried his face in the top of her head.

267

'Actually, you don't,' he said, releasing her, clasping her cheek warmly in one hand and smiling. 'You never have. It's just taken me till now to accept it. You don't need anyone. Look at you. You are the most frustrating, most tenacious, stubborn, reckless person I know. You have dreams, hopes, ambitions beyond anything I even imagine. A hopeless heedlessness I'd never be brave enough for.'

Callie felt it then. Right, wrong, iniquitous, she loved him. The pain splicing her body, mind, very being, would carry with her long after the pain of what she was about to face. She gulped the ball of tears in her chest away.

'In another life?'

'In another,' he nodded. 'We need to finish this.

'You'll come?'

Ben took her hand and turned it in his. He kissed her index finger gently, then the others when she did not complain, a gently whisper of his lips across the tips of her nails. Then he held it tight in his own.

'I'll come.'

They tried to make small talk as they walked back to the medical facility: oh-ing and ah-ing at unique and insightful recycled projects they passed that they had missed previously; passing the cage and commenting on how much they had feared and learned since then; wondering when those sent for Dealga would return. Short, blunt statements mostly, neither in the mood, the small talk just making it all the more unsettling. It wasn't just the thought of what Callie was about to endure, it was the knowledge their time together was nearing the end.

Maya met them at the entrance, her expression warm, serious. She too was acutely aware of the sacrifice Callie would make and the finality of it. When they drew level she nodded, unspoken, and the three once again entered the hospital. This time their journey took them down an empty corridor to a large, brightly lit theatre. Ben drew up sharply.

'Is it in there?'

'It is,' Maya's voice was grave, understanding. 'We have to begin.'

Callie took his hand and looked up,

'It's ok. You're here. That's all that matters. Stay here for me.'

'I'm sorry,' Ben started, 'I just can't watch you.'

'I understand. It's just another reason why I love you. You'll wait?'

He nodded, his eyes glazed and swimming.

Callie stretched her shoulders and, neck long and tight, stepped on.

'Always,' Ben said, reaching out and pressing his splayed fingers against the door. 'Always.'

Behind it, Callie tried to shake off the pressure looming down on her, pushing weight into her body, almost driving her into the floor so she felt like she sludged and struggled with every step on heavy, heavy legs.

Maya wrapped Callie in an embrace, then pulled back and maternally pushed strands of hair out of her face, behind her ears.

'This is your decision. You need to be sure.'

'Yes,' Callie nodded. 'I am.'

'There may be other options.'

'Nothing so safe. So definite. Let me. It's best for everyone.'

'Very well.' Maya gestured to the woman arranging cold, shining metal instruments on the trolley. 'Callie, this is Adeline.' The woman smiled, silently. 'She will be…She is…' Maya, for the first time, seemed to stumble, uncertain over the words to use. Adeline sensed this and took over,

'I will be performing your wrist disarticulation.' Her voice was stern and clinical, personifying the situation. 'I don't agree with the process; there is no trauma or disability to the limb; we have no operating team or access to sophisticated prosthetics or rehabilitation. However, I have been assured of the grave need and assure you, promise you, I will treat you with the upmost skill, security and care.'

Callie felt as if she was back in class, with Mitez scrutinising or scolding her. The weight of the situation remained in her shoulders and she too, struggled to know what to say given the momentousness of what was coming. Her 'thank you' floated weakly in the air.

'You will change into this gown,' Adeline held up a thin, pale blue tunic, starched to sharp edges. 'We have no safe means to put you under completely, but you will not feel the procedure: we have the means to provide that level of anaesthesia at least.' She paused, waiting for Callie to gesture for her to continue. 'A tourniquet will be strapped just above your carpal bones.' When Callie squinted her nose and appeared confused, she rephrased, 'above your wrist. Then the procedure. The operation should be over in less than 45 minutes. The skin leftover from your palm will turn back over the stump.' Callie winced at the word and rubbed her palm, looking perhaps for the last time at the lines, hacks and callouses that lay there. A whole map I've never really paid attention to before, she thought morosely. 'Hopefully, we will be able to keep your wrist and at least you will have that movement. Am I clear.'

'Yes,' Callie said, 'Very clear. I'm ready.' As if in demonstration she began undoing her clothing and shrugged her shoulders out of the top. A few moments later she stood, feet cold on the floor, in the gown and, with a deep breath of uncertain certainty, sat on the bed. Almost as if waiting on cue an attendant appeared at the side of the bed. Mute conversation and understanding passed between herself and Adeline as she passed thick straps at Callie's shoulder, elbow and forearm, clamping her arm straight and tight. She continued, filling a syringe with clear, polished liquid and rubbed Callie's upper arm clean.

'This will remove all feeling from your shoulder down your arm,' Adeline explained. You will feel nothing of the laser bar a slight warm pressure. Try to ignore this and the noise. It can play tricks with your mind and convince you of feelings that are not there.' She spoke as her assistant pressed the needle of the syringe against Callie's arm. She felt a momentary spurt of pain then tingling, cool numbness like cooling pins and needles run down her arm to her fingertips. This seemed to increase in pressure until her arm was a useless weight limp and motionless at her side.

The nurse positioned a small, curtained stand over Callie's elbow, blocking her lower arm from view.

'What's that for?'

'The screen prevents you from viewing the procedure,' Adeline replied. 'Stops any untoward panic reactions.'

'Please, I want to see.'

Adeline glanced and Maya, who remained motionless in response, then turned and looked long at Callie. 'I do not recommend it.'

'At least give me the option.'

Adeline considered for a moment then signalled to the nurse to remove the stand.

'As you wish. It will remain here in case you change your mind.'

'I won't.' Callie did not know if she believed her own words or not.

The sound overcame Ben as he sat, knees up, hands bent at the elbow pushing in on his ears as the tears ran down his clenched, folded face. The dull, electrical whirr of the laser had signalled the point of no return while he stood, facing the door. His head had bumped gently against it, eyes down pinpointed at a mark on the floor as he whispered her name, his love, his feelings of compassion, wrecked emotion, sorrow spewing out nonsensically into the solid door.

It was when the tone changed and became rougher, more aggravated as the laser bore down crunching burning, tearing of cartilage, of muscle, of bone that he finally crumpled and folded. He had shouted uselessly then, beating on the door and shouting her name through his tears. Begging her to change her mind, promising he would find another way. That hadn't lasted long; the sensible part of him scared of disturbing the surgeon and remembering his promise. There was no screaming out, he thought, the one saving grace.

Finally, Maya opened the door and Ben scrambled to his feet, an insect scrabbling upright after sprawling on the ice. He rubbed his hands quickly over his face, removing the damp, sticky signs of his crying from his eyes and nose. Desperate, tormented eyes met Maya's as he waited, almost unable to hear but wanting nothing else but to listen to her voice.

Her voice was slow and clear, the enormity of what had just happened etched on her face.

Ben shook, 'Is she?'

'She's fine. Sleepy, uncomfortable. She lost a little more blood than anticipated.' Ben's eyes winced then stretched wide in alarm, not reducing much as Maya quickly added, 'But she will be ok.'

'Can I see her?'

'Yes. But,' Maya took Ben's shoulder, 'remember this was her choice. Irreparable. Callie needs support. Understanding. Our reverence.' Ben sniffed, his eyes betraying him. 'I give you my word. She will be ok. On my oath. On my life.'

Ben did the only thing he could, unable to speak. He put his hand on Maya's and let her lead him to Callie.

Despite her pallid face and straggly, sweaty hair clinging to her forehead, she looked angelic, almost serene. Ben thought the indent her head made in the pillow unfolded into a lined, white halo around her. An angel she was, he supposed, sent to save and endure. He sat down gently on the bed, not wanting to disturb her. She would need this rest. He looked down, her right hand lay out, flat against the sheets. Under it was, Ben wasn't sure how to think it. Was what was left. A dull stump curled up, waiting for its new owner to awake. He thought for a horrible second he was going to be sick as his chest contracted and turned, twisting viciously. The discomfort in his body was enough to disturb Callie and her lashed fluttered from sleep. He saw the instant when she woke, innocent, forgetting where she was until the cruel memory catapulted her to alertness.

'Hi', Ben smiled gently.

Callie smiled back, weakly, Ben noticed she held his gaze. Was this deliberate? Fear of what she would have to face? 'How are you?' he continued. Embarrassed at the stupidity of the question he stumbled on, 'Sorry, don't answer that.' He put his hand on hers and squeezed softly.

Callie flinched.

'Sorry!' Ben jumped.

She shook her head slightly, 'It's fine. It's not you, it's just, sore you know.'

Ben had no answer. He felt her begin to slide her left arm out and pressed down slightly in response.

Callie stopped. 'You know you have to let go. I need to see. It's ok.' She began to pull again at the same time squirming to sit up.

'Here, let me…' Ben reached behind her to pull up her pillow while she leaned forward on her right elbow and raised herself up slightly.

'Thanks.'

Callie took a deep breath and blew out slowly and deeply, her mouth forming an 'o'. 'Here goes.'

She raised her left arm up, elbow bent, looking through slitted eyes, her lashes reflecting light and casting a hazy film over what was in front of her. With another deep breath she opened them properly and looked.

Her arm was heavily bandaged from between the elbow and the wrist to what was now the end. Thick gauze wound round and round making a bulbous mushroom shape. The bandage increased in volume towards where the hand should be, the swollen stump nodding as Callie turned it around in front of her. She reached out and folded her right hand over the stump, before bringing them both down to her lap again. Her eyes met Ben's and he could see that, despite the tears of grief she was holding back, she did not feel any regret.

'Do you want me to get you anything? Do anything?' he asked, uncertain where to go from here or what he should or could do.

'No,' she said.

'Okay,' he didn't want awkwardness seeping in, but didn't know what would happen next or when 'next' would happen. After this it wasn't his right to move forward, it was all up to Callie.

Callie appreciated his uncertainty. She was weak, needed to rest, but he needed to continue.

'Ben?'

'Yes.'

'I need to sleep, need some painkillers and some rest.'

He bounced off the bed, looking around for any medicines. 'Let me find some. Find someone.'

Callie interrupted, 'No, Ben. Look at me.' He stopped and turned. 'I didn't mean that. I don't need you to find me pain relief. I'll get that when Adeline comes back. I need time to,' the words escaped her – weren't enough to explain. She raised her stump to Ben, 'To…this. And I need you to find Maya. Find out what is happening with the Dealga. You need to move this forward. Without me.'

CHAPTER TWENTY-EIGHT

He found Maya sitting outside in the courtyard, straight backed on tightly packed rubble of stone and plastics, her, head up towards the sky, eyes closed. He had no idea if she was relaxed, thinking, sleeping, listening. He felt partly as if he should berate her for what had happened, his petulance almost rising to the fore, before remembering Callie's words and wishes. Maya may not have proved herself a trusted ally, he doubted his wariness would ever go, no matter how long he spent here, but he had to work with her now. He had no choice.

Ben felt truly alone for the first time since those seconds at the dreadful lake when he was sure Callie would not survive. He hated the fear it rose in him – a mixture of lack of experience and a need for adult reliance that grounded him back in reality. He was not yet a man, not yet able to manage the situation on his own. He needed Maya, needed to believe her.

He coughed lightly as he approached and her eyes open. As he was so used to now, they looked straight through, reading his thoughts, his temperament and body language.

Her voice was resolute, purposeful, 'You need to go. It is time to prepare, organise for your return.'

'I know. You will look after her.' His words were more of a statement than a question.

'She is one of us. Callie is home now, Ben, truly at one with us. No harm will come to her here.'

Ben opened and closed his left hand, feeling each finger. 'No more harm.'

Maya did not argue, 'No more harm. Her decisions are all her own, as are yours.'

'The ones she left me with.'

'You might find them excruciating, awful, but they are yours to take.'

'And the first is the hardest. Leave her. Trust you.'

'Then the rest will follow. Take the leap of faith. See she was right. Make this sacrifice for her. You have come this far, heard me out and believed me before. Not for much longer. By tonight you will be on your way.'

He could not afford to hesitate and wait. His head filled with rushing, buzzing air. Without thinking, knowing if he did he would run back through the doors and take Callie in his arms he faced the exit.

'We need to go. I need to go to the Dealga.'

It didn't look like much, Ben thought. People were meant to believe this insipid, bleak looking plant would save the world, salvage humanity? Mind you, he figured, it couldn't be any more ridiculous than what they were already brainwashed to think.

The plant was thick stemmed, a rusty brown, twisted bark grew short and stocky from roots that now lay white and naked against the sky, soil still clinging here and there in clumps. It looked bolshie and obstinate: willing to put up with the elements here rather than face the easy idyl of a greenhouse. The leaves were wide and curved, a dull, tepid green colour which lay lank against the roots. Ben had no idea if this was because they had been dug up, or if this sickly look was natural. It didn't matter, this was the horde he had, this was what they had asked him for.

Was there enough? He had no idea. Certainly, no-one could deny they seemed to have been generous. Callie's pack bulged, leaves poking out of the top. Ben felt a pang of intense pain; everything she had carried here was now removed and the pack prepared for him to return with. It's full emptiness a reminder how she would not need it now. His own kit had been carefully layered on top with the Dealga, surely leaving no scope for Takot or Prane questioning what had been gathered.

'It's doubtful it will last too long out of the earth,' the man who had handed it over to Maya and Ben had explained. 'This is fresh, any longer than 36 hours out of the ground and there will be little chance of any plant surviving. It's already drooping in places.'

Maya reassured him, he obviously felt this was nothing more than a complete waste of resources. 'There will be time. Our leaving is imminent, we just have last minute preparations,' she said, then, perhaps more to herself than anyone else, 'Besides, they might not realise, might not know time is limited. Who knows if they have ever actually seen this large a yield before.'

Ben zipped up his suit, thoughts of going it alone on the return journey at the forefront of his mind. How would he cope without her tracking skills? He suddenly realised the fundamentals of what Callie not being there would mean.

Almost as if she had read his thoughts Maya spoke.

'I have assigned Laggan to support you on the trail back, at least until you are safely on your way. She will track, lead and keep you from harm. You can't go all the way together of course, that would not be safe for either of you in case you were seen together, but you will be under our watch and under no harm. She will remain with you this evening and return tomorrow when she is certain you are in no danger.'

Ben looked both shocked and uncertain.

'I was expecting just to leave myself, find my own way back.'

'I realise that, but it was decided that is not be the best idea. To ensure your safety and the security of all of us, I've asked Laggan to accompany you.'

'You decided?'

'Yes, although the idea was suggested to me rather forcefully.'

'By whom?'

The voice behind him scuttled up his spine, the nerves tingling in its ring. Calming and determined despite its usual weakness.

'What are you doing here?' he said, turning to face Callie. She sat in a wheelchair, tall in defiance at needing to use it, a blanket wrapped round the hospital garb she still wore.

'You shouldn't be here,' Maya scolded. 'You are still too weak from the aftermath of the procedure.' At the words Ben's eyes skimmed over the bandage, still hidden under Callie's right hand.

'I had to come. See you one more time.' Her words were directed to Ben, not Maya. 'You need to take Laggan with you. You know you can't get back yourself.'

Ben joked, tenderly, 'Still think you're in charge and you can't trust me on my own, don't you.'

'Something like that,' she smiled and tried to rise out of the chair, slamming her remaining hand down infuriated on the arm rest when her legs began to give way, still shaking from the trauma. And hopefully the effects of some kick-ass painkillers, Ben thought. He had leapt forward to catch her and now knelt at her side.

She ran a finger down his face.

'I don't have much time,' he said.

Callie nodded. As if on cue, Laggan appeared, a pack strapped across her back, spear in hand. She nodded briefly to Ben, more deeply to Callie, a thin, line of a smile appearing on her lips.

'I know. I just wanted to see you one more time. Make sure they didn't let you go stumbling off on your own.'

'Stumbling! Gee, thanks!' he joked. 'Is that what you think of me?'

'You know what I think,' her eyes looked deep into his and he really did. The words were too painful, too treacherous now, but they passed silently between them.

'And I had to tell you it's ok. I forgive you.'

He hung his head, shaking it slowly.

'Ben, look at me.' He raised his head again. 'I do. I have to. I needed to tell you before you go. Needed to make sure you knew. Now go. Get back. Find your own path.'

'You mean find this rebellion? We both know Maya has hinted at it. Of distrust in Salthea. People from the Wilds infiltrated there even.'

'That doesn't matter now,' Callie continued. 'No, I don't mean just that. You'll know your path when you find it, like I have. All that matters now is you returning safely, convincing them of why you are alone. Keeping us all safe – on both sides. That is your goal. Later can come later.'

The medic who had brought Callie began to turn her chair,

'We have to return. It is time for your wrist to be attended to.' Callie sighed.

'I need to go. Be safe. Maybe one day in the future.'

Ben took her hand, pushed his own against it until all their fingers pressed against each other.

'Until one day,' he said, standing up. Callie was turned and taken. She did not look back.

Laggan appeared at his side, his kit in her hand.

'It is time. Let me help you with this.' He shrugged once more into his pack. Callie's was then strapped across his front.

Maya approached.

'You have everything you need. Your story?'

His voice was monotone, grave, 'I know what I need to tell them.'

'The proof. The…'

'Where is it?' he asked before she could finish. Ben had not seen the hand, nor did he want to until or unless it was absolutely necessary. He wasn't sure he was steeled enough for that.

'Carefully packed within the front section of her kit. Safe and secure.' Her next words were slow, carefully chosen, respectful. 'Adeline has made sure the circumstances appear to have been naturally created in a tragic accident. This was done with complete deference and care. There will be little doubt.'

Ben snarled the words out through his teeth, in woeful disgust. 'To prove she is dead.'

'To prove she is dead,' Maya continued. 'It is time for you. I know you won't let her down.' She clasped Ben's upper arm and squeezed in both approval, comfort and trust.

'Then now we leave,' he said.

Laggan stepped out, pointing towards the direction they had been dragged through by Ankor and Fly,

'This way.'

Ben had to admit, although only to himself, that it was highly doubtful he could have found his way back without this support. He couldn't tell if Laggan was as gifted a tracker as Callie, or if she was just so aware of the terrain and location that she didn't feel the need to trace the land but passed through it with ease. There were no halts to adjust direction, no doubts of marker point. In fact, despite his own athleticism, he struggled at times to keep pace and avoid tripping over nodules of earth, trailing vines or twisted stumps.

He recognised, with a spark of adrenaline, the point at which they had been accosted by Ankor and Fly, another world ago. His head was bursting with the enormity of what had passed since then, the age now piled on his shoulders. Laggan wasn't exactly a great conversationalist either, not that Ben had any real desire to talk to her. She was fulfilling a purpose, he trusted enough to know she would see him safe but had no doubt if her orders had been to deliver him to the biters, he would have been shredded into pieces hours ago.

Looking around Ben tried to feel the same wonder and awe for the journey they had both felt on the trek in. He couldn't do it. It wasn't just the haze within his mind, it wasn't just that the initial sheen had passed in his limited experience so far. It was Callie. It was her light that had enthused him so much, their shared experience that had meant so much. When Laggan broke through some branches and startled a vibrant gold, jade and crimson bird, sending it protesting into the trees he wasn't excited by the wings, each feather alive and dazzling, which rose up. His first thought was how Callie would have reacted. He couldn't help but smile at her voice in his head calling out, gesticulating, capturing the image in her mind. But it was a melancholy, taunting smile.

Sometime later, sooner than he had expected, Laggan resolved that they were ready to camp for the night. The light had all but faded and they needed to eat. Ben also figured she was not convinced he would travel safely in the darkness. Although, he was not going to argue, the thought of food, rest and sleep was too strong.

The shelter wasn't great, but it was enough for one night. Laggan had found a reasonably flat spot within the trees, with enough even ground to lie comfortably without contending with too many rocky mounds or lumpy roots. Ben helped her stretch and tie the shelter corners around the trunks of four trees. Three sides hung down, more or less touching the ground and at least offering some privacy and shelter from any breeze. The last lay open against the fire she deftly lit, blowing gently on tiny twigs and sharp, dried leaves to burst the smoke into flames that licked and tasted the air, eager to be alive.

Ben took his sleeping bag out and, keeping it rolled, sat on it, unlaced his boots and rubbed his feet as they relaxed at the heat. The whole day had been awkward, grunts mainly as Laggan drove forward, directing him here and there, warning him of divots or hidden burrows and the like. Clearly, she didn't rate him or relish the idea of returning with him injured. Laggan reeked of sheer nonchalance, but Ben felt discomfort pushing down on his shoulders, embarrassment at being stuck here with this grumpy, strange woman.

'How long have you been living out here?' he asked, the relaxed tone sounding contrived and stupid in his head.

Laggan looked across the flames and chewed her nutrient bar carefully.

'A while. Long enough.'

'So, did you harvest back home?'

'We just left my home.'

'You know what I mean,' he pressed, not giving in to her obstinance.

Laggan chewed, Ben felt for a deliberately long time, before eventually answering.

'I did. I harvested.'

'And then you left?'

'Evidently.' She took an apple from her pack, crunched into it noisily and leaned back on her elbows, shaking her hair down her back. This was obviously as far as Ben was going to get with the conversation.

Wanting to appear unphased he took pains to open his pack slowly, retrieve the rations there and unwrap his own nutrient bar. He looked down at the torn wrapper, fire burning in the background as he ate, his eyes out of focus but at least not resting on Laggan. As he chewed, he ruminated over what he would face tomorrow when he met Takot and Prane again, how he would approach them.

Keep it vague. Keep it short. That avoids any doubt or confusing questioning. They had been over it- Maya, Callie and himself. Stick to the truth as much as you can – that story you can tell unfabricated. The creature in the loch had got her; she had not stood a chance; he had tried but he had barely survived himself; he had reached out to save her one last time but then... Well, they would see. Why had he kept it? Grief. Love. Mania. He couldn't explain, Say nothing about proof. Nothing that could arouse suspicion. Where was the rest of her? Who knew, probably in the belly of that vile beast.

Why hadn't he run? Run to what, he would suggest. To face the biters or the Wilds alone. How could he run without finding Dealga and returning with the last hope? He couldn't do that. That would have been the easy way; he collected Dealga in her memory. He'd taken someone she loved from her, now he would give life in her name.

It sounded plausible in his head. More than that, it sounded real. Authentic. The kind of bullshit he could come out with, and they would buy. Ben took confidence from the thought as he drew back into the shelter and encased himself in the sleeping bag for the night. He knew he would need all his energy, wit and sharpness to make it through the next 24 hours.

The night passed, a mixture of wild dreams which jerked him suddenly awake with head spinning, confused thoughts and long spells lying awake brooding, regretting, badgering himself for allowing this situation to happen, knowing most of it was out of his hands, He woke up cold and aching, his head bent at a strange angle which left him with an annoying pain in the side of his neck. He sat up, still in his bag and kneaded it deeply with his fingers, trying to wake up and shake off the feelings of foreboding. The confidence from the night before was gone. It was too close to reality now.

Laggan must have wakened earlier; her bed roll was already back in her pack, and she had carefully made sure the fire was definitely out. Ben figured she must have gone to the bathroom or to scan ahead. They would soon enough be closer to the drop off point so she would want

282

to make sure there was no sign of them being followed or tracked together.

Ben munched on an apple. He sucked at the natural, poly free juice and relished the fresh, tangy taste realising this could be the last real meal he would ever have. He was taking his time, wiping juice from his chin and licking it off his fingers, not willing to miss a drop, when Laggan returned. Ben immediately felt useless as she looked with disdain at his unpacked kit, dishevelled appearance and inactivity. She sat impatiently, crossing, uncrossing her legs, fiddling with straps on her pack, surreptitiously eyeing Ben and sniffing, coughing and tapping her hands or feet noisily in frustration.

As quickly as he could he stumbled around, still chewing the hard core, stuffing his bag into his pack, the ends splurging out, stubbornly, till eventually he had it sealed. Shoving it purposefully on his back he announced, as casually as he could, his voice only slightly breathless,

'Ready!'

Laggan almost bounded to her feet and set off. After a few minutes she partly turned and waited the few steps till he caught up.

'I will need to explain where I will leave you. The route you need to follow so you hopefully don't get lost.' The cynicism in her voice was clear to Ben. 'Today's distance is much further. You have to make up time. Little room for errors.'

'I'm sure I'll be fine,' he mumbled.

Laggan paused, doubtful. 'Be that as it may. Maya instructed me to see you to probably safety. So that is what I intend to do.' When Ben said nothing she added, 'That will not be an issue will it?'

'No.' His voice was flat, inside the frustration of knowing she was right eating away at him.

'Then we continue,' she motioned through a tightly wound curtain of winding vines, reaching out, curled around each other. Shoving and ripping slightly at the plants she pushed herself through, a few rough, straggly ends snapping back towards Ben's face. He pulled his head quickly from side to side, avoiding a smart across the cheek or poke in the eye.

Ben felt a tear in his trousers and, once through, looked down to check the rip. Finding nothing he put it down to imagination. Standing up and heading on again he took a half step back, stunned.

Before him lay the shore of the loch.

The water sat, the light once again shimmering and beckoning, luring him forward. The surface lapped gently, tiny bubbles breaking along its edge. The sky and trees looked back on themselves once again, reflected almost perfectly in the stillness of the glass surface.

Laggan, hands on hips, stared out, reaching her head back then from side to side, enjoying the stretch in her neck. Ben wondered, glad she wasn't looking as he also shuddered slightly, if she was considering whether to go straight across or make their way around. He knew which he would prefer. As he walked towards her, he returned to the trip across the water he had had with Callie. Remembered the beast: the look of its putrid eye, its vicious, snarling jaws, the sound of its pained smashing through the water as he stabbed it. It was dead. Yet the words lay fragile in the base of his stomach. Was their doubt? Could it have survived? Did this enticing crystal surface hide a more gruesome reality?

Laggan's voice shocked him slightly in its considerateness. 'We will need to cross. It is far, far simpler than going round.'

'It's dead.'

'You're sure?'

Ben thought carefully, knowing what his answer meant. Squatting down he picked up a pebble, tossed it from hand to hand like a potato taken from a fire, stood up and tossed it as far as he could. It landed with a deep splash, rehomed perhaps forever in the sand at the bottom.

'As sure as I have been of anything since we got here,' he answered, leaving Laggan to decide what to do with the answer.

He saw her considering, weighing up the dangers, the time. Probably the hassle too he wondered ruefully. At least both of them knew what to expect, the surprise and paralysing terror it had brought not an advantage this time.

'I take it you can swim reasonably well if it came to it? Fast. Strong enough?' Laggan asked, her decision clearly made, adding a gibe at the poly world beyond the Wilds, 'I mean, in real water?'

'You'll find out, won't you? It's not like it's the first time, is it?' Ben said before boldly marching out, on, into the loch. 'Besides,' he added glibly, looking back over his shoulder, 'We had more to contend with last time than swimming.'

He shivered as he splashed through the shore, deeper into the water. Partly from the coolness, immediately swirling around and trapping his legs, licking eagerly. Partly from the fear at what could be. The cold drove up his skin to his shoulders where it released in a shake. He concentrated on supressing the discomfort and on maintaining his balance as he adjusted to the flow and drift of the water. As it reached up to waist level he held fast to his spear, scanning the area wider and closer for any change in texture or colour. Nothing. Yet.

Laggan, this time behind him, did the same. It wasn't until now Ben wondered if she had done this before, or if this was one experience new for her where he had the upper hand. He harumphed out loud at the thought: of all the places to have it.

They stepped on tentatively, holding their arms up out of the water, bent at right angles so they appeared like torn, stripped wings. Their hips moved, rocking side to side as they kept balance and strode on, both of them stepping as far as possible with each step, knowing they should get across and on dry land as soon as possible.

After a short time, no more than a quarter of a way across Ben spun, splashed and drove his stick down with a roaring exhale. His eyes spun round the water, searching. Laggan braced and seemed to stop breathing altogether.

'There,' Ben pointed with his free hand, slightly off to his left. His voice was not much more than a relieved pant, 'It was nothing.' Laggan made out a dull darkening in the water which moved slowly off in a ripple. She caught up with Ben who still stood, scanning, and looked at him expectantly.

'Just a large fish,' he said. 'Nothing bigger than us.' As if justifying his attack he finished, 'I'm not taking any chances.'

'No,' she agreed. 'No, we're not.'

They proceeded on, easily chest height in water now. It was a numb comfort Laggan was equal to him in height, Ben realised, she could stride faster and easier than Callie was able. He had relaxed slightly when there was no sign of anything in the water longer in length than he was in height. Now he knew he was around midway across, and the water pushed against his chest and up around his armpits he was acutely alert once more. If there was a weak point, a time of peak danger, then this was it.

But nothing appeared. After another long ten minutes he realised the depth was subsiding, the water gleaming across his top as it slowly began to dry, the level now somewhere between his chest and lower ribs. The push against his legs became easier to counterbalance as the level dropped and he felt like he could see deeper down, not quite to the loch bottom, but further down. This could have been Ben's imagination, but it gave him comfort anyway – the further he could see the less surprised he could be.

'I think you can be certain. It's gone.' Laggan sounded reluctantly impressed.

Ben remained cagey, guarded. He disliked water at the best of times, even the real, natural stuff he had decided. He wouldn't be happy until both his feet were back on dry land, well out of reach, eyeshot even, of the loch.

As the water moved down further, no higher than his upper ribs now, a group of small fish darted around, parting only as they suddenly avoided collision with his body. He started, every sense probing and examining the water. He tried to obsess on every fish, paranoid they were streaming together away from some as yet unseen attacker.

They flew under the water, pushing through and around, flashes of green, brown, grey and bluish flecks illuminating the water. Ben realised with relief they were not streaming off in distress, fleeing a predator. Rather they were journeying through and now, in actual fact, searching him out, passing through his legs and around curiously, tasting and studying. As quickly as they arrived, they were on, off to search for more viable food or playthings.

After an age, they reached the other side, Ben not caring how he looked as he ran the last few metres from knee deep until he could turn and sit, well up the banking where the grass stopped abruptly, and the pebbly shore began. Laggan was less obvious, although she too picked up her pace the last stretch.

She sat next to him, no doubt contemplating her return journey; were they certain, or should she resolve to return walking around the loch. No matter. This was almost where they would part.

'If they are searching, they will find you half a day trek from here,' the word 'they' laced with hate and disgust.

'You're leaving me here? Now?' Ben tried to sound blasé but felt nerves wrench inside.

'It wouldn't be safe for either of us, if I went much further. There could be scouts, lookouts waiting for your return. You have no idea of the suspicion and mistrust in Salthea. The lengths they take to keep order. Control.' I will see you safe within the wood, then I will return. Maya did tell you.'

Ben cut her short, 'Yes, she did. Fine. It's fine.' He hoped his voice did not give himself away.

Laggan reached into her pack and took something out of it, wiping it absentmindedly on her trouser leg before offering it to Ben. He couldn't quite see what it was as he reached for it, the light shining on it awkwardly. When he realised what it was, he lunged and snatched at it greedily, cupping it in both palms. Callie's compass. A precious prize.

Ben wiped it himself, removing all traces of Laggan from the surface, cradling it again and looking at it tenderly.

'Where did you get this? Why do you have it?' he asked.

'She gave it to me. For you. Insisted you took this one in particular. Said you would understand.' Once again, her voice was uncharacteristically compassionate, no doubt more out of respect for Callie than for him.

He gazed on her words then rubbed the surface again, as he had brushed hair from her face.

Ben smiled despite himself, his voice light and full of humour. 'That's trust, eh? She didn't even believe you could get me to safety!'

'Mmmm. I'm not sure that was the only reason.'

'What do you mean?'

'It's hers.'

'I know that.'

Laggan looked at him incredulous. 'Are you kidding me? It's hers. She didn't give it to you just to get you home, she gave it to you because it was hers. 'To have something of hers.'

'Do you think? I mean, I think that. I feel like that, but…'

'Yes. That's why. Now, we need to go. You need directions.' The fleeting sensitivity dissipated. Laggan launched into her plan and instructions. She would lead him within the wood then support him on to follow a definite southern direction. After than she could go no further. He would need to make his own way through the forest. Laggan assured him this would be the trickiest part. Afterwards the plain would follow, with a clear, obvious target, the crescent mountain again. This time Ben need not fear the caves at the foot of the hill and would be able to follow a clear track from them straight up which should be easier than the unmarked route he and Callie had taken on their initial journey. If he kept a reasonable pace and avoided errors he would, she assured him, be able to reach the pickup point as evening became night.

If he made it directly. Ben did not care about being out here alone. Laggan assured him there were no living creatures that would endanger him in any way. No people from the settlements were foraging this far and even if they were they would be aware of his journey. Just in case, Laggan handed him a written pass embossed from Maya. The only thing that could possibly provide a threat would be random, travelling,

'Biters.' Her voice was weighted with gravity. 'They are increasing in number and although they do not normally evade our monitoring, well…' She did not need to carry on. But Ben had not come this far, Callie had not sacrificed what she did, for him to die now.

He could do this. He would do this. Not for him, but for Callie. For all of them.

288

The ground dried as they neared the woods. The damp smell of the water was replaced with the woody, heady smell of the trees and greenery within the forest. Leaves began to crunch; twigs snap noisily underfoot as if exemplifying the dryness. Plants became taller, trees thicker and soon there was no sign of the loch behind them, the forest had closed around them. This time there was no awe, no time to stand and examine, experience the life here. Ben was not able to reach out and run his hand along the bark, exploring the curls and wrinkles winding round the trees. His job was clear. Stay alert. Stay South. Get home. Quickly.

Laggan seemed to become increasingly edgy, checking for sounds, lifting her head often. Ben did not know if she was sniffing the air, listening or watching for something hidden out in front. She was clearly a veteran tracker, scanning for threats. Thankfully none came. With a pang of longing Ben wondered if Callie would learn from her, become even more assured, an expert in the terrains of the Wilds. He would never know.

Despite his determination, all too soon she announced at this point she would go no further. Throwing her pack from her shoulders she secured it to his.

'Your tracking will get you from here, I can assure you.' She said, joining both packs together tightly. 'Stay alert. Keep south. Review your story. This is on you now.'

'Tell her I will do it. Tell her I will never forget her. Tell her if I can, I will find the Rebellion.'

Laggan was facing him now, adjusting the straps across his waist and shoulders. Without blinking she looked into his eyes.

'I will.'

Ben was uncertain how to leave, he stuck out his hand awkwardly. Laggan looked at it, herself uncertain, then took it and they shook a tight, knowing handshake.

'South' she beckoned.

'South'. Ben turned, as she did, and alone for the first time, began to work his way through the forest. As the immediate time passed, he became obsessed with the compass, following it rather than looking ahead, so determined not to stray even a degree off course. He tripped over tree roots, was whacked across the face with vines and branches and scratched with thorns before he realised how ridiculous and rash he was being. Break, even twist or damage something out here and he would not reach the pick-up. Plus, he thought, bursting the bubble he had of feeling assured and confident he was guaranteed to return, if he was preoccupied with Callie's compass, he would not notice any creature, human or worse, until it was too late.

He continued in a new state, his head bobbing up and down like an awkward timekeeper, as he looked from the compass to the forest, then back again. These intervals became less and less as he realised he didn't need to rely on the compass and was looking on it only as a memory of Callie. He saw her face in it, heard her words as his eyes drifted across it, watching the murmurs in the arrows.

But she was in his head anyway, guiding him forward and going over his story- the details he would so soon share with Takot. She had died at the hands, well jaws, of the creature as they returned. He had proof – a shiver ran up into Ben's heart at the thought. What had happened to the rest of her? How the hell would he know? He had the Dealga, no they had not met anyone else. Had found arrowheads and been disturbed but split up and evaded whoever or whatever it was. He could do it. It wasn't lying per se, just missing out huge chunks of information. As if they would give a shit. They would have the Dealga and one less thing to worry about. Ben wasn't daft, he knew he was disposable now and potentially in danger. Takot would more than likely be grateful when he returned alone.

Ben was shocked and panicked when it became clear there was no doubt – the trees were thinning, and he was leaving the forest behind. He was sure he must have gone wrong, off track despite all his efforts. There was no way he could have passed through so quickly. Yet he checked the compass, tapping it lightly and the dial stuck stubbornly. He had definitely stuck to heading South, slightly South West. But the shadows were definitely longer, the air not so thick and stuck, shrubs and plants becoming less and less.

Then he reached it, the edge of the wood. Hoodoos and plains lay stretched in front, before the mountain. The last trek before the return. He stopped for a short breather, drinking deep and looking back into the forest.

He would perhaps never see this real, pure nature again, at least in such quantity. Ben ran his hand over the trunk of a tree, as he and Callie and done when they reached here at first. He too one last look at the mottled floor, the shade and colour created by the branches and leaves overhead which helped protect the secrets and life within. He listened for any signs of life: the crackles, rustles and movements that gave away the vivacious energy inside. Then he turned to leave, stopped and turned again. Taking his knife out of his pack he carved a deep B and deep C into the bark of a tree, and leant his forehead against it, eyes closed.

CHAPTER TWENTY-NINE

It's funny how reactions and instincts are near impossible to shake off completely, Ben considered, as he began the hot, dusty walk back across the plain. There was little need for him to need shelter or disguise. Maya had almost completely made sure he would not be disturbed or harmed. Any biter that he had the unlikely misfortune of encountering would be seen so far off they would not worry him. In fact, he could more than likely outrun them to safety with minimal effort. Any spies from Salthea would see him just doing what he had been ordered to do. Yet he still kept close to the hoodoos, considered his distance from rocks and large stubby bushes. Kept a relaxed but armed, visible hold of his Khalto stick, with all its recent knocks and scratches and bumps.

The late afternoon stretched before him in all its heat and headiness, stubborn and resilient against the approaching twilight. The packs were uncomfortable, the weight digging in at his shoulders and waist. His back felt damp and sticky with sweat and he was glad when the occasional breeze, warm as it inevitably was, crossed his face. Ben marched on, feeling paranoid that he perhaps wasn't making as good time on this leg of the walk. The forest at least changed, a large, decaying trunk here, a slushy, sloppy mound there, a disturbed creature exploding quickly across his path or disappearing invisibly in the swaying undergrowth or tree.

Here there was nothing, Metres and metres of tumbleweed, hoodoo to hoodoo, before yet another appeared. The land was arid and cracked, crazy shapes criss-crossing the dead loch.

 But cross he did, the caves they had both previously been so nervous of becoming more than dark, thumbprint smudges in the difference. Eventually they drove up before him, gaping mysterious caverns battered into the side of the mountain. They did make Ben feel uneasy, he had the feeling the dark darkness indicated an enormous depth where a myriad of things could be hiding. It was little wonder he and Callie had been warned of them – they were a perfect hiding place for Wildings protecting their communities from people from the cities and the farms. People like him he supposed. Whatever he was now.

This would potentially be the last time he was safely alone with his thoughts – his true thoughts – for a very long time. He would, he knew beyond certainty now, deliver the Dealga, what little use it was. He figured there would be some sort of interrogation or deconstruction of the events of his trip and what they had seen and found. After that both he and Callie had resigned to the fate of being returned to harvesting at best, death at worse. Or perhaps there were worse things than death, he worried now. Callie had certainly thought so.

Before he had met her, before all this. Who was he kidding, even during part of all of this, he had always wanted just to return to the farm, return to harvesting. What happened with Tax was not something he wanted to be alone with in his head. He had relived it over and over in gruesome detail which had ripped it apart. No, he was not ready to even attempt to deal with it yet. But that world, the world of the farm, had given him stability, focus, routine. The mundaneness was comfort. And penance perhaps.

The realisation of the possibility there was a Rebellion, all the details Maya had given them about Dealga and the truth about the polys, had destroyed his brain. It had all been at first too ridiculous, then too mind-boggling, then too horrifying and tragic. Could he join? Should he join? If he had been asked just days ago he would not have conceived it possible. How often had he berated Callie for her itchy feet, recklessness and thirst for more. But should he survive this, know what he knew, could he honestly believe life back on a farm was enough?

Ben didn't know. Couldn't even imagine where to start. It wasn't like he could sidle up, casual, to someone in Salthea and ask if they were part of a Rebellion, looking for any new members. The dangers he would be in were almost incomprehensible.

But look at what Callie had done.

As this image swirled, cruelly teasing in his head, Ben reached the very foot of the caves. The dim, dim light barely gave much away except the very entrance to them, and Ben was glad he didn't have to worry about what could lie within. All he had to do was find the pathway Laggan had advised him was there and head up towards the crescent. Passing in front of two gaping mouths in the mountain he saw a scabby patch of trampled, squashed grass and figured this was the start.

A crunch and skitter, the sound of a stone scuffling swiftly across the earth jolted him. Grabbing his Khalto stick across his body, Ben hunched over his shoulders and braced. He took a few steps backwards up the path, giving himself the benefit of distance and height. Standing for long, careful seconds, there was nothing. No sound, barely even any movement except his quickening, edgy breathing. Could he have upset the ground himself? Ben doubted it, the noise hadn't come from under his feet. But he had to continue, he couldn't stand here staring out, listening at nothing.

Warily he began following the track up the side of the hill. He couldn't yet shake off the idea he had heard something, that he was not alone, but there was no other sign, no other cause for concern and slowly, as he pressed on, the feeling dissolved.

The track was certainly much easier than the one he and Callie had created for themselves. Here any lose shingle or trip hazards were more or less obvious and the going, although steep, quicker and easier. At the steepest point Ben had to navigate his way over large boulders, some requiring he use his hands as well as his feet to balance and climb further up the hill. Not the easiest task while carrying two loaded packs on his back and a staff, ready in his hands. A last final burst of stretched lunges finally took him to the top, the crescent shaped plateau he had reached bent round before him.

His shadow was now beginning to stretch out, his legs a ridiculous, elongated, caricature of themselves. The sun was dipping now, afternoon slipping away. He stopped to stretch and rest his gangling legs for a moment and taking a deserved long gulp of water, surveying his past journey. The forest was far, far off, but Ben looked down at the blonde, empty plain scanning for life and in self-admiration at how far he had come today. He didn't give a shit if he kept anyone waiting, he would negotiate the crescent and down to the pickup point tonight of that there was little doubt. And he would do it in his own time. They wouldn't wait forever, but they would wait.

The crescent curved in a meandering arc, Ben followed it, enjoying the level path and the breeze. He could smell nature in the air, not sure he had noticed it before. The coolness in his nostrils drew his attention to it and made him aware of its journey. Maybe it was his imagination but these last few breaths of true freedom he would have seemed sweeter, more alive and urgent as they ran through his nose and into his lungs. The air seemed to expand lighter inside his body.

As he reached the end of the curve Ben considered how long was left of his journey. He thought it had taken them maybe three hours to reach this point initially – here he was doing it downhill and in reverse. He was fairly confident in two hours max he would be back. There was light left. Granted the shadows strung him out, thin and wiry even more, but there was life in the sun still, sunset had not yet bloomed. If there was a need to walk in any darkness, he had light with him.

It wasn't needed. As the flushed blush of the pink sunset began to fade Ben saw the helicopter. He stood, face contorted and skyward, gasping in his last free air. His body ached, muscles and mind cried out silently. Ben shrugged off the pack and walked forward. Waiting to find out his fate. Wondering at this point if he even cared.

Takot got out of the helicopter, flanked by two guards and waited; his face emotionless as Ben covered the last few metres of ground. Both stood, silent, eyeing each other, waiting for one to make a move.

Without warning his face twisted in fury and he punched Ben once, cruelly in the stomach. Ben fell back, doubled over, one hand clutching his abdomen, the other trying to steady his fall.

'What the f...?' the words flew from his lips, shaping instead into a groan as a sharp kick tossed him back, face up, onto the ground. He looked up in wrath and confusion as two guns pointed low, inches from his face.

Takot righted the collar of his suit and dusted off the sleeves, his crisp, flawless cream suit cutting a sharp outline against the surroundings.

'You're late.' The words were a command for explanation rather than a question. 'The consequences of which might not be ah, fulfilling for you.'

The guns continued to stare and threaten as Ben rose to sitting, opening his palms and raising his arms above his shoulders in a gesture of capitulation.

'Miss me?'

At that a guard kicked a cloud of sand into his face and he spluttered and wiped at his eyes and mouth.

Takot spoke, his voice curt. 'You are late. Why?'

Righting himself to his feet and sighing, Ben rolled his shoulders and composed himself. The time for smart arsing and wise cracking was gone. He needed to deliver a performance. One that may well decide if he would live or die. If others would be safe, hidden for longer. Ben became a youth, withered and hopeless, thankful for any adult presence taking charge – even Takot.

'I'm sorry. We. I did my best. A day. I did what you asked. Please…'

'The Dealga?' Takot's voice was colourless, there was no expression of hope or regard.

'I have it.' Ben pointed to the base of his pack.

Takot brought his fingertips together. One at a time the thumb, then forefinger of each hand, followed by the rest, tapped against each other. As he reached the small finger he spoke again.

'And the girl?'

Ben's voice growled with indignation and hate. 'Callie. Her name was Callie.'

'Was?'

Ben nodded. He wasn't going to give up details on his own.

'How?'

Ben shrugged his shoulders. 'Does it matter? She's gone. That is down to you. On you. I have the Dealga. That was the deal.'

His attention was diverted as he heard a door slam on the other side of the helicopter and footsteps approach.

'How did she die?' Prane's voice curdled in his stomach. The woman approached him, examining him with a long, considered look. 'It appears you have done well.' She ran a perfectly manicured finger across his cheek. 'Now tell me what happened.'

The words spewed out of him easily, his emotions taking over in release of tension and of regret and of love. He felt bile and twisting rage rise inside as he spoke of the monster and the attack. Real tears made his tongue and lips salty as he recounted how he had tried to help; tried to drag her from its grasp but was too late. Too weak. Too small. By the time he had finished he was exhausted, the pain of losing her physical inside his heart and mind.

Takot eyed him, watching the tears and the wringing hand and the panting sobs, becoming more painful with every detail.

'There is proof I presume?'

Ben looked up, his cheeks scarlet and his wet eyes ringed with red. He swung his packs off and opened the top one. With reverence and adoration, he took out the parcel containing Callie's hand. It was wrapped tight, shrouded in material from her own pack, cushioned respectfully to ensure safe transit.

'Proof?' Ben ran at Takot, shoving the package into his chest. The guards braced and aimed, lowering their weapons only after Takot raised his hand. The man looked down, his face twisting in disgust at what it could possibly contain. 'Here is your proof,' Ben shouted. 'Here's the only bit of her left. The only part it would give me back. Take it. Take her. I don't care anymore. That's what she did. What she did for you.' He let go and stepped back, stumbling. Takot caught the package in both hands before it slid to the ground.

Maintaining composure he handed the package to a guard, wiping his hand down the front of his jacket as if to remove any trace of it.

'Check it.' The guard nodded and took it out of view, back on to the helicopter.

'You think I'm lying now?' Ben glared. 'Then where the fuck is she?'

Takot's lips pursed, and Ben could see a slight pulsing twitch at the side of his eye. His words were ignored as Takot went on.

'The Dealga. Show it to me.'

'Get it yourself, I'm done now.'

Takot sniffed deeply, his nose wrinkling as he clasped his hands behind his back. 'It would not do to cause any unnecessary fuss after everything you have completed. Out here.' His voice was placid, but Ben could feel the warnings lacing the unruffled tone. Holding back a further outburst he grabbed and pulled at the ties on his pack and tipped out a Dealga plant.

Takot and Prane both took a step towards it, the woman picking it up delicately and turning it around between her hands, taking care not to damage any roots or remove any more of the soil.

'It has travelled suitably well,' she decided. 'Are they all in the same state?' she asked, turning to Ben.

'No idea. I guess so. Look. I did what you asked. It's there. As much as I could pack. Roots. Soil. After that, I think my job is done, don't you?'

'Indeed it is,' Prane purred. 'I assume you are ready to return.'

Ben did not get a chance to answer, the guard who had taken Callie's hand returned, a grave look on his face. He stood, legs apart, arms at his side, until acknowledged to speak.

'The scanner data request confirmed a 100% match, Sir.' The extract came from Rassay.'

'There can be no doubt?' Prane answered.

'Absolutely none. I ran the test twice, both times it returned a reading of 100% accurate. They are her remains. The DNA coupled with her birthmark data make it irreputable. We also have aerial footage of him.'

Ben's insides flooded and froze, his shoulder blades shuddered as if stabbed forward.

'Footage?'

The officer turned his helmeted head and with one step batoned Ben in the stomach to silence his interruption.

'The perimeter drones confirm he was alone. He left the forest unaccompanied and was not assisted.'

Takot was satisfied, motioning to the guard to secure the Dealga onto the helicopter. This was done while another officer escorted Ben to the craft and secured him to a seat. Ben shoved his waist forward and back, trying to find a comfortable position against the restraint, too tight against him.

'Take him to Interrogation Level Five.' Takot instructed.

'Five?' Prane looked alarmed, shocked. 'Is that necessary?

'That is what I want to find out.' Takot replied. 'I assume you are not questioning my decision making?'

'Of course not. I just hadn't deemed him that notable. Anymore. A mere child again. I thought after some time in Reassimilation he could perhaps be of some use back in a factory line of some description.'

'We'll see.' Takot ended the conversation. 'We'll see.'

The helicopter rotors began to spin and chug into life and those inside rocked slightly as it left the ground. Prane looked out of the window at the receding hillside as they began crossing the arid floor which would lead them on to Salthea. Laggan, camouflaged against the hill, stood up from a low ditch behind a stubborn, windswept bush and bobbed her head towards her.

Almost imperceptibly Prane returned the nod.

The next instalment in the DEALGA series will appear Autumn 2023

Printed in Great Britain
by Amazon